Absolute Zeroes

by

K. Jered Mayer

Dedications:

To Jenna, always, for starting me down the path.

To Chelsea, always, for keeping me on it.

To Ian and Eric, without whom there would be no Absolute Zeroes.

To Derek, who I can't wait to swap stories with again come the next life.

To my dad, who did his best.

Foreword

Greetings, readers! If you're looking at these words right now, you've either managed to get yourself a copy of Absolute Zeroes, first book in the Causeways series, or someone has inexplicably torn the Foreword out and you've managed to stumble across the pages. That would be curious for both of us, I'm sure.

Either way, let me give you a real brief history on the book you're about to read, if you're interested.

I first came up with the idea for Absolute Zeroes around 15 years ago. I was working in a comic book shop at the time, and my friends and I constantly bounced ideas off of each other: how to make existing comic books better, which characters we would kill or bring back, what concepts would make for a neat comic. At some point, I came up with the idea of three friends who couldn't be more different living and working together on a spaceship in a largely dead-end job. Childhood friends who worked each other's every last nerve, forced to have each other's back to survive.

At the time, I thought it would be a cool comic book. I hadn't really delved into writing novels yet, and wouldn't for several years, so I just jotted down a few notes that never went anywhere, some story threads I never developed, and some character names that went through some tweaks. Ark Carnahan became Archimedes Carnahan (Ark for short). Greyson Toliver became Grey Toliver. Caesar Anada… well, I nailed that one on the first try.

And then, of course, there's the *Sol Searcher*. Every good space-y science fiction story has a great ship at the center of it. Firefly had the *Serenity*. Alien had the *Nostromo*. Star Wars had the *Death…* wait, I mean, the *Millenium Falcon*. I knew even back then that the *Searcher*, a beat-up little transport ship that the boys would both live on and use for their work, would be the heart of the story.

Life happens, though. I never found a comic book artist (or learned how to write comic books). I moved to Los Angeles when I was 21, and Seattle a little over a year after that. I hit a personal low in my life and, lost and directionless, turned to writing.

The project was not Absolute Zeroes.

In the span of about three years, I wrote Waypoint, Death Worth Living For, and As the Earth Trembles, collectively known as the Convergence trilogy. They're a little rough around the edges, but I like most of what came out of it. I discovered through them a renewed passion for writing, and I had proved to myself that I could do novels. Actual books, with plot and descriptions, character arcs and dialogue!

About halfway through Death Worth Living For, I started tossing around ideas for what I wanted to do next. I found my old notes for Absolute Zeroes in an abandoned email folder and used them to put together what would be the first actual outline, a rough little thing that… to my tremendous surprise, has actually held up over the years. And, once I had finished As the Earth Trembles, I started polishing the outline up. I wrote out the first three chapters.

It was fun! The Convergence trilogy had been pretty grim: a lot of betrayals, and violence, and tragedy, and though there were moments of levity, the harshness of that world was the point, as was what it would take to survive in it or to rise above it and be better. By contrast, Absolute Zeroes was supposed to be about adventure and ridiculous situations, and the humor that can be found in terror or fear or horror, even in anger. It was a *fun* book, and a funny one, I thought.

And then I met a girl. And I wound up breaking my own heart. And in the process of that, I got the kernel of an idea to channel my sadness and disappointment and lingering romanticism into. That kernel burst into the popcorn love story that is Read in Denver. I've since become proud of what that story became, and what it apparently means to people, but it was a nightmare for me to write, confronting and facing and trying to articulate a lot of complicated emotions I was experiencing at the time. I was more than ready to be done with it by the time I finished it, and the last thing I ever wanted to do was pick up a pen and write a story again. What was the point, you know?

But stories never die for a writer. They just sit in a corner and scream until you give them attention again, which is obnoxious, but here we are.

So check it out: fifteen years after I first imagined the *Sol Searcher* flying among the stars with Ark, Caesar, and Grey sniping at each other and getting into wild scenario after crazy adventure, here is Absolute Zeroes, the first book set in a universe full of aliens and bandit moons, extraordinary wildlife and mad science, with criminal networks and bumbling dreamers. Seven years after I first outlined it, here's a finished novel. Four years after I wrote the prologue, I'm typing up a foreword to introduce the complete story to you who have decided to take a chance on me.

For the first time in nearly three years, I'm presenting a new story to the world.

In those three years, I've lost my stepfather, my closest writing peer, and one of my best friends within weeks of each other. This year I lost my dad and my dog within a week of each other. It hasn't been easy. But it has been worth it, I hope, to channel *those* energies into this book, a book full of wonder.

I had two goals for Absolute Zeroes when I decided to return to it:

1. Tell a story about friendship, brotherhood, and adventure.
2. Make it fun, and funny, for the readers.

I believe I've accomplished the first thing. It'll be up to you to decide if I've accomplished the second. I hope I have, and I'm grateful to you for giving me the opportunity to entertain you.

With all that said, strap on your seatbelts! Keep your viewports clean and your airlocks hermetically sealed! Open your eyes, and your minds, and get ready to take off for the stars.

--KJM

Absolute Zeroes

Prologue

Lessons in Irresponsibility

Before he had reached his thirteenth birthday, Grey discovered three things about himself that would define the rest of his life: he liked working with his hands, he liked fighting with those very same hands, and he loved going fast. He pushed the throttle of his skimmer further forward, cutting through the blackness of space, and felt at peace.

For all of four seconds.

Then the comm on his dashboard crackled, giving him a split-second warning that someone was about to patch through.

"It sure is quiet out here," came the tinny voice through the comm speaker.

"Well, it was," Grey said, rolling his eyes.

He looked out of the cockpit to his right. He could make out the flashing lights at the far end of his wing. Further out and farther down was Archimedes' DeVorian skimmer, the same model as his, blue instead of black. The crafts weren't meant for deep space travel, but they were comfortable and reliable enough for transportation to and from Salix's three nearby moons.

Or joyrides. They were damn fine for a joyride, too.

"Do you think anyone has noticed a couple ships are missing yet?" asked Archimedes.

"I doubt it. If they didn't see us leave with them, I don't think they're going to be paying close enough attention to notice I put their cameras on a loop. Even if they did, they're going to have a monster of a time unraveling the blocker I put on our transponders."

"I can't get busted for boosting skimmers, Grey. It would kill my future. You know how many polis have records for GTS? None. Maybe one, there's always at least one, but I can guarantee their names are lost to the annals of time."

"It was *your* idea to boost the skimmers, Ark. You knew the risks. Besides, getting slapped with a grand theft spacecraft rap might be the best thing that could happen to you. A life in the political arena would be unrelentingly boring."

"Maybe for you, pal, but ladies love a man with a silver tongue. I don't want to miss out on a life of luxury and lasciviousness."

Grey pinched the bridge of his nose and sighed. "It's just like you to come up with a moronic idea and then find a way to twist the blame," he muttered.

"What was that?"

"Nothing, Carnahan. The cameras are looped. The trackers are blocked. Now, we're coming up on the starting point. You want to shut up and race or keep bitching?"

Archimedes grinned from his own cockpit and straightened into a ready position. "You're a real ass, my friend," he sang into the comm. "But I am ready."

He watched as Grey's ship dropped down and angled to the left. They had reached Gaster, a moon full of industrial rigs and ever-opening labor jobs. It was also littered with some stellar pubs known for their cheap drinks and the kind of people who had large personalities and short tempers. On any other night, they might have landed and seen which of them could drink the other under a filthy, splintered table first. Tonight was meant for something different.

Gaster was notorious for its roughneck nature, but it had one other distinguishing feature as well: a ring of minor asteroids around the poles. It was Salix's only moon to have one and one of the few places that had been discovered to possess a field so dense. Transports to and from the surface would navigate to the left or right of the jagged space rocks, avoiding them completely. Archimedes and Grey, on the other hand, found it a perfect place to race recklessly.

The rules were simple. The first person to fully circumnavigate the moon would win. Leaving the field above, below, or on either side was an automatic forfeit, even if doing so was only to protect the skimmer and — by default — their life from being shredded into oblivion. And that was it. The race was dangerous, no illusion about that.

As they turned their skimmers into the ring, Grey thought to himself that it wouldn't be any fun if it weren't.

The race began. The speed at which they were traveling only allowed for a brief respite in between each large body. They dipped and climbed, swerved and even stalled a couple times when their zealousness got perilously close to overwhelming reason. The orange and white hues of Gaster streaked by in their periphery, looking much lovelier at a glance than the flat, dusty moon was in actuality.

"Don't waste my time with your sight-seeing," laughed Grey. "This is supposed to be a competition."

"Up ahead, dipshit!"

Archimedes watched as Grey jerked his ship upward and dragged the bottom of his skimmer across the upper edges of an asteroid before barrel-rolling between two others. Archimedes banked into an opening on the right, skirting the rock with his wingtip. He had time for a few deep breaths before the next obstacle came up; he flew under it and then swooped up on the opposite side like a swallow.

"Better start paying attention, buddy," he said through the comm. "You're going to tear that thing apart and die in space. I hear it's a miserable way to go."

"Ah, it was just a little comet kissing," said Grey.

"Do you not know what a comet is?"

"I know I'm kicking your ass right now."

"I'm better on the straightaways," Archimedes protested.

Grey snorted. "Everyone's better on a straightaway."

They came around to the dark side of the moon. Both of them flicked their hands out instinctively, toggling a few switches. The exterior lights of their ships lit up and their radar display moved to the right of their windshields. Asteroids appeared as blue blips that they zipped around, and the young men fell quiet again in their concentration.

Archimedes slowly edged up on his friend, cutting closer corners than was probably wise in order to better his time. Grey responded by pushing his skimmer even faster. His eyes flicked to his speed meter and fuel control. Most pilots wouldn't run a skimmer so hard, but he knew DeVorians inside and out. They were capable of a lot if you just gave them a little tough love.

After several tense minutes, an alert popped up just below the radar, flashing in orange. They had come around the bend and were nearing their starting point. The lap was almost complete.

The two friends caught a quick glimpse of each other and bared their teeth. No words were necessary. Both crafts accelerated. They missed the rocks by meters as they twisted and dipped. The difference in distance between them was minimal.

Archimedes could see that he was slowly taking the lead. He grinned in triumph and swerved around an asteroid only to flinch and slam his hand down on the control that would reverse his thrusters, stalling him. Behind the obstacle had been another, close enough that they had registered on the radar as a single blip.

He had almost crashed into it at full speed.

"Dammit!" he snapped as Grey cackled over the comm.

"Next drinks are on you, Carnahan!"

"I almost had you. I was so close! So, so close."

"You'll never have me, Ark, no matter how close you get. I'm too damn good. How are we doing on time?"

Archimedes piloted his way out of the ring and looked at his watch. He had kept the cycle adjusted for Gamemon, the city on Salix they had departed from. They had clocked the trip and the race time accurately enough but finding the skimmers and making off with them had taken longer than they had expected.

"Not bad, actually. We'll have four or five hours of sleep before class if we leave now."

"Did you factor in finding some place to drop these babies off without getting pinched?"

"…ah…"

"So we're kind of screwed, aren't we?"

"Well…"

*****

Caesar Anada stopped mid-question as a snore ripped through the classroom. He forced himself not to betray the exasperation and embarrassment he felt, continuing to stare at the professor and slowly closing his mouth instead. A few titters broke out amongst his classmates. Behind him, a shock of white hair and two pink ears were the only parts of Archimedes' head that weren't buried in his arms. Grey was stretched out in his chair, arms crossed over his chest and head thrown back cringingly far. It was he who had released the nasal rumble.

The professor was not nearly as amused as his students. "Mister *Carnahan*. Mister *Tolliver*," he said sharply. The two men jerked awake, frantic expressions plastered on their faces. Caesar rolled his eyes. "Do you mind either paying attention to the lecture or leaving the class? My course room is not a rest stop. I'm not positive but I *am* pretty sure that whatever recycled mattress you have nestled in your undoubtedly disgusting dorm room is more comfortable than the chairs you're seated in. For the love of God, you only have two days left with me."

"Sorry, teach," muttered Archimedes. Grey said nothing. He smacked his cheeks a couple times to wake up.

The professor gestured for Caesar to continue.

"I was just wondering," the young man began, brushing moppy blond hair out of his face, "what the likelihood is of the Causeways either collapsing in on themselves or reverting back to black holes. Any spacecraft using them or traveling near them would be completely destroyed, correct?"

"Well, that's the leading theory. To be honest, even though we've had hundreds of years to study them there is a lot we still don't know about the Causeways, including their stability or what they would become if they stopped being what they currently are. Their very nature seems to indicate that they were created or at least reinforced by some kind of... I am hesitant to say higher power. Some sort of advanced mind or minds, let's say. Of all the species we've come across and had dealings with, none have taken responsibility for them in any provable way so far. There are plenty of questions yet to be answered.

"As you pointed out, we do know that a lot of them used to be black holes. We know that several more appeared at roughly the same time, seemingly out of nowhere, and we know that something changed with or within them that transformed them into something more akin to wormholes."

"Allowing us to travel to all kinds of places," Grey broke in.

"Yes," the professor deadpanned with a warning glance. "Several previously unknown galaxies opened up to us. We have since been exposed to incredible worlds, including some with inexplicable similarities to Terra Alpha, like the home worlds of the Dyr and the Ryxan."

"See? I'm paying attention."

"Everybody knows that part, Grey," said Caesar. "Shut up."

"To answer your question, Mister Anada," the professor continued, "all of the studies that have been done so far do seem to indicate that the Causeways *are* stable and will continue to be so for the foreseeable future. We hope. But because the hows and whys of their existence still elude us, it's possible that they may indeed just shut off or revert themselves someday without warning. That would—as you say—result in a tremendous loss of life. Now, we've developed enough colonies and relationships with other worlds in other star systems that society would likely continue to thrive around the universe. It would just come down to our ability to adapt and endure." He smiled sheepishly. "We just have to hope it doesn't ever happen. If it does, we probably won't know it's happening until it's done." The professor gave a sheepish shrug. "Sorry that my answer is more of a non-answer, but there it is."

"I thought you were paid to know this stuff," said Grey.

"Mister Tolliver, I'm this close to failing you on principle."

"I fixed your car!"

"And I remain grateful, but you will see exactly how little water that actually holds with me."

"He's saying you're useless," Archimedes chimed in.

"I'll show you useless, you foppish—"

"Enough!" the professor roared.

Caesar rested his elbows on his desk and sank his face into his open hands.

*****

Cynosure Academy was the jewel of Gamemon, its multiple stories and crystalline spires stretching out over the cityscape. Wide, flowing lawns unfolded around the grounds, the grass glowing a deep teal. Concrete pathways criss-crossed through them, filled with students hurrying to and from class. Others laid out in the sun, soaking up the warmth, reading books and playing instruments.

It was an inclusive school, designed to be open to men and women of all social and economic backgrounds. Once accepted, the students would choose from a variety of classes and teachers. The prices would vary depending on the quality of the class, but even the more affordable alternatives offered a well-regarded education. The tricky part came after graduation, when employers would scan an applicant's past transcripts and that person had to convince them they were still a better alternative than the guy who shelled out a few thousand chits extra for the professor with more letters behind his name.

It was a busy campus in a busy city on a busy planet. Salix's moons tended to be more diverse in their populations, but cities on Salix—and Gamemon in particular—had always seemed more tailored toward men and women of the Human race who were looking to grow up and move on to promising careers.

It was that idea, and the dream of working alongside the brilliant minds of the SciTech Industrial Lab Organization, that preoccupied Caesar's mind as he weaved through the crowds of gossiping academics. In two days, he would take the last exam he ever needed to take and then the world was wide open to him, rife with opportunities to make his mark in the world.

"Caesar! Hey, man, wait up!"

He stopped with a wince and a sigh. Against his better judgment, he turned to face the direction of the call. People frowned at him as they were forced to move around him, and he apologized for taking up space in the middle of the walkway. Archimedes reached him moments later, breathing heavily.

"Ark," Caesar greeted curtly.

"You left class in a hurry."

"I've got a lot of studying to do. Where's Grey?"

"Ah, he screwed off to catch some more shut-eye. We had kind of a late night."

"No kidding."

Archimedes grinned. "Yeah, we—"

Caesar held up a hand, cutting him off. "Please don't tell me. If and when the police come around to interrogate all of your known associates, I'd prefer not to have any knowledge that would implicate me in whatever the hell you two idiots got up to."

"You're jealous."

"I'm really not."

"You are. You heard about fun once and you really want to try it, but you can't. You will literally die if you have even a small amount of fun. The tiniest amount. You try to smile, whatever grotesque mockery of human emotion that might look like on your face, and you have a heart attack. Right there. Boom, dead."

Caesar sighed again and shifted his weight impatiently. "Ark, what do you want?"

"Let's go grab a drink. Grey's being an old lady and I'm bored."

"I have studying to do. As should you. Especially you. Nobody's going to want to elect you to speak if you're leaving here with middling test scores."

Archimedes laughed. "You're kidding, right? Nobody gives a damn whether or not a poli scored high on his exit exams. It only matters if they can talk themselves out of having to prove it. Come on, man." He held up his index finger. "One drink. Just one. We used to have the time of our lives, the three of us. Raising hell, having adventures."

"We were kids, Ark. At some point a guy needs to grow up and find some direction for his life."

"There's plenty of time for that when we graduate. We've got a few nights left to enjoy our youth. Then you get to go be a big science geek, I'll be charming the pants off the rich and powerful and beautiful, Grey will… do whatever he does, probably poorly, but the kid's got heart. You'll cry into your beakers because you miss us and because you can't live vicariously through us anymore. It'll be you and your geeks sitting around, not having fun together."

Caesar scowled at his friend. Still… he had known Archimedes a great many years and his words held a little truth. It was well known that graduation tended to result in the growing distance between friends as life pulled them along different paths. He glanced over Archimedes' shoulder to the beautiful academy glinting in the afternoon sun. He pivoted and looked towards Stagger Street, a nicknamed road lined with pubs tailored toward the university crowd.

"One drink," he said. "You're buying."

Archimedes grinned and wrapped his arm around Caesar's shoulders. "Of course. What are friends for?"

*****

The atmosphere on Outer Springer wasn't natural. The first settlers had touched down two hundred and thirty-seven years before on a mission from the planet it orbited—then called Springer, since renamed Inner Springer even though it would have been perfectly fine left alone—and worked tirelessly to create a sustainable environment in which to build a society. Seven different races collaborated together, and it was through their combined efforts that they were able to erect a collection of domed cities and an extensive rail system with which to connect them, all in a mere thirty-two years. It was a resource-rich, multi-species feat of engineering and coexistence that had rarely been seen before and never with such speedy results. The settlers became a community, the community a thriving town. Before long, the empty domes became bustling cities and further expansions were constructed as quickly as the materials could be shipped from Inner Springer.

The only shadow on what they had achieved was that it took nearly seven decades before any kind of structured law enforcement attempted to regulate the population.

In that time several of the domes had developed reputations as anything-goes locales, safe havens for dealers, smugglers, and murderers. Despite the initial acclaim and celebration that surrounded the moon's colonization and despite the popularity and esteem of the planet it orbited, Outer Springer had come to be known as a backwater sort of place to visit. Sure, there were laws. There were even more general rules to follow and some semblances of an organization that enforced those rules, but that enforcement was questionable at best. Anyone who lived there was almost guaranteed to be running from something. It took a certain type of person to even intentionally visit.

Euphrates Destidante was not that type of person. He preferred refined and intelligent discourse, not dealing with the type of people who holed up in shanties and played cards in hopes they could win enough chits to buy whatever watered-down beer would get them the drunkest the fastest. He had people for that kind of work. Professional, dependable people who *did* prefer the underworld of the galaxies. They got done the things he was unable or unwilling to do himself.

Even so, a distaste for getting one's hands dirty did not mean one wouldn't do so when pushed. To step out like this, to this place, took a special kind of offense. One that could not be ignored. He had thought about that offense the entire trip and though it didn't show, it incensed him more with each passing hour.

He found himself in Camoran, a city on the northern end of the moon. It was known as one of the more violent domes, rife with street fights and senseless killings. It was where the man he was looking for lived. When Euphrates sent six of his most trusted retrievers, it was in Camoran that they found him. The retrievers contacted Euphrates once the target had been properly subdued and relocated from his home, and he caught the first private transport he could arrange away from the curious eyes of his peers.

Upon landing, he utilized a black-market body scrambler to hide his appearance from any surveillance or sousveillance equipment he passed by. It did not take him long to reach his destination: a small storage shed behind a seedy nightclub called Fracture. Four of his men stood guard outside. The other two flanked a burly man strapped to a chair.

Euphrates closed the door behind him and pulled a second chair over until it sat a few feet across from his captive. He removed his coat—a finely tailored dark purple satin piece—and draped it over the back of his seat. One more moment was spent straightening his cuffs and then he lowered himself onto the chair. One leg swept up and over the other. Relaxed. Casual.

The prisoner's muscles swelled with the evidence of regular calisthenics, and it took twice as many cords to restrain him as it would have a lesser Human. More pressingly, this man was more than just a meathead. There was a prideful glint behind his eyes that indicated the kind of shrewdness necessary to not just survive but thrive in Camoran. To dominate. To stake a claim as some kind of slum lord.

A saying came to Euphrates' mind: pride goeth before destruction. He didn't subscribe to that belief personally. He believed that pride elevated confidence. It drove a man to set goals, work hard, and become accomplished. When a man was proud—properly proud—he wouldn't allow what he had succeeded at and acquired to be torn away, broken down, or stolen. A prideful man would keep an eye on his assets, his allies, his enemies, his resources, and he would make sure all of them were manageable.

A properly prideful man would admit he had flaws and would do his best to defend those flaws against attacks. A man like that could be wounded, because even a prideful man isn't invulnerable, but he would also be resilient.

Corrective.

No, Euphrates was not a man who shied away from pride. To him, pride was a wildly different animal from hubris. Looking at the man he had ordered bound to this chair, he reminded himself that it wasn't pride a man should be wary of. It was arrogance.

"You know who I am," he said.

"I've got an idea," the man replied. He spat a glob of spit and blood off to the side.

"I didn't ask a question," Euphrates said. "I stated a fact. You know who I am."

"…yeah. You're a public figure, after all."

"So I am. Albeit with private dealings." Euphrates drummed his fingers along his kneecap. "You are also a man with private dealings. So, you know who I am. Being a public figure, that's to be expected. But I know who you are, too. You, who live in an area that I should only know by the reports I receive. Paper reports with numbers on them instead of names. Papers that I then shred, and then burn, and the ashes of which I then scatter to the whims of the air passing by my office window. I should not know your name. I shouldn't know you even as a figure, a placeholder, an icon or anything similar. And yet."

"And yet," the other man sneered. "What do you want me to say, Destidante?"

"Nothing. You've said enough. That's why we're here."

Euphrates glanced at one of his guards. The man gave a tight nod and exited the shed. A few minutes later he returned with a folder in his hand. Euphrates took it, opened it, and flipped through the papers inside.

"Colby Tzarkev, also known as Skel. Male, obviously. Somewhere between forty and forty-three years of age. You don't know how old you are? Nobody else seems to know, either. Nobody cares. Not about a youth addicted to just about every drug he could get his hands on." He glanced up at his prisoner. "How have you lived this long? You should have stumbled into a fatal overdose by now. In fact, you nearly did, hmm… four times, it looks like.

"One of the few things I don't have here is how you managed to kick the habit. Couldn't have been a family intervention; you don't have any family left. Lucky for you, lucky for me. Whatever it was, you sobered up. Why spend money on drugs when you can *make* money by selling them? So you picked apart your competition in a methodical fashion. Infiltrating their ranks, ambushing them, brutalizing them. You sent messages. That, I like. I can get behind that. Onwards and upwards you rose until you found yourself as one of the many little spiders playing in the outer threads of my web. It's a cushy place to sit, where you were. Profitable. But that wasn't enough for you, was it?"

Tzarkev said nothing.

"Let me ask you a different question. Do you know what power is?"

"Of course I do," Tzarkev sneered. "I *have* power. Camoran is mine. It's been mine for years. The people here answer to me. They act in fear of me."

"That isn't power. You have—sorry, had—*influence*. You gave orders. People followed them. If they didn't, you served up a swift and brutal lesson. You had a tenuous control bolstered by your reputation." Euphrates lifted a hand, palm out. "Don't get me wrong. Building what you have after coming from where you did, it's impressive. That isn't what I'm talking about. I'm talking about *power*. Real power. The kind that means a man sitting a full Causeway and a galaxy away can compile a full dossier on some junkie thug beating his chest atop a filthy scrap pile on a filthy moon orbiting a—from what I can tell—perfectly mediocre planet. I know what your *blood type* is, Colby. Do you even know what your blood type is?"

"…Delphi-2."

Euphrates' brows rose. "Incredible. You actually managed to surprise me."

"You polis never know how to turn your damn mouths off," Tzarkev said, eyes flaring. "If you want to kill me, just kill me. I built something great here. My name'll last beyond my life. My legacy is in the blood and the stone of this dome. S'cool. I'm good with that. But your name? Your name will get out, too. And it won't look so good for you."

Euphrates uncrossed his legs and leaned forward, clasping his hands between his knees. "Colby, I want to tell you something. The shipments that come out here? I don't like them. I don't use drugs. I don't employ people who do, and my employees don't hire any users either. If I could get around selling the stuff entirely I would, but there are certain business associates who insist on it. I acquiesce because it's a deal-breaker for them, and the resources and information I gain from keeping them as allies are far too valuable for me to force the issue. Additionally, they give me a cut of the profits. That never hurts. Being in business with them is lucrative in a great many ways. It allows me to branch out far and wide, creating—as I said before—a web, with myself at the center.

"As with any web, there is a problem when something or someone snaps a thread. The disturbance creates a ripple. It threatens the integrity of the very thing I've spent so much time weaving together. I can't have that.

"If you had simply stolen one shipment and sold it, you might have been able to get away with it. If not, you'd have simply been killed quietly and dumped in an alley. If you had stolen a shipment in a clever way—and I mean *really* clever—you may have found yourself becoming an official resource. I like creative people. That would have been a good position to have. Too bad for you, you were clever in all the wrong ways and in all the wrong directions. You took too many shipments. You dug too far into where they were coming from, and you hurt too many people putting the pieces together. You found my name. My mistake was having a weakness in my protection that you could exploit. I admit that. Your mistake was crowing about what you had learned, using my name as if it were some kind of trophy or bargaining chip."

"But I did crow and other people know now," Tzarkev said. "There's even a data chip. You take me out, my people will release it. Your career will be over. You'll be disgraced, you'll get tossed into prison, and you'll get to see how tough you really are. I'm guessing not very."

Euphrates leaned back. A smile crossed his face, slowly, almost sad. "There is no chip. You certainly should have made one. That would have made things a bit more interesting. Your people? They're taken care of. They were touched first, before we even found you. That's power versus influence, Colby. I don't need to dig through the streets for hours and knock down doors to try and frantically stop some kind of leak. When I turn my attention to a problem, that problem ceases to be. That's what this meeting is about. That's what I wanted to drive home to you: when I leave here, *you* will cease to be. Colby Tzarkev? Never heard of him. Skel? Is that some kind of drink? This legacy you think you've built is nothing but paper reports. Shredded, burned, the ashes scattered to the wind."

Tzarkev opened his mouth to scream a retort but one of the two guards stuffed a thick cloth into it before he could get a sound out. The rag had been soaked in kerosene for no other reason than to make the experience more insufferable. Euphrates stood and donned a pair of purple satin gloves that matched his jacket. His second bodyguard handed him a heavy pistol.

Not too far away, a man who had successfully evaded the law after embezzling thirty million chits from his employer decided to share the wealth by buying the entire patronage of Fracture a round of drinks.

The resulting cheer of approval drowned out the gunshot.

<u>Chapter One</u>

What's Illegal, Anyway?

Three years later…

The courier's office had lines, but they didn't go anywhere. They were products of restless bodies arranging themselves in a visible manner while they waited impatiently for their turn to be called. Chairs would have been nice, and indeed there had been some in previous years, but the Aventure Courier Group found that when a spot of leisure was available to the public, it was only a matter of time until transients filled it. Instead of dealing with the hassle of keeping the riff-raff out, it was decided that job acquisition would stay an in-and-out, business-focused arrangement involving people who actually needed to be there.

Which did nothing to placate Caesar's tired legs. He sighed and glanced around the crowded common room. Members of a half-dozen races crossed their arms irritably, sighed loudly, shifted their weight from foot to occasionally clawed foot. Through a pair of glass doors they could see several large desks with ACG employees seated comfortably. That was where the jobs were selected, and each time a courier stood up with a commission ticket in hand the rest of them held their breath in anticipation.

Vvvvttt.

Whup-whup-whup-whup.

A hatch above the doors popped open and a device emerged. It was oval in shape and constructed from polished chrome save for a single blue lens front and center and the four aero-polymer wings at the back that allowed it to flit around the common room. They looked up as one—as they had every time a seat freed up—and followed its flight path while it made its rounds.

The drone stopped at Caesar's place in the line. It descended at a controlled pace until it was even with his head, then turned so the lens could get a proper angle on his face. A red light blinked to life at the bottom.

"State your name, ship classification, and the name of your craft," it buzzed.

"Caesar Morelo Anada. C-ranked courier ship. Designated *Sol Searcher*."

"Captain Anada, please make your way to Center Twelve. Aventure Employment Agent Bazregga will see you."

"Thanks, robot thing."

Caesar nodded sheepishly to the others as he shuffled past them into the next room. They weren't particularly quick in getting out of his way and he felt a twinge of guilt despite having waited just as long as most of them. Once he was past the glass doors, he turned his eyes away from his peers and toward the columns placed between each desk. Each one had a brass plate fixed to it displaying a number in progressive order. He made his way past eleven of them, but it wasn't until he had reached his destination that he realized he had met Agent Bazregga before.

He sighed.

"Hello again," he said, forcing a cheer he didn't feel from his ribs and out through his teeth.

"Sit down, Captain," said Bazregga. She waved one clawed hand towards the seat in front of her desk. He plopped down into it and squirmed in an attempt to get comfortable. It never worked, and he continued believing the chairs were designed to be unpleasant so couriers would be encouraged to leave as swiftly as possible.

The agent was a Skir, with mottled purple skin denoting her gender. Her bunched face seemed small in comparison to the ridged cranial crest that stretched behind her. Four nasal holes shared a gap above her mouth and the skin around them flared when she exhaled sharply.

So she wasn't in a good mood. Great. This was going swimmingly already.

"Pilot's license and ship registration."

"Certainly." Caesar fished from his back pocket a pair of data cards—the edges long worn down into smooth curves—and slid them across. Bazregga scanned them and squinted down at the information scrolling along her side of the desk. She grunted.

"Any outstanding warrants for you or your crew?"

"Uh, no." He scratched behind his ear. She had an ability to make him nervous even though he had done nothing wrong. He suspected she knew this, too, by the way she continued to stare at him without blinking. Skir had eyelids. He knew they did.

"Any no-fly orders for your ship?"

"No, is there… does it say that there?" he asked. "When you scanned my cards? Because I swear, I can't think of--"

"It does not."

"Oh, good. Then—"

"But computers make mistakes."

Caesar raised an eyebrow at that. "How often does that happen? My cards are current."

"Often enough that I feel the need to ask, Captain." Bazregga typed something into her system, stared at him again. "What is the current number of your crew?"

"Three permanent, including myself."

"Do you pick up temporary crew often? Do you sublet jobs to freelancers?"

"I wouldn't say often, no."

"How regularly, then? And are you aware that when subletting jobs you need to file with an Aventure agent before pick-up is made so that arrangements can be made regarding occupational insurance and liability agreements?"

Her eyes burned into him as she spoke, so Caesar avoided eye contact. He focused instead on the edge of the desk closest to him and picked at the arm of the chair. "We don't sublet jobs. As far as crew, I don't know. We have a friend on board every now and then."

"But not a certified courier?"

"No."

"Nor a freelancer?"

"I don't think I even know a freelancer on a first name basis. Grey or Ark might, but-"

"So by not often you meant never," Bazregga interrupted with a scowl. "So you could have just said three."

Caesar tried a smile. It had no effect. "I suppose I could have just said three. You're right. I'm sorry."

"That would have sufficed."

"Got it."

"Captain Anada, do you have any idea how busy this agency is?" She gestured around the room to illustrate her point. "Were you blind in that waiting room? How did you manage to find your way to my desk? I wasn't aware the columns called out their numbers as you passed by them and I'm terrified to inquire as to your capabilities as a pilot."

Caesar folded his hands in his lap and stared at them. It seemed the safest course of action.

"Would you like to look at the job list and pick something now, or would you like to continue wasting everyone's time?"

"I'd like to look at the jobs," he said meekly. "May I see the list?"

Bazregga showed off her pointed yellow teeth in a grin that took up half of her face. She pointed at him and he flinched involuntarily. "You should see the options on your side of the desk. Use the arrows to scroll. Select a job for more information on it and when you find one you like for your crew, select the Approve button and sign on the line. Keep in mind that everyone you were waiting with is also a courier looking for a job and that delaying acceptance may result in a job being acquired by someone else."

Caesar knew the routine but he wasn't risking anymore of the Skir's ire by saying so. He leaned forward instead, taking in the list. Each job appeared initially as a single line with a pick-up location, the drop-off location, the total package weight, and the payment offered for a successful delivery. His finger hovered over the Down arrow and tapped it when his eyes reached the bottom of the list. Three screens later, he rubbed at his eyes to make sure he was seeing clearly.

"What is this? Half a million chits to deliver a small item? I've never seen the same weight go for even half that."

"I don't look at all the jobs, Captain. That's your responsibility."

"Right. Forget I said anything."

"If only I could."

Caesar scowled—downwards so Bazregga couldn't see it—and tapped the job. He skimmed over the details, trying to grasp the important information before some other crew could pull it out of his hands. It was a single item, meaning if the listed weight was right it was probably a parcel or a small crate. Maybe some kind of antiquity, given the payment offered. Delivery was

set for a private residence on Peloclade. That was only a single Causeway away, meaning the

half-million payout would cover fuel enough for the trip several times over. Hell, it could even

cover the repair costs for half a dozen problems that had been plaguing their ship.

He hit the Approve button with enough force to hurt his thumb. It flashed green, an indicator

that no other captain had taken the job while he was reading. The signature line popped up next

and he drew his index finger along it in an approximation of his full name.

A paper printed out on Bazregga's end, a physical copy of his contract approval, and she

handed it to him. She started speaking again, either congratulating him on finally making a

decision or admonishing him for not already being on his way out of the building. He honestly

thought it might be a clever mix of both, but he wasn't really listening. He clutched the contract,

already thinking about how he would break the good news to his friends.

*****

Three feathered drakes circled lazily overhead, nipping playfully at each other's tails. They had

flown in roughly the same spot for almost an hour, seemingly in no hurry to move on either to

find food or even a quieter placed to roost. Archimedes could relate. Since waking, he had sat in

the co-pilot's seat with his feet propped up on the control panel. The sun was a warm blanket

over him as it filtered through the *Sol Searcher's* viewport. He felt like a cat. A really good-

looking cat.

"I don't know how you can watch those things. They creep me the hell out. I kind of want to go out and potshot them."

Archimedes turned as much as he could in his seat without compromising his comfort. Grey stepped into the cockpit with a data screen in hand and plopped his full weight into the pilot's chair, letting out a loud belch.

"Firing a gun on a public landing station always goes well," said Archimedes. "I say go for it. Also, good morning, Grey. So glad to see you up."

"Yeah?"

"Yeah. I was worried I'd be able to enjoy a quiet morning to myself for once. Thank God you're always around to snatch away a good thing."

"If you want quiet," said Grey, scratching his belly, "go back to your room."

"I'm already settled in here. And it's warm. And look at the view."

Grey made a face over his data screen. He pointed out the window. "What view? It's a bunch of rusted buckets out there. I'd be surprised if the majority of them aren't scrap metal and fire the first time they try to take off. If half those captains knew what kind of potential was purring under their asses, those could be fixed into *actual* ships. Then it wouldn't be so depressing every time we came in for a job." He shook his head. "It's like landing in a fucking graveyard."

Archimedes closed his eyes and rolled them under the lids. "What've you got on your screen there?"

"The news."

"You don't read the news."

"I do when it's interesting," Grey said. He keyed on the audio system and linked in his favorite playlist. The first song to crow out of the speakers was *Worldwide Outlaws* by the Datacasters.

Grey considered it a classic; Archimedes considered it the equivalent of trying to dice something with a meat tenderizer: a blunt, destructive disaster that left everyone disappointed and resulted in a goopy, disgusting mess.

"And interesting to you is…"

"The Gamma Men got a new bassist."

"Don't care."

"Umm, new personality cores announced for personal service robots."

"Useless," said Archimedes. "No, wait, that's actually awesome. I can use that. I'm buying one."

"What the hell are you going to put a personality core in?"

"I'm obviously going to have to buy a robot, too, Grey. Keep up. What else is in the news?"

Grey glanced down. "Bandit activity around Dephros."

"That's not even *news*," said Archimedes, throwing his hands up. "There's always bandit activity out there. They call it the 'bandit moon', for God's sake."

"Caesar would care. And it isn't always so bad out there. Estie says it has charm."

"Estella is obviously biased, and you know it. And Caesar wouldn't care. He'd fake it, maybe, if he weren't out thanking every god he can think of that he isn't in here being forced to listen to what you call music."

Grey tossed his data screen onto the control panel and turned in his seat. "You know what, Carnahan? If you don't like it, you can hop your ass off the ship. If you keep yapping about the things I like, though, I'll drag you off myself and you can kiss your dumpy little hole of a room goodbye. I'll convert it into another bathroom so something useful actually happens in there."

Archimedes stood, the frustration of having his tranquil morning interrupted turning into a full-blown anger. "I'd like to see you try, shitheel. Don't forget that a third of the *Searcher* is mine. The creditors won't, I can promise that."

"Ahem."

Both men turned to look at the entrance to the cockpit. Caesar stood there, a familiar paper in his hand. He leaned against the door frame looking unimpressed. The expressions on his friends' faces quickly matched his own.

"Did you just *say* ahem?" asked Grey.

"I, uh, didn't have to clear my throat for real. Don't you want to know what I was doing?"

"We can see you got a contract, Caesar," said Archimedes. "You couldn't even fake clearing your throat? We're arguing. That was the weakest, most half-hearted…"

Caesar scowled. "Well, you've knocked it off for now, right, so listen to me. The job I picked up for us is great. Maybe the best we've ever landed. Small weight, short distance, big pay-out."

"How big?" asked Archimedes.

"Half a million chits to hop down to Akers' storage, pick up what looks like a box or something, and take it to Peloclade."

Grey frowned. "Let me see that." Caesar unfolded the contract and handed it over. Grey scanned it and looked up at the ceiling, calculating. "You're sure the weight is listed right?"

"I mean, we'll know for sure when we pick it up, but I don't see why it wouldn't be."

"Peloclade isn't too far," said Archimedes. "That would leave us quite a bit left over. I could get a new bed."

"Forget your bed. We can finally get a pair of light cannons and the permit to arm the *Searcher* with them. I'm thinking under the front, mounted on a pair of cupolas to allow for a wider range of defensive coverage. I'll have to wire controls up through the hull, but that's the easiest part."

Caesar cleared his throat, this time for real. "*I* was thinking we could get the stabilizer fixed, seeing as how the one we have right now is unreliable at best."

Grey scowled. "Who needs to waste money on a stabilizer when you've got a pair of crack pilots that can balance the ship out."

"If you find a couple, I'll stop worrying about it, but until then I think it's a valid concern. This job is the best opportunity we have to get it sorted without starving between jobs."

Grey sighed and kicked lightly at the pilot's console. "I just really want--"

"You want cannons," said Archimedes. "We know. It's because you're a sociopath. Caesar, my morning's already ruined. Let me take a shower, hope Grey doesn't interrupt that, too, and we'll go."

Caesar nodded and made room for his friend to pass by. He looked over at Grey and opened his mouth to offer some kind of commiseration to make up for shooting down his plans to add cannons; he clamped it shut again when the stocky man reached out and turned the music up further. *Supernova Messiah* by Daniel Baltennan pounded through the halls of the *Sol Searcher*.

Somewhere near the bathroom, Archimedes swore loudly.

*****

In person, a gathering of the Universal Council could be overwhelming, especially to the uninitiated. Each of the seventeen dominant races sent at least one Speaker. The average was two or three, while the Wanos sent the most, at five. Each Speaker also had at least one Advisor present to take notes, keep them on track, and even speak for them on occasion in their absence. After that came the time-keepers and record-makers. Adjudicators were necessary: impartial, elected members of one of the many less-influential races. They had their own seconds and thirds and small councils. There were also journalists and a small crowd of the general public. In the latter case, these spots were always filled on a first-come, first-serve basis and served as a form of transparency for the population of the connected galaxies who wanted to keep up to date on current affairs.

All told, a Council meeting would consist of anywhere from three hundred to five hundred bodies. For that reason, they only met in person on a quarterly basis, defined by a year on Elagabalus. That was where the massive Council headquarters had been constructed: a densely populated planet that served as the hub for some of the most prosperous interspecies commercial interests.

Elagabalus had sixteen months to its year. For each of the remaining twelve months, the Council would meet via holoconference. Each race had their preferred location to broadcast from and each room was customized by that race to fit their preferences, though the presentation was largely the same. In the center of a large conference room, the three-dimensional image of whichever Speaker had the floor would be displayed alongside relevant reports, graphs, or evidence they wanted to have showcased. A second screen would be laid out on a desk or personalized tablet; this would have a complete list of those present in the meeting. Whoever was speaking would have their name illuminated in blue. The next Speaker or Advisor queued would be yellow. After that, barring interruptions to discuss whatever topic was currently on the table, those queued would be listed in numerical order.

Many preferred the digital congregations. They weren't as loud or as hot—though the Council hall on Elagabalus allowed for plenty of open space, the sheer amount of people present often raised the temperature to an uncomfortable degree—and the listing system for waiting contributors was far more organized. The virtual meetings also cut down on travel costs and the room and board reservations that went with the trip. Though the meetings came often and the life of a Councilmember was a hectic one, the ability to conduct large portions of business from the comforts of home was a welcome perk.

Rors Volcott, Speaker for the Human race, was one of the few who felt more alive when he was in the same room as everyone he addressed. He felt energized when surrounded by his peers; he had joined the military instead of a theater troupe in his youth at the pressure of his mother, but he had expressed several times throughout the years that he thought he would have made for an exemplary thespian.

Be that as it may, it was the military that had shaped him into the imposing figure that presented himself today. In his late fifties, he maintained the fortitude of a man two decades his junior wrapped up in a tall, burly frame. His head and chin were shaved bald while thick, gray chops bristled out from his cheeks and connected via a well-oiled mustache. His eyes were the light blue of early winter frost and he gave voice to the calculated thoughts behind them in a deep baritone.

He paced back and forth across his air-conditioned office. The rest of the Council would have him in full display where they sat. He had his own display separated into two images. The first was Graxus, the Ryxan Speaker he was currently debating; the second was a rotating cycle of several other members, selected by Volcott's Advisor so he could gauge their reactions as he spoke. Though Volcott's words were technically directed towards Graxus, they were *for* the rest of the Council.

From where he sat at the back of the office, Euphrates admired Volcott's technique. They both knew Graxus' brutish size and appearance belied his intellect, and that he was uncharacteristically patient for a member of the *adum* caste; when it was his turn to speak, he said his piece in full and waited for his opponent to do the same. He never interrupted and he never forgot the points and counterarguments he wanted to address, something few other Speakers were able to do without the assistance of an Advisor. Despite this, Volcott was less concerned with irritating the Ryxan and more concerned with winning the opinions of the other Council members.

The point in contention today was the tripling of the export price for an industrial oil unique to the Ryxan territories called celaron. The severity of the escalation itself would have been cause for annoyance but would have been somewhat understandable if it had at least been spread equally among the other races. After all, when one is the sole provider of a resource, they have free reign of how to price it. Instead, the Ryxan had chosen to pin their exorbitant fees on the Humans alone.

That's not completely true, Euphrates thought, flicking through his reports. They had imposed the new prices on the Serobi as well, but as the Serobi had never before expressed any interest in the oil, it was a pointless gesture serving only as the faintest argument that they weren't specifically trying to target Humans.

The snub was seemingly unprovoked and Volcott was trying to rectify it—or at least minimize it—before tensions between the races escalated into something more serious. He strode across the floor with his hands behind his back, casting the occasional piercing glance at whoever needed to be drawn back into the discussion.

"As has been demonstrated here today and over the past few months, we have been diligent, respectful, and punctual in our business dealings with the Ryxan peoples through tens of thousands of corporations and through millions of trades and transactions. Indeed, it has been proven over the last two centuries that though there have been varying personal and political tensions between us, our commercial collaborations have always risen above such squabbles. Those incidents were unrelated and should remain so instead of tainting the healthier aspects of our relationship. Instead it seems that other interests, perhaps even wounded feelings, are at the heart of the matter here. The result isn't one of prudence. It is an attack.

"Or… perhaps it is only a misunderstanding. Perhaps the prices were simply miscalculated. Maybe we did something to unintentionally slight the noble Ryxan and reparations should be made. We, of course, would be more than happy to field a more thorough explanation from either Speaker Graxus or Speaker Tarbanna. Before that, however, we would like to present specific details on how the trade agreement as it currently stands has negatively affected the Human race's corporate, commercial and industrial interests and investments.

"This is normally where my esteemed colleague, Speaker Suvis, would step forward to address the Council. Unfortunately, Speaker Suvis has taken ill and is currently doing her best to rest and recover so that she can rejoin us soon. In the meantime, she has placed her trust in her Advisor, Euphrates Destidante, to speak in her stead. If you would be so kind as to give him the floor now and direct your attention to him, he will go over his reports with you all."

This was the moment Euphrates had been waiting patiently for. He had spoken in front of the Council before, but it never grew less exciting for him. He reveled in having the attention of some of the universe's most powerful individuals centered on him; he lived to have them cling to his every word.

Euphrates ignored the other Advisor as he stepped up to the center of the room. Volcott retook his seat and pressed a button on the inside of the left armrest. A podium rose from the floor directly in front of Euphrates; Euphrates tossed a slight nod of gratitude Volcott's way, then laid his notes out.

He took a moment to still his heart and compose his thoughts. There was no need to rush. To be a member of the Council was to exercise control. If there was one thing he enjoyed above all else, it was exactly that.

"Speakers and Advisors of the Council, assembled keepers, adjudicators and witnesses, thank you for your attendance and attention. The task assigned to me is a sobering one: bringing to your attention the statistics regarding our dealings with the Ryxan and the position they have put the Human race in. However, this task is also an important one. Only through understanding the facts can we then attempt to find a satisfactory compromise that will restore stability and civil discourse between our peoples. Now, if you'll direct your attention to the infographics I'm bringing up on your displays…"

*****

Nothing was resolved by the meeting's end, but these things seldom ever were. Not in a handful of hours on a single afternoon, no matter how many charts and numbers you threw at a wall. A stand-off of this magnitude was less a tea-time disagreement and more a war to be picked apart over a series of battles. It was up to him to prepare for the next engagement. He had under a month to do so.

The hallways of Thorus' Parliament of Universal Interest were significantly brighter than the conference room had been. Euphrates used the reports in his hand to shield his eyes as he weaved through the attendants filling the passageways. The day had been long enough, he didn't need to add a headache to it.

"You're in a damned hurry, Destidante."

Too late. Euphrates sighed to himself.

It was a testament to the years he had spent training for the political arena that he didn't flinch when Talys Wannigan stepped up next to him. Volcott's Advisor was a thin man with wispy brown hair that he kept parted down the middle. His suits always seemed to hang a bit loose from his slight frame, leaving him looking inept and ill-prepared. Euphrates knew it was a calculated move that left other politicians overlooking and underestimating him. That was a mistake. Talys was frightfully intelligent and he had a nasty habit of always being in the last place you wanted him to be.

Like right next to you.

"I thought you handled yourself well in there. Better than your first couple times. I'm sure most people left feeling you had actually accomplished something, that your reports were accurate, and they'll probably leave it at that. But what do you think? How many will actually take a good look at your reports?"

"*Our* reports," said Euphrates. "We're on the same side, Talys. Human solidarity and all that."

"The same side. Sure, sure. How much of that information did you come up with on your own and how much did Magga hand down to you? Is she even sick or was she trying to drown you in the deep end?"

Euphrates stopped in the middle of the hall and turned to the other Advisor. He waited until attendants had passed by on either side, leaving them alone for a few moments. "What do you want, Talys?" he asked in a low tone. "Why are you nipping at my heels?" He folded the reports in his hands and slid them into his inside breast pocket.

"Professional competitive interest. I want to know what you said that convinced Magga to let you speak for her on this issue. Why didn't she just hand everything over to Rors and let him handle it?"

"*I'm* Magga's Advisor, Talys, not Rors. I'm the one that spends dusk to dawn working with her, and in so doing have proven to her that I am capable of operating independently, and that she can trust me to do so. That's why she allows me to speak in her absence and why I'm sure Rors never steps aside to allow you."

If the words struck a nerve, Talys' grin refused to acknowledge it. "Perhaps, Destidante. Perhaps. Trust is a valuable, powerful thing. It's probably good, then, that Magga is too sick to realize at least some of the reports you offered up were doctored."

Euphrates' eyes narrowed. "I don't know what you're talking about."

Talys nodded to a pair of passing women and waited until they were out of earshot. He stepped in closer and lowered his voice. "Maybe you don't. Maybe you just went up and read off whatever she put together for you before she got too sick to attend the one meeting a month she's actually expected to be present for. Terrible timing. Really quite sad."

"I resent your implication that her illness was either falsified or manufactured. I resent your accusation that the reports I presented were anything less than genuine as well."

"And I'm sure that most people will give them a casual glance and believe them to be so. There would be several layers of peeling needed before something seemed amiss. You're a thorough man."

Euphrates straightened slowly, his expression growing black, cold. "Talys, the situation we find ourselves in, *as a race*, has the potential to leave us in scrambling for purchase on the Council hierarchy if a more favorable resolution isn't found. It's something that transcends petty rivalries or peacocking or whatever kind of angle you're trying to get your tiny hands on. The Ryxan understand that and will be looking for any cracks they might widen, any flaws they might exploit. You know that, which means you know that I have a limited amount of time to prepare Magga, Rors, *you* and myself for whatever arguments and accusations come from *the Ryxan* at the next meeting." Euphrates narrowed his eyes. "I did accomplish something in there today, Wannigan. *I bought us time*. Be careful not to spoil what goods we have gained."

Talys' grin widened, and he nodded enthusiastically. "Quite right, quite right. When you put it that way, I suppose I see your point. I hope you've seen mine too: it's important that us Humans are all on the same page. That we know where we stand. That we know where the secrets are and what might be exposed if someone were thought to be acting against the good of us all. Or if someone were to step on the wrong toes."

"I hear you loud and clear," hissed Euphrates.

"Perfect. Again, well done in there. Masterful performance. I do so admire your work."

Talys winked and turned back towards the conference room. Euphrates watched him go, the other man's words echoing in his ears. It took him a minute to realize his hands were balled into fists by his sides. He forced them into his pockets and stretched his neck.

It did little to clear his head.

*****

Akers' Storage was the larger of two sanctioned courier pickup lots in Catalasca and one of seventeen on Salix. It was a family-owned business five generations deep and was run by a Human, old Gabber Akers, who had inherited it from his father some years before. When it had first opened, it was a handful of shacks with sliding metal doors and thick metal padlocks—you could bring your own, but the ones Akers' sold were often more secure than the options at the nearby stores—and a couple of family friends that worked for cheap who kept an eye and a rifle on things. They were humble beginnings, but Atrus Akers wasn't so humble a man. He had a knack for finding the right circles to spread a word, and that (coupled with a reputation for honesty and reliability) helped the business expand.

The storage units filled up quickly, and Atrus invested carefully. As demand grew, prices inched up until more units could be built to accommodate the customers. More units meant more clients meant more money. Pretty soon a wide variety of spaces were open to rent or store packages until they could be sent or delivered. Atrus Akers dropped *Reliable Repository* from the space above the door and replaced it with a garish blue neon display of his own name. It was his and he was proud.

The business continued to grow, so the staff did as well. Fences were constructed around the lot. Wooden buildings were replaced with metal ones. The doors were replaced with thicker steel ones. For the larger units requiring the sliding door variants, auto-lock mechanisms were installed to stop any unauthorized breaches. Security cameras kept an eye on the aisles separating the units. Password locks replaced padlocks, with software installed to shut down any invasive programs and an alert that would sound when a wrong code had been entered too many times. Even the security personnel had been increased once it was decided that Akers' would be open all day and night.

Five generations later, the storage lot was even older than a few of the courier companies that contracted out to it. Gabber didn't rest on his laurels, though: he would eagerly snatch up a deal with any new prospects that cropped up. Gaining new clients was good business. Good business was good money. Everyone liked money.

Caesar preferred Akers' to the other courier stops on Salix. Location, for one reason— Catalasca was temperate and busy, a real city with a generally well-behaved populace—but also because the other local pickup lot (Skyline Imports and Exports) was cramped, rarely cleaned, and sat under an ancient bridge in a low-lit part of the city with a history of crime.

The woman behind the desk had her hair tied back in a ponytail and looked up from her paperwork at them through squared-lens glasses as they walked in. The little metal tag on her lapel read 'Morgan'. The expression on her face read 'mildly inconvenienced.'

"May I help you?" she asked.

"We're couriers with ACG," said Caesar. "We're here to pick up a package for delivery." He stepped up to the counter and slid his identification card across to the woman, along with their printed contract for the job.

"Alright, thank you," said Morgan under her breath, all routine. Her eyes slipped over the details on the paperwork. Her fingers were a blur across the keyboard as she pulled up Caesar's profile. "You're all good to go through, but I need to see their IDs as well, please."

Grey fished his card from his back pocket and handed it to the desk clerk. She glanced at the front and back, pulled up his file and nodded. Everyone turned to look at Archimedes. Ark was chewing the inside of his cheek as he checked his pockets one at a time. He set a collection of items on the counter: a handful of chits, one of the ignition keys to the *Searcher*, a VIP pass to a nightclub on Peloclade.

Noticeably absent was his identification.

"What the hell are you doing?" asked Grey.

"I think I left my card back on the ship," said Archimedes. He poked his fingers into his inside coat pocket. They came out with an expired transit pass. It was a year old.

"We waited for you," said Caesar, "so that you could get ready. How are you not ready?"

"Must have slipped my mind. Could have been the terrible music beating me over the head that distracted me, I don't know."

"I swear to God," growled Grey.

"Look," said Archimedes, leaning over the counter. "I can give you my courier code. You can pull up my profile with that, right? Compare my mug shot to the mug standing in front of you."

Morgan shook her head. "I need your identification. I have to make sure it's authentic and up to date. I need to make sure there aren't any restrictions or revocations on it, too. It's policy."

"We've been coming here for two years, Ark," said Caesar. "You know you need your ID."

"After two years, I would have hoped we'd be more recognizable. What time are you off? If you could just make an exception for me, I promise I'll be right in and out. I would be incredibly grateful and more than happy to make it up to you with dinner or a show."

Morgan gave a thin smile. "I'm not interested. Even if I were, I wouldn't be interested enough to risk my job."

"Am I not handsome enough?"

"You aren't *woman* enough." She appraised him. "Although you're close."

Grey snorted loudly. "She's got you there, Carnahan."

"Just wait in the lobby, Ark," said Caesar.

Archimedes slumped into one of the chairs set against the wall. "I'll just wait in the lobby. I guess."

"Yes, you will," said the desk clerk. She gave a wide smile to the other two men and handed Caesar a slip of paper. "Your pickup is in unit P-312. I've written the code for the lock on the paper there. It's good for twenty-four hours."

"Thanks, Morgan," said Grey. "You've been a great help. Don't let that guy talk to you anymore."

Caesar pushed through a door at the back of the lobby and walked out amongst the long aisles of storage units. Different colored letters marked the aisles for easier navigation. A handful of other couriers and customers passed them by and milled about in front of the units their contracts had led them to.

As they walked, Grey glanced up at the security cameras. He did it out of habit; he had broken enough laws in his life that paranoia kept a snug seat on his shoulder whenever he was in public. The cameras each had a tiny bulb just below the lens. None were illuminated, and Grey figured they had their security systems set for live surveillance only. He chalked it up to power conservation, but it still didn't make much sense to him not to be recording all the time.

"What do you think it is?" he asked, bringing his eyes back down to the path.

"Come again?"

"What do you think the package is?"

Caesar pushed some of the moppy hair from his face and frowned. "Something valuable, obviously. Jewelry or antiques, I'm guessing."

"Antiques fetch that much? Even something that small?"

"Antiques and art, sure. Fibrelli eggs, for example. They're about the size of your fist and fetch an easy ten million chits each. At least."

Grey whistled. "Good thing we're honest."

"*I'm* honest. You and Ark are iffy. Besides, it pays more in the long run to keep our reputation as reliable deliverers. We can build a career off of that."

"There are career thieves, too. We just need a couple Fibberal eggs to give us some capital."

"Fibrelli, and you wouldn't know how or where to sell one." The scowl on Caesar's face looked like it was chiseled there. Grey grinned and shrugged. It was too easy to get his friend riled up. How Caesar hadn't snapped and tried to kill Archimedes or him yet was a mystery.

They rounded a corner and almost ran into a trio of men, two Humans and a massive Bozav. Grey and Caesar stepped around either side of them and mumbled an apology. The Bozav grunted and shook out his silver mane, then continued on out of sight with his companions.

The couriers kept walking, eyeing the numbers on the storage units as they counted upward. P-312 was tucked between two spaces large enough to fit a speeder in; they missed it during their first passing and had to backtrack to find it.

Caesar pulled out the slip of paper Morgan had given him and glanced at the digits to make sure he remembered them correctly. His fingers tapped each of the eight numbers in sequence, the pad lighting up yellow as he touched it. Once the code was complete, the pad flashed green twice. There were a series of clicks as the metal door unlocked and then a whirring noise as it slid upward.

A single light flickered to life, bright enough to illuminate the entire space. The unit itself was unimpressive, bare save for a table situated exactly in the center. A small blue cooler with a number lock of its own sat on top.

"Huh," said Grey.

There were a pair of loud clicks and Grey's attention was torn from the package. He glanced up at the door, but it hadn't begun to descend again. The lock pad's status remained the same as well. He turned to glance back the way they had come and spotted the group they had nearly collided with. The two Humans led, handguns extended in their direction.

"Company," hissed Grey.

Caesar glanced up, curious. His eyes widened when he saw the approaching gunmen. He crumpled the paper with the code on it and tossed it into the unit. His fingers dragged down the lock pad next, causing it to flare red with the incorrect entry. The door slammed closed, sealing the cooler back inside.

"What are they packing? Pulse guns? Lasers?"

"No. Those ones shoot bullets. Stun rounds if you're lucky."

They fell quiet as the three men cornered them. The Humans cast a glance either way, looking for security. With none in sight, the Bozav grabbed Caesar by the neck and lifted him off the ground. Grey stepped forward in protest but the man to his left put the barrel of his gun into Grey's chest and pushed him back.

"Open the unit," said Lefty.

"Piss off," spat Grey in return.

"Come on, guy," said Righty. "Taghrin can pop your friend's head right off." The Bozav grinned, serrated fangs standing out. Caesar had both of his arms wrapped over the arm holding him suspended, trying to take the pressure off of his airway.

"The package isn't yours," said Lefty. "We're not taking *your* stuff. It's probably insured. You can tell whichever company you contract out of that you got stuck up. It happens all the time.

You're in the clear."

"You would shoot us in the middle of Akers'?" asked Grey. "That's gutsy."

"We don't want to, but the payday is worth it."

"Grey," gasped Caesar. "Let them take it."

"Shut up, buddy," Grey said lightly.

"No, keep talking," said Righty. "Tell me what the lock code is."

"Caesar…"

"The lock code is—"

"In my jacket pocket," interrupted Grey. He held his hands up in surrender. "Alright? You win. Don't hurt my friend. I'm going to reach into my pocket and grab the damn code. Keep your guns on me if it makes you feel better."

"It does," said Righty. "Hurry up."

Grey reached into his pocket and fumbled around. As he pulled his hand free, he dropped a silver sphere about the size of an orange. It bounced twice and then rolled to a stop between Lefty's feet.

"Ah, hell," said Grey. "That's what happens when you rush me. I panic."

"What is it, Dawson?" asked Righty.

"It's some kind of ball."

"It's not exactly a ball, Dawson," said Grey.

"Then what is it?"

"It's a novelty wallet. The blue button on top, you push it, it opens up. I've got a couple hundred chits in there and a meal card to Lorcciano's. Go ahead and take it while I look for the damn password. I'll have the company reimburse me for damages or something."

He eyed Dawson in his periphery. The gunman's curiosity got the better of him. He held the pistol steady in his right hand and switched the sphere to his left. His thumb found the inset button and depressed it.

"Eyes and ears, Caesar," said Grey. He didn't quite shout it, but he put enough of an edge into the words that his friend immediately took note. Caesar removed his arms from the Bozav's and clapped his hands over his ears. His eyes clenched shut. Grey did the same.

A second and a half later, there was a booming noise loud enough that Grey could feel it in his chest. His eyelids lit up yellow, briefly, and he gasped at the intensity despite taking only a fraction of the glare. He must have forgotten to carry a one somewhere when he was calculating the output. Math had always been more Caesar's thing.

Grey opened his eyes and saw that the Bozav, though stunned, still held Caesar aloft. Grey kicked the massive creature between the legs, hoping Bozav males had similar anatomy to his own; the wheezing bellow that followed filled him with delight. Caesar dropped to the ground and rubbed at his eyes with his forearm.

"I'm blind, Barrus," Dawson croaked. He clutched at his face with both hands. His pistol and Grey's sphere both lay at his feet.

"What?" asked the man to the right. "What?" He waved his gun around and then lowered it, apparently considering the risk to his companions should he start firing wildly.

"You lied to them," Caesar choked out. His throat was a deep red.

"We can talk about the merits of honesty later, pal."

"What was that thing? It wasn't a wallet."

"Really? What gave you a hint, the bang or the brightness?" Caesar opened his mouth to say something else. The words were choked off as Grey grabbed him by his arm and pulled him into a brisk jog. "It was just something I cooked up in my lab. Not exactly illegal, but not legal enough that we should wait around and try to explain ourselves."

They left the three muggers dazed behind them as the concerned shouts of Akers' security rang through the air.

The concussive boom could be heard as far as the front office. Morgan started in her seat and alternated looking at the display monitor to turning to the door each time a courier passed through in a hurry to exit. Archimedes watched her from where he sat, more interested in her reaction than whatever had caused the commotion. He drummed his fingers on the seat of the chair next to him.

"Will you stop that?" the desk clerk finally snapped at him.

"*That's* what bothers you?" Archimedes asked skeptically. "Not the loud, explosive noise?"

"You're *not* bothered by the explosive noise?"

"I mean, this isn't a place I would expect to hear something like that, but I don't see any smoke. You haven't jumped up to swear and scream about a fire. Nobody has run through here covered in blood or missing any limbs. No tears are flowing, nobody's saying anything about bodies. I can wait until I know what's going on a little more conclusively from the, I hope, relative safety of this lobby before I break my neck over it."

Morgan paused her panic to narrow her eyes at him. "Do you always talk so much?"

Archimedes gave his most winning grin. "Pretty much."

The woman huffed and turned away. Archimedes craned his neck to see what she was doing. On her screen, the software used to pull up authorized entrants to the storage units was minimized. Replacing it was a large grid of video feeds. She selected one and enlarged it; Archimedes could make out a concentration of bodies engaged in some kind of scuffle.

"What's going on there, in that square?"

"Mind your own business."

"Can you rewind it? We can see how the fight started."

"I've been trying and it hasn't been—*will you mind your own business?*"

Sighing loudly, the courier started to sink back into his chair. The door at the back of the lobby whipped open again and Grey and Caesar piled in. The former grabbed Archimedes by the arm and jerked him out of the chair.

"We're going."

"Hold on, what happened?"

"Wouldn't know," said Caesar a little too quickly, a little too unconvincingly.

"Where's the package?"

"Caesar and I were feeling a little peckish," said Grey. "We decided to get something to eat first and come back later. In case it was heavy or something."

Archimedes started to ask another question but something in Caesar's eyes convinced him it would be better to wait. He let Grey push him through the front door and out onto the street. He cast one last glance back at the desk before the entrance closed and caught Morgan staring after them from behind it.

*****

It was late when Euphrates finally arrived home and he was mildly surprised to find several

lights on. He closed the door gently, letting the lock arm itself, and took his jacket off. Instead of

using one of the ivory hooks on the wall to hang it, he folded it over his right arm. He used his

left hand to pull a small pistol from the back of his waistband and slipped the gun into his right.

The coat concealed it nicely.

Talys wouldn't be so bold, he thought. *Especially not so soon after showing his hand. He's too*

cocky, too eager to play games, too ready to blackmail. He considered the other Advisor for a

moment. *And too much of a coward.* There were a great many other people without the same

hang-ups, however. It would take a tremendous amount of wealth, resources and intelligence to

trace his extracurricular dealings back to him, but he hadn't made it to this point in life by

discounting trace possibilities.

He put the toe of one shoe against the back of the other and quietly slipped it off. He repeated

the gesture with the other and then stepped quietly through the rooms of his house, his socks

masking his steps. The hallway light gave a soft glow over the empty corridor. To the right, the

living room was also partially lit. A single lamp—a golden post topped with glass petals

surrounding a tear-shaped silver bulb—stood next to an expensive mulberry recliner. There was

no one in the chair, nor did anyone appear to be waiting behind it. In fact, he couldn't see

anybody in the room at all.

Euphrates' brow furrowed. He continued down the hall and glanced into the next doorway, the

dining room on the left. That room was dark; the kitchen beyond it was not. *If I were going to set*

a trap for someone, this is one way I would do it. Use the lights as a distraction, and then…

But if it was truly an ambush, it was a poor one so far. They would have had a better chance

blindsiding him on the front porch. Now that the door was closed, they wouldn't be able to come in from that direction. Not quickly, anyway. The locking mechanism was keyed to only two biometric scans and the materials it was made from could withstand a battering ram. Inside the home, there were no real hiding spots in the living room. None at all in the dining room.

He took a deep breath and stepped past the hand-crafted chairs, past the avorwood table that had cost almost as much as his personal cruiser. His feet pressed into the carpet, prepared to pivot and run. The metal of his pistol was growing hot in his hand. A swallow caught in his throat as he moved into the kitchen.

"There you are. Where have you been all night?"

"Oh, for the love of--" Euphrates cut himself off and closed his eyes.

When he opened them, it was to Nimbus Madasta's smile from the kitchen's island. That smile dazzled him. It always did, those beautiful white teeth and the way her cheeks dimpled and the way her skin crinkled by her eyes. She had lilac bangs and the color deepened the further back it traveled in her hair until a rich waterfall of violet spilled down her back. It was a striking contrast to her tawny tone and made Euphrates' heart beat a little bit faster each time he saw her.

Coupled with the adrenaline he had had pumping when he first got home, it nearly killed him.

He took two deep breaths and then forced himself to smile, hoping it looked convincing and didn't betray any of the creeping panic he had felt moments before. "For the love of the job," he said, switching tacks, "I found myself working long hours today. I had a Council meeting. Our people left upset, the Ryxan left upset, plenty of other members besides the primaries weren't particularly pleased or left not knowing how to feel. I decided to work late in hopes I could find a way to make the next meeting end more favorably."

"It was that bad?"

"It actually went better than I made it sound, but there's always room for improvement. Talys Wannigan decided to meet me afterward. The man could find a way to suck the joy out of a wedding."

"You shouldn't let him get to you."

"Some people have a gift. His is getting to people. It put me in a mood, the mood put me in my office. Believe me, though, if I had known you'd come home early, I would have gladly pushed that paperwork nightmare off until tomorrow."

Probably, he thought. *I would have done my best, anyway.*

A bottle of McEvoy's 32nd Parade sat on the island. Nimbus held a glass of the pink wine in hand. Euphrates nodded appreciatively. "Good choice."

"I was reading a romance novel earlier and somewhere between the third and sixth overwrought sex scenes, I realized what I needed to fully appreciate them was an impaired sense of judgment."

"You picked a refined method for that."

Nimbus smiled again. "You really didn't know I was back from the hot springs?"

"I really did not."

"But you saw the lights."

"I saw the lights."

"Were you worried?"

Euphrates laughed. He set his coat on the island, careful to wrap the handgun within it so that the metal didn't clink off of the marble surface when he let it go. He took her in his arms and kissed her neck. The smell of apricots filled his nose. He couldn't tell whether it came from a lotion or a conditioner but liked it either way.

"Never," he murmured into her shoulder. "Worry is a foreign entity to me."

"It's only irritation, dissatisfaction, and determination that are familiar to you." She kissed the top of his ear. He pulled his head up and matched her lips with his own. They stayed that way for a long moment, the stillness of the house drawing them further into each other. When Nimbus broke away, it was to smile wide and take a draw from her glass. "My, my. I missed that."

"Love," said Euphrates.

"I'm sorry?"

"I also feel love for you. Sometimes it even relieves the irritation."

Nimbus swatted his arm lightly. "Only sometimes?"

"Alright, most of the time. I guess."

"You guess. Come to bed with me and we'll see if that guess finds itself on more solid ground."

"One glass and you've already achieved the proper amount of impaired judgment."

"That's assuming this is my first glass or that you're an overwrought sex scene."

Euphrates' lips turned up faintly. This smile, slight as it was, came naturally. He found the tension had left him, relieved by her presence. "There are just a couple things I need to do before calling it a night. I can meet you in bed or come get you when I'm done, if you'd like to keep reading."

Nimbus nodded. She set her glass down and ran her fingers through his hair. She was accustomed to his mannerisms and how much importance he placed in his work. He had proven to her time and again, however, that if she pushed him, he would choose her. He always would.

But she didn't want to push him. Or perhaps she wanted to but never did. Euphrates was filled with gratitude. Gratitude and guilt.

"Go," she said softly. "I'll be reading. Find me when you're done."

"I'll always find you."

"Do you want me to hang your coat?"

Euphrates glanced at the bundle at the end of the island. He could picture the pistol slipping out and clattering to the floor. He shook his head slowly.

"No. No, I'll take care of it. I have some notes in my pockets."

He stepped away and grabbed the bottle of McEvoy's. She hadn't quite finished what she had poured, but he refilled her glass anyway. She took it and kissed his cheek. One hand trailed across his chest as she made her way around him and back toward the living room.

Once she was out of sight, he scooped his coat and weapon from the island and exited the kitchen in the other direction. He passed the short hall leading to his bedroom and continued on to the double doors that opened up to his home office. Despite the extensive measures taken everywhere else in the house, he kept this room locked in the traditional way, and he had to get a key out to gain entry.

Where his office at the Parliament building was arranged to appear clean and sleek—white walls, white tile, black furniture, crystal art pieces—his work space at home was built for comfort. The walls were devla wood, imported from one of the Wanos worlds, burnt red and naturally sound-proofed. The desk at work was a black frame with an IntuiGlass surface, the advanced systems he used wired through it with network mesh. His desk at home was a heavy thing, thick wood and wide angles. The computer atop it was designed by a number of technicians, independent of each other and with the kinds of materials one wouldn't find in respectable stores. Put together, the device's network was impenetrable, its investigative capabilities incomparable. He had back-up files and two other devices just like it in secret locations, just in case of emergencies, but this one was the primary hub for his power brokering.

Two low chairs were positioned in front of his desk, backs curved and armrests padded. He threw his coat over one of them and took his seat across from it, behind the desk. His own chair had been custom-built, designed to accommodate a slight curvature at the top of his spine and an extended tailbone unnoticeable to any but him and only when he sat.

The gun found itself on the edge of his desk. He opened a drawer and removed a faceted bottle filled with a light blue liquor and a glass. Two fingers' worth was poured into the latter; the former was returned to its confinement.

He pressed the tip of his index finger against the upper right side of his computer box. A red light scanned it from top to bottom and then a thin metal square unfolded itself from the top. Moments later, a digital screen flickered to life within the frame.

As he had hoped, a glowing orange exclamation point bounced in the lower left corner of the screen, indicating unread messages. He tapped the air just above it and his display was replaced with a transparent gray background. Lines of light green characters flew across the screen. Several layers of encryption rendered them indecipherable. He waited patiently as his own programs translated the message, sipping his drink and rolling the blueberry alcohol over his tongue.

The decryption didn't take long. Euphrates set his glass down and leaned forward.

Package existence confirmed.

Package contracted for delivery confirmed.

Contract commissioned on behalf of 1.82.2 suspected, but not confirmed.

Package delivery recipient confirmed.

Package contents pending, confirmed high value, confirmed discretion specified.

Procession parameters requested.

He read the message over several times, allowing each line to weigh on his mind and further fill out the puzzle. He had almost missed the rumor when it first fell into his web. Even later, when he went back and gave it a glance, he hadn't thought it would reveal any tangible worth under scrutiny. So many similar gossip pieces fell apart once time and money were put into investigating them. This message indicated something different. It was filled with confirmations.

Euphrates was intrigued now. Deeply so. He *had* to know what was in that package.

He downed the rest of his liquor in a single gulp and set the glass aside. A casual wave of his left hand brought up a keyboard projection. His reply was curt, to the point. Details could wait for the morning.

There was a woman waiting for him, after all.

Chapter Two

Contract Work

Dusk fell on the city.

Catalasca had a healthy night life, with groups of people guaranteed to be wandering the streets looking for a place to drink the twilight hours away until the taverns closed and they had to find a place to crash. It was only after last call that the action would spread out to the launch pads for a few hours more. Captains and crew would stumble back to their ships, some with dates, some to fight, nearly all of them to keep drinking. Impromptu parties would break out as crews shared food, music, and beverages with each other, using the light of the moon and the bulbs that rimmed the landing pad to illuminate them. Occasionally a captain would turn on the exterior lights of their ship to provide a larger spotlight.

Yes, the pads would get lively, but that was still some time off. For now, the area was mostly empty. A handful of folks used portable lights or headlamps to aid them in late-night maintenance on their ships. A pair of captains were drinking beers and shooting the breeze next to the wing of a Wescoran 04S model transport ship. Grey leaned back quietly in the pilot's seat of the *Sol Searcher*, watching them. He wondered if either of them would bring up how Wescoran's love of using obenswick metal in order to cut production costs always led to higher maintenance expenses in the long run, each atmospheric breach wearing the material down more and more.

A hand patted him lightly on the shoulder and he glanced back. Caesar stood there with some documents in hand, looking as severe as he had ever seen him and with hair even messier than usual. It struck him as funny that Caesar, the oldest of their trifecta, had somehow managed to stay looking the youngest.

"What's up?"

"I got the scans back."

"Where's Archimedes?"

"He's in the kitchen. I asked him to cook dinner tonight."

Grey winced. "Why, ever?"

Caesar sighed loudly. "Because I was running the scans! Not all the records are public, Grey. Do you have any idea what it takes to break into law enforcement databases? Without detection? As quickly as I did?"

"Oh, knock it off." Grey pushed himself out of the seat and stepped past his friend. "You've been breaking into databases since Cynosure. I remember when you got flagged for it the first time. You had redirects to kick them off your trail. How much harder could it be?"

Caesar followed him silently until they reached the kitchen and dining area at the center of the *Searcher's* top level. The kitchen cabinets had been outfitted with metal latches and security hooks that clipped under the bottom. It was a small hassle to access each one every time an ingredient was needed, but it was a small price to pay to keep everything from flying all over the room should the ship ever need to make an unusual maneuver. For the same reason, the table at the center of the room and the six swivel chairs around it were bolted into the floor. A long sofa the color of dried blood was attached to the right side of the room. It was perfectly suitable to lounge on, but it also served as an extra seat for turbulent flights, with several tight safety harnesses that passengers could pull out and strap together.

Caesar slid into a seat at the table and spread the papers he had printed to the right of his eating space. Grey sat across from him. Within minutes, Archimedes had placed plates in front of them containing a hearty chunk of some kind of fish, Salixian carrots, and mashed purple potatoes. Archimedes sat down at the head of the table with his own meal and dove into the food without a word.

"It *was* harder," said Caesar.

"What?" asked Grey.

"It was harder this time. That's why it took me longer. Catalasca's arrest and imprisonment records are public, but the facial database of prior offenders is mostly private. Redirects weren't an option this time, either, because if I got caught, it would just shove off to one of these other ships. The authorities would show up to the pad, start asking around. It wouldn't take them long to narrow it down to us."

"You're talking about the scans, right?" Archimedes asked around a mouthful of food.

"Yes, I am."

"So what did you do instead?"

Caesar cut a piece of the fish free and forked it into his mouth. "I had to do it the old-fashioned way. Create a backd—echh." He coughed. "What kind of fish is this?"

Archimedes was unfazed by his friend's reaction. "Local sailfish, is what the merchant said."

"More salt," said Caesar, applying some to his meal. He slid the shaker across the table to Grey. "And a liberal amount of lemon juice next time. Anyway, I created a backdoor into the database and applied an algorithm I designed that basically made my user signature an echo of authorized users. For the most part, it's undetectable. If it is discovered, though, it just looks like a delay or an echo from one of the people logged into the same system. It should hopefully allow me the option to use it again in the future if we need to, which I very well hope we do not."

"I take it you found something, though," said Grey. He poured a judicious amount of salt on his own food, tasted it, then added some pepper to top it off. He pointed his fork at the papers Caesar had laid out, questioning.

"Well, it wasn't easy, but we had their first names to work with, and Catalasca's system is put together well. I typed in the closest spelling approximation I could think of for their names. Then race, skin color, hair color, height and age parameters. I didn't mess with the age so much because I'm horrible at guessing, and—"

"I take it you found something though," Grey repeated, deadpan.

"Uh, yeah." Caesar scooped up a few of the pages and tossed them across the table, between his friends. The top sheet had a mugshot of a dark-haired young man in an olive turtleneck. Grey recognized him as Lefty. "That's Dawson Wesley. He has a record for home invasion, burglary, armed robbery, and cyber-crime. He wasn't the one with the gun in the robbery case, but the gunman got away while Dawson was beaten and subdued by the shop owner. Because Dawson was complicit, they stuck him with the armed charge anyway."

"Huh," said Grey.

"Huh, what?" asked Archimedes.

"Well, that vibes with what Caesar and I saw. It looked like Dawson's friends were mostly calling the shots. He seemed like he was just the guy they recruited to come along with them. Kind of a follower type. Did you find anything on the other two?"

"Not locally, so I branched out. If they're tracking courier jobs, I figured the most likely place they might catch a record was Thorus or thereabouts, so I managed to worm myself into their database next. That was a nightmare. I did find a file for one Taghrin Grydor. Assault, robbery, grand theft auto, grand theft spacecraft, and, uh, wanted for murder."

"Sounds like a really swell guy," Archimedes swallowed.

"I couldn't find anything on Barrus," Caesar continued, "but I doubt it's because he's never committed a crime."

Grey sat his fork down on the edge of his plate and leaned forward to look over the papers. "Well, I figure one of two things happened. Either the girl at the front desk has a crew just wandering around waiting for tips on decent contracts coming through…"

"But she was so nice," Archimedes said drily.

"Or Dawson, their resident cyber-crime committer, got into Akers' system somehow and found the contracts himself."

Archimedes began to argue but reconsidered. "I remember the clerk, Morgan, saying she wasn't able to rewind the tapes. I thought it was weird that the cameras were set to a live feed only."

"I noticed that, too, right after we checked in," said Grey. "I thought maybe it was a new routine for them or something. I'm thinking now that it was these three guys shutting the recordings down until they could ambush us and take the package."

"It wouldn't be a bad business, tapping into the system like that," said Archimedes. "Pretty brazen, but you could come away with some good money whenever it works out."

Caesar nodded. "Be that as it may, that good money is supposed to be ours. We've already lost a day because we couldn't grab the package. We'll try again after dinner. That way we can at least take off in the morning. Ark, it's on you this time. Things should be calmed down, but Grey and I will stay nearby just in case."

Archimedes' fork stopped halfway to his mouth. "Come again?"

"You're going in on your own," Caesar repeated. He had cut his fish fillet into several smaller pieces and surveyed them carefully, wishing he had cooked it after all. "Grey and I can't risk being recognized so soon after the stick-up."

"We just established that the cameras were down."

"Maybe," Grey acknowledged. "Maybe not all of them. Look, I left a device there that I don't particularly want to get tied back to. It's *probably* legal, but on the off chance I broke some kind of ordinance and there are guards around, I don't want to get locked up just because I defended myself."

"What if they think I built it instead? And that I'm coming back to pick it up."

Grey laughed. Caesar, a master of tact by comparison, coughed and blamed it on the dry fish. "No one's going to think you've built anything," said Grey. "Your hands are too soft, for one. Like baby hands. You sound like a moron, for two."

Archimedes cranked up his middle finger but gave up the argument. He finished the rest of his meal in silence. He cleaned his dish and utensils in silence. He gathered the papers Caesar had quite illegally acquired and read them in silence.

Grey rolled his eyes.

"So are you good with the plan?" Caesar asked.

"I'm taking my gun," offered Archimedes in return. Grey nodded his approval.

"Good. Do it. I would."

"Is that really necessary?" Caesar asked. "I doubt any of them would hang around Akers' after all the commotion today."

Archimedes tapped the stack of papers with a rigid finger. "Grey kicked a huge, murderous alien in the balls this morning. If that were me, I'd find a way to stick around. I'm good with the plan, but I'm taking my damn gun."

*****

Not much changed at Akers' after dark. Security doubled in size. The door to the front lobby was kept closed with a custom vacuum seal that only relinquished when the clerk pressed a button on the underside of his desk. Bright bulbs affixed to each of the storage units kept the aisles lit for easy navigation. Other than that, the storage company operated the same as usual.

The handful of police cruisers scattered around the front lot were new, though.

Their presence reignited a sense of unease in Archimedes' gut and he shifted his weight back and forth between his legs. Grey cuffed him upside the head in hopes a little tough love would get his feet moving. Archimedes responded by wrapping him around the waist and wrestling him to the ground.

"Stop!" Caesar ordered, kicking Grey in the seat of his pants. "Stop!" he said again, planting his boot in Archimedes' ribs and pushing him away from the other man. "Your response to seeing the authorities respond to an altercation is to *start another altercation right in front of them*? You're fucking armed! Get it together, Ark! You aren't breaking any laws. You're a courier. You've got a job. Just go in, grab the package, come out. We'll go home and get some sleep."

Archimedes stood and brushed himself off. "All this just because Grey is cooking up illegal explosives in his lab."

"A semi-legal *stun* device," corrected Grey. "And I used it to save Caesar's life. I'm hardly at fault. You should see some of the other stuff I'm working on, by the way. I've got an electric current stunner that could take down an Ilo Eronite."

"You've never even met an Ilo Eronite."

"GO!" Caesar yelled. An officer across the way was about to get into his vehicle. He stopped halfway in and looked over at the trio. Caesar smiled, trying not to look embarrassed, and waved a greeting. There was an awkward set of heartbeats where nobody moved, but when no further outbursts came the officer waved back and went on with his business.

Archimedes shuffled off to Akers' lobby. There was a square blue button next to the door. He pushed it, and a *fwuuump* noise came a moment later as the door unsealed. A buzzing sound followed, telling him he was able to open it and enter.

The lobby area was more or less the same as when he had left it that morning. Less panic, for sure. More armed men. An Akers' security guard was in the chair Archimedes had sat in early, a rifle laid across his legs. A Catalascan officer leaned against the wall to the right, arms crossed, one foot up to brace himself. Despite being licensed to carry a firearm, the gun on Archimedes' hip felt wildly out of place under their scrutinous eyes.

Morgan was no longer behind the front desk, her shift long over. A gaunt man with a sickly yellow pallor and thick stubble that ran all the way down his neck sat in her place. Instead of a name tag, he wore a mustard stain. It glistened.

"Good evening," the man said in a croaky smoker's voice. He seemed to focus on Archimedes' mouth when he looked up at him. "Dropping off or picking up?"

"Picking up. I'm with ACG." Archimedes slid his identification across the countertop. Grey and Caesar had separately demanded he triple-check his pockets to make sure he had it before they departed the ship.

Mustard pulled up Archimedes' profile and compared it to his ID. "Says here your unit was accessed earlier today."

"It was. Right around the time some kind of tussle was going on. I heard a lot of yelling, something that sounded like a gun or a bomb going off. I figured it would be best not to risk my cargo and decided to come back later. So… here I am."

"Yep, that was a mess all right." Mustard handed the ID back. "Sorry about that, partner. All sorted now. Can you find your way back to the unit?"

"You know, I get turned around enough here when it's light out. Do you mind writing the directions down? Password too, if you could. I misplaced it somewhere on my ship, and I don't trust the ol' noggin to remember it correctly." In fact, Caesar had repeated the password multiple times and made him repeat it back. Still, better safe than sorry.

While Mustard tore off a piece of scrap paper to write on, Archimedes turned to the guard with the rifle. "Were you here when all the trouble started?"

The guard scratched his chin and shook his head. "Nah, man. I just clocked on. Which is fine by me, because that Bozav put two of our guys in the hospital before they left."

"Before who left? The Bozav? He wasn't captured?"

"None of them were, but we'll get them soon enough," said the officer behind him in the voice of someone who comfortably believed they wouldn't have to be a part of said capture.

"Right, right." He felt something poke his elbow, turned to see that the clerk had slid the paper across the counter. He was also staring at Ark's mouth again. "Uh, thanks." To the armed men, he added, "Good luck, guys," then grabbed the paper and stepped out through the back.

The lights over each unit in the storage yard dropped a thick glow over the branching paths. They also filled every corner with deep shadows. A handful of other couriers and private citizens conducted their business nearby, and while most of them did so with a singular focus a few cast their eyes to and fro to make sure whatever they were taking out, putting in, or messing around with remained a private affair. Archimedes—hair standing at attention all over his body—was glad that he didn't seem to be the only paranoid person there, convinced some threat would leap out at him from unseen angles.

He liked to think of himself as a prankster personality. A trouble-maker. The life of the party. He wasn't the kind of guy that got into fights, he thought, ignoring all of the fights he had been in, most of which he hadn't exactly won.

I'm a lover, he thought to himself. *Right? That's how the saying goes?* His mind walked to a memory of being wrapped in bed sheets with a woman on Beldus. Then climbing out of a window in the early morning hours on Agnimon. He recalled fondly the way that blonde exchange student whistled while she slept, all the way back during First Year at Cynosure.

He would have much preferred to be back in any of those times and locations than at Akers' in the middle of the night. Especially when three dangerous lunatics were on the loose. Especially when those lunatics could just swap out any additional people they might be affiliated with to get back into the storage yard, much like Grey and Caesar had done with Archimedes.

The shadows leaned in on him a little further, and he shuddered.

He found P-312 tucked in between two larger units. For a brief moment, he became one of those wary workers, glancing both ways and waiting to catch a glimpse of a gun barrel. Seeing nothing, he keyed in the code and waited patiently for the door to slide open.

Inside the unit, a panel in the ceiling registered a lack of ambient light and flickered to life. The space was awash in white and he had to blink a couple times before his sight adjusted. Before him sat a cooler, precisely as Caesar had described: blue metal sides; a flat maroon lid, also metal; a numeric lock pad that crossed the seam where the lid closed; and a single steel-gray handle with which to carry it. It was hideous to behold.

Archimedes darted in and grabbed the case (it was lighter than he expected, maybe ten pounds), then left quickly, not even bothering to close the door behind him. His eyes darted back and forth and over his shoulder as he headed toward the lobby. No one seemed to much notice him as he walked, save for a red-haired woman he recognized from a couple visits to the ACG office. He smiled at her and she noticed him then just enough to roll her eyes in response.

It's probably the low light. If we had run into each other earlier today, I've no doubt she would be happier to see me.

That thought carried him through the rest of the yard. It carried him through the lobby where he gave a quick wave to the guard, the officer, and the man obsessed with his mouth. It wasn't until he got outside and saw his friends that the fear and the briefest lust left him, replaced with the overwhelming desire to go back to the *Searcher*, pour a nightcap and pass out. For their part, Caesar and Grey were just relieved that Archimedes was returning unharmed.

And so, distracted on their return trip home, not one of them noticed the eyes that followed them.

******

This early in the morning the boardwalk was empty, many of the businesses yet to open. Jeth Serrano strode confidently, long coat flapping behind him. Shuttered windows lined the buildings to his right. The Reishus Sea sang softly to his left, the surface of the water glittering under the newly risen sun.

Beside him, Crajax Madan grumbled under his breath. He had forgotten the tinted lens for his optic implant and the very same sun that was creating a masterpiece of the sea was wreaking havoc on his senses. It felt like a week-long hangover without the benefit of the booze, but were he to shutter his augmentation completely, he would be deprived of the data-feed alerting him to items of interest and potential threats.

"How much further?" he growled.

"Not far. Relax."

Serrano looked sideways at his partner. Crajax was far from what one would call handsome, even for a Human. Deep scars crossed both sides of his face, creating a patchwork of his beard. The optic implant had been inserted by a back-alley surgeon somewhere on Dephros. By all accounts it functioned as intended, but the hack-job operation left the puckered skin around the metal a disgusting shade of purple. The man's demeanor was equally ugly, but he had been a good partner to Serrano for nearly three years and a trustworthy peer for five more.

"Have you never been here? I could have sworn I'd brought you at least once."

Crajax shook his head. "I ain't much for these kinds of places."

Neither was Serrano, but 'these kinds of places' were good for finding employment and information once the drinks started going down and the lips started flapping. And when it came to these kinds of places, you could do far worse than the Ruby Swell.

Located near the end of the boardwalk, the Swell was an exotic dance club with expensive but potent drink specials and an opening gimmick: the doors only unlocked and admitted customers when the sunset over the Reishus was low enough that the entire sea looked like a bed of rubies. Hours of operation, therefore, fluctuated by the season. Some days, the club didn't open at all. Lines at the door would start in the early evening and continued on through the night, with the first twenty people given a drink called the Undertow free of charge. Two parts blossom rum, two parts mango juice, and a dash of a mild hallucinogenic just to make things interesting.

Indeed, one could certainly do worse than the Ruby Swell for an evening. In the morning, though, it was just a soulless building like any other.

Serrano stepped up to the door and gave it a two-knuckle rap. Flakes of faded red paint floated down to his feet. A Human cracked open the door and looked out with bloodshot eyes. He sized up the two freeguns, then sneered in Serrano's direction.

"We don't serve Murasai," he spat.

"Yes, you do."

"Well, we're closed fer business, anyway. Get you gone." The man tried to close the door. Serrano wedged his foot between it and the frame just in time.

"We're not here to drink," said Serrano, his nostril holes flaring. "We're cashing in on the Ruby Swell special."

The man in the bar narrowed his eyes and looked over at Crajax; Crajax's headache had blossomed into a full-blown migraine and his face bunched into an inscrutable grimace. The man in the bar nodded once, then kicked Serrano's foot out and slammed the door shut.

"Special's cancelled," they could hear him yell from inside. "Get you gone!"

Crajax stepped back from the door and turned so that the sun was fully at his back. His hands slid up and down his body, patting different areas. His knives were in place. So were the guns in his shoulder holsters. He pulled the pistol from the holster on his thigh and checked its readiness to fire.

"What are you doing?" Serrano asked.

"Generally being prepared for anything," he snapped. A second later, more quietly, he admitted, "I'm just distracting myself, really. Fuckin' head is killing me."

"Yeah, well… put the gun away." Serrano glanced up to the corner of the door frame. A shiny black box had been affixed there, angled toward the step. No doubt some kind of facial identifier. No doubt running scans on them right then.

"I take it we're supposed to wait for him to come back."

"You assume correctly."

"Nice fuckin' guy, he is."

Serrano snorted. "Got to keep up appearances. Although he is probably like that all the time."

They waited. Minutes ticked by. They turned away from the building to take in the morning. Some kind of gull with long talons circled over the golden waters. It dove as they watched, snatching a fish twice its size from the sea. Minutes more passed.

Finally, the door creaked open behind them.

"Get in, then," said the man in the bar. "Hurry up now."

"Nice guy," Crajax said again. He grinned mirthlessly up at the bouncer.

"Go fuck yourself."

The bouncer closed the door and led the freeguns into the club through a hallway lined with mirrors. The club was a boxy place, filled with square booths, square tables, and three square stages with poles set into them. At night bulbs in the edges of the platforms would light up the dancers performing. Crajax would have seen red, blue, purple, green, orange, and yellow; Serrano knew there were other colors, too, invisible to the Human eye. The bulbs would shine those as well.

This early in the morning, they were dim; the stages, empty. A thin Human stood behind the bar, wiping down the counter with a filthy red rag. He kept his eyes on the newcomers, a Nutrov Copper Pot handgun close at hand. It was a nasty gun. One round just about anywhere would take somebody out.

The bouncer led them down another hallway. No mirrors in this one, but polished wood. One small office set halfway down the length, empty save for scattered stacks of paperwork. One more door set at the end, flanked on either side by two more armed men.

"In there," said the bouncer.

Serrano didn't pause. He led Crajax into the back room, a much more expansive office with dark blue carpet and blue chairs on either side of a stunning white desk. Shelby Hewitt—the owner of the Ruby Swell and a man who looked like chewed leather—stood to the right of the furniture. Euphrates Destidante sat behind it, hands clasped neatly on the desktop.

"Well, this is a surprise," Serrano said, grinning. He plopped into one of the chairs across from the poli without waiting for an invitation. "Long time, no see. You look tired, Euphrates, but well."

"Mm. I had to wake at the crack of dawn to get a flight here. A call might have sufficed, but this job is important to me." Euphrates motioned for Crajax to take the other seat; the freegun complied, rubbing lightly at the skin around his implant. "You've picked up a new partner since the last time I needed your services, Jeth."

The Murasai shrugged. "Three years isn't exactly new. Maybe you should hire me more often."

"I've been fortunate enough not to need to." Euphrates' slate-gray eyes moved over to the other man. Crajax, not unused to discomfort, still felt as if the poli was ripping him open layer by layer. "Mister Madan. You were highly recommended even before you joined up with my… friend. What made you decide on a partnership?"

"Figured it was a good idea to pool our professional contacts."

"More jobs that way," Serrano added.

"Bigger ones, too."

"More money that way."

"Pros all around," Crajax said, then cleared his throat. He pulled out a half-empty pack of cigarettes. "Not many cons. Do you mind if I smoke?"

"No," Shelby Hewitt said, at the same time Euphrates said, "Yes." Hewitt didn't meet the poli's eyes when Euphrates looked up at him. "Shelby, do you mind giving us the room?"

"Um, of course. Use it as long as you like."

The club owner moved around the desk, pointedly avoiding looking at either of the freeguns. He didn't say anything to the gunmen just outside the door when he stepped out into the hallway. They looked in and started to step into the office, but Euphrates waved them back. He waited until the door was closed, then gave both freeguns a smile as warm as the winter wind.

"I'm very grateful to the man for the use of his office, and for your discretion in meeting me here, but this place smells rank enough without the addition of cigarettes. You understand."

It wasn't a question. Crajax didn't take it as one. "Of course," he said, and made the pack disappear.

"To business, then?" Serrano asked.

"To business, so I can get the hell out of here." Euphrates pulled from his inside jacket pocket a thin silver data drive. He set it on the desk with a click and slid it across. Jeth Serrano picked it up between two fingers and slipped it into his pocket.

"The job is on that drive, as well as the pay. Ten thousand chits are in an account under your name as an advance. The necessary information required to access that money is also on the drive. If you need to contact me at any time, the method to do so safely is on the drive. Everything is on there, but the gist is this: I am looking for a package that is currently in the possession of a courier ship. I do not want any of the couriers dead, but I am not concerned with casualties if it is unavoidable. Just as long as the package is intact and none of your activities are in any way traced back to me. I do not know what the package looks like. When you find and recover it, under no circumstances are you to open it or discuss it with any others."

"Of course not," Crajax said, scowling. "We're professionals, ain't we?"

"History points to that being the case, Mister Madan." Euphrates leaned back in the chair and laced his fingers across his chest. "Even so, I have never worked with you. I've worked with Jeth on several occasions. He has built trust with me, which is the only reason you're even here, but let me be clear about my seriousness regarding this contract: if the package is threatened, or opened, or if you attempt to betray me, or if I believe something you have said or done—or will say or do—becomes a threat to me, I will have you killed. Is that understood?"

Crajax studied the poli leaned back in the expensive chair, soft hands woven together over a vest that probably cost more than his rent. Nothing about the man was overtly threatening, and yet there was something in the way he spoke that positively exuded menace. Crajax nodded once. "It's understood."

"Good. Track the ship. Get the package from the couriers, preferably before delivery. Bring it to me. Good day, gentlemen."

The freeguns took that as their cue to leave and did so without a word. They were stopped only briefly at the door by the security until Euphrates was confirmed unharmed. On the way out of the club, Serrano noticed that the man who had been wiping the bar down was gone, replaced by a young Human woman with shimmering green hair. One of the show girls, but likely armed as well, and likely trained to use the weapon. He did not return her smile. Crajax didn't even notice it, busy sheltering his implant before they walked back into the sun.

Traffic along the sea had picked up since they had gone into the Ruby Swell, but the passersby were more focused on their own commute than they were on the sight of a Murasai and a Human walking like chums. The waters still sparkled. The birds still swooped.

"You know," Crajax said in a low voice once they were a healthy distance from the club, "I've accepted work from a lot of lowlifes. Gang lords. Murderers. Jealous lovers. All types, right? I don't know that I've ever contracted out to a dirty poli."

Serrano was slow in responding. "Look, I've been doing jobs for that man on and off for twelve years. Since well before he was a poli at all. In that time, I've learned two things about Euphrates Destidante. First, he pays well. Really well. Especially if it's something he feels the need to be personally involved in.

"The second thing I learned is that he can and will follow through on any threat he makes. Somehow. Some way. Even if it takes years, and especially when you think you're safe. A politician, dirty or not, is the least of what that man is."

*****

The decks of the *Sol Searcher* were quiet and filled with the lingering smells of breakfast. The cabinets were closed and locked. The halls were cleared of clutter. The old ship was never cleaner than when prepping to launch on a new job.

It was a good craft, if a little rough around the edges. It had been repossessed and slated to be broken down and sold for scraps when three disillusioned young men happened across an ad for it. Grey had insisted that it would be worth the investment, that even a busted transport ship would be good for contract work and a place to live no matter which company they signed up with. All it needed was a paint job, some proprietary software installations, and the bulk of their earnings going toward repairs and general maintenance.

Occasionally they came across enough of a windfall to do some custom fitting. Grey had managed to piece together a thrust drive from spare parts and the occasional black market dealings. It wasn't Peregrine-branded, but it was nearly indistinguishable outside of the absence of a serial number, so that's what they called it when it was finished.

Now he sat in the same workshop where he built that drive, hunched over his desk, safety goggles on and soldering iron in hand. There was a part of him that was still bitter about being turned down for a loan to start his own shop some years before, but the life he had found instead brought a surprising amount of contentedness. He got to pilot his own ship more often than not.

He got to spend as much time as he wanted in junkyards and scrap markets. He even had his own space to experiment with crafting his own… well, he would call them toys. All in all, things had turned out better than he could have imagined.

The *Searcher* thrummed to life as Archimedes activated the ignition key from the top deck. Ceiling lights in the workshop flickered to life, and Grey used the moment to set his tools down. He wiped at the sweat on his forehead.

"Alright, alright, alright," Archimedes said over the intercom. "This is your captain speaking. Strap yourselves in and get ready to ride, boys. Peloclade is a few days away, but it should be a nice and easy trip. If you do find yourself with any questions or concerns about the flight, feel free to take them to the commode where you can flush-"

Grey slipped on a pair of headphones. Hard drums and gnashing guitars filled his ears, drowning out his friend. Just as it should be. As it should always be. He pulled the goggles back down over his eyes and returned to work.

Chapter Three

Things (Metaphorically, Hopefully) Blow Up

The Causeways. Rips in space that granted faster-than-light travel to galaxies that had—for millennia—gone undiscovered until the Unveiling. Nearly a thousand years previous, astronomers on Terra Prime and the surrounding colonies looked to the stars in bafflement as black holes around the universe either disappeared entirely or transformed into something… else. Something quite different. These new creations existed as shimmering portals of sorts that defied scientific laws and explanations.

Panic had set in at first as the news was relayed to the general public. Alarmed, intensive studies followed when nothing else happened immediately. Scientists struggled to figure out what this new development meant in the cosmic sense. Was their galaxy doomed? Was death around the corner?

And still nothing seemed to change.

More experiments kicked off. Satellites were sent out to test the gravitational pull around the anomalies. They found no pull at all. More satellites were sent to test for elemental compositions. None of what they found registered on any comprehensible scale. Obviously the next step was to shoot things into it, so rockets with video and recording devices were sent into the tears. They passed through without trouble at first, but as streaks of light seemed to shoot by at unfathomable, unceasing speeds, the cameras gradually broke down. The rockets were lost soon after.

It took decades and billions of dollars to design a machine capable of withstanding the strange energies existing within the rifts. Further and further, the spacecrafts would push through. And then, one day, an unmanned shuttle dubbed *Heritage 12* found itself in another galaxy.

Another thriving, populated galaxy just as confused as Humankind's own.

Things moved quickly after that. The Dyr—a race of Humanoids (though they would resent this description) evolved from animals almost identical genetically to those on Terra Prime, and from a home world equally similar—were the first to make return contact, reverse-engineering the hardware that allowed travel through the breaches. War broke out soon after, then halted as more races began to arrive, and then war began again.

For a hundred years, the universe was in conflict as members of several species, all alien to each other, struggled to gain dominance even as they failed to understand their evolving situation. It was unity through ignorance that finally slowed the bloodletting. Dialogue was opened. Resources were exchanged. Slowly, a Council was established.

Once a relative peace and understanding had been reached, the richest in resources among them set out to make the Causeways safer to travel through. Massive floating arches were crafted and carefully placed on either side of every breach they could find, to help prevent hapless travelers across the cosmos from flying into one unprepared. Specific ships were fitted with the failsafe technology required to survive passing through. Each race devised their own name for it in an effort to take ownership: Humans called them gate guards; the Dyr called them latchkeys; the Murasai referred to them as *sal harnak*. The only holdouts were the Ilo Eronites, who were powerful but solitary by nature and had little interest in petty power struggles or naming conventions.

Soon the vastness of space found itself moderately congested by these black-turned-wormholes. Lines formed, waiting for the arches to flash a confirmation that it was okay to pass through. There had been no documented crashes in a Causeway yet. Nobody knew if it was possible, or what would happen should a collision occur. No one wanted to find out.

Lines. Flashing green lights. Wait times.

Behind the pilot's controls of the *Sol Searcher*, with Archimedes snoring in the seat behind him, Grey Toliver flipped off the massive freighter in front of him with both hands. "Least goddamn favorite part of this goddamn job," he muttered.

Destiria Gate's lights flashed red, caring not at all about the plight of couriers.

*****

"Now say ahhh…"

The little girl on the table opened her mouth wide and followed the instructions loudly and to the letter. She giggled when the depressor hit her tongue, and then winced when it was taken away. Her hand shot up to her throat, rubbing it gently.

Nimbus patted her young patient on the leg. "You did very well, Fiona. Thank you for being so brave. How does your throat feel? Does it still hurt to swallow?" The girl nodded. "Would you like a citrus drop?"

Fiona brightened. "Yes! Yes, please!"

Nimbus smiled and stood. Her bright blue latex gloves came off and tumbled through the air to the trash can. She thumbed a plastic-wrapped lozenge out of a jar on the edge of the sink and handed it to Fiona's mother to unwrap.

"It's a little red back there. Her tonsils are a bit swollen, but I believe it looks like a cold right now and not anything more serious. Keep her home from school for a couple more days, stick to cold medicines and cough drops for now. I'm going to prescribe some antibiotics just in case, but don't pick them up unless she gets worse or she's not better within a week."

"Thank you, Doctor Madasta. Truly. I cannot tell you how much happier we are with you than we were our last physician."

"I'm just happy you and Fiona have a place where you feel you can be comfortable. All I want is for her to get well quickly and for both of you to get back to having fun. Now, did you have any other questions or concerns for me before I set you two free?"

Fiona's mother shook her head. "I don't think so, Doctor. If something comes up, I can call?"

"Absolutely. Please do." Nimbus smiled again and opened the door for the woman and her daughter. "Goodbye, Fiona!"

"Guh-bah, Doggtor," the girl managed around the cough drop.

Nimbus closed the door after them and set about tidying up her exam room. The box of sterile gloves went back into a large white cabinet by the door. Rubbing alcohol, gauze, swabs, and a pack of tongue depressors went in with them. The thin paper pillowcases and sheets on the exam table went into the trash without a replacement; Fiona had been her last appointment for the day, so the table would be fine as-is until morning. Once she was finished, the lights were turned off and the door left unlocked for the cleaning crew.

At first glance, Nimbus Madasta was the very essence of aristocracy. Even in doctor's scrubs. Even without make-up or jewelry or any of the other glamorous trappings one would expect from a socialite. She just held that aura of refinement, that sense that she floated across the room, removed from the petty problems of the 'common' people.

Until she smiled, anyway. Then it slid away, the gentleness running from the corners of her lips all the way up to her eyes and igniting the same kind of warmth one would get by the hearth after coming in from a frosty night. Nimbus embodied compassion, as anyone who spent more than a minute with her would say. The very essence of humble gratitude, her station left at the door, never to be brought up or considered when dealing with the infirm. Her patients were her first concern. Her only concern.

She was very popular at the hospital.

Any feelings of comfort and safety she had there, however, did nothing to prepare her for the sight of Talys Wannigan leaning against the pillar just outside the hospital's front doors. She was struck with the sudden uneasy assumption that he was there to see her. His face lit up at the sight of her, confirming her suspicion, though now she was at a loss for a reason why. Sure, she had met the man a few times, but it was always in passing at some sociopolitical event she had attended with Euphrates. Hardly any words had been shared between them, but she couldn't forget the… slimy impression he had left behind.

"Advisor," she said cordially. "This is a surprise."

"I know, I know." Talys pushed himself off the post wearing a smile that, much like his outfit, was much too large to look natural. "Truth be told, I wasn't planning on coming here. Not specifically here, anyway. I go on walks when the stresses of the workplace become overwhelming, and my walk took me in this direction today. It wasn't until the hospital sign came into view that my mind got to working on a possible solution to my current woes." He stopped and held both hands up, apologetic. "I'm being rude, I'm sorry: how have you been, Miss Madasta?"

"Doctor Madasta, if you please," she corrected. "I put in the years and racked up the debt. The least I could get in return is the honorific."

Talys gave a bow that didn't necessarily look sarcastic but sure felt like it. "My apologies, Doctor."

"Think nothing of it. What brings you to my hospital, Advisor?"

"Talys is fine, if you like. I hate the idea of having to be so formal all the time. To answer your question, though, I've been having some trouble reaching a colleague of mine. Euphrates Destidante? It's become a bit, ah… I don't want to say irksome. Inconvenient? Inconvenient. But I recalled that Euphrates isn't so much the lone wolf he pretends to be, and I recalled that the love of his life just so happened to work at the hospital I was passing by. Long story short, I stopped by in hopes you could help me get in touch with him."

Nimbus hooked a rebel strand of hair behind her ear and shifted her weight. "I'm afraid I don't know where he is, Advisor. I wish I could be more helpful."

"He didn't tell you where he was going?" Talys asked, tilting his head. "Perhaps I could meet him there."

"He did not."

"That doesn't strike you as odd?"

Nimbus' mouth twisted in distaste. "Euphrates is not a pet that I would keep him on a leash. As you well know, he has a job that requires a tremendous amount of attention and energy. If he isn't responding to your calls, it may very well be that he is simply out for a walk, overwhelmed by the stresses of the job."

Try as he might, Talys couldn't quite keep from smirking at that. "You might be right. If that's the case, maybe you could—"

"Advisor, let me stop you right there," Nimbus said, raising a finger. "In the same way Euphrates would never deign to come into my exam room and diagnose one of my patients, I would and will never involve myself in his work. He is my lover. I am not his secretary."

A dry moment of silence stretched between them. The poli smiled slowly and gave a bow. This time, it was deeper, and felt more respectful on a surface level at the very least.

"That has never been clearer to me than now. My apologies, Doctor Madasta. May the rest of your day be easy."

"And you, Advisor Wannigan."

Nimbus' lips stretched tight in a smile born of practiced courtesy. She walked past the man with a grace that belied the tension in her body, keeping her eyes on her vehicle. Talys hadn't threatened her, hadn't even come close, but there was something there all the same. Something off. A tickle at the back of her mind made her suddenly worry for Euphrates.

Talys watching as she drove away served only to make that feeling worse.

*****

Archimedes' focused mind was aching as he tried to make sense of the battlefield in front of him. His opponent was a clever one. One wrong move would surely spell his quick destruction. Every decision needed to count.

With the weight of that responsibility fully settled on his shoulders, he took one trembling hand and moved a black horseman three circles to the left.

Caesar's eyebrows lifted at the same time Archimedes' fingers did. "That's your move? Huh. Okay. If you want to change your mind, though, I'm willing to make a one-time exception to the rules."

"I know what you're trying to do."

"Hey, if you're sure, I don't want to--"

"You're playing mind games," Archimedes said. He narrowed his eyes, suspicious. "Mind games typically come in when somebody's feeling scared."

"Yeah, alright, Carnahan," Caesar said, laughing. "What's there to be scared of? You've never beaten me. That's not a mind game, it's a fact."

And it was, despite hundreds of games spread over nearly two decades. Ever since Archimedes and Caesar had found an old *dakarrat* board at a yard sale in their neighborhood. It had come cheap as several pieces were missing. Grey helped them fashion replacements out of scrap metals but had little interest in the game itself. It became Archimedes' and Caesar's pastime, one they both grew savvy at, but though there had been a handful of occasions when he had come close, Ark really never had beaten his friend.

"I feel good about this one," he said, nodding to himself.

Caesar snorted. "You say that at least once every game."

"And yet I notice you still haven't made your move."

"I'm savoring the moment," said Caesar. He took another look. His brow furrowed. He reached out and hovered his hand over a blue chaplain, pulled back without making contact. The second time he caught himself before his hand actually reached a piece, but his indecision was clear. Maybe Archimedes had a shot after all.

The intercom in Caesar's room crackled to life. Grey's voice piped through, moderately concerned. "Hey, I need you guys in the cockpit."

"We're a little busy at the moment," said Archimedes.

"Busy your asses to the cockpit!"

He shut the intercom off, leaving Archimedes and Caesar to stare at each other in silence. Caesar moved to put the *dakarrat* pieces away. Ark slapped his hand.

"Don't you dare. You're not getting out of this that easy. If you still can't figure out a move, though, maybe you can get some pointers from our esteemed pilot."

Caesar grumbled and pushed him out of his room.

Grey glanced from the control board out into the space beyond the viewports of the *Sol Searcher*. The traffic that had congested the entry point to the Causeway had dissipated not long after they had all passed through the rift, with ships headed to different planets or moons. Some would continue on to another Causeway and another star system beyond. Others would go searching for new asteroids to mine or a spaceport to conduct business in. With so many different directions to go in, it was a reminder that the universe was very, very vast, and it wasn't long before the *Searcher* was alone again.

Or maybe not.

Grey's eyes flicked back down to the blinking orange light to the left of his steering rig. He hadn't noticed it going off until after the *Searcher* had passed through the Causeway and had no idea how long it had been active. That could be a problem.

"What's the big deal, Toliver?" Archimedes asked, ducking into the cockpit. "I had Caesar on the ropes." He peered through the viewport, saw nothing of interest. He turned to Grey. Caesar came in behind him, rolling his eyes.

"The comm signal has been going off," Grey said. "For a while, I think."

"Who's trying to hail us?" Caesar asked.

"No idea."

"Have you tried directing the signal back? Hailing them instead?"

"Yep. Nothing." Grey scratched at his jaw. "The thing is, I don't think they're trying to communicate with us at all, whoever it is. They're just using the signal to target us. It comes off less alarming than, say, a weapons targeting signal."

Archimedes looked thoughtful. "They're locking on to the ship so they can follow us, then. Authorities?"

"No," Caesar said. "The authorities would hail us, stop us if we didn't listen. Board us, probably, if they were really agitated. But the authorities don't have any reason to follow us. We're just doing our job."

"Maybe they know something we don't," Archimedes said. "Or maybe this is about what went down at Akers'."

"That still doesn't explain why they wouldn't just talk to us. Or stop us, even."

"Caesar's right," said Grey. "Whoever it is, it isn't the cops."

Archimedes frowned. He leaned in toward the passenger's seat and craned his head, trying to get a glimpse of the space behind the *Searcher*. It was a futile effort; the craft's body extended out to either side to compensate for the narrow hallways and crew bedrooms that made up the interior. Normally the ship's control board would have a video display running for the top-mounted camera, but the lens had broken months ago. It was yet another item on the not-inconsiderable list of pending ship repairs that were needed.

"Do you have any thoughts on who it might be?" he asked.

"Sure," said Grey. "They could be rival couriers. Scavengers. One of your vengeful ex-girlfriends. But they're probably someone else."

"What do we do?"

"Well…" Grey pointed a finger at Caesar. "*You* keep shooting me down every time I suggest arming this bucket, so we aren't going to be manning the guns. Our best bet is probably to haul our asses to Bax Tavilian Gate, get some other ships around us, and hope our tail is content just to follow."

*****

As a child, Euphrates could never sleep while on the move, and certainly never on a spacecraft. Growing up in poverty the idea of stars just outside the metal walls he was pressed against excited him, and the unfamiliar jostling during take-offs and landings kept him skittish and a little nauseous. With car rides across the country, it was a little different; his impatience to reach his destination kept him energized and awake up to the point his young body couldn't take it anymore and he finally succumbed to exhaustion.

It took years for him to discover the usefulness of an in-transit nap. Not everything could be solved with a video call or a holo-meeting. His obligations both legal and otherwise had grown to encompass so many different things that he found himself traveling constantly. Catching a brief moment of shuteye gave respite to a mind that was constantly turning over, relentlessly searching for opportunities to exploit. By the time his foot hit pavement after a long drive or he descended an off-ramp, he was back to operating at full capacity.

His return to Thorus after his meeting with Serrano was no different. The freegun's employment effectively took the package off of his list of concerns until the time came that it was actually in his possession. He was able now to devote his full attention to the trade issues with the Ryxan.

"Who is driving?" he asked the steward once his craft had landed. He pulled a cushioned ring from around his neck and tossed it onto the seat next to him. His briefcase was pulled from beneath his seat, the latches checked to make sure they were secure.

"Rollo, sir."

"Good. Call ahead so he's ready. Tell him I'll be going to the CED."

The steward led the way to the open door of the aircraft and pulled a nearby lever. A thick box at the base of the entrance slid away from the craft and unfolded into a thin staircase leading down to the ground. Euphrates stepped out into a bright, cool day. A smattering of gray clouds in the distance hinted at the possibility of rain later in the afternoon.

That would be fine. The planet could use some water, and he planned on being in an office for most of the day, anyway. The Center for Element Distribution was a notoriously droll place full of scientists who wanted little to do with politics, but Euphrates had demanded an emergency meeting. He needed to know what the absolute bare minimum amount of the Ryxan's celaron was necessary to prevent any serious problems for Human industry.

All this for oil, he thought and scowled. *The more things change, the more things stay the same.*

The left side of his chest vibrated. Left inside pocket. His personal comm unit, then. Rollo stood by the back seat of a long, dark blue car and held the door open. Euphrates waved at the driver with his left hand and retrieved the comm with his right.

"This is Destidante."

"Hello, my love," purred the voice from the other side. His body flushed with a sudden warmth. "Are you home?"

"Just landed, actually. What's going on? Did you manage to get in a break from work?"

"I got off early today. Which was nice, honestly. I love my patients, but sometimes I just need an afternoon to myself." Nimbus took a deep breath as if she were about to add something else, then held it. She let it out a moment later, off to the side, away from the comm. Euphrates heard it anyway.

"What's wrong?" he asked. He slid into the back seat of the car and waved Rollo to the front, opting to close the door himself.

"Nothing. Well, I was just thinking… I was hoping to expand the gardens this summer. I was given some new strains to plant as a gift from some of the ladies in the office."

Safely away from her view, he raised a hand in bemusement. "What—yes, of course. You don't need to ask me for things like that. It's your home as well, Nimbus."

"Even so, I wanted to talk to you about it first. Communication in a relationship is important, even for things like this." She paused again. Euphrates half-expected her to ask what color flowers he would prefer she plant next. Instead she said, "Talys Wannigan stopped by today."

Euphrates felt the world freeze around him. He blinked a few times, sure he had heard her wrong. She added nothing to convince him. "He stopped by, what do you mean? Stopped by the house?"

"The hospital."

"He came by your *work*?" He heard his voice crack with incredulity and cringed. "What did he say to you?"

"He wanted to know where you were and why you were ignoring his calls."

"That's it?"

"Yes." Concern edged into Nimbus' voice. "Is everything alright, Euphrates? Is something going on?"

Maybe. That fucking weasel. "No," he said, "nothing is going on. What did you tell him?"

"I told him I didn't know where you were, because I *didn't*, although even if I did, I hope you trust that I wouldn't just tell somebody that."

"Of course I know, love. Of course I do. Look, I'm going to let you go. I'll see you tonight at the house."

"Is everything alright?" she asked again. Euphrates bit the inside of his cheek.

"Everything is fine. I love you."

"I love you, too." There had been a brief pause, and he knew he hadn't fully convinced her. Still, she let it go.

Euphrates switched off the call and slid the comm unit back into his pocket before he could throw it against the window. His hands clenched and unclenched around the leather curvature of his seat. He took deep breaths. He counted to ten. He continued on to twenty.

Once he felt enough control had returned to him, he called up front to Rollo. "We're going to have to reschedule with the CED. Take me to Parliament instead. Another meeting has taken priority."

*****

The three co-captains of the *Sol Searcher* stared fixedly at a blue screen in the center of the control console. The screen displayed a graphic representation of their ship with a grid overlay indicating the separate shield panels. It also functioned as a proximity alert and an indicator for any nearby energy signatures. It was how they kept the *Searcher* from crashing into anything while their external camera was damaged.

It was also how they knew that the ship pursuing them had grown uncomfortably close.

"They're really gunning it," murmured Grey. "They're pushing their ship harder than I'd trust this hunk of junk to do."

"It's a hunk of junk that *you* picked," Archimedes pointed out.

"And one that I love," Grey shot back, "but I'm not going to pretend it's something that it isn't."

Caesar cleared his throat. "Is anyone else wondering if they're going to tell—" The comm came alive with a crackle. "Never mind."

"Couriers," said the voice over the comm, rough and ugly. "Couriers, come in. Come in. Are you receiving this message?"

Caesar sat down in the co-pilot's seat so he could access the switch that would allow him an outgoing response. "We hear you loud and clear. This is Captain Anada of the *Sol Searcher*. Who am I addressing?"

"You're addressing the captain of the *Grim Pagoda*. Glad to let you know ahead of time that we're planning on blowing you into oblivion. You boys got any last words?"

Grey smirked and leaned in toward Archimedes. "I think I know who this is." Louder, into the intercom, he said, "Blowing us, you say? This is Taghrin, right? How are the gonads I kicked up into your belly, they still sore? Or what do you call them? What's the Bozav word for balls?"

Beside him, Caesar held his hands out in the universal sign for *What the hell?*

Taghrin's voice came back in, uglier even than before. "The only downside to blasting you into pieces is that I can't personally pluck your eyes out while you're still alive to hear me eat them."

"Hey, moron. You realize you can't blow us up, right? If you do, the package goes up with us and you're out of a payday. So how about you just keep on following us to Peloclade and we can let the authorities help us hammer out Right of Possession?"

"Or we could just knock a hole in your hull and grab the package after you freeze to death."

Archimedes nodded to himself. "That would probably work."

"Shut up, Ark," Grey and Caesar both snapped. The static of the intercom disappeared, the bandit's ship ending the transmission. The blinking light went dead with it.

"They're all talk," Grey said after a moment.

Caesar shook his head. "You do recall one of them has a rap sheet for murder, yes?"

"Bah," said Grey. "Killing someone planetside is one thing. Wrecking a ship and murdering the crew is different. There are audio logs and travel records involved. It would take some serious balls, and we've already established that I kicked—"

The rest of his sentence was drowned out by an obnoxiously loud buzzing sound. Archimedes slapped an orange button, shutting the alarm off. The control panel lit up with red emergency lights, a secondary alert that took the captains' hearts and dropped them into the pits of their stomachs.

Weapons had just been locked on the *Searcher*.

*****

Rollo pulled the car into the private lot beneath the Parliament building. Several spaces were open—most of the politicians gone for the day—and he found a spot to park near the elevator. Euphrates was out and moving before the vehicle was fully stopped. A woman held the elevator door open for him until he was able to get inside.

He glanced over to thank her and realized he knew her. Carol Sharma. She was some kind of custody lawyer. Euphrates had purposefully made her acquaintance on the slim possibility he might one day need to know the best way to leverage someone's children against them. Euphrates nodded at her and pressed the button for Talys' floor.

"Councilman Destidante," she said, beaming. "I'm surprised to see you here so late in the day. How are you?"

"To be honest, Carol, I am positively seething with rage."

"Oh, I… okay."

The rest of the elevator ride was quiet.

Euphrates reached his destination first and strode through the rows of desks and straggling workers with a singular focus. At the back end of the floor was Talys Wannigan's office. A young woman with bleached-blonde hair sat just outside the door. She was setting the phone down when she caught sight of him. Her eyes widened.

"Advisor Wannigan is busy right now," she said, standing. "If you want, I can—"

"Quiet, intern," he responded, breezing past her. His hand gripped the doorknob and it twisted freely in his grip. It occurred to him in a fleeting thought that he would have looked absurd had a locked door stopped his righteous indignation in its tracks.

"I'm not an intern, Advisor. I'm a full-time—"

He closed the door behind him and turned the deadbolt, muffling her response. Talys Wannigan was standing over his desk, examining a handful of reports. He looked up at the sound of Euphrates' entrance. If he was surprised, he didn't show it.

"Why, Euphrates, it's good to see you. I've been looking for you all day. Lucky you caught me before I left."

"It wouldn't have mattered," Euphrates snarled. "I would have found you. I always know where you are."

Talys smiled. "Is that so?"

"It's so." Euphrates rounded the desk and approached the other man. Uncomfortably close. Dangerously close. "You are audacious, Wannigan, to invade my lover's work."

"It was hardly an invasion. I reached out to you multiple times and you didn't respond. I feared for your well-being. I happened to be passing the hospital and I thought the kind doctor might be able to ease my concerns."

Euphrates resisted the urge to grab the man by the neck. "There are some unspoken rules to what you and I do. They are important ones. Especially as regards to dragging unaffiliated family and friends into conflict. Whatever your problem is with me, it should stay focused on me."

Any sign of geniality left Talys' face. "It doesn't work like that, Destidante. Not with a snake like you. It's important you understand that I see you exactly for what you are."

"Stay. Away. From Nimbus."

Talys leaned in until their noses were nearly touching. "Or what?"

There was a thin metal rectangle in Euphrates' right pocket. His finger traced the outline of it through the fabric of his pants. A small button on the side, when pressed, would release a sharp little blade from one end. Carbiron, capable of cutting through flesh like paper.

It would be quick, he thought. *A swift blow to the solar plexus to knock the wind out of him. Hit the carotid, twist the knife. That's all it would take.*

The right side of his chest vibrated, pulling him out of the fantasy. Other thoughts rushed in to fill his mind: the secretary, Carol Sharma, surveillance cameras. It would be difficult to guide the Human race from a prison cell. His lip curled in disgust.

"And here I thought you were at least smart enough to know that when you recognize a snake, you shouldn't step within striking distance."

Euphrates backed away until he was no longer in danger of reflexively stabbing the Advisor. It was time to leave. If Jeth Serrano was calling him already, it had to be something important. He gained nothing by prolonging this pissing match with Wannigan.

"No foreplay and only ten seconds of action?" Talys called after him. "It's a wonder Doctor Madasta stays with you at all."

The barb meant nothing, and Euphrates let it fall behind him as such, heading for the elevator. The secretary tried to admonish him for barging past, but he simply barged past again. Once the doors of the elevator closed, he pulled the comm from his pocket and snarled into it.

*****

"What is it?"

Euphrates sounded pissed. Jeth glanced across the cockpit to his partner, but Crajax was focused on the action through the viewport.

"There's been a development."

"What kind of development?" Euphrates snapped.

"Well, it wasn't hard tracking down the couriers," Jeth said. We're through Destiria Gate and into Pryantris, but it looks like, ah… well, it looks like somebody else has it out for these guys. There's an unidentified ship currently lighting them up, and we're not even halfway to Bax Tavilian."

A sharp inhalation of breath from the other end of the line. "I already told you what I want. Make sure that package isn't destroyed. Reach me when it's finished."

The call cut off abruptly.

Jeth tucked his comm unit away and gripped the steering rig of his ship, the *Mathra D'abai*. Crajax pried himself away from the one-sided dogfight to look at his partner.

"What did he say?"

Jeth shrugged. "He said proceed like normal."

"Whoever is flying that courier rig is a hell of a pilot," Crajax mused.

"I do not care. We've still got to bail him out."

*****

"Now!" cried Archimedes.

Grey jerked the controls to the right and a set of blaster bolts streaked past the *Searcher*. Archimedes was watching the display intently, waiting for signs of energy output spiking behind them. Grey was using his prompts to make evasive maneuvers. They were still alive, but they hadn't been able to dodge everything, their shield panels just hanging in there.

"What's that?" asked Caesar, pointing at the bottom of the screen. A larger blip had popped up where there had been nothing before.

"I think that's another ship," said Archimedes.

"Is that good or bad?" Caesar asked, wide-eyed.

"How the hell am I supposed to know?" Archimedes snapped. "Left, Grey! Now!"

Grey shifted the steering rig but wasn't quite fast enough. A bolt connected with the back end of the *Searcher* and a shudder rolled through the ship. The navigation system blinked out, replaced by a blank black screen. The image returned a few seconds later, this time flickering intermittently.

When the bandits had started firing, Grey knew it wasn't likely that they would make it to the Hesperos system, much less Peloclade, without a miraculous intervention. The Pryantris system was full of planets, though, and he had picked up speed toward the nearest few, hoping he could reach something before the *Searcher* was disabled or destroyed. He could see one of the planets coming up on their starboard side.

Archimedes leaned closer to the control board. "Energy output on the screen... it looks like the newcomers are firing on our bad guys!"

"That's great," muttered Grey. He glanced past Caesar, through the viewport. "But that doesn't amount to much at the moment." He slapped Caesar's shoulder with the back of his hand. "What's that?"

"What?" asked Caesar, startled. "What's what?"

Behind them, the bandits banked their ship hard to one side right as the third party fired again. Two more crimson blasts passed them by completely and slammed directly into the *Sol Searcher's* hull. The alarm lights flashed across the control console once more. A low shriek sounded from the engine room.

"Planet," shouted Grey, dragging the word out. "What. Planet. Is. That?"

"Uh. Um. Based on the duration of our trip and our relative location between Destiria Gate and Bax Tavilian, it's likely one of two planets. I think."

"Oh, you sound confident," said Archimedes, his voice tight. "Go on."

"It's, um, either Aggrath. Heavily populated by the Dyr."

"Great. Because the Dyr love us so much. Or?"

"Or Astrakoth? I think? It isn't occupied so far as I know, save for maybe a science base or two."

"Even better," growled Grey.

"Why is that better?" asked Caesar.

"I was kidding. Both are bad. We've got to go down there, though. We're too vulnerable in space." There was a loud cracking noise and the *Searcher* shuddered hard.

"Stabilizer's out," warned Archimedes.

"Yep." Grey turned the ship away from their pursuers. They broke the atmosphere moments later. Flames licked up the front of the craft and it felt like every part of the ship was shaking independently.

"Shit! Move, Caesar!" Archimedes yanked his friend up from the co-pilot's seat and strapped himself into place. "Get in the back! Buckle yourself up quickly!"

As Caesar staggered out of the cockpit and towards the extra crew quarters, Grey continued to wrestle with the steering rig. "I was going to bring us down so we'd have better evasive maneuvering, but I've only got about half of the control we need."

"To do what?" asked Archimedes. He flipped a series of switches, rerouting emergency power to the flight controls.

"Uh, to pull us back up," laughed Grey humorlessly. "I'm thinking it's not an option anymore."

"Stellar." A jagged crack stretched across the glass. The cockpit began to heat up and a shrill whistling caused both men to wince. "There's a split in the viewport!"

"I can see that" Grey snapped back. "It's right in front of my fucking face." His eyes lit up with a sudden idea. "Toggle the Peregrine drive."

Archimedes stared at him. "Come again?"

"Stagger the Peregrine! One second intervals. The start-stop might let me balance us out."

"It might also blow the whole engine! Or rip us in half! Triggering a thrust drive *during* a dive—a thrust drive, mind you, that is *not* a Peregrine, but a patchwork monster you made that has never been under this kind of duress—that's a mad plan, Grey."

Grey shook his head wildly, frustrated. "Look, the *Searcher* might be our ship, but she's *my* baby right down to the drive. I know her better than anybody, and I'm telling you: we either try this and maybe die, or we don't try it, crash into the planet nose-first and *definitely* die."

Archimedes let out a curse with a mouthful of air. "We're going to feel mighty stupid if we told Caesar what great pilots we are just to blow ourselves up."

Grey grinned.

Trying not to think about the many, many things that could go wrong, Archimedes reached one unsteady hand across the control console and let it hover over the switch that activated the *Sol*

Searcher's thrust drive. Some small part of his brain desperately trying to detach itself from the situation marveled that a simple metal lever could regulate enough power to propel a spacecraft across the cosmos at high speeds. Giving in to reckless abandon, he began to toggle it back and forth.

The *Searcher* began to undergo a series of jolts, jerking the two pilots back and forth in their seats. Grey yanked the controls back, wrestling with the ship for some semblance of control even as two more cracks in the viewport split off from the original. Below them the world flashed by in streaks of color. The *Searcher* began to level out, still dropping, not slowing.

"Grey," Archimedes said worriedly. He kept the thrust drive off and gripped the co-pilot's controls.

"This is as good as it gets, man," Grey said through clenched teeth. "I'm aiming at that clearing up ahead."

"What clearing?"

"The one! There!" Grey flapped his hand at the display screen. A chart had recalibrated automatically to show the clearest flight path, the surrounding terrain, and the nearest plausible landing options… of which there were none.

"That's not a clear—there are trees down there!"

"Do you see a better alternative, Ark? *Because I am open to options!*"

Archimedes' eyes flicked from his controls to the viewport to the monitor. He reached over and pressed the ship's comm button. It lit up immediately. *At least that's not busted*, he thought.

"Caesar, you hooked in back there?" he asked.

"Yeah," came the tinny response. "What's the situation?"

"We're going down. Prepare for a crash landing."

"Oh, *god*."

"Whichever one you pray to, pal."

Archimedes turned the com off again and focused on the matter at hand. He and Grey looked at each other, gave a single nod, then strained to steer the ship toward the clearest patch of forest available to them.

The *Sol Searcher* plunged into the foliage like an apocalypse. The sound of trunks snapping around the wings of the ship was near-deafening. Greenery slapped against the viewport, staining it. The *Searcher* gave one more loud, distressed moan and then slammed into the ground with calamitous purpose.

Archimedes' shoulder belt tore at the buckle, launching him forward. His forehead slammed into the corner of the control console. There was a brief moment where he could hear the sounds of scared and angry wildlife somewhere outside. The moment passed, and he knew then a blackness deeper than space.

Chapter Four

A Little Gunfire Never Hurt Nobody

In the *Sol Searcher*, across from Archimedes' room, there was a compartment built to seat six. Being a courier ship, the *Searcher* didn't often take extra passengers off-planet, but every once in a while a situation cropped up and so contingencies needed to be considered for them in the event of an emergency. Each seat had a safety harness that buckled across the waist and a pair of thick straps that came down over the torso in an X to further secure the passenger. Several panels around the room held capsules of flame retardant impact foam, designed to deploy and rapidly expand at the moment a crash was registered, further protecting anyone in the room by absorbing kinetic injury that might otherwise prove crippling or fatal. Altogether, it was a sound set-up meant to handle any situation outside of a sudden decompression or exposure to the vast unforgivingness of naked space.

None of that put Caesar Anada at ease. Crashing while in a windowless box was a hellacious nightmare. Not having any way to judge how close the ground was put a hitch in bracing for impact. Caesar's imagination wasn't helping things, either, picturing with perfect clarity a scenario where shrapnel ripped through the impact foam, turning him into julienned courier. Or maybe it would be fire that killed him, the flame retardant being more of an advertisement than an actual feature, the flames melting his clothes into his flesh. Even if the inferno didn't get him, oxygen deprivation would, choking the life out of him with black, incorporeal hands.

Could sheer panic kill you? He'd heard it said.

The thought flew from his mind before he could explore it, evacuated by the first collision and replaced with blind terror. The blow hit the ship from somewhere behind him, followed by a second, sharp bump and then a ceaseless stream of impacts. He started to yell, his voice growing

in decibels and rising in octaves until he was shrieking with his eyes screwed tightly shut.

When the *Searcher* finally slammed into the planet, Caesar's head was jerked hard into the

wall. There was a flash of white behind his eyes, then stars, and then a bellowing pain. He could

feel the ship sliding beneath him, felt it pick up on one end and then settle back down. Caesar's

eyes stopped shaking in their sockets a minute later. It took a minute more before he actually

realized he wasn't dead. A shocker, truly, as the impact foam never released from its

compartments.

"I fucking hate this ship," he muttered.

His hands moved clumsily over the clasps that kept him buckled in and he unfastened them one

by one. His first step was accompanied by a flare of pain from inside his skull, sending him

stumbling into the wall, slamming his funny bone into an edge somewhere. He swore, pushed

himself back to an upright position, saw the corridor ahead of him tilted at an angle. Caesar

considered the idea that he was concussed.

No, the ship *was* tilted. The *Searcher* hadn't landed evenly.

This is worse than I expected, Caesar thought. *Wait, scratch that. I fully expected to die.*

He staggered down the hall to the cockpit, using one hand on the wall to keep him standing.

The lights kept flickering between their normal power scheme and the one reserved for the back-

up generator. A low whine was coming from somewhere below.

The cockpit was a horror show. A large branch had broken off from one of the trees they had

flown into and speared through the viewport, piercing the pilot's chair on the left. On the right,

blood had sprayed all over the glass and Archimedes was slumped over the control console,

motionless.

"Caesar!" croaked the branch. "Thank God, you're alive. Help me."

As Caesar neared the pilot's chair, he saw that Grey was still breathing, pinned against the wall of the cockpit, pushing as hard as he could against the branch. He had just missed being impaled, the makeshift javelin scraping by, tearing open the flesh over his ribs and trapping him. The skin around the laceration was already beginning to purple. A shallow pool of blood had settled into the seat.

Caesar tried to pull the branch from the seat first, the bark scratching at his palms as he gripped and pulled, but it didn't budge. He and Grey worked together, him pulling it toward himself while Grey pushed, and between the two, Grey was able to scrape and squeeze his way to freedom. A moment of quiet relief followed, during which Caesar keyed off the ignition. The distant whining stopped, replaced by a sudden, heavy silence.

Archimedes took that moment to snort himself back to consciousness.

"Oh, my *fucking* head," he moaned.

"I thought you were dead," Grey said, stepping off of the pilot's seat to inspect his friend. Ark slapped him away.

"Me, too," Caesar chimed in.

"Sorry to disappoint." Archimedes touched his face with a pair of shaky fingers. They came away warm, wet, and red. "Whose blood is this?" He turned, caught his reflection in the broken viewport, saw his face as a crimson mask stemming from a long, deep gash in his forehead. "Aw, man. It's in my hair!"

"If you're able to walk, let's get going," Grey said. "Those assholes will be coming down to pick our bones clean soon. We don't want to get caught with our pants down."

"Why don't we just give them the box if they want it so bad?" Caesar asked, thoroughly

shaken. The pounding in his head seemed louder now that the ship was quiet. His stomach turned

over. "They've already shown that they're serious about taking it."

"We're serious now, too," Archimedes said. "About keeping it. Look what they did to the

Searcher, man. Grey's right. We've got to get prepared."

'Prepared' was Archimedes trailing blood all the way to his room to retrieve his gun. Grey was

already carrying his, and Caesar didn't own a firearm, so Grey took him down to the lab to fit

him with some tools to defend himself with. This consisted of a knife with a five-inch blade,

instructions on which body parts were best to stick it in, and a sphere not unlike the one he had

used in Akers'.

"You already know how to use a Boom Sphere, but this is a prototype that I've been tweaking,

so listen closely: after you press the button, you drop it and you run. Same as before, but you run

harder and faster this time. Got it? Don't wait for it to go off."

"Okay," Caesar said, nodding.

Grey took him by the shoulders and looked him in the eye. "Caesar, it is very important that

you run."

"I *got* it, Grey."

Archimedes, meanwhile, had either been unable to find a bandage or was too rattled to

consider it. He had torn a scrap of cloth from one of his shirts and fastened it to the cut on his

forehead with a wrap of electrical tape. He met Caesar and Grey in the loading bay, gun at the

ready. Grey had his pistol out as well, tight in one hand, the handle of the cooler they were

transporting gripped hard in the other. They looked at each other, took a few breaths to collect themselves. The situation settled on them: hurt, shipwrecked, pursued. Cornered, outnumbered, outgunned.

When they opened the loading ramp, it scraped against the dirt wall the *Searcher* had propped up against, leaving just enough room for the three couriers to wiggle through and drop down to the ground below.

Bullets ricocheted off of the hull just above their heads. Taghrin, Dawson, and Barrus had landed their ship in the ragged clearing the *Searcher* had torn open during the crash. The three bandits advanced on the couriers, weapons barking.

The fear is real, shouted Caesar's brain.

"Scatter!" shouted Grey's mouth. He ran toward the woods on his right. Archimedes bolted to the left, firing a couple shots at the bandits that went wide, thudding into the dirt somewhere. Caesar bounced from one foot to the other, thinking, panicked, then took off after Ark. Better to be with the guy not carrying the item everyone else was trying to get.

Swearing and bullets and bandits followed him all the same.

From the *Mathra D'abai*, Jeth Serrano had to admit that he had officially joined Crajax in being impressed by the pilots of the *Sol Searcher*. The weapons on Jeth's ship were no-joke, top-of-the-line fuck-your-shit-up blasters designed for extended dogfights. When he had accidentally shot the courier ship, he thought he had bungled himself out of a massive payday. Then the *Searcher* pulled off a controlled dive somehow, and while the clearing below was long, wide, and ugly, it didn't contain a fiery pile of wreckage.

"Told you," Crajax said, catching Jeth's expression.

"Guess you did."

"Looks like our competition still wants in." Crajax pointed at a medium-sized ship positioned at the start of the rut. Their tag scanner identified the craft as the *Grim Pagoda*, but both of them would have bet a thousand chits that it was a fake register.

"Guess they do," Jeth said. "Let's set down next to them."

"You think the couriers survived?"

"Ten minutes ago, I wouldn't have thought so. Now… well, I wouldn't be surprised. I don't particularly care either way. The real question is whether or not the package survived."

Crajax adjusted the *D'abai*'s controls, angling the ship in for a landing. "What's the plan?"

"I was thinking we go down, get whatever information we can out of whoever we can, and then shoot everyone." Jeth considered what he said, decided it did indeed sound good, nodded to himself. "Just to be safe."

Crajax chewed on his lip. "Well," he said, "at least we can stretch our legs."

The forest was a trial and a half to run through. Thick, knotted roots uncoiled from the ground at odd angles and inconsistent intervals, threatening to trip them up at any moment. Caesar and Archimedes pushed through groups of chest-high plants with serrated leaves, their clothes ripping, dozens of thin cuts materializing like magic across their arms, chests, shoulders. Something or things were breaking through the branches above them as they ran, disturbed by the motion on the ground and either taking flight or leaping away.

"Where… where are we supposed to go?" Caesar asked, breathless. He had never really taken to athletics at any point in his life, and his lungs were going to great pains to remind him of that. *Probably doing wonders for my core, though*, he thought.

"Forward and away, dude, until we can find a spot to stay low. Shit!"

The heel of Archimedes' boot caught in a divot in the ground. His ankle twisted, and a bolt of lightning flashed up his leg. He hopped awkwardly over to a nearby tree, put a hand against the trunk to steady himself. A loud report sounded from behind him and the wood next to his face exploded, showering his cheeks and forehead with splinters.

Dawson broke through the foliage, pistol out in front of him, and Caesar cried out in alarm. Finally with a clear shot, the bandit pointed the gun at Archimedes' chest and pulled the trigger. It clicked on an empty chamber.

Ark let out a laugh of disbelief. "You were supposed to be the nice one."

"What the hell are you talking about?"

Archimedes shrugged, started to lift his own pistol to take a shot. Dawson was faster. While Caesar stared, rooted to the ground in shock, the bandit rushed forward and grabbed Ark by both wrists. The gun went off. A bullet whizzed past Caesar's ear.

"You almost shot me!" he cried, aghast.

"Maybe if you weren't just fuckin' standing there," Archimedes snapped back through clenched teeth, struggling with the bandit.

What can I do? Caesar thought. The Boom Sphere weighed heavy in Caesar's jacket pocket, but with the two men grappling it seemed like it might do more harm than good. Maybe he could grab Dawson from behind? Surely two against one was better odds, but Caesar wasn't a fighter. He couldn't remember the last time he had even been in a fight. The most he could do would be to hold on for dear life and hope that was enough to turn the tides in their favor.

The steady stream of options and excuses not to pursue them continued playing through his head until it was too late. Archimedes' ankle gave out, sending him tumbling backward. Dawson, pulled off balance but refusing to let go, went with him. They continued scuffling on the ground, rolling over each other, trying to gain an advantage, throwing punches that deflected off of shoulders, the tops of each other's heads, failing to land even. Their guns had both disappeared somewhere in the foliage.

"The knife!" Caesar shouted to himself in sudden recollection. He scrambled to free the blade from the sheath on his hip.

And then Archimedes and Dawson disappeared.

Caesar blinked. Neither man reappeared. A loud rustling sound was in their place, one that quickly gave way to thrashing, crashing thumps, and that grew fainter as the seconds passed, He stepped closer to the spot he had last seen his friend and found an edge jutting out over a steep decline,. With so much green around him blending into itself, they had all missed the drop-off entirely.

"Ark?" he called meekly. No answer. "Archimedes?"

The only sounds greeting him were those of the forest: wind through the leaves, the crunch of twigs underfoot as he adjusted his stance. The alien calls of whatever passed for wildlife in this godforsaken place. He considered going down after them but couldn't find a safe way to start. What if Ark was hurt? What if he was dead?

What if Dawson isn't*?* he thought. *I need help. I need Grey.*

He turned back toward the *Sol Searcher*—or where he remembered it being—and ran.

Archimedes felt like he was living in a kaleidoscope. Browns and greens whirled by as he pinwheeled through branches and thick stalks of thorny plants. Sharp stones dug into the skin of his hands, his sides, his face. Every couple seconds he caught a glimpse of one of Dawson's limbs nearby as the bandit rocketed down the hill beside him, equally out of control. Ark wasn't sure if that made him feel any better. He was more concerned with not breaking his neck.

The ground dropped out from under him. He twisted in the air, trying to get his bearings, and succeeded only in landing face-first in three inches or so of water, not nearly enough to soften the impact. Something crunched beneath him and he hoped it wasn't anything inside him. He groaned and pushed himself up to his knees. At some point during his tumble, the makeshift bandage on his forehead had ripped off and the gash had begun bleeding anew. The drops of blood that sprang forth sent ripples in the water around him. To add injury to injury, a crooked stick had lodged in his forearm. When he pulled it free, a fresh stream of blood coming with it, he nearly passed out.

They had fallen into some kind of shallow marsh. Tall grass and flowers of all shapes and colors stretched up from the ground. A waterfall poured down the side of a cliff not far away, tall and majestic, terminating in a deeper pool the color of sapphires.

"We just want the fucking box. I don't want to kill you, but I will if I have to."

Archimedes turned on his knees, sweeping away a loose collection of hard objects under the water. Dawson stood nearby, an ugly knife out and pointed at the courier. Ark grabbed one of the underwater items by his leg, something heavy and oblong with jagged edges, and stood.

"What are you planning on doing with that?" Dawson laughed, revealing a bloody hole where one of the bandit's teeth had been knocked free. Archimedes looked down at what he was holding and found himself staring into the empty sockets of some kind of animal skull.

"I guess I was hoping you maybe had a... some kind of a bone phobia. No luck, then?"

"No, idiot, no luck. Now tell me where the... where the package..."

Dawson's eyelids sagged and he shook his head sluggishly. The arm holding the knife drooped, then dropped completely. He looked past Archimedes, distracted by something.

Maybe it was the music. That was strange, wasn't it? How had he missed that, music all the way out here on an uninhabited planet. It was beautiful, raindrops on guitar strings. Drops. Water drops. The waterfall? With tremendous effort, Archimedes turned to look at the curtain of water cascading down the cliffside. Prismatic colors streaked through it and bled out into the world around it. Captivating, those colors that seemed to ebb and flow with the notes that sprung from the lake's surface.

In the back of his mind he thought it might be prudent to get away from the bandit, find his way back to his friends. He would. In a minute. He could move any time he wanted, he could, he just didn't want to. It wasn't important just yet. He could take a few moments, listen to the music a little longer.

Thick red vines at Archimedes' feet began to rise from the water and coil around his ankles and legs. Like worms. Like snakes. Thin barbs along the lengths of the vines pushed through his tattered clothes and into his flesh. Shallow punctures.

He hardly noticed.

Grey's frantic run away from the bandits was a wild, twisting one until he finally burst from the woods to find himself at a dead end, a clearing at the edge of a canyon. Exhausted, arm throbbing from the weight of the cooler, he shuffled closer to the edge to see if the drop might be survivable. He saw a river, though it must have been two hundred feet below.

"Okay, so that's out. Maybe if—"

A commotion behind him stopped the thought cold. He had slowed too much, allowed his pursuers to catch his trail and close in. Grey fired blindly and hit nothing, but the shot was enough to startle Barrus and send his returning fire wide as well. Taghrin came barreling around his partner. Grey hurled the cooler out of reflex and the corner caught the Bozav directly in the crotch.

Barking a laugh, Grey tried to bring his gun around to finish off Taghrin while he was bunched over. Barrus was suddenly there, full of rage, charging and shooting at the same time. The first two bullets missed entirely, but the third punched through Grey's right shoulder. He grunted with the impact but barely had time to register the pain before Barrus plowed his head into the courier's chest.

Can't breathe, he thought. *Can't stop myself.*

His balance was off. His body felt like it was on fire. Despite his best efforts, he couldn't keep his feet from pedaling backward. Grey reached out desperately, looking to right himself, looking for anything that might stop him. His fingers hooked into the neck of Barrus' shirt. For the briefest of moments, it seemed like that might be enough. He was safe.

But his body found one more step in it, out into the open air, and bandit and courier alike tumbled over the edge.

All was quiet and relatively still by the three spacecraft in the trench. The gunshots rattling the peace of the forest had stopped, signaling empty magazines or dead bodies. Either way, Jeth Serrano expected someone to head back at some point. The question was how many, and for which ship. The Bjaeger Black Tactical Rifle he had spent most of his last job's pay on was nestled comfortably in his arms, safety off, ready for all comers. Like a chrome baby. One that could blow a hole in the side of most hulls.

Crajax was inspecting the outside of the *Sol Searcher*. The entry ramp was open, but there was no telling what the crew had left inside. Some kind of tripwire. Internal weapon systems. Another courier with a gun.

"What do you think?" Jeth called.

"I think it's a miracle that this thing is in one piece," Crajax said. "We hit them pretty hard. I wouldn't mind knowing how they managed to land, to be honest. If we get the chance to ask, I mean." He pointed at the thick shaft of wood piercing the viewport. "What do you think that is? A branch? A fuckin' tree trunk? How much you want to bet there's a dead packet jockey on the other end of that."

"Why don't you go in and look?"

"I don't even know what we're looking for," Crajax said, scowling.

A rustling of foliage at the edge of the trench turned into a full-on crash as a figure burst out from the woods. Human. Male. Blond. Head over ass as his feet betrayed him to the ground. Jeth fired his gun on reflex. The gun roared, but the bullet missed the tumbling form, hitting the ground just behind the man, kicking up a large storm of dirt.

"Whoa! Whoa!" the man cried from his knees. He held his hands up in surrender. "I don't have any weapons! Well, I have a knife, but it's sheathed. See? Empty hands!"

"Which ship are you with?" Jeth asked.

Crajax approached the kneeling man cautiously, the barrel of his gun trained on his torso. "Go ahead and pull that knife off of your hip. Toss it away, to the side there."

The man complied, chucking the blade out of reach. "I'm on the *Searcher*. The courier ship. I contract with Aventure."

"You got anything else on you?" Jeth asked. Like his partner, he kept his gun ready, though his was pointed off to the side, at the ready in case they were joined by anyone else. "No hidden guns, no extra knives? It's best to tell us now, because if he finds something on you, he's going to put two bullets into your head without a conversation about it."

"I don't have anything," the man said, hands raised over his head. "Just an ignition key for my ship and, like, a ball."

"A ball," Jeth deadpanned.

"A sphere. It was the job we were hired for. The package. We took it out of the cooler it came in before we left the ship so it wouldn't be so hard to carry. I was coming back to stash it somewhere. I couldn't do it in the woods because I'd lose it. Have you gone in them yet? I'd forget where I put it, you know? Everything looks the goddamn same. I barely found my way back here."

"Do you always talk this much?" Crajax asked. He tapped the courier's sternum with his pistol.

"I'm nervous, sorry. You guys have got two large guns, and I'm on my knees. I've heard stories like this, and they don't typically end well."

"Whatever," Crajax said. He adjusted his position, inadvertently putting himself between Jeth and the courier. "Look, we ain't assassins. We're contractors, just like you. Give us the orb, we'll leave you and whoever came in that other busted piece of shit to settle your differences."

A sudden inexplicable shred of panic gripped Jeth. "Wait. Crajax, you should—"

"That sounds fair enough to me," the courier said. Jeth caught a glint of silver as he tossed something to the mercenary. Crajax turned it over in his hands, trying to figure out what made it so valuable. Jeth's eyes were on what parts of the courier he could see, waiting for him to try something. Crajax moved just enough that Jeth could see the courier's eyes were clamped shut.

"Now we can get the hell—"

Opaque panels laid into the sides of the sphere flashed a white so bright and pure it could have been mistaken for a star. Speakers at the top and bottom belted out a concussive sound that sent both mercenaries rocking back on their feet. A massive group of avian creatures lit out from the nearby canopies. Jeth's eyes watered, everything a vague blur, but his partner's body had absorbed most of the flash. It was the sound that had truly rattled him; he touched his ear lightly with a trembling finger and it came away dark blue with blood.

He registered a motion somewhere in front him, a quick motion. The courier. He had been prepared for this. Jeth raised his rifle to blow the back out of the man before he could reach the tree line, but the sphere at Crajax's feet had one last ugly surprise.

First, the panels lit up again. Not bright white this time, but a deep, neon red. A shrill whistle followed and got louder by the second.

Then it exploded.

Crajax disappeared in a black ball of smoke and flame. Jeth felt the heat on his face next, a harsh, biting, furious thing filled with the smell of burnt flesh. The force of the explosion rushed behind it, pummeling his torso and launching him far enough back to land beneath the nose of the *Grim Pagoda*, or whatever it was really called.

With no small measure of effort and a pain he had only ever known twice before in his life, Jeth Serrano rolled onto his side, vomited, and passed out.

Archimedes had never truly appreciated instrumental music—that was Caesar's thing, composers like Loni Carmichael and Zachary Chantil—but this he could feel right down to his bones. The hair on his arms and the back of his neck stood at attention, tingling, like a static shock. Waves of warmth massaged him from his temples down to where his ankles broke the water. Ribbons of color danced before him like frolicking lovers. He grinned at them, a laugh of joyous disbelief trapped somewhere between his chest and his Adam's apple.

He wished his friends could see this. See the sparkling lake and the rainbows, feel the life thrumming from the waterfall and the way the music wrapped around you like a blanket, smell the flowers rising from the shallow waters, those amorous scents that washed back through the sinuses like milk and honey. Caesar would appreciate it; he had an eye for beauty. It might even be enough to crack through Grey's grumpy exterior. Where were they, his friends? What could they be doing that was anywhere near as glorious as this? At least his friend Dawson was here, enjoying the moment with him.

An insane booming disrupted his reverie. It was just enough to drown out the sound of the waterfall hitting the lake, like someone clapping next to his ear. His eyelids flickered. The haze over his mind parted. He closed his eyes in a long blink, shutting the colors out. He hadn't realized how dry and itchy they had been. Archimedes reached up to scratch his eyes and felt a heaviness wrapped around his arms, his legs, his torso.

He looked down at himself and screamed.

Tight, barbed vines twisted around his extremities. They pulsed to the beat of his heart and he could feel the strength leeching from his body with each throb. The sweet sounds of the waterfall began creeping back in. Archimedes screamed again, drowning out the noise, refusing to let himself sink back into that stupor. He ripped at the tendrils, sending small jets of blood flying. The vegetation around him shivered wherever the ruby drops landed.

The vines had been much more successful with Dawson, climbing the length of his body and wrapping around the crown of his head several times over. The bandit's eyes were fully covered. He stood facing the direction of the waterfall with a slack jaw, another vine wrapped around his mouth, between his teeth. His legs were spread, individual ropes wrapped around them, but his arms were strapped to his torso, making him look like a singular, neatly packaged snack.

For the third time in thirty seconds, Archimedes screamed. He clapped his hands to his ears and ran in the opposite direction. Bones of all shapes and sizes crunched under every step.

The first breath Jeth Serrano took upon regaining consciousness was a ragged gasp that felt like inhaling shards of glass. His throat and lungs had been burnt by the scaling air of the explosion. The event came back to him in bursts as jarring and traumatic as the blast itself.

Well, nearly as traumatic.

Once he had regained his feet, a painful undertaking, he turned his attention to Crajax Madan. His partner was curled halfway into the fetal position, one hand stretched out, clutching at the sky. His optic implant shone silver, the only hint of color left in the blackened husk. The gun he had been pointing at the courier had warped and broken in the explosion. Any chits or other belongings he might have been carrying were burned beyond recovery.

That blond little wimp had done this. Wily bastard. Jeth wondered if the other couriers were just as dangerous. If so, what the fuck were they doing carrying packages when being a freegun was an option? He glanced back, saw the *Grim Pagoda*, remembered there was a second crew to worry about as well. And him half-dead and down a partner. Still, he had never abandoned a job before.

Somewhere in the woods, something massive roared.

"Fuck this," he muttered. He had just found his limit.

Well, he wasn't dead yet. That made two times in less than an hour that dying had been a distinct possibility, and while he was happy to still be breathing, Grey's tolerance was wearing thin. When Barrus had tackled him off the edge of the cliff, he had managed to use the momentum to twist his body just enough that his left side was facing the cliff. That arm had lashed out wildly, desperately, and got caught in a group of thick vines growing along the rocks. The sudden stop, coupled with the bandit's brief grip on Grey's boot, nearly tore his arm out of its socket. His other shoulder, the one with the bullet hole in it, had settled into a cold ache.

Barrus was nowhere to be seen. He had managed to snag Grey briefly with a handful of fingers but no thumb, no real grip, and then he plummeted on down to the river below. The fall had likely been enough to kill him, but the current swept him away regardless. Grey's gun had gone with him, half a decade's worth of memories with it. Not great. He took his time securing footholds in the vines and the cliff face, whichever offered more stability at each step, and headed carefully back up to the edge. Taghrin was waiting for him, cooler in one hand and shotgun in the other. Grey finished pulling himself up and over the edge, then settled back on his haunch.

"Guess you got me," he said. He spat off to the side. "I suppose it was touch and go there for a minute, though."

"Not really," Taghrin said. He slipped his finger onto the trigger. "Where's my partner?"

"Washing the stink off him, but he's probably too dead to realize it."

The Bozav's lips curled over his lower canines. "See, that was probably the last thing you should have said to me."

Taghrin set the cooler down and used both hands to anchor the shotgun. Grey nodded to himself and lowered his eyes, so resigned to his fate that when a horrific bellow came from the woods he expected pain to follow immediately after. Instead a massive beast made of matted hair, bright yellow eyes, and so, so many teeth exploded into view. It was twice the size of the Bozav and took the bandit by surprise; Taghrin never had a chance. His shotgun dropped next to the cooler, almost gracefully in comparison to the way he was yanked and thrashed out of the clearing and into the growing dark. He screamed. And kept screaming.

Grey stared at nothing, shocked, the breath caught in his chest. His eyes went to the trees next, slowly, dreading and almost expecting to see another giant monster there. Nothing. Just the torn brush and uprooted trees that marked the creature's violent exit. He inhaled deep and long, then picked himself up and snatched up the cooler and shotgun from the ground.

DeSylva 610, he thought, *Ammo is pricey, but the shot is worth it. Which is just fine, because this place fucking sucks.*

But the shotgun hadn't helped Taghrin any, had it?

He pushed that thought to the back of his mind and limped off back toward the *Searcher*.

The scorched body of the freegun was crumpled in plain sight of the tree line. The other one had retreated back to his own ship, a relief to Caesar who was tired of running and fresh out of tricks. A surge of emotions ran through him: relief, revulsion, rage, guilt.

A rustling of leaves to his left made him flinch back against the stump he was crouched against. He grabbed up a branch and lifted it over his shoulders, ready to strike whatever came forth. That whatever was Archimedes, damp and covered in dirt and blood. Startled at the sight of someone else, Ark lifted his arms reflexively to deflect any blows directed his way. None came. When he realized it was Caesar holding the branch, he reached out and pushed it down until it brushed against the ground.

"You look terrible," Caesar whispered.

"Shockingly, I also feel terrible." Archimedes settled down between the roots of a nearby tree and leaned his head back against the trunk. "What about you? How bad are you hurt?"

Caesar shook his head, gave a pitiful shrug. "I'm not."

"Not badly hurt?"

"Not hurt at all."

Archimedes gaped. "…*how* is that possible?"

"Lucky, I guess." Caesar took a deep breath and let it out. A full-body shudder escaped with it. "I, uh, I killed a guy, Ark. That guy out there in the clearing. I used one of Grey's spheres… his Boom Spheres, he calls 'em? Apparently he makes one that explodes."

Archimedes pushed himself up, shoulder back against the tree, until he could glance out at the clearing and the burned body in the middle of it. He studied it for a minute, got a good look at it, then slid back down to the ground. "Was he pointing a gun at you?"

"Yeah," Caesar said softly.

"Well, then I'd try not to let it bother you. Self-defense, you understand? Nobody in the universe would blame you for doing what you needed to do to survive, and you shouldn't blame yourself either, yeah?" Archimedes closed his eyes and let out a long breath, settling in, trying to relax. "Speaking of Grey, you seen him?"

"Not since the shoot-out," Caesar said, shaking his head. "I've been wandering around the woods trying to find either one of you. I've been pretty much lost since you tumbled down that hill, aside from the… aside from what happened out there. Dawson?"

Archimedes shook his head.

They sat in silence for a moment. Caesar wanted to know more about what had happened but was almost afraid of the answers. Archimedes was thinking about the other bandits and what they'd have to do to find Grey. If they *could* find him. He tried to ring out parts of his shirt, but the dirt and blood had seeped in too deeply and he gave up the whole thing as ruined. Across from him Caesar's stomach rumbled. The rumbling grew louder, and louder, and it took a minute for the couriers to realize the sound was coming from the trench.

The *Mathra D'abai*, the ship that had shot them down, had keyed its ignition. Archimedes and Caesar watched as it rose from its position behind the *Grim Pagoda* and fired on the bandit's ship, destroying the engines and blowing off its supports entirely. The *Pagoda* dropped hard to the ground, listed to one side, then settled down, derelict. The *D'abai* hovered for a few seconds longer, then ascended, heading for the stars and leaving its crisped crewman behind.

With one freegun dead, the other gone, and the bandits nowhere in sight, Archimedes and Caesar decided to risk heading back to the *Sol Searcher* to wait for some kind of development rather than wander back into the woods blind and at the mercy of whatever stalked at night. Archimedes took the opportunity to shower and change his clothes, discovering that his body was already a mess of dark blue and purple bruises. Scores of shallow holes covered him from where the vines had fed, and the sight of them made him retch. Once he had composed and dressed himself, Caesar helped him fix a proper bandage to the gash across his forehead and around the hole in his arm.

"What do you think?" Archimedes asked. "Do I look any better?"

"Well, the blood is out of your hair," Caesar said.

"The most important thing."

"You've got to walk before you can run."

Night settled in on Astrakoth. Archimedes stood guard at the loading ramp. Caesar cooked them dinner—potatoes from a box, a can of corn, some fish jerky, something simple to get them through the night without dipping too deep into their food stores—and did a quick check on the perishables inside the ship. To his surprise, little had been lost or broken. The kitchen, for example, was nearly immaculate.

"Small miracles," Caesar said softly to himself, stirring the pot.

A few hours passed during which Archimedes and Caesar keyed the *Searcher's* ignition and turned on the exterior lights, hoping it would help lead Grey to them. Hoping that was the only thing they'd lead to them. They ate by the open loading ramp and passed the time by playing *dakkarat*, once Caesar was able to find the pieces that had been strewn about his room. Caesar had insisted they start a fresh game, refusing to grant Ark his first victory from their paused match before the crash.

In the middle of the night, as the expense of adrenaline throughout the day finally began to wear them down, a series of clangs against the hull of the ship roused them once more. Cautiously, nervously, the edged up to the ramp opening in the bay. Grey stood there, a shotgun held under one arm and a handful of rocks in his hand. Mud had been packed into a wound at his shoulder. The cooler sat next to his feet.

"Thank God, it's you," he said when they came out to greet him. He accepted their hugs, careful to keep his wounded shoulder clear, then caught a good look at Caesar. "Are you… how are you literally unscathed?"

"I asked the same thing," Archimedes said.

Grey shook his head slowly, eyes tired. "Never mind. Doesn't matter. I need one of you to patch me up. After that, it is well past time we found out what the hell is in this box."

Chapter Five

Breaking and Entering

The cockpit of the *Mathra D'abai* was too quiet, and it made Serrano's injuries feel more pronounced. The impact of the explosion had stretched a number of muscles and every single one gnashed at him. The burnt patches of skin throbbed, glossy and painful to touch. He just sat there, not too far out of the forest planet's orbit, scowling down at the planet. Part of him wanted to head back down so he could retrieve Crajax's body and give him a proper burial. The man had been a good partner, reliable if not the best conversationalist.

The other part of him knew it had been Crajax's impatience that had killed him, nearly killed Serrano, and cost them any reliable opportunity they'd had to recover the package they had been hired to find. If he hadn't moved in so close to the courier, or if he had considered for a single second that the sphere so willingly handed over might not actually be the prize they were looking for, then he might still be alive.

Now Jeth was left alone, replaying the near-death experience in his head, furious that his perfect record as a freegun was about to be marred by an incomplete mission.

For Euphrates Destidante, no less, he thought. He let a low breath hiss through his teeth, then leaned forward to tap in the number he had been given on the data drive. It was better to just rip the bandage off.

"What news do you have?" The voice came through the cockpit speakers without inflection. No telling his mood this time.

Jeth decided to go on the offensive, putting some steel in his voice. "Did you put anyone else on this job?"

"If I had, I would have told you. Doing otherwise would be reckless, and I'm not—"

"Reckless, yeah, I know," Jeth said, cutting him off. He rubbed at his eyes carefully, the skin around them raw. "The job went to hell. The second ship, the one following the couriers, it had fake tags. I'm guessing the crew were thieves or smugglers looking for a score. Both the couriers and the other ship took hits in the orbit of an uninhabited planet and crashed. Crajax and I followed them down. The ships were wrecked, but most of both crews survived. It turned into a clusterfuck of a firefight, but we managed to take them out one by one 'til we got the last courier. He took us to the package, but he'd... he had trapped the container it was in. Some kind of bomb. Crajax and the courier were killed, and I got hurt. Everything else was destroyed in the blast. Unrecoverable."

Close enough to the truth, the lies came easier than expected. But would Destidante buy them? He held his breath and waited.

"I see," Euphrates said, finally. "Disappointing news. Not what I was expecting to hear. Did you at least find out what the package was?"

"You told us not to open it," Jeth said.

"True, I did. It sounds like things got rather exciting on your end, though. I wouldn't blame you for becoming curious."

Jeth was offended. "We took your contract, Euphrates. I follow contracts to the letter, *you* know that. Now I'm down a partner and a payday, so at least pay me enough damn respect not to accuse me of breaking my word."

"Alright, Serrano, alright," Euphrates said, although Jeth knew there wouldn't be any kind of real apology coming. "The courier didn't say anything about what it might be?"

"No. He didn't."

"Mm. What planet did this happen on?"

"I don't—hold on." Jeth leaned forward, stifling a groan, and typed a command into his control console. The display of the space around his ship shrunk and slid to the left side of his screen. On the right, a second image appeared, a visual analysis of the planet below.

"Some planet called Astrakoth. There are a few notes about the place hosting a few science outposts, but we didn't see any when we went down there, and nobody came running when shit kicked off. Says here that nearly all of the local animal species encountered have been registered as exceptionally hostile. Some of the flora, too. It's some kind of predator battleground, which seems about right from my limited experience with the place."

Another long pause, one that seemed to stretch through Causeways.

"You still there?" Jeth prompted.

"Yes. Just… thinking. There may still be a way for you to collect the back end of your payment, though I'll be holding on to Mister Madan's half. You understand. Would you be interested in the job?"

"I don't know," the freegun said, hesitating. "Are you sending me after more couriers?"

There was a soft snort from the other end of the call. "No, though I imagine it won't be any less dangerous. I want you to continue on to Peloclade and find the man meant to receive the package. Find out everything he knows about it by any means necessary. When you're finished, cut ties with him. I do need to know your answer now. Time may be an issue."

Serrano bit at the inside of his cheek. What Destidante had already paid him up front was more than enough for him to feel comfortable walking and taking the time he needed to heal. It was the safe option. Then again, his pride was hurting even more than his body and taking the job could go a long way toward restoring good will with Destidante.

"The address of the recipient?" he asked.

"In the same file I gave you. I'm not sending you into a trap. Probably, although the couriers weren't supposed to be an issue, either. I advise you to exercise caution. You're a lone agent now."

Jeth grimaced. "I'm in. It'll take me a couple days to reach Bax Tavilian and get to the Hesperos system."

"Very good," Euphrates said, and hung up.

The freegun stared at his control console, disarmed by the abrupt dismissal. He glanced out his viewport at Astrakoth. He wondered if Destidante would send someone to verify Jeth's story. He knew that both ships *were* derelict. He figured their crews would either kill each other or get finished off by the planet. It was a calculated risk, one he would just have to take.

Jeth Serrano fired up his thrusters and took hold of the steering rig. The *Mathra D'abai* slid gracefully in the direction of Bax Tavilian Gate. The quiet in the cockpit remained stifling.

*****

With everyone that had been after them seemingly dead or departed, the *Sol Searcher's* crew made survival and escape from Astrakoth their priority. They ransacked the *Grim Pagoda* for their tools, food, and first aid supplies (of the latter, there had been thoughtlessly little), and set about looking for anything they could use to start repairing their ship. To Grey's deep annoyance, the *Pagoda's* weapons system had been turned into an unsalvageable melted mess, but he saw promise in the shield panels along the hull.

It was slow-going work. Grey was the one with the eye for mechanics and engineering. The hands, too; Archimedes' were soft, uncallused, unprotected from the rough materials and sharp edges. Grey watched him work, aware that Archimedes was probably smarting something awful from the scrapes, bruises, and bloody holes that covered his body, a little proud that Ark pushed through it anyway. Caesar, meanwhile, had triggered both the ACG emergency beacon 'for courier agents in distress' as well as a general Need of Rescue signal before settling into his workshop to take a crack at unlocking the cooler.

A loud clang sounded as Archimedes wrenched another metal panel free from the *Grim Pagoda* and hurled it toward his own ship. He had pulled a magno-clamp ladder from the *Sol Searcher* and was putting it to good use, clambering up and down the bandit's ship and systematically stripping pieces off it according to Grey's instructions.

For his part, Grey was propped up under the hull of the *Searcher*, miserable and barely able to move the arm he'd been shot in now that the adrenaline had worn off. He could still shoot one-handed, though, and kept watch with Taghrin's shotgun cradled in his lap. A pair of pistols they had found onboard the *Pagoda* rested on the ground next to his leg.

"We're going to need their viewport at some point," he called up to Archimedes. "That'll be the big grab, since ours is totally fucked."

"Is it?" Archimedes asked from atop the *Pagoda*. He wiped a sweaty hand across his sweaty brow to no effect. "I think the thing I hate the most about you, Grey, is the way you talk about things as if I hadn't been sitting right next to you when they happened. Quick question for you: say I get the viewport off by myself, somehow, and reinstall it on the *Searcher* without destroying the seals, somehow, how are we going to launch her without blowing ourselves up?"

"You don't trust me to keep that from happening?" Grey grinned.

"Not particularly, no."

Grey patted the shotgun. "How about you just shut up and keep stripping parts before I fuckin' shoot you?"

Dinner that night was carefully rationed by caloric content, cooked and dished out by Caesar. The portions were small and none of them were happy, but they kept any complaints unspoken, Archimedes offered to do the dishes, grateful for something to do that wasn't manual labor. Grey closed out the day with a couple of circuits around the *Searcher*, trying to figure out how they could lift the ship enough to start repairing the parts of the hull that had been damaged in the crash. No obvious solutions presented themselves.

As the sun set once more on Astrakoth, the couriers sealed up the loading ramp for safety. Grey and Archimedes' dressings were changed, with Grey taking two small yellow pills—Dagrofil— that Caesar had given him for the pain. The cooler was left in the workshop for morning. Archimedes sat in the cockpit, listening to the sounds of the alien wild through the broken viewport until sleep stole mercifully upon him.

*****

Peloclade—like Salix—was considered a hub world of sorts, one that might, in casual conversation, be described as 'one of the nice ones.' Members of all races were welcome, housing was affordable, the nature reserves near its equator were highly recommended, and most major cities were considered pleasant places to live.

Jeth wasn't interested in any of that. He liked Peloclade well enough, but he had a job to do, one that took him to the river-filled city of Zeanum. Romantics called it the Flowing City. It was

Bridge City to everyone else. It had taken the freegun three days to reach Bax Tavilian Gate, pass through into the Hesperos system, and reach the planet, and he was ready for some fresh air.

And he would get it, but not to the extent he wanted.

"What the hell do you mean I can't leave the landing pad?" he snapped at the officer.

"I'm sorry, Captain Serrano. You're free to walk *around* the landing pad, of course, and mingle with the other captains and crews, but everyone here is restricted to the area for the next couple of days at least. That means no departures and no going into the city proper. If you need provisions, arrangements can be made."

Jeth gaped at him. "I know you're speaking Trader to me, but it doesn't make any sense."

"I understand your apprehension," said the officer, nodding, "but this really is for your safety and the safety of others. There has been an active serial bomber for—"

"A *serial bomber*? I thought I landed on Peloclade, not fucking Dephros! You couldn't tell me about this when I hailed the pad to land?"

"I mean, all arrivals are welcome. I suppose it may have been courteous for whoever it was you spoke with to have mentioned something, but really, we don't expect this to be more than a minor inconvenience. It's just a couple of days, just until the threat has been resolved."

"So which is it?" Jeth snapped. "A minor inconvenience, or a threat serious enough to lock me in my fucking ship? It would have been nice to have had the option *not* to land, and *not* to be in a city with a goddamn terrorist. I just *spent* three days—" He closed his eyes and massaged his nose slits, trying to calm himself.

"It's for your safety," the officer said again, unable to keep hints of frustration from creeping into his own voice.

"Yeah, you keep saying that. What do you expect me to do in that time, restricted as I am to the landing pad?"

The officer shrugged. "I don't know, Captain. Play cards. Watch a movie or something. I'm just doing my job, which is keeping people alive, and which is not being a nanny."

Serrano let that go unanswered and watched the man move off. He wondered if he could find someone more amendable. Or, if not, maybe someone bribeable.

Euphrates won't be happy about this, he thought. But then, wasn't a couple days of rest and relaxation exactly what he had been thinking he'd need? *After all, who am I to argue with the law?*

*****

"I got it! Guys, I cracked the code, we can get it open!"

Caesar squeezed himself outside through the *Sol Searcher*'s ramp and rounded the ship. He found Archimedes and Grey near the nose, screaming into each other's face. As far as he could make out, they were arguing about the same pack of six-legged reptilian hounds that had dragged off the scorched freegun's body a couple days earlier.

"Why wouldn't you bring the bag back inside with us?" Grey was yelling. "How are we supposed to repair the ship with no fucking tools?"

"Why *would* I bring it in?" Archimedes shot back. "We're the only people here, moron! I'm supposed to think, hey, these non-opposable-thumb-having animals might want to build a spacecraft in their murder jungle? No, that would be far too lofty a goal. Maybe they'll just build a house. A murder house."

"You ever consider that maybe someone trained those things? Sent them here against us?"

"Or, hear me out, they're savage beasts that just want to grab and chew on whatever catches their beady little eyes. How would I know that what caught their eye would be a meatless bag of tools? Why would that even be a thing that crossed my mind?"

"You're right," Grey said, sneering. "I should have expected that, seeing as how *no* thoughts *ever* cross your mind."

Archimedes reeled at that, incredulous. "You're one to fu—"

"Hey! Idiots!" Caesar clapped his hands loudly, having set the cooler down at his feet. "I've got the code to this thing. We can see what's in it together, or I can come back after you two murder each other and just look at it on my own."

Grey spat at Archimedes' feet. "Now is fine. At least we can die on this shithole with our curiosity sated."

"Don't spit at me, or I'll—"

"You'll what?"

Archimedes floundered. "I'll... kick it back at you."

"Shut up, Ark, for the love of God," Caesar said, rolling his eyes.

They moved out from the sun to a clear spot under the *Searcher* and sat down on the ground in a row, their backs pressed against the hull. Caesar, in the center, set the cooler down in front of him. A small circular device had been magnetically attached to the lip of the numeric lock pad, a tiny light at the top blinking green. Caesar pressed the ENTER key on the lock; two *clack*s and a *swish* sounded, and the seal to the cooler—bisecting the number pad between the second and third rows—slid open a notch. Caesar gave it a gentle push and the lid fell backward. Thin ribbons of frosted air filtered up from the box.

All three of them leaned in at the same time to look.

The cooler was empty, save for a translucent green sphere about the size of a man's fist. A small pedestal had been fixed to the bottom of the container; the sphere sat atop it, held in place by a wire frame. Caesar reached in, unfastened the frame, and pulled the sphere free.

"Cold," he murmured. "Really cold. The cooler must be modified somehow, turned into something more like a freezer. Must be some kind of internal mechanism built into—"

"What the hell is it, Caesar?" Grey interrupted.

Caesar held the orb up in front of his face. He could make out a vague shape inside, suspended near the center. What *was* he looking at? Were those limbs? A tail?

"It's a lizard," Archimedes said, sitting back.

"I don't think so," Grey said. "It looks like a—"

"No, it's a lizard." Archimedes reached out and tapped one side of the sphere. "You can make out its dumb little head. There's the tail. Get in close, you can see it's got webbed feet. There, see? The little toes are spread out? People have been trying to kill us over a lizard. Caesar, do you know what kind of lizard it is? It's got to be exotic, right, with that price tag?"

"I don't know," Caesar said softly, turning the sphere in his hands, studying it.

"A lizard," Grey deadpanned. "That's actually infuriating."

"Maybe," Caesar said. He slipped the orb back into the cooler, secured it to its pedestal, and closed the lid. "We don't know anything about it. A valuable object is a valuable object, and we'd all be pretty pissed if they were trying to kill us over a painting or a sculpture or a precious stone the same way we are about whatever that thing is. 'That's it?' you'd say. 'Killing people over that little thing?' You don't want an explanation, Grey, you want something to complain about."

Grey's jaw dropped, stunned. "*Excuse you?* Where did *that* come from? And frankly, I think people trying to kill you is a perfectly legitimate reason to complain."

"Shut up," Archimedes said suddenly, holding a hand up. He tilted his head back, eyes fixed on the underside of the *Searcher*, but he wasn't looking for anything. He was listening. "Sounds like a ship is coming. Caesar, put the cooler back inside, somewhere it doesn't look out of place. Grey—"

"Gun, yeah. Got it." One of the pistols he had taken from the *Grim Pagoda* had been just about a perfect fit for his thigh holster. He lurched to his feet and yanked it free. Archimedes went and grabbed the shotgun.

They reassembled in the trench moments later, out in the open, halfway between the *Pagoda* and the *Searcher*. They watched, one hand shielding their eyes from the sun, as the arriving ship began its slow descent.

"Sure taking their sweet-ass time about it," Archimedes said.

"Who do you think it is?" Caesar asked, fidgeting. He was the only one that wasn't armed, uncomfortable handling the other pistol they had available.

"Mm, hard to say. I think bandits might be a bit more in a rush to see to our needs. We sent out a distress signal, that's pretty much a flashing neon sign saying easy prey."

Grey grunted an agreement.

"Guns down, you think?" Archimedes asked him.

"Maybe. I ain't looking to get accidentally shot. Getting shot on purpose hurt bad enough."

Caesar, trying not to let their conversation make him more anxious, kept his eye on the ship. It had finally descended enough to block out some of the sunlight and give him a proper look at it.

"That… I think that's an IRSC flyer!" Caesar said. The navy blue patches painted over the silver hull were clue enough, but the star-shaped gold insignia painted on the nose of the ship was a dead giveaway. He couldn't make out the words just yet, but he knew they would read Intergalactic Research and Science Craft at its four points. "They must have been assigned to the planet!"

The ship finally settled down in the trench, just to the left of the *Pagoda*. A ramp on the side lowered itself a few moments later, and a dozen armed soldiers followed it down in a well-practiced march, rifles up and pointed at the couriers. Archimedes and Grey kept their guns down, pointed at the ground.

A thirteenth figure strode confidently through the arrangement until he had taken point, about five paces or so from the couriers. He wore a steam-pressed cobalt uniform with silver patches over his broad form, and sleek boots that stretched up to his knees. His hair was midnight black, well-oiled and slicked back to sweep across his ears. He looked to be an old 30, maybe a young 50, and held the air of an officer.

"We received a distress call," he said.

"We triggered it," Caesar said. "Five days ago, actually."

"Well, the research ship isn't… we weren't monitoring for that kind of activity, or we would have tried to get here sooner." He glanced over at the *Pagoda*, took in the *Searcher*'s condition, looked back at the couriers. "This also wasn't the best place for us to land."

"Not an ideal landing place?" Archimedes gasped, looking around at the ragged rut torn into the ground.

"Alright," the officer said, lifting a hand. "Point taken. So, you triggered the distress signal. Who are you exactly?"

"Captain Caesar Anada," Caesar said.

"Captain Grey Toliver."

"Captain Archimedes Carnahan."

The officer glanced around again. "Where's the third ship?"

"One ship, actually," Caesar said. He jerked a thumb at the *Sol Searcher*. "That one, specifically."

"Three captains for one ship?" the officer asked, making a face. "How does *that* work?"

Archimedes held his hand up. "I'm the most captain. I just let the other two call themselves captain so they don't grow despondent. Space can pretty dour from time to time, I'm sure you know."

"Uh, okay. And what kind of ship are you flying?"

"A busted one, sir."

The officer bit back a response, took a deep breath, asked, "What *rank*, Captain?"

"C-rank, sir," Caesar chipped in. "The ship isn't armed, though we may be reconsidering that. The *Searcher*'s a courier ship, contracted to Aventure. Haven't had any trouble to speak of until now. We've got our licenses and related paperwork on board. I can bring them out if you'd like to see them."

"That would be great. I can see the Aventure logo, but if you wouldn't mind, I'd like to run the licenses. Standard procedure."

The rest of the men stood in awkward silence while Caesar ran back inside the *Searcher*. The soldiers lowered their guns, but only halfway, as if expecting Archimedes and Grey to try something suicidal. The officer nodded his head in the direction of the *Grim Pagoda*. "What's the deal with that?"

"Bandits, I guess," Grey said. "Tried to corner us in Catalasca, then took off after us. We didn't notice they had followed us until we'd passed through Destiria Gate. They shot us down here, chased us into the woods, stole our cargo. Took us some time to find our way back, haven't seen hide or hair of them since."

"What happened to their ship? Looks like someone blasted it."

"No idea, sir," Grey said, shrugging. "It was like that when we got back. Maybe the bandits had bandits of their own."

The officer frowned, looked around, saw the wide patch of charred ground where the Boom Sphere had gone off. "And that?"

"Campfire."

"Looks more like an explosion."

Archimedes gave a sheepish smile. "What can we say? We're couriers, not camp counselors."

The officer studied him for a long moment, a wave of exhaustion washing over his expression. He sighed and, spotting Caesar returning from the *Searcher*, said, "You know what? If the paperwork comes back clear, I don't even care."

Caesar reached the group and handed over the licenses, registrations, and the confirmation letter of their most recent job to the officer. He called one of his soldiers up, a baby-faced young man named Fitzroy, and had him run the documents back to the flyer. With nothing to do but stand around and wait, an awkwardness settled between them.

Catching sight of the bandages on Grey and Archimedes, the officer said, "Well, you boys certainly have been through it." Pointing at the bandages coming up from Grey's shoulder to above the collar of his shirt, he said. "Shot? Stabbed?"

"Shot," Grey acknowledged.

"I was stabbed," Archimedes said cheerily.

The officer grunted, looked at Caesar. "Not a scratch on you, looks like. You must be the dangerous one." He looked past them to the *Sol Searcher*, noticed the massive hole in the viewport for the first time, and the large branch laying on the ground nearby. "You boys got lucky. Been working on repairs while you've been waiting?"

"We were until this morning," Grey said. "Pack of wild dog things took off with our tools."

"Yeah, those bastards are all over the place," the officer nodded. Fitzroy returned and handed the papers and licenses back to the officer. They leaned in and had a quick and quiet dialogue, then Fitzroy stepped back into position with the rest of his fellow soldiers. The officer handed the paperwork back to Caesar. "Everything checks out, so we're more than happy to take you up. I assume you're going to want to salvage your ship. To that end we've got vacuum sealant for the breach in your viewport, and a mag-clamp we can attach to the hull so's we can tow you up, but you'll need to find a way to close your ramp. Gonna need enough power to guide the ship into our cruiser's bay and set it down. Think that's manageable?"

"The ramp's fine," Grey said, "as long as we can get her pulled up off the embankment there. I've got the power back up and running enough for just that, but then she'll be about tapped. I figure she can use the free tow with the power in reserve until we get to your ship, and then I can take over and lead her in."

"Great. I guess strap down what needs strappin' down, then. You got a—"

"A space suit?" Grey nodded. "Yeah, we've got a few."

"Just in case the sealant doesn't, ah, quite seal all the way." He turned and whistled at his soldiers, sending them marching back up their ramp and onto the flyer, then turned and pointed at Caesar and Archimedes. "You two are coming with us. Couple of my boys will come back out and help with sealing the breaches, and then Captain Camp Fire can take control." He eyed Grey. "You going to need help getting in that suit with your busted wing?"

"I might," Grey admitted.

"Alright. Most Captain can assist you." To Caesar, he said, "Captain Manners, go on and board my ship. And all of you, cheer up. You've been rescued."

The bullet wound did indeed make for an unpleasant experience, but Grey was eager to get back behind the *Searcher*'s control panel. He and Archimedes both did a full walkthrough of the ship, starting at opposite ends, and secured everything that hadn't already been strapped down or destroyed in the crash. Afterward, Grey double-checked the sealant that had been applied to the viewport by the IRSC soldiers (they may have been a bunch of grunts, but they had been thorough) and Archimedes did the same for Grey's space suit. After Ark left to join Caesar aboard the flyer, Grey spent some time transferring primary controls to the co-pilot's seat and then hailed the rescue ship to let them know he was ready.

The larger ship lifted off, slowly, its powerful thrusters and the mag-clamp dragging the *Searcher* foot by foot out of the rut it had dug. As soon as it was clear, Grey keyed the backup power and closed the loading ramp. To his relief, the ship's sensors indicated that everything sealed tightly, no breaches detected.

"At least one thing on this damn ship isn't busted," he muttered.

He flicked the switch that operated the *Searcher*'s thrusters, taking some slack off of the tether and giving him more control over steering. Archimedes' dried blood still covered most of the co-pilot's control panel, flaking off wherever Grey worked.

The *Searcher*'s oxygen levels continued to stay consistent as the ships left Astrakoth's atmosphere. Grey allowed himself to relax for the journey, making only minor adjustments on the way to the IRSC cruiser. When they arrived, Grey read the bold red letters across the hull to see what the vessel called itself: *Imagination*.

Archimedes must be pissing himself, Grey thought. *I can hear him now. 'How little imagination do you have to have to settle on that?'*

He took the flight controls awkwardly, one-handed, and angled it after the flyer. They passed together through a gravity field and into the landing bay. A number of armed soldiers and unarmed crewmen waited patiently for them to land. After a couple minutes of careful maneuvering the flyer settled down, then the *Searcher*. Grey dropped the loading ramp and keyed the power off once more. The suit came off next, piece by piece, each with prolonged and creative strings of expletives.

A crewman met him halfway up the ramp when he was finally ready to disembark. "Welcome to the *Imagination*, Captain. Do you require assistance?"

"Five minutes ago," Grey growled. "Where are my friends?"

"Sergeant Yant escorted them to the medical bay upon landing. We have four doctors on board and an entire hall for recovery. I've been told you had suffered injuries planet-side as well, and I am to escort you the same way for medical attention.

Grey nearly made a snarky remark but the exhaustion and fear he had kept at arm's length the last few days finally ganged up on him. His breath rushed out of him in a long, tired flow and he sagged. The soldier caught him around the torso, kept him upright.

"Lead the way, crewman," Grey said, but he was already being carried along.

Chapter Six

Imagination

Like all major IRSC spacecraft, the *Imagination* was absolutely massive. The ship's docking bay—located at the bottom of the cruiser—was filled with military escort flyers, mobile science ships, land and sea transports that could be loaded up and taken down to the planet's surface, speeders and sky hoppers for sub-orbital transportations, racks upon racks of maintenance equipment, and even a handful of empty spots for any unscheduled craft that might arrive during one of their months-long research expeditions; the *Searcher* was one of these ships and easily the ugliest craft in the bay.

The bulk of the cruiser's occupants were either researchers or the crew required to maintain the vital functions of the ship. The crew quarters were arranged irregularly along the top two decks, all individual rooms for the minimum required number of staff, plus an additional twenty for back-up and emergency crewmembers, and two 6-bunk rooms in case of unforeseen circumstances.

Then came the soldiers brought along to maintain security and provide protection for planet-side excursions. Each of their rooms held four beds and each occupant was given a standing locker and a footlocker for their things. Only the officers had individual rooms, and only the officers held keys to the armories positioned at each end of the deck. The armories were filled with several variants of environment-specific tactical gear and a wide range of both lethal and nonlethal weapons. Due to the advanced dangers of unloading high-caliber firearms and explosive devices in the void of space, these rooms were only unlocked directly before a mission and only under close supervision.

The third deck, being roughly the center of the ship, also contained the mess hall and the storage rooms for the *Imagination*'s provisions.

Below them, and above the docking bay, were two levels fully devoted to the rest of the *Imagination's* populace: scientists and academics, their assistants, and the *Imagination*'s doctors and nurses. Each of these individuals were afforded their own private rooms as well, and there were additional rooms here again for contractors, special visitors, and emergency residents. There was also room for the research laboratories, computer labs, and study rooms, the medical bays, workout stations, additional locker rooms, and storage compartments. If there had been a shopping center, the IRSC vessel could have been classified as a small town. It was on these levels that Caesar, Grey, and Archimedes had been assigned their rooms, positioned somewhere above the separation between the docking bay and the engine room.

Caesar and Archimedes had been separated upon reaching the *Imagination*, not forcefully but with little room for argument. Ark had been hauled off to one of the medical centers while Caesar was taken the opposite direction on the same level, escorted by a young woman with dark skin and blonde hair that fell down to her shoulders. The last inch or so was a ring of black dye.

"Um, excuse me," he said. He kept looking back at his friend until Archimedes was pulled around a corner, out of sight. "Who exactly are you?"

"I'm Koko," she said, smiling.

"Right. I'm Caesar, nice to meet you. But… where exactly are we, um, going?"

"To your room. They didn't tell you?" She shook her head, smile still playing at the edge of her lips. Her expression seemed to say, *Oh, those guys*, like they just dropped people off to wander aimlessly down the halls all the time. She realized something and stopped, and he nearly tripped stopping with her. She said, "Where is your stuff? You lose it all planetside?"

"No, it's… my stuff is on the *Searcher*. We came up separately, so I didn't really have any time to grab anything."

She pointed at him. "The junker that was getting towed up! That's your ship? I figured that bucket was just getting brought up for scraps."

Caesar made a face. "That's a licensed courier ship, I'll have you know, and one with a stellar record. And no matter what it looks like after a *crash landing*, the inside is just as good as..." He trailed off, looking around. He gestured at the hallway around them. "As this place, for example."

Koko nodded, letting him finish. She asked, "There are three of you, right? All men?"

"Uh."

"Do you guys live in the ship fulltime, or do you have apartments somewhere?"

"Um."

"I'm sure it's absolutely pristine," she said, laughing. Caesar flushed red. "Maybe your room is. You seem the put-together type. The rest of the ship? Not a chance. I'd bet on it. Anyway, if there's something you really need off of your craft, we can go back down and get it. Otherwise, if you're as exhausted as you look and just want to clean up and get some rest, your room's got a shower and some generic IRSC uniforms you can change into. Once everyone is settled in, you'll have more access: the hanger to grab stuff on your own time, the mess hall to, you know, eat."

"You do a lot of these tours?" Caesar asked, trying to recover from his embarrassment.

"Not really, no. I'm usually exercising piss-poor posture in one of the labs upstairs." She jerked a thumb toward the ceiling. "Professor Eppleheim gave me the day off, though. I heard you guys were getting picked up and had to find out what was going on, seeing as how Astrakoth isn't really known as a vacation locale." She grinned, gave a big shrug. "What can I say? I'm a curious girl. Probably what makes me such a great scientist."

Caesar blinked in surprise. "Come again?"

"What? Never seen a lady scientist before?"

"No, sorry," Caesar said, waving a flustered hand. "I didn't mean… did you say Professor Eppleheim is on board? As in Professor *Sonus* Eppleheim?"

It was Koko's turn to be surprised. "The courier knows his academics."

"I'm something of a scientist myself. I read his paper on quantum displacement. Big fan of his work."

"*A Better YOUniverse*? If there's a better version of me out there, which I highly doubt, I'd have to kill her."

Caesar laughed. He found himself warming to the woman, put at ease by her demeanor. It wasn't until that moment that he fully embraced that he had been rescued and that he could finally relax again.

Koko turned and resumed walking, Caesar following close behind her. He read the digital displays next to the doors as they passed them, each one listing the names of the room's occupants or the nature of the lab within. It wasn't until he was standing in front of his own quarters that he realized he hadn't spent a single moment during their walk worrying about Grey or Archimedes.

I'm sure they're fine, he thought. *And so am I.*

"Thank you, Koko," he said. "After everything I've been through recently, it's nice just to have a warm welcome."

Koko pulled a white card from her pocket, swiped it over a gray block next to the door. When the door slid open, she handed the card to Caesar. "I'm better than a killer planet? Can I use that as a back-of-the-book quote if I ever get published?"

"You have my explicit permission," he said, chuckling. He took the card and slipped it into his back pocket. "Hey, how much do you know about Astrakoth?"

"I mean, nobody knows much," she said. "People have come and gone, done up some maps, taxidermied some animals, but this is the first real science expedition, I think. The *Imagination* has been studying different areas for a couple of months now. We keep getting samples brought up, the samples keep surprising and frightening us."

Caesar snorted. "Sounds about right." He stepped past her, into his room, hesitated. He looked back. "The labs on this ship, are they nice?"

Koko's eyes glittered. "This is an IRSC vessel. I'm pretty sure it's required by law for our labs to be exceptionally nice. You want to see one? You want to meet the professor?"

"Is that allowed?" The question came out in a squeal of excitement. Koko graciously pretended not to notice.

"It is when I'm your escort." She looked past him, nodded at the bed. "You sure you're not too tired?"

He *was* tired, could feel the exhaustion snaking through his bones, but the opportunity was too great to pass up. "No, not at all, but should I... I should shower, right? Not that I haven't been showering, the shower was working on the *Searcher*, but these clothes—"

"Caesar," Koko interrupted, "it's a science lab. Half the things in there smell worse than you do."

The nurse hovered over Archimedes like a human canopy, adjusting the glowing suction pads covering his body. Most of them were glowing green. A few, firmly and achingly pressed against scrapes and bruises, showed yellow. A pair positioned on either side of where the branch had stabbed him (that wound was now stapled shut, another exercise in misery) were red. The nurse would move a few of the suction cups at a time, look at the lights, lean back to check a terminal display, and then jot down notes on a clipboard.

"I can just tell you where I hurt," he said.

"Is it everywhere?" the nurse asked without looking up.

"I mean… okay, when you say it like that…"

"The sensors are there to register the *severity* of an injury to the area of your body to which they're applied, Captain Carnahan. You've pulled a number of muscles, you have several contusions, several abrasions. These are mostly minor, things you'll recover from in a matter of days, maybe a couple of weeks. What I'm more concerned about are fractures, breaks, infections, any internal bleeding." He glanced at Archimedes over the rim of his glasses. "Have you ever had septicemia?"

"No," Ark said, shaking his head.

"Ever seen someone suffering from it?"

"No, I haven't."

"Blood poisoning. Nasty stuff, I assure you. It can spring on you quickly, and hard, and then your survival rate drops pretty drastically after that depending on how fast you decide to see a doctor." He waved a pen at the pattern of puncture wounds that wrapped around his body. "Keeping that in mind, what happened here? We've been chasing nasty beasties all over the planet, but I haven't seen or heard of anything that would do this."

"Yeah, well, don't go chasing waterfalls," Archimedes muttered.

"Excuse me?"

"Nothing, never mind." Ark pushed himself up on the hospital bed, wincing at the concert of aches that sang at him. "Look, can you at least give me some drugs or something? For the pain?"

The nurse gave a look of disapproval. He set his clipboard aside, pushed his glasses back up the bridge of his nose. "I'd like to, but unless you're going to give me more information about these marks, I think it's best we wait until your blood work comes back. We can't risk any medication adversely reacting to whatever else might be swimming around inside you."

Archimedes scrunched his face, disgusted. "Blood work. You have to take my blood, too?"

"Oh, right! I haven't done that yet. I really am sorry, Captain Carnahan, but it's standard procedure."

The nurse stepped over to a counter at the far side of the room, to a tall black box with a red heart decal on it. He pushed open the lid, hovered his hand left and right over whatever was inside, then reached in and pulled out a long, thin syringe. The needle at the end was thick, the kind of needle you might murder someone in prison with.

"Hey, now," Archimedes said, pushing himself further up the bed. "Where do you think you're sticking that?"

"Don't panic," the nurse said. "Like I said, this is perfectly routine."

"That isn't an answer. Also, the fact that you stab people with that on a regular basis does not put me any more at ease."

The nurse returned to the side of the bed. He held the syringe up, checked it for air. "Let me ask you something, maybe it'll help you relax: if money weren't an issue, what is the one place in the universe you'd want to vacation most? Me, I think I'd take a Stardew cruise. Gamble a little, I've always liked that, maybe pretend I'm somebody else for a week."

Archimedes blinked, bemused. "I—I'm not sure. I guess maybe—"

The nurse jammed the syringe into his thigh.

Archimedes yelped, eyes bugging out. "*What kind of fuckin' doctor ARE you?*"

"I'm just a nurse, Captain Carnahan, and a considerate one I would like to think. Surprise seemed a better course of action than to prolong the dread you were already experiencing."

"First off, *no*. Secondly, now there's another hole in my leg!"

The nurse set the syringe down next to his clipboard and grabbed a thick bandage. He tossed it to Archimedes, who snatched it out of the air indignantly.

"Keep pressure on that until it stops bleeding. The injection was a chemical cocktail designed to stave off any dehydration. That way I don't need to hook you up to a saline bag. If your leg becomes numb, don't be concerned. It will pass. As far as the puncture wound goes, well…" The nurse smiled cheerily. "Once it's healed, it will fit in perfectly with all the rest, don't you think?"

"Wonderful," Archimedes grumbled.

"You lay back and relax now. I'm going to run down to the lab, and then I'll be back soon."

"You're a goddamn savage," Ark said to his back as the nurse exited.

The room hummed and whirred with the sound of machinery. Archimedes laid his head back and stared at the ceiling, hands pressed to his thigh. He had only been gone from Astrakoth for a couple hours, but it already seemed like a lifetime ago—the gunshots and explosions, the smell and taste of blood, the heat.

To be honest, he kind of missed some of that heat. The room was freezing, and he had been left to endure it in his lucky boxers, white with little pink hearts patterned all over. He hoped the whole ship wasn't set at the same temperature, some kind of regulation or command, maybe to conserve energy. Maybe this was just another one of the nurse's 'routine' medical practices.

He shivered and closed his eyes. Within seconds, he was fast asleep.

Archimedes woke some time later to a light rapping on the door. He opened his eyes just as Caesar stepped through the threshold, closing the door behind him.

"Hey," Caesar said.

"Hey."

"How are you feeling?"

Archimedes shrugged. "Like I crashed a spaceship, got the shit kicked out of me, got the blood sucked out of me, and nearly broke my neck. You?"

"Pretty good, more or less," Caesar said. "You know, on the bright side, I don't think you came away any uglier."

"Small miracles," Archimedes grinned. "What are you doing up? I figured you'd have been the first one to tuck in."

Caesar moved around to the side of the hospital bed, found a stool, and pulled it over to take a seat. "Yeah, I would have. Koko's been showing me around some of the labs." He looked over the suction cups still attached to Ark's torso, flicked one just above his nipple. "What are these? These new?"

"Never mind those," Archimedes said, swatting his friend away. "Koko's the blonde? She's a looker."

"And an accredited scientist, you cad. It was nice, you know? The tour? I had really forgotten what stimulating conversation was like. And Professor Eppleheim is on board! Do you know how long he's been a hero of mine? I saw him speak once, about the migratory patterns of insects versus avians following a—" He trailed off, seeing Archimedes staring at him. "You don't care."

"Not really, no."

Archimedes lifted the bandage from his thigh to see if the puncture wound was still bleeding; a dark red bubble of blood welled up almost immediately. Caesar saw this and got up, moving around the room, rummaging through drawers until he came up with a roll of purple adhesive gauze. Archimedes tossed the bloody bandage toward a small trash bin under the sink. It bounced off of the pipes hanging below before going in.

"That's deeply unsanitary," Caesar said. He pulled up the end of the tape with his thumbnail, started wrapping it around Archimedes' leg. There is a box on the wall specifically for things relating to bodily waste.

"I don't c—"

"You don't care. I know. Keep in mind that we're guests on the ship, Ark." Caesar tore the tape from the roll and tucked it under the rest of the wrapping, securing it to his friend's leg.

"Thanks," Archimedes said. "You really should get some rest, you know."

"According to the *Imagination*'s time cycle, it's currently morning. I figured I could get some breakfast, maybe grab a few things out of the *Searcher*. Settle for a nap later so that my sleep schedule doesn't get all screwy." Caesar returned the gauze to the drawer he had pulled it from. "I was headed to the mess hall but wanted to check on you first."

"How sweet," Archimedes said. He lifted his leg from the bed, gave it a few trial bends of the knee. "You seen Grey?"

Caesar shook his head. "Not since we got on the flyer. I'm sure he's holed up in another one of these exam rooms, probably being unpleasant."

"If there's any justice in the universe, he'll get the same nurse I did."

Archimedes sat up and started pulling off the suction cup sensors, grunting at the few that took chest hairs with them. When they were all removed, he swung his legs over the side of the gurney. A dozen knives cut him up from the inside. Felt like they were on fire, too. And coated with angry bees. He swayed, lightheaded, and fell forward. Caesar caught him before he could hit the ground and helped him up to his feet.

"What are you doing?" Caesar hissed.

"I'm coming to get breakfast with you."

"Really? And what if you're dying? Have you considered that?"

Archimedes snorted. "Well, I don't want to die on an empty stomach. We won't know either way until my blood work comes back. Apparently. But I'm not waiting, because I am in dire need of a morningcap."

Caesar paused, waiting for Ark to elaborate. When he didn't, he asked, "What the hell is a morningcap?"

"It's like a nightcap, but around breakfast time." Archimedes looked at him as if it were obvious. "It's a thing. Right? It has to be."

"That sounds like something an alcoholic would say," Caesar muttered. "You're not even wearing any clothes, Ark. Where are your clothes?"

Archimedes stepped back, sat on the edge of the hospital bed. He waved the question away. "I think someone took them to wherever my room is supposed to be. Just grab a robe. There's got to be one in here, probably wherever they stashed all the blankets."

Caesar waited a moment, making sure his friend wasn't going to fall on his face, then got back to rummaging. Before long he found a short stack of robes and a pile of thin, cornflower blue blankets in a bottom cabinet. He snatched up one of the robes, looked at it. It was cotton, ankle-length, tied together in the back. He took it over to Archimedes and helped him put it on.

"Am I going to have to carry you?" Caesar asked.

Ark tested his balance. One of his legs was fine, but he couldn't feel the one that had taken the syringe. "You very well might, my good buddy. But on the bright side, imagine what Koko will think of you when she sees you being so strong and supportive."

Caesar paused, considering.

"Ha! You're too easy."

Grey Toliver couldn't remember the last time he was this lost.

The *Imagination*, due to its size and purpose, was designed to be utilitarian and easy to navigate. The walls of the corridors were all white, the floors and ceilings silver, but brightly colored and thoughtfully placed lights and signs were there to help one get around the twists and turns of the science cruiser.

Which was all well and good when painkillers didn't make those lights flare, the colors bleed, and the walls, ceilings, and floors blend together and swim away,

"These will help with the pain," the nurse had said after fitting him for a better sling. "Or at least considerably ease it. I would tell you not to operate heavy machinery, but I heard what condition your ship was in, so it doesn't sound like she'll be usable any time soon."

"Har har. Am I going to need surgery?"

"Just give it a couple days of rest first, and then we'll see. For now, the infected tissue is gone and all your vitals are right where we want them to be."

"My friend, did you give him any drugs?"

The nurse had laughed, probably a lot louder than he really needed to. "Oh, God, no. Something weird went on with that boy. We can't just give drugs out to everybody."

"He got in a fight with somebody near a waterfall," Grey said, not sure if that helped or not.

"Yeah, he mentioned the waterfall," the nurse said, and then went back to his clipboard.

Grey had taken the medication with a glass of water and followed it with several more glasses, the pills leaving his mouth feeling like it was full of cotton. Now he was shuffling around the ship to his best ability, hungry, needing to pee, but blissfully free of pain.

"The nums," he said to a woman passing by.

"What?" she asked, flinching away.

Grey touched his ring and middle fingers to his thumb, then touched them all to his lips. "Num nums."

"Are you looking for the mess hall?" she asked, still uncertain. "Two lefts down, then a right, then another two lefts."

You understood me! Grey tried to say. *You are a blessing.*

Instead, he put his fingers to his lips again in the same gesture until the woman walked away.

The mess hall was a massive open room, a hangar in miniature, designed to hold at least half of the *Imagination*'s full crew at any given time. Three long lines wound around circular food stations. Each station had trays and buckets filled with fruits, eggs, gravies, salads, sausages and bacons from a number of different animals, waffles, pancakes, breads, and more. A kitchen tucked somewhere out of sight regularly sent runners to replace any of the pots or pans that were nearing empty, alerted by a switch under the server's side of each station counter. Scientists, soldiers, and other crew mingled together, greeting each other softly as they filled up their plates. Those whose shifts had ended usually took a seat at one of the tables. The rest took their food to go, filing out of the hall back to their work stations or their rooms.

It had taken most of the distance from the exam room to the mess hall for Archimedes to get used to walking with one numb leg, but once he sucked up the rich smell of food through his nostrils he found the will and the way to limp along unassisted. He and Caesar piled on as much food as their plates could endure, nodding to what few strangers they caught staring at them. At the drink station Archimedes filled up a glass of scotch to the brim. Caesar grabbed orange juice for both of them, tucking one glass between his arm and chest so he could carry everything. They walked together and sat at a table in the far corner of the room. Even among the scattering of eaters, they were isolated.

"You were serious about the morningcap," Caesar noted. He pushed one of the glasses of juice across the table to his friend.

"I never joke," Archimedes said.

"You do nothing *but* joke."

"You got me there." Archimedes grinned and took a swig of the liquor. He closed his eyes and held it in his mouth, savoring it before swallowing. "God bless the military."

Caesar shook his head. He pushed the food on his plate around with his fork, selected a piece of turquoise melon, some fruit he had never heard of, and popped it into his mouth. Sweet, full of juice. "Not the military. The IRSC didn't think mixing soldiers and booze in space was a good idea. They wanted to keep liquor off entirely, but a coalition of scientists came together with an, ah, extensive list of examples where scientific discoveries were made under the influence of drugs and convinced the higher-ups to allow liquor as sort of a compromise. Didn't you study this?"

"The IRSC?" Archimedes asked. "I mean, kind of. I studied government, but science organizations, even government-funded, that stuff never really clicked with me. I tended to zone out until we moved on to something more interesting. The Bozavian Solar Crusades that led to their abolishment of all religion, *that* was more my speed." He swirled the liquor around in his glass. "God bless scientists. Present company excluded."

"You really are an ass."

"But I'm alive! And so are you! Can we drink to that?"

Caesar sighed and lifted his juice. "To not dying a horrible death," he said, and drank. He set the glass down, stared at it for a second. "You know, I can't stop thinking about that bomb going off. And having a gun pointed—"

"Don't," Archimedes said, suddenly serious. "Don't think about that. We've got our ship, busted as it is. We've got our lives. We're on a secure, government-backed spacecraft full of armed soldiers. No matter how hacky their medical staff is, we're getting free meds." He picked up his fork, tapped his plate with it. "And free booze! We're good, Caesar. We're gravy. Don't think about the other stuff."

"It bothers you too, doesn't it?" Caesar asked, realizing.

Archimedes didn't answer. He picked up his glass, took another swallow of scotch, and waggled his eyebrows over the rim instead.

Caesar sighed. "Okay, well, we still need to contact ACG and let them know we're alive. We've opened the package, which is obviously a breach of contract, so we should just say it was stolen and file a report to that end. What happened, who was involved. They'll probably make a fuss, and the client will probably lodge a complaint, but we didn't do anything wrong. We were attacked, so that's our ass covered. The client will be covered financially if they applied for any insurance on it."

"We still don't know what *it* is," Archimedes said. "Could wind up kicking up a storm of attention."

"Maybe," Caesar acknowledged. "I still think we'll be alright."

"You want me to make the call?"

Caesar shook his head. "Your talent for spinning shit into gold notwithstanding, you still look like ten miles of bad road, and Grey doesn't have any patience with ACG employees. I'll do it."

Archimedes nodded, then caught sight of Grey at the far end of the room. He had entered the mess hall at some point and was standing by the food lines, staring at them. Ark called out to him and waved.

Grey turned his head slowly, almost sleepily, until he caught sight of his friends, then walked toward them with stilted motion.

"Did he hurt his leg, too?" Caesar asked in a low voice.

"I don't know. I don't think so. And I didn't hurt my leg, dude. I hurt my ankle. The *nurse* hurt my leg."

"How's it feeling?"

"The fact that it's feeling anything at all is an improvement over half an hour ago, but it's that static feeling, like when your circulation is just starting to return? Drinking should help, I'm thinking."

"Ark—"

Just then Grey reached them and plopped down next to Caesar. His eyes immediately found Caesar's plate of food and fixated on it. Archimedes set down the scotch without taking a sip and studied his friend.

Caesar edged his plate away. "If you're hungry, they aren't charging for the food, and there is plenty of it."

"Kinda hungry," Grey said.

"Yeah, I bet," Archimedes said. "You put away more food than anyone I've ever met, Human or otherwise."

"Wanted t'see my friendsh first. Friends. Freeendz."

"Okay, what's wrong with you?" Archimedes asked. "Look at me. Are you high? Let me see your eyes. He is high off his ass, Caesar."

"Where did you get drugs?" Caesar asked.

"Nurse gave 'em to me," Grey said. He smiled, slowly, very slowly, very much to himself. It creeped out both of his friends. "Give me your drink, 'medes."

"No, dammit," Ark said, slapping Grey's hand away from his glass. "That son-of-a-bitch nurse."

Caesar placed his arm on the table between Grey and his plate of food and proceeded to continue eating. "Back to what we were talking about, I think we should all get some rest first. Especially you-know-who. I'll call ACG in the morning, and we can figure out where to go from there."

"We need to figure out what to do with the *Searcher*," Archimedes said.

"I'll handle it," Grey murmured. He reached for the scotch again. Ark swatted him again.

"You'll handle it. You don't even know what moon we're on."

Grey's eyes lit up. "Outer Springer!"

"We're on a spaceship, you fucking idiot." Archimedes drained the rest of his liquor, set the

glass down, and stood up. "Right, I'm off to bed. Good luck with this."

Grey bobbled his head so that he could smile at Caesar.

Caesar sighed.

*****

Jeth Serrano studied himself in the mirror. The flash burns that covered his face had mostly

healed, though the skin was still tender; applying the make-up around his eyes to make himself

appear older had been an ordeal. The contacts had been much easier. Ice blue eyes on a Murasai

with a red and black complexion was a rarity. The goal, of course, was that he wouldn't be

noticed by anyone. If that should prove unavoidable, the contacts would stand out and send

anyone searching for him later down a very specific path in the opposite direction.

He stepped away from the mirror to reach into a thick brown chest he had dragged out of the

D'abai's storage unit. The inside of the chest was composed of several different compartments.

On the left, mostly make-ups, but there were also a number of creams, dyes, and prosthetic

molds (he had once used the latter to build himself an actual nose, but it hadn't worked well over

his nasal folds and he'd had to fake an illness to excuse his heavy mouth-breathing). The drawers

on the right side were filled with an assortment of authentic-looking fake jewelry (rings,

cufflinks, necklaces, earrings), as well as a number of official-looking badges and insignias from

important organizations. The center of the chest was reserved for clothing of all different styles

and functions; Jeth pulled a thick black jacket with a high collar from this area and put it on.

It had been several years since Jeth had opted for subterfuge over bravado and reputation, but the disaster on Astrakoth had wounded his confidence. To his delight, he found the art of disguise came back to him as naturally as breathing. He allowed himself a moment of self-admiration and then left the *Mathra D'abai* for the streets of Zeanum.

The lockdown on the landing pads around the city had finally been lifted that morning, two days later than expected. It had taken that long to find and capture the serial bomber that had been terrorizing Zeanum's populace, a Human named Gorska Hart, and to confirm that he was acting alone. Seven bombs had been successfully detonated by the time of his arrest, destroying five bridges, the top two floors of a printing press (the building was later written off as condemned), and the townhouse of a socialite, Zeanum's #6 Most Eligible Bachelor, Charles "Charlie" Heuser. Five more explosive devices had been discovered and successfully disarmed, but Charlie and thirty-four others were dead. Three more were killed by gunfire during the apprehension of the bomber. Hart had been shot six times himself—once each in both of his arms, once in the stomach, once just above his ribs on right side, once just above his left knee, and once in the face, tearing off part of his left cheek—but was expected to make a full recovery.

The danger was over, but the city was still tremulous in the wake of it. Jeth sympathized but also found the fear useful as the streets were mostly empty come late evening. Most of the people walking out and about were folks like him, trapped on a landing pad during the lockdown, now seeking out the business owners and entertainment centers brave enough to keep late hours.

Brave, Jeth thought, *or opportunistic.*

The freegun walked briskly, keeping his eyes down, directed at the dark pink and ivory colored cobblestones. He crossed Verity Bridge, the river below placid and clear. Several large fish swam in a group, their scales shimmering blue and green. The handheld GPS beeped faintly, alerting him to a change of direction. He cut through a small residential neighborhood by the river where the houses all had porch lights and the front yards were framed by tall hedge fences. Jeth walked through them, past them, and crossed Trapper Bridge, and then a small arch bridge lined with paper lanterns in a repeating yellow-orange-red-orange-yellow pattern. He looked both ways, saw no one, and ducked into an alley.

Jeth began to move with an efficiency a small, nagging part of him had feared he'd lost. He pinched the corner of his collar, hard: the chip wired within registered the pressure and sent a soft current through the jacket that turned it from black to a light cream color. A sharp tug on a cord at the inside middle unraveled a part of the jacket that had been packed up inside the back, turning it into a duster. A surgical mask was pulled from one pocket and fixed over his nasal slits and mouth. It was the kind of thing germophobes would wear in public, or perhaps someone with a lingering fear that Hart's bombs had released something toxic or carcinogenic into the city. From the other pocket came a pair of black gloves. Jeth tugged them on, then reached up and pulled free a hidden hood that had been sewn into the back of his collar.

Seven seconds is all it took for Jeth Serrano to walk out of the alley a different man.

The address Euphrates Destidante had given him for the contact led him toward a tenement building at the center of the city. As he neared his destination, he reviewed the things he had learned about the man.

Turner Materas was forty years old. Twice divorced, once from the daughter of a respected lawyer, once from an up-and-coming confectioner, both of whom decided at some point that their prospects were better with someone that could hold a job for more than six months. Over the last ten years Turner had worked as a travel agent, a speeder salesman, a banker, an exotic pet keeper, and a vacuum salesman (*They still have those?* Jeth had wondered, surprised). His longest job had been as a freelance journalist, although after a blog of his surfaced online heavy with racism against the Ryxan, no respectable outlet offered him further assignments. Still, through his commission-based jobs and his short-lived career, he had managed to keep enough money squirreled away from his ex-wives to keep him afloat while he searched for whatever work he could find next.

His criminal record was nearly spotless—a couple counts of petty theft in his early twenties, and an arson count that got pled down to breaking and entering back when he tried to set his ex-wife's bakery on fire. The man seemed desperate but not particularly dangerous, the kind of guy who would do anything for a quick buck as long as it didn't require him to stick his neck out too far,

A woman stood in front of the tenement, fussing with a baby carrier strapped to her chest. A red-faced infant boy was nestled within, screaming directly in her face. Jeth slipped around them and into the building unnoticed. There was a cylindrical elevator just inside that had begun to rust both at the top and bottom.

Jeth took the stairs. From the stairwell window, he could see the evening lowering itself gracefully into night.

Turner lived on the third floor, in an apartment two doors down from the stairwell entrance. The hallways were empty. Jeth slipped a small roll of opaque tape from his pocket, struggled to pull a strip off with his gloves, finally managed to tear a small piece free and pressed it over the door-viewer. If Turner looked through, he would be able to see a form, but one without definition. Blacking out the viewer entirely might have aroused suspicion; this way it would seem like the lens itself was faulty.

Jeth knocked. No one came.

He leaned his head in close and listened for a hint of anyone moving around inside, possibly waking up from a drunk or a nap. He heard nothing. Jeth checked the hallway once more. He saw no one, so he drew his gun and knocked again.

Still no reply.

He considered the possibility that Turner was one of those brave, opportunistic souls out on the streets looking to turn a quick chit. Maybe he had landed a job at one of the stores that stayed open late. Jeth took the doorknob in hand and turned it slowly. He was pleasantly surprised when it didn't catch on a lock. One more glance both ways down the hall (*Never too safe*, he thought), then he pushed the door open and stepped inside.

And immediately raised his gun in alarm.

Every inch of the apartment had been ransacked. Couch cushions were spread about the room where they had been flung. The couch itself had been lifted and propped up against one wall, the bottom of it shredded open. The dining table had been turned into a pile of four separate legs and a flat slab of splintered wood. A desk lamp had been shattered. A standing lamp had been split in two, the cable inside still running between the two metal segments, allowing the bulb to flicker inconsistently. Books and papers were scattered all across the floor, partially covering a body that was sprawled out in the middle of the room, limbs akimbo.

Jeth gripped and turned the inside doorknob and closed the door behind him as quietly as possible. He kept his gun in front of him with the other hand, finger on the trigger. Cautiously, he stepped around to the right, careful not to tread on any shards of glass or crumpled papers. He found himself in an empty kitchen, the refrigerator and freezer doors open and all of the drawers pulled out of the cabinets. The floor was littered with thawed food, silverware, and the rest of the junk that accumulates in the kitchen drawers when you have nowhere else to put it. Everything had been arranged in neat little mounds.

He stepped out of the kitchen and crossed the room, checking the bedroom next. The scene was more of the same: dresser and closet emptied and torn apart, the mattress pushed up against the wall and shredded, the bed frame disassembled. The ceiling light had been removed, the air vents unscrewed and their gates set aside.

Frustration must have set in by the time the burglar reached the bathroom. The shower curtain had been torn down and thrown into the tub with the rod. The bottom cabinet doors had been kicked in, the mirror above the sink shattered. Jeth could see no spots of blood, no other evidence of the intruder or intruders that had preceded him. He reluctantly holstered his weapon and returned to the body in the living room.

Nice to meet you, Turner Materas, he thought, kneeling over the corpse. Turner was staring at the ceiling with one half-lidded eye. The other eye was a pulped ruin where some kind of blade or spike had been driven in, back into his brain. Turner's cheek was bloody under the entry wound and there were dried trickles of blood from his nostrils and the corners of his mouth, but that was all. Not too messy a murder.

Jeth searched the body, knowing it was futile, knowing that whoever had beat him to the punch had already done the same thing, gone through the same moves. Judging by the state of the apartment, they had apparently not found anything useful. The pockets were indeed empty; he looked around and saw the edge of an open wallet poking out from under one of the sofa cushions.

"Alright," he said. "Got to go through the motions."

He straightened, walked over to the tabletop, and lifted it from the scrap pile. He locked the

door and lodged the table under the knob as an extra precaution. It wouldn't do to get caught at

the scene of a murder.

With the entry secured and no immediate threats present, Jeth holstered his weapon and

engaged in a search of his own. It was relatively quick—the heavy lifting had been done for him

already—and was really just so that he could honestly say he had done everything he could to

find information. The results were mostly what he expected.

The kitchen: nothing.

The bedroom: zilch.

The bathroom: nada, but he did nearly cut himself sifting through the glass.

"No loose ends," he muttered, making his way back to the living room. "But at least you didn't

leave anything for those what killed you, huh, Turner?"

He gave a soft kick of mock frustration to the bottom half of the fallen standing lamp.

Something rattled around inside. Jeth ignored it, chalking the noise up to broken pieces of the

lamp itself. He pulled the tabletop free from under the door and put his hand on the knob.

Hesitated. Looked back.

It's nothing, he thought.

Couldn't be anything, he thought.

But what if, he thought, removing his hand from the knob, *what if the lamp fell during the*

ruckus and just… escaped notice?

Jeth stepped quickly over to the lamp and lifted the lower end, holding it upside down. There

was definitely something in there rolling around, scuffing the sides and the cable it shared space

with. He shook it, softly at first and then harder when nothing rolled out. A small gray object popped out at the end, then withdrew back into the tube. *A tether*, he thought. It took a few more shakes and some precise timing, but Jeth was able to clamp the item between his forefinger and thumb. One swift yank snapped the elastic band holding the object and Jeth came away with a perfectly intact data drive. He gave the corpse an approving look.

The data drive was slipped safely away into his pocket. Jeth looked around the room one last time and decided it was time to leave. He headed to the door, unlocked it, slipped into the hallway, and closed the apartment behind him. No one was around to greet him.

Jeth Serrano took the stairs again and disappeared into the night.

*****

"And that's what happened. Grey, Archimedes and I are alive and without critical injury, but the *Sol Searcher* is currently damaged beyond operation. The *IRSC Imagination* has another three months before leaving Astrakoth's orbit, so however you look at it we're going to be out of commission for a while."

Caesar was speaking to Calgo, a Peran representative of the Aventure Courier Group. Calgo's dark gray skin didn't furrow with concern, disbelief, or confusion. His lidless, diamond-shaped black eyes gave away nothing, either.

"You look fine," Calgo said.

"Have you ever had a gun pointed at you?" Caesar asked.

"I have not."

"Well, it has a way of putting things into perspective. My crew and I, for example, decided no matter how great the pay… well, you know how the rest goes."

"I do not," Calgo said.

Caesar blinked. "Oh. Uh, no matter how great the pay, it's not worth dying for. Or, it doesn't matter how much the pay is if you're not alive to spend it. There are a few variations. Basically, we're not in a huge rush to get back to work when a break seems prudent, forced upon us as it may have been."

"And the package," Calgo said, "it was destroyed?"

"Or taken by one of the two bandit teams," Caesar said. "Like I mentioned, between the crash, the animal attacks, and the gunfight between the competing parties that ambushed us, it's hard to say. My crew doesn't have it, but you might reach out to the clients and tell them if it's something with resale value, they might want to keep their eyes open on whatever markets are appropriate."

"Yes, we will take all appropriate actions in regard to the client. Any time a package is lost it is an unfortunate experience, but the captain of the *Imagination* reached out to us as they were bringing you on board and everything seems to be in order. We will, of course, have to mark the incident down in your file, but there will be no disciplinary actions taken. The clients may leave a poor review; that is out of our hands. When the *Sol Searcher* is back in suitable operating condition, or once you have acquired an appropriately credentialed replacement craft, contact us and we can see that your work is resumed." The Peran moved to disconnect the call, paused, and said, "On behalf of the Aventure Courier Group, we are relieved that you aren't seriously injured, and we wish you a swift recovery."

Caesar grinned. "The call is being recorded, huh?"

The viewing screen flickered and went black.

"That's quite an ordeal you and your friends went through." This from Professor Eppleheim, who had rolled his chair back from his research table to study the young courier. Caesar had scoured the decks looking for a reliable room to make the call to ACG, one in which he'd have a measure of guaranteed privacy. The professor had found him frustrated in the hall and graciously offered up his laboratory. While some of the other labs had specialized focuses (geological testing, separate rooms for land and marine flora and fauna, stress testing equipment and so on), Eppleheim's lab was the main research area and the largest, open to general studies of anything and everything. Experiments would cycle through to and from the other labs as needed, but for the most part only a handful of scientists spent much time in the big room.

Sonus Eppleheim was one of those. He had taken one of the corners as his own open office, complete with a desk covered in textbooks, scientific journals, reports from his subordinates, and heaps of personal notes. When he wasn't at his desk, he spent the bulk of his time in the lab at two other stations: a long, white dissection table made of lightweight but durable plastiron with a million-chit shell decontaminator that could be lowered over it, and a smaller table with a cutting-edge nanoscope worth more than the *Sol Searcher* had cost. Several steel lockboxes filled with slides and vials containing biological specimens sat next to the nanoscope, along with an adjustable digital map of Astrakoth loaded with notes and observations. A large silver box with a closed-grip locking handle on the front was positioned on the floor to the right of the smaller table. The handle was used to open the entire front of the box like a fridge, or maybe a safe. Of the many cabinets, specimen displays, and expensive technological marvels scattered around the room, it was this tall unmarked box that caught Caesar's attention the most. It was the only item whose purpose remained a mystery to him.

"It's been a trying experience," Caesar answered. "Being friends with Grey and Archimedes comes with its own set of stressors, and our youth was filled with plenty of ill-advised adventures no matter how hard I kicked my feet, but we've never run into anything like…" He gestured vaguely in the direction he thought the planet was in. "Certainly not since we started running the *Searcher* as a courier unit. It's a fairly straightforward job, you know? Pick up stuff, drop it off. Get paid. We're basically mailmen. Nobody attacks the mailman. Except dogs, maybe, and union-busters."

Eppleheim chuckled. "Well, the worst is past, I hope."

"Yeah, we'll see," Caesar said. His mind drifted back to the condition of his ship.

Eppleheim removed his bifocals and tucked them into the breast pocket of his lab coat. "Do you mind if I ask you a question?"

"Not at all!" Caesar said, surprised. He pulled his chair over so that he could sit facing the professor. "Ask away."

"What made you want to work as a courier?" Eppleheim held his hand up, palm out, as if to say there was nothing wrong with the job. "I only ask because when we met earlier, you seemed genuinely interested in our laboratory arrangements and in the work we're doing. So are you a courier because it's, as you said, a straightforward job? Or are their personal benefits as well? I have many friends who work in sales or with customer-based industries, my grand-niece included, who seem to thrive on making a difference in a stranger's life. Or even a single day. No?"

Caesar smiled at that. "Don't take this the wrong way and pardon my language, but if I had to work in sales, I'd probably fucking kill myself. Even working as a courier pushes it sometimes. I don't really care about cheering up people I don't know. I've never been much of a people person, never been much of one to go out of my way to make friends. Ark and Grey and I, we grew up in the same neighborhood. We became friends more because of proximity and lack of options than anything else."

Eppleheim laughed. "That reminds me of a group of scientists that I came up with through university. We hold these quarterly get-togethers called, regrettably, The Men of Minds. We drink and play cards, smoke cigars, that sort of thing. One fellow, Albright Wylard—"

"I know him!" Caesar interjected. "He wrote *The Brown Dwarf Addendum*, right?"

"Yes! You've read it? Utter tripe, but Albright always brings cigars from a different planet each meeting, so I keep my mouth shut. I mean, most of them taste awful, but the experience makes it worthwhile. To your point, though, those chaps are really the only ones I spend any regular time with. It sounds like my feelings as pertains to people are very similar to your own."

Caesar chuckled. "People aren't that interesting, right? My friend, Grey, he feels the same way. He would rather spend his time building things or taking them apart, fixing up the *Searcher*. Archimedes, he's the people person, but I think sometimes that while he likes socializing, he can't stand the people he's socializing with. He likes playing with them."

"Sounds like he'd make a great poli."

"Yeah, maybe," Caesar said, nodding. "That's what he wanted to do. And he's a lot smarter than he lets on, but it feels like he likes to waste his talent sometimes."

"Then he would *definitely* make a great poli," Eppleheim said, and they both laughed. "Okay. So you've told me about Grey and Archimedes, but what about you? Why are you doing this?"

Caesar shifted in his seat. "Well, you were right to note earlier that it's science for me. That's my interest, always has been. Did I want to be a courier? Hell, no." He pointed at the professor. "I wanted to be like you. I wanted to be doing stuff like this, on a ship like the *Imagination*. I graduated twelfth in my class at Cynosure. Top Ten would have been nice, but out of sixteen thousand students? I'll take it." He shrugged. "Still wasn't good enough to get admittance into Hervatyne. Wasn't good enough to get an internship at STILO, either.

"It reached a point where I needed to find something just to get by. Grey… I don't know, thrives in poverty. Ark could con money out of a children's charity if he put his mind to it. But both of my parents are gone, you know? There isn't a safety net for me, and my only marketable talents weren't marketable enough, apparently, so…"

"So you bought a ship," Eppleheim said.

"*We* bought a ship," Caesar corrected. "Because of me. Archimedes and Grey would have been fine on their own, but they pitched in with me, *for* me, and pretended all of us needed it. We patched it up, contracted out to Aventure…" He trailed off, reflecting, reliving the past. He said, "Being a courier isn't, you know, a glamorous job, but it pays well enough and I get to work with my friends. Even if I want to kill them most of the time." Caesar smiled.

Eppleheim drummed his middle and ring fingers against his knee. "You got a few rejections," he said. "So, what? You just gave up?"

Caesar opened his mouth to respond, thought for a moment, closed it again. Then he said, "Has anyone ever stolen anything from you, Professor? Not money, or a watch or something. Nothing like that. Has someone stolen credit for something you've written or created or discovered?"

"No," Eppleheim said after some consideration. "All of my work has been published under my name or never went anywhere at all. Perhaps I'm just lucky."

"Perhaps," Caesar said, smiling sadly. "I must not have been. I came up with something my senior year, a new kind of fuel distribution system for spacecraft. Long story short, it got picked up and I didn't. That was about it for me. I don't even talk about it much anymore, don't see the point of it. You said you played cards, right? With your friends? I'm not much of a gambler myself, but I know enough to walk away from the table when I keep losing hands."

As close as their mutual interests had drawn them together, the reminder of their professional differences opened as large a gulf between them. Caesar shuffled his feet awkwardly, smoothed out his pants, and stood.

"Anyway, Professor, it's been a pleasure chatting with you. Thank you for letting me use your lab to make my call."

Eppleheim smiled up at him. "Of course, dear boy, of course. Feel free to stop by anytime. A pair of fresh eyes might be useful with some of the junk floating around here. In fact," he said, arching an eyebrow, "might I convince you to stay behind and engage in some mad science with me?"

Caesar laughed. "Another time, maybe. I haven't been able to sleep for the last several days without worrying I might get shot or eaten alive. I've been looking forward to the rest." He lifted a grateful hand and turned toward the door, had a thought, turned back. "I do have one question, Professor."

"And I am sure I have an answer."

Caesar pointed at the tall silver box next to the desk. "What is that? It's the only thing in here that I don't have a passing idea as to its purpose."

Eppleheim grinned at the box and patted the side of it. "This thing? You don't know what this thing is? I'll tell you, but only if you promise to keep it a secret."

Caesar zipped his lips shut with his fingers, pantomimed locking them and tossing away the key.

"This beautiful machine is the result of scientific progress marrying government funding. Each IRSC vessel is fitted or will soon be fitted with a molecular deconstructor."

"It's a disintegration machine?" Caesar asked, blinking.

Eppleheim laughed. "No, son, everything stays quite intact. This machine is the most comprehensive molecular analysis computer in existence. So far as we know, anyway. Created by Humans, exclusive to Humans. It takes any type of organic material and analyzes it layer by layer, molecule by molecule. They're ridiculously expensive to produce, marginally less expensive to maintain, but invaluable for our understanding new flora and fauna. It's very much a government secret, though, so I'm hoping your love of science is enough to secure your confidentiality."

"That's both incredibly awesome and also a genuinely terrible reason to break security protocol, Professor," Caesar said.

"Who are you going to tell?" Eppleheim laughed. "Grey and Archimedes? They're so terribly interested in science. Relax. It's nice to be able to surprise someone who actually cares about something like this."

"No kidding. Listen, we're going to be stuck on the ship for a while…"

Eppleheim held up a hand, cutting him off. "Anytime. I mean it."

Caesar nodded and glanced around the lab on his way out. Lots of interesting things in there, lots of interesting tools, but it was the silver box that stayed on his mind. *A molecular deconstructor*, he thought. *How curious.*

After multiple screenings and a battery of tests, Archimedes' blood results came back perfectly normal, with the exception of a minor potassium deficiency. The nurse provided a small bottle of supplements to help balance him out, and a second small bottle full of painkillers.

"Finally," Archimedes said. "Why'd you hook up my shipmate earlier and not me?"

"Your friend was shot, Captain Carnahan. He wasn't attacked by a waterfall."

"Okay, it wasn't… you know what, never mind."

His ankle still throbbed from when he had twisted it, and he tried not to put any weight on it as he navigated the halls to where his room was supposed to be, still clad in the robe and his boxers. He wanted to pop a pill, longed for it, but the thought of Grey being borderline affectionate was enough to convince him to wait until he was safely locked away in the bedroom.

The room that, apparently, had a beautiful woman waiting outside of it.

"Uh, hey," he said, his talent with opening lines another casualty of his exhaustion. "Koko, right?"

"That's right," she said, smiling.

Stars above, that smile, he thought. "Caesar's room is down the hall, to my understanding."

"Oh, I know. I took him to it earlier."

Archimedes grinned. "Did you, now? That wily dog. He didn't tell me that."

Koko didn't elaborate. She said, "I was just stopping by to make sure your keycard worked fine. Sometimes when they set up new rooms there's a glitch or two. From what I've heard you've already been through enough without getting stuck in a hall."

"Does nobody care about Grey?" Archimedes asked, a little angrier than he intended. "First Caesar didn't check on him, then you. He crashed, too, you know. He was torn up, flew up here by himself, got doped out of his mind. Why isn't anyone making sure he's alright?"

Koko took a step back, surprised. "Caesar led me to believe that your other shipmate didn't like to be bothered."

That isn't wrong, Archimedes thought.

"If you're concerned, I can send someone to check on him. I'll even go myself, if you'd like."

Archimedes shook his head and sighed. He switched both pill bottles to his right hand and swiped the room key against the lock pad with his left. The door whooshed open. He stepped through the threshold and waved Koko in after him.

The room, larger than his quarters on the *Searcher* by half and free of his clutter, made him feel like he had checked into a hotel. There was a large bed, neatly made up with white sheets, burnt orange blankets, and a cream comforter that looked thick with down. A pair of nightstands flanked it, each with their own lamp. An open door set in one wall led to a private bathroom (*private!!!*) while a writing desk sat against the wall opposite. A mini-fridge was plugged in on the left side of the desk.

"Do you think there's liquor in there?" Archimedes asked.

"In these rooms? Statistically," Koko said. "These are meant for guests. But it's the middle of the day, and you probably shouldn't be drinking if you're planning on taking any of those painkillers."

"At this point I think the general weariness coupled with the morningcaps should be enough to put me to bed. The pills can be something to look forward to tomorrow."

"What the hell is a morningcap?"

Archimedes ignored her. He set the pill bottles on the nightstand closest to him, tossed the key card on the bed, and moved to the mini-fridge. A dozen bottles of water were stocked inside the body of it. The shelves on the door had a half-dozen shooters each of whiskey, vodka, and tequila. Ark grabbed four of the whiskeys, two bottles of water, and closed the door. He split the drinks between Koko and himself.

"It's the middle of the day," she repeated.

"Koko, something horrible happened to me down on that planet that is going to give me nightmares for years. You're a scientist, right? How about we stop worrying about the time of day and try instead to find out what liquor does to a body on a spaceship in orbit."

"There's artificial gravity on the ship, Captain. It would be the same thing as—"

"You can call me Archimedes," he interrupted. "And that's a fascinating hypothesis, but there's only one way to test it."

He winked and unscrewed the lid on one of the tiny bottles, flicking it to the floor with his thumb. Koko watched him impassively as he drank it down. When he wouldn't stop grinning at her, she relented and drank one of her own. Her swallow came with a hard wince. She opened her bottle of water and took a large swallow.

"God, why," she said. "For the record, I'm a vodka woman."

"Then I appreciate your sacrifice," Archimedes said. He set the empty bottle on the writing desk and took a seat on the foot of the bed. "What are you doing here, Koko? Really? Anybody could have come and checked on the keycard, or just left me to it with the expectation that I could find someone if it didn't work."

Koko set her empty down next to his, paused for a moment, then unscrewed and downed the second shot. She set that bottle on the desk, too. Archimedes, gleefully surprised, followed suit. Koko held her hand out for his bottle, took it, and lined it up with the others.

"The thing that happened to you on Astrakoth. Caesar said you were attacked by some kind of vampire vine?"

"Did I tell him that? I don't remember." Archimedes rubbed a tired hand over his face. "It was something like that, yeah." He pulled the side of his robe around enough to show the puckered puncture wounds that crossed his side and back. The swelling had gone down enough that the pink circles resembled an unfinished connect-the-dots. "My blood work is with the nurse, but they said it came back fine if that's what you were interested in."

"I was actually wondering if you had managed to retain a piece of it somehow."

Archimedes stared at her.

"Like, if you cut a piece off or something, or part of it got caught in your clothes. One of its teeth, maybe."

Archimedes continued staring.

Koko spread her hands. "I'm sorry! I'm a scientist. My curiosity knows no bounds."

Archimedes thought of Caeser. A smile touched the corners of his lips. "Rarely have I been handed such a goldmine of a line, but I'm going to have to disappoint you. The last thing on my mind was keeping any part of the thing that had been feeding off me. By the time I got back to my ship, my clothes were soaked, covered in blood and dirt, and riddled with holes. If anything did break off and stay with my shirt or pants, it burned with them."

"You burned your clothes?" Koko asked, surprised.

"We burned a lot of stuff. We were trying to conserve energy on the *Searcher* because we didn't know how long we'd be stuck there, so we kept warm by a campfire at night until we tucked into bed. The clothes weren't salvageable, so they were the first to go." Archimedes shrugged.

Koko looked genuinely disappointed. Archimedes gave a small chuckle, surprised that he was relieved she had only ambushed him for the sake of scientific pursuit.

"Well," she said, "your key card works."

"It does," he said.

"You must be tired."

"I am," Archimedes nodded. "Very much so."

Koko opened her mouth to say something—'Goodnight,' maybe, or 'Goodbye'—but turned on her heel and headed for the door instead. She looked back, halfway into the hall.

"But really, what the hell is a morningcap?"

"You had a couple," Archimedes said, pointing at the empty bottles on the desk. "Just a couple hours late."

Koko rolled her eyes. "You're ridiculous."

"And ludicrous, irresponsible, harebrained, foolhardy, and a bit of a slut," Archimedes added. "And those are my good qualities. I advise you to stay well clear of the likes of me."

She shook her head and left, the door whooshing shut behind her, leaving Archimedes with the first full silence he had experienced since… goodness, how long had it been? The night before they left for Peloclade?

He tugged off the hospital gown and tossed it on the floor. After a moment the boxers went, too. Archimedes crawled up the bed as gently as he could, pulled the blankets down under and then back over his weary body, and closed his eyes.

His slumber was deep and dreamless.

A number of mechanics drifted around the *Imagination*'s docking bay. Most were doing tune-ups on the surface vehicles, hosing off the grime and slime and occasional splashes of blood they had picked up during planetside excursions, sending the muck down into drains that led to one of the ship's waste tanks. A few workers sat on footstools and folding chairs around a wooden wheel that had been turned on its side. Opened beers were drained and replaced from a pair of red and white coolers. Cards were splayed out among the bottles.

The *Sol Searcher*, battered and scraped, the viewport covered nearly entirely by vacuum sealant, had been moved to the back of the bay. It sat by itself in a corner where several of the bay's lights didn't quite reach, the loading ramp still open from when Grey had disembarked. It looked sad and abandoned, like a scrapyard junker forced to watch the newer models fly off to adventure.

Grey, unsure if he was even allowed to be in the area unescorted, stood next to his ship and surveyed the exterior damage. Her name had been painted on the side in bold, swooping orange letters bordered in dark blue. Black streaks gouged through the letters now, creating a striped effect. It hurt to see his pride and joy so wounded. He boarded her, prepared for a fight if anyone came looking to stop him.

If anyone noticed, they didn't seem to care.

The *Searcher* felt emptier than normal knowing he was the only one on board. He walked through the halls, gently touching the angles and grooves of the doorways and walls as he passed them. Since they bought the ship, Grey had studied every inch of it, familiarized himself with every dent, every stich in the seats, every flaw in the mechanics. The thrust drive had been the first thing he'd replaced. After Astrakoth, it would be one of the first things he repaired. The drive was technically illegal, having been pieced together from three different models and tweaked constantly until it was as good or better than something listed as top-of-the-line. It just didn't officially follow regulations or have any of the approved certificates from the Department of Interstellar Safety and Caution, that's all.

Grey had sold off the *Searcher's* old underwing thrusters, too, and used half of the money to

buy a quad-set of busted replacement thrusters off a B-ranked Skellyton light cruiser. He rigged

them for the back of the ship and fixed them up until they were giving twice the output of the

originals. The rest of the money went into adding an extra half-capacity fuel tank with a

reinforced shell to the undercarriage of the ship. He regularly swept the halls, washed them,

polished them. Reinforced the outer hull panel by panel. Even painted her name on himself.

There were three names on the loan for the craft, but the *Sol Searcher* was his baby. No doubt

about it.

Grey poked his head into his workshop and flicked the lights on. It had been a small miracle

that more of their belongings hadn't been destroyed in the crash. Oh, the kitchen had been tossed

around a bit and their bedrooms had been upended, but for the most part only inexpensive or

easily replaceable things had suffered lasting damage.

In their rooms, anyway.

Caesar kept most of the experiments and research he was conducting in the lab locked away in

secure cabinets, freezers, and chests (built and installed by Grey, naturally), but most of his

equipment, kept out for easy access, had been made of hinges, brittle plastics, and glass. Most of

his work had survived but the rest of his tools were trashed.

Grey's workshop had fared much better; he never kept anything out and he worked with nice,

durable materials. There was only one item, a half-completed lab chair he had been building for

Caesar, that had been caught at just the right angle between his desk and the wall, snapping the

seat back free from the base. The chair had been a gift he was building in secret, so Grey had

said nothing about it. He simply piled the pieces into a corner and resolved to fix and reinforce it

when he got the time.

As he looked at the workshop now, everything seemed to be as it was when he left it. Locked tight. Untampered with. Which was good, as he had some items tucked away that the military presence on board might have some issues with. The cooler, sphere inside, sat under his worktable with the lock pad pressed against the wall, out of sight.

"The security here really kind of sucks," he muttered to himself. "Not that I'm complaining."

His finger hit the light switch and the shop fell back into darkness. Grey moved on, past Caesar's lab, past the row of cells bolted into the back. The five cells were another addition Grey had added, prompted by a drawn-out presentation by Caesar illustrating the profit that could be made from transporting live cargo. They had done so around twenty times since with no complications, although the clean-up afterward was always a chore. Archimedes, in his infinite wisdom, had insisted they get credentialed for outsourced prison transfers, but Grey refused to take any of those contracts until he could arm the *Searcher*. This latest job served only to strengthen his resolve; if strangers would shoot them down for a mystery box, he wasn't going to brave any vengeful friends or relatives seeking revenge or some trigger-happy outlaw coming to save his captured buddy.

Grey moved up the ramp to the upper deck. He avoided the central common area, circling around to the left corridor, passing Archimedes' room, passing Caesar's bedroom and the emergency room he had used. He would need to figure out why the impact foam hadn't deployed and fix that, then clean out and repair the emergency room in the other hall as well, refilling the foam compartments.

He paused at the cockpit, checked out the damage there. The entire viewport would need to be replaced, and the side panels, just to be safe. He would need to go over the entire control panel and make sure it was in working order. It looked untouched and had seemed to operate just fine on his brief flight up to the *Imagination*, but that wasn't a stress test by any measure. Glass and blood and splinters of wood were everywhere still. That would need to be cleaned, and both the pilot and co-pilot's chairs replaced.

And, of course, the stabilizer. That had been put off for too long, largely because of money. If he played his cards right, though, he might be able to get access to the *Imagination*'s resources. If he could do that, everything else was probably doable.

The *Sol Searcher* was a disaster, there was no doubt about it. It would probably be easier to make a list of things that *didn't* need to be cleaned up or repaired.

Grey was thrilled.

He moved on, continuing around the ship until he reached his room. It was simple and efficient, like him. There was a single bed, carefully made, with thin blankets because he would rather be chilled than too hot. A single dresser sat against one wall, packed with black shirts of varying sleeve-lengths and two spare pairs of jeans. This had tipped over onto the bed during the crash, breaking off one of its legs; it was righted now, and stable, but sat just a little bit crooked. A duffel bag full of toiletries and other bare essentials was shoved under the bed. It was perfect.

Once the drugs had worn off, Grey had found the room assigned to him aboard the *Imagination* without much effort. He'd scanned the card, checked out the digs. It was nice. Really nice, even, but it wasn't home. This, here… this was home.

Grey shut his bedroom door, propped his pillows up against the wall, and climbed into bed, careful not to jostle his injured arm. It took a couple minutes of fidgeting before he was able to find a position that felt comfortable, but he had slept through worse. The week and a half of scratchpox came to mind, when every movement, no matter how minor, made him want to claw his skin off. This was a walk by comparison.

His head settled back against the wall, neck supported by the pillows, and he faded away.

Chapter Seven

Movers, Shakers, Secrets

WELCOME TO YNDA PALATIAL ESTATES, a community where you're guaranteed to live a *CHAMPION LIFESTYLE.* With our acres of lush, meticulously landscaped grounds, the Ynda experience has something to offer everyone!

1. Take leisurely walks beside the babbling brooks!

2. Have a picnic next to one of our *THREE* vibrant lakes!

3. Go for a run around the brand-new track!

4. Play high-serve on one of our state-of-the-art courts!

5. And more! We have a pool!

Located within convenient travel distance of high-end shopping centers and the beautiful purple waters of Graffri Beach, our carefully vetted, incredibly secure gated community will give you the life of luxury, calm, and safety that you so clearly DESERVE!

Euphrates rolled his eyes at the advertisement and set it on the seat next to him. He was sitting in the back of his private car with the window rolled down, Roll driving. He turned back to the empty security booth and waited for the guard to return with his credentials. It only took a moment, and Euphrates' identification documents were handed back through the window without incident.

"There you go, sir. Thank you for being patient. Everything looks good, so the gate here will lift in just a second and you'll be able to pass on through. Do you know where you're going?"

"Yes, I've been here before," Euphrates said. "Question for you: do you have to hand out these little flyers to every visitor that comes through? Is that new?"

"Yes, sir. We're trying to increase interest among potential new buyers," the guard said. He was leaned forward, both hands on the windowsill.

"It just seems like a waste of paper if those people are already coming through to see the property for themselves, don't you think? I assume all relevant information could be found online, right?"

"Never really thought about it, sir, but I suppose that's right. I can't say it bothers me much. Ain't never been a tree that ever did something special for me, you know what I'm saying?" The guard grinned. Euphrates' eye twitched at the sight of the man's crooked and yellow dental condition.

"Aside from providing oxygen and enriching the ecosystem," Euphrates said, "if there were no trees in this community, you would be left guarding a glorified lawn."

"Ain't no skin off my teeth," the guard said, still grinning.

Euphrates squirmed in his seat, adjusting his position to take some weight off of his tailbone. "Tell me, are you authorized to use lethal force while conducting your duty?"

"Oh, yes, sir!" The guard lifted his collard uniform shirt and patted a heavy-looking handgun he had tucked into his waistband. "Got a Blue Echo right here. When you get hired here the company lets you either take some factory-assembled piece of junk, or they give you a 200-chit stipend to use for something of your own. I took the stipend, dipped into my savings a little, bought this beauty. Ain't had a chance to use her yet, not outside of the range, but I'm hoping something happens soon, you know what I'm saying?"

"Yes, I'm sure that will be a thrilling day for you," Euphrates said, and rolled up the window before the conversation could continue any longer. The guard stepped back and pushed a button somewhere out of sight. The wrought iron gate in front of the car rose seconds later. Rollo drove on through.

The Ynda community's road was built with efficiency in mind. The single lane that led inside split into two some fifty feet from the gate. The lanes made an elegant loop through the full length of the private neighborhood before eventually terminating at an exit gate. There were a number of turn-offs that cut through the loop, allowing the residents access to the many amenities paid for by their extravagant annual residency fee.

Eighty estates were built in the community. No more, no less, and most of those belonging to either physicians or polis. The waiting list existed on a first-come basis, full of people unashamedly waiting for someone to grow too poor to stay or to die without heirs. There were other gated communities in Thorus, of course, and you would see a lot of the same names on those waiting lists as well, but Ynda held a certain level of prestige.

Each of the estates had their own turnoff, something that could generously be considered a long driveway, and each was spaced far enough apart from each other that next-door neighbors were a foreign concept. The massive lawns that separated each property were maintained by community-employed landscapers unless replaced by the resident's own choice. Private pools were installed on some properties for those who preferred not to risk the germs or socializing that came with the community pool. Other properties had installed gardens, hedge mazes, isolated meditation chambers, or any of a dozen other things to personalize their territory. When someone moved into Ynda, they got every square foot of the property and as long as they weren't overreaching into someone else's zone or impacting other residents, they could build or demolish whatever they want.

Magga Suvis, Speaker for the Human race, lived on one of the coveted properties, seventeen left turns from the entrance. The entire winding way back to the house was lined with trees covered in brilliant pink grapefruit blossoms. Euphrates admired the color through the window and watched for the one with a weathered swing hanging from its branches that would let him know they were getting close.

The house itself was a marvel, one of the thirty-seven original houses belonging to the founders of the community, designed by the famous architect Hael Cho nearly a century earlier. Magga's grandfather had been one of those founders and had been central to convincing Cho that creating eighty unique floorplans for Ynda was worth his time. Meyer Suvis, a gem baron, helped seal the deal with a sizable monetary contribution.

When the schematics were finished, Meyer had his pick of the litter. The one he settled on was relatively modest by the standards of the rest, which is to say that Euphrates' home could fit into it at least twice, and perhaps halfway again. Translucent green moldavite reinforced with firming minerals made up the staircase that towered over the cobblestone driveway and the crystalline fountain that sat in the center of it. The balustrades sweeping off to either side were made of the same beautiful substance and was used as a composite for the two pillars framing the front door and supporting the stone canopy above it, creating pale green swirls that wrapped around them.

"Every time one of these rich idiots tears one down to build their own flophouse, they should be arrested for crimes against Humanity," Euphrates muttered.

"What's that, sir?" Rollo asked, glancing back over his shoulder.

"Nothing. Pull off to the side there, away from the fountain. I don't want to risk you accidentally dinging it with your door."

If he was offended, Rollo said nothing. He parked as instructed, got out, and opened the back door for Euphrates.

"Do you think I could come inside, Mister Destidante?" he asked. "I'm awfully parched."

Euphrates smoothed out his suit jacket and adjusted his cuffs. He glanced over his driver and gave a curt nod.

"You can come with me, but you'll stay in the lounge or wherever it is that Magga's people want to put you. If they tell you to come back out to the car, you'll do that with no complaint. Understood?" Rollo nodded. "And next time keep the car stocked with bottles of water or something, hmm?"

They walked up the stairs together without speaking, and a pair of butlers pulled the thick wooden doors open once they reached the top. Euphrates strode on without hesitation. Rollo was two steps behind, staring at everything with wide-eyed fascination; Euphrates cleared his throat without looking back and the driver hurried to catch up with him.

The foyer was hexagonal, a single staircase at the back. An open archway on the left led to a lounge, while a matching arch on the right opened up to the entertainment room. Two more doors sat in recesses on either side of the staircase. The foyer floor was white flecked with red, with a deep black circular ring in the center. A small table against one wall to the right held a stack of books related to Salix's history, and a vase full of dark violet flowers. A chandelier above them dazzled, a globe of light reflecting through waves of pink and crimson crystals.

The butler who walked them in (*Sanchez? Santos?* Euphrates struggled to remember. *No. Carlito. The Head of Staff.*) touched Rollo's elbow. "If you wouldn't mind, please wait in the entertainment room while Master Destidante meets with Lady Suvis. Refreshments will be provided in short order."

Rollo looked to Euphrates—who nodded—then moved into the room on the right. Carlito waited until the driver was out of sight and then led Euphrates up the staircase and down a long hall with maroon carpets and gold wallpaper decorated with exotic flower bulbs. This hall terminated in another door, one Euphrates did not recognize. Carlito opened it but did not enter.

"This isn't the study," Euphrates said, hesitant.

"No, sir, it isn't," Carlito responded. He did not clarify any further.

"Hmm."

Euphrates walked into the room and was met with the smell of cherry clove smoke undercut with some kind of herbal balm. Though the space was roughly the size of a dance floor, he realized he was in a bedroom. Most of the furniture—dressers, a vanity, a sofa—had been pushed off to the far side of the room to make space for a number of medical machines, but the bed remained, its messy blue lace bedspread matched by a low-hanging canopy overhead. A small medical staff remained huddled around the bed, fiddling with the machines and logging the biological readings that were coming across the screens.

Two massive panes of glass were set into the wall on the left, offering up a beautiful view of the backyard. Small channels ran on either side of the lawn, bordering the two dozen gardens set up in their own neat little boxes. A pair of armchairs with thick cushions sat facing the windows. A small ivory table sat between them, its three legs curling out elegantly beneath it. On the table was a bottle of wine, two glasses, and an ashtray.

Magga Suvis sat in the chair furthest away from the door. A brass cigarette holder looped around her index finger and she puffed contentedly at the Lekenex Cherry tucked into the end of it. Her favorite brand, Euphrates knew, one that went for a thousand chits a carton.

She had always been a thin, severe woman but her illness had made her nearly cadaverous. Her skin was pulled tight against her knuckles and wrist bones, and across her skull. Her lips were thin lines surrounded by the creases that came from six decades of sneering and frowning (and, statistically, probably a few smiles here and there). The hair on her head was thinning; what remained was the color of steel wool streaked with white. Euphrates had made a mistake once of asking if she had ever considered dyes or a restoration procedure, thinking the signs of her age might lead some to think her weak. He had promptly been treated to a lecture on the uselessness of artificial enhancements and a reminder that while there might be power in perception, there is more so in competency and, "actual fucking brains, you presumptive fop."

Euphrates' respect for her grew even deeper for that.

"Don't hover, Destidante," Magga called from the chair without looking at him. "Come and sit down. Try my wine." She took a deep drag on the cigarette and let the smoke filter through her teeth.

There was a click behind Euphrates, starling him. He looked back to see it had only been Carlito closing the door. The medical staff had filtered out as well, allowing two of the most powerful Humans in the universe some privacy.

Relative privacy, Euphrates thought. *This is Magga Suvis, after all. The wine bottle is probably bugged.*

He smirked at the thought, moved to the empty chair, settled down into it. He flared out the bottom of his suit jacket and smoothed out the sleeves. "Where's the doctor?" he asked.

"Oh, I sent the fool away." Magga waved her hand dismissively, then used the same hand to pour wine into both glasses.

"Is it because he told you smoking and drinking weren't a recommended rehabilitation system?"

"Leave the witticisms to someone else, Euphrates. You're no good at it. Now," she said, lifting one of the glasses, "try the damn wine."

Euphrates took up the other glass dutifully and tapped the edge of hers with it, then drank a generous amount. His flavor receptors immediately went wild with pleasure as the taste of several fresh fruits—not all of which were familiar to him—rolled over and through each other. His eyes widened in alarm, then softened as he savored the deliciousness. He could feel himself salivating and gulped the wine down, setting the glass back on the table.

"What," he gasped, "the *hell* is that?"

Magga's eyes twinkled. She took her time with her own mouthful, then swallowed it with a sly look. "Fantastic, is it not? It's a closely-held secret among some very rich, very influential people."

"Is it a new brand?" he asked. "Or made with some kind of new process? My better half is much more the wine connoisseur, but I'm surprised I've not heard something with this, this kind of flavor profile."

"It comes from a small town full of nobodies on Elagabalus. A speck on the planet, really, but big enough at least for two wineries. One is a Broderman's, though what kind of business prospects a chain like that saw in a population of only five thousand is beyond me. The other winery is a locally owned hole-in-the-wall that gets by undercutting Broderman's with cheaper vintages of better quality. The townsfolk eat it up. Or drink it up, as it were.

"They hold back some limited, more expensive bottles for collectors and merchants passing through, which is how we eventually heard of them. One of the merchants turned around and sold one of the bottles he'd picked up to a billionaire—no, I won't tell you who, but he's a well-known musician who has spent the last decade trying to curry favor with certain lawmakers you detest—and word began to pass through certain niche circles. A few conversations and compensations later, it is discovered that this nobody vintner has yet another tier of stock: significantly rarer, significantly more expensive. And, as you've noticed just now, worth every chit for the drinking experience."

"And the technique?"

"A very closely guarded family secret."

Euphrates frowned. "They're only one family, yes? I'm surprised Broderman's hasn't beaten the secrets out of them or forced them out of business some other way. Nobody has purchased the process?"

"You misunderstand me. Broderman's does nothing, because the family secret is closely guarded by the exclusive group of buyers the vintner has attracted. We have a particular interest in seeing that the fruits of those labors stay fermenting and stay secret. Broderman's knows better than to argue the point.

"As far as buying the process?" Magga shrugged. "We're less concerned with recreating it than wallowing in the thrill that comes from having this exotic delicacy all to ourselves. It's like eating an endangered animal. It loses something if you can just walk into anyone's front yard and shoot the thing. So we keep it our little secret, ours against the universe."

"A secret you've now invited me in on," he pointed out.

"Mm, yes, well, you've always liked secrets, Euphrates," Magga said, smiling. "Almost as much as I do. Someone new ought to know before I shuffle off this mortal coil."

"Not your children?"

She pulled the cigarette free from its holder and ground it out in the ashtray. The brass ring was next, pulled from her finger and set down next to the wine bottle. "My children are idiots, Euphrates, and you know that they're idiots."

He wasn't exactly sure what to say to that, so he changed the subject. "As nice as this is, the wine and reminiscing, it isn't what you invited me over here for."

"No, it isn't," she agreed. "Maybe someday, do you think? It might be nice to just take in the gardens and enjoy a drink, some charcuterie without having to worry about the future of the Human race and all the universal bullshit."

"You don't have the passivity in you, I don't think."

"No, no, you're probably right. And nor do you." Magga turned in her chair so she could look at her Advisor directly. Her body may have grown frail, but her eyes were as sharp as ever, and the weight behind them was heavy on Euphrates. "Tell me, Destidante. What is Rors up to?"

Ah. The meat of the matter.

Euphrates stretched his legs out and slowly cracked his knuckles. He stopped halfway down his left hand when he realized he was doing it; it was uncharacteristic of him, a sign of uncertainty, and he knew she would notice it, too.

"I think Rors might be trying to start a war with the Ryxan."

Magga studied him for a long moment, looking for any other tells. She said, "It was the Ryxan who started the trade war."

"Was it? I'm not so sure. I think he's been instigating things piece by piece, an executive order at a time. I didn't notice it at first. My attentions were… elsewhere. Doing the things expected of me to make the things expected of you easier to get through. When the Ryxan became aggressive with the celaron prices, it surprised me as much as anyone. Then I started looking into it."

"What do you think his reasoning might be? The military side of him, perhaps? Rors falling

back on the stereotype of an old soldier looking for a war?"

"That would be a concerning quality in a Speaker," Euphrates said drily. "I'm still figuring it

out. There are pieces missing that I am in the process of tracking down."

"Perhaps your new proximity to Speaker Volcott will prove a boon for your investigation,"

Magga said.

Euphrates paused before responding. Though Magga was practically bed-ridden, she had

plenty of resources at hand beyond his regular reports to keep her apprised of the goings-on in

the political arena. He tried to read her voice, detect if there was anything in it that sounded as if

she were suspicious of his relationship with the other Speaker.

"I don't think he trusts Talys," he said cautiously.

"Only a fool would," she responded. "You don't trust him, do you? Talys Wannigan is a

grease-covered weasel. He wasn't chosen for the position like you were. He blackmailed his way

into the position and Rors has never forgiven him." The bluntness of the statement caught

Euphrates off guard, and he tried not to let his surprise show. He had heard rumors but hadn't yet

figured out how Talys had done it or who he had done it to. Magga continued, saying, "You can

tell by the way Rors prefers to handle his own work rather than relying on Wannigan.

Unfortunately, that leaves Wannigan free to do as he pleases with all of the resources his position

comes with. Not really ideal."

"Rors seems to trust me enough while you're absent."

Magga gave a thin smile. "Don't let this go to your head, Destidante, but you're a valuable

resource. You might be a deceitful, manipulative, conniving little bastard, but your allegiance

has never been in question." Euphrates stared at her. "The Human race, Euphrates. Above anyone and anything. I'm sure you tell others the same, not caring whether or not they believe it. I *do* believe it. Talys, on the other hand… he wants only for himself." She tapped her lower lip with a long, thin finger. "And very likely he wants what you have."

"What's that?" Euphrates asked, nearly choking on the words. His throat had suddenly gone very dry. He nearly reached for the wine, remembered how a single swallow had left him, and thought better of it.

"Power," Magga said. "And whatever resources you have that he doesn't."

He turned to look at the Speaker directly. She was nearly skeletal and still radiating power, still magnetic. She likely had trouble walking to and from her bed unassisted and yet she was still capable of a rare feat: frightening him.

"He has exactly as much power as I do," he said evenly. "And the same access to resources."

Magga didn't move, her expression didn't change. Her eyes seemed to tear apart every layer of Euphrates all the same, every year building up to the man he had become. Every dirty act, every crooked connection. He remained impassive under her scrutiny, frightened but comfortable with the decisions he had made.

"Well," she said finally, leaning back. "Perhaps he just hasn't learned how to utilize them as well as you have just yet. Be wary of him, though, Euphrates. Talys is a fast learner with a lot of time on his hands. He may not be the scalpel you are, but even a dull knife can cut."

Magga picked the brass cigarette holder back up from the table and slipped it back around her finger. A cigarette followed suit, and a match to light it.

"Do you think a war with the Ryxan would benefit us?" she asked mildly.

"No, I do not," Euphrates replied. "I don't think a war with anyone would benefit us at this point in time."

"Mm, as I said: you aren't a fool. Continue learning what you can. If your suspicions are correct, stymie Rors as much as possible, regardless of how much justification he may have on his side, and no matter how riled up the Ryxan get. You fancy yourself a problem solver, yes? So go and do that."

He nodded. "Yes, ma'am."

Magga raised an eyebrow. "By that I mean you can leave me to my smoke."

"Yes, ma'am," he said again, and rose. Carlito had the door open by the time he reached it, and Euphrates wondered if the butler had heard everything or if Magga had triggered some kind of signal without him noticing. He paused at the door and looked back at the Speaker.

"I just wanted to say," he started, but she cut him off.

"Save the goddamn flattery for someone who needs it, Destidante." She waved him off, the smoke from her cigarette trailing along like a streamer.

Euphrates smiled to himself and allowed Carlito to lead him back to the foyer, all the while thinking of the two concerns he had had when coming into the Ynda estates: that Magga might be complicit in whatever it was Rors was getting up to, or that she would believe Euphrates was and had tricked him into coming so that she might confront him. The old lady still had teeth, and they bit, but it looked like they were still operating on the same side, working toward the same goals.

For now.

But another concern had come up during their conversation: that Magga knew more about Euphrates' extracurricular activities and reputation than he had known. It was mildly alarming but not particularly surprising; you don't become the leader of an entire race without extraordinary canny. On the other hand, she seemed content to let him operate unchecked. A loosening of the leash, so to speak, should it come to it. It wasn't necessary just yet.

But it is always nice to have options, he thought.

*****

Tens of thousands of spaceports populated Salix, all of them alive with incoming and outgoing traffic. In an effort to keep accurate records without becoming overloaded, the databanks for the ports were separated into twelve networks based off of regions of the planet. These regions kept their own records, cross-referencing them with the other sections every two weeks to check for inconsistencies, hoping to crack down on illegal entries, erroneous or outdated tag reporting, smuggling, kidnapping, other criminal enterprises of lesser degrees, and plain ol' humdrum Human error.

Each spaceport had a portmaster, and each portmaster the ability to access records from any other port in their region as well as the bi-weekly fallacy reports. To hear it described by one of them or by any dock supervisor, it would be like a singular complex organism with twelve identical limbs working in concert.

Talk to any dockworker, though, and for two mugs of ale and a five-chit dinner, they would tell you it ain't the region that matters, it's the port itself. They'll tell you each port has a life of its own, a soul. They'll tell you each port has a personality.

And while you reconsidered your decision to treat that dockworker to drinks and a meal, they would list all the reasons why their port was the best. Which probably wasn't the answer to whatever your question was, but there you have it.

Lloberam Station did indeed have a bit of a heart, if a tad grimy and coated with rust, and a bit of a soul, if cracked around the edges. Located on the outskirts of Thorus, it looked at first glance like it was ready to fall apart at any moment. The pads, brown with dirt and neglect, were sturdy enough but the massive hangar reserved for ships in need of maintenance was all exposed girders, abandoned crates, and idling machinery. The roughshod and scattered appearance of everything belied the hardworking nature of Lloberam's crew; out of all the ports in Thorus, it was ranked year in and year out as one of the most consistently efficient in security, repairs, and seamless cycling through arrivals and departures.

The portmaster, Holt Simon, surveyed his domain from a boxy glass office secured to the ceiling of the hangar, accessible via a thin titanium spiral staircase. The windows of the office could be tinted by scrolling a small blue ball set into his desk but that was rarely done. Holt preferred the transparency, believing it lent him an air of approachability while keeping his workers vigilant.

Talys Wannigan slipped in and around the station as naturally as if he had worked there for years despite not looking the part. He had swapped his ill-fitting suits for a loose maroon shirt that hung down nearly to his thighs. His pants, black, were made of equally soft fabric and flared out around his ankles. Not at all the attire one would see on the rabble making their living at Llobearm Station. Also not the attire one would expect on an Advisor for the Human race.

In another life, years before he had become a man of influence, Talys had grown up around chop shops and hangar bays despite having no interest or talent working with anything contained within. The familiarity of the environment stuck with him, though, the comfort in existing somewhere he didn't belong. He smiled his knowing smile at workers as they carried cargo past him, as they tested their blow torches and reviewed shipping manifests. His smile unsettled them even as they felt they should know him, as if they had seen him somewhere before.

Nobody was quite able to place him, though, until he stepped from behind a light cruiser into clear view of the portmaster's box. Holt looked down, brow furrowed, trying to make sense of the casually dressed man staring up at him. A new arrival? Someone lost?

Then sudden recognition hit him and Holt blanched. He shook his head.

Talys grinned at him and headed for the stairs. A handful of workers, curious now, watched as he climbed the spiral staircase. The windows turned black before Talys was halfway up.

Holt Simon's office was modest almost to the point of absurdity: a large desk with three monitors (one running Lloberam's stat sheets and records, one with access to the region's record database, one for personal use), his chair, a seat for guests, and a standing lamp. The floor was polished silver metal. There were no sculptures, no sentimental pictures, nothing else at all. This was very much a work-only space.

Holt was standing when Talys entered the room, nervously wringing his hands together. Talys ignored this. He took a seat in the cushionless visitor's chair and crossed his legs.

"What are you doing here?" Holt asked. "You ain't been around in what, five years? Six? I thought we were quits, you and I."

Talys pointed at the window behind Holt, toward the spaceport, though neither man could see through the tint. "I helped you get here, my old friend. This port, this position., This woefully naked office. I told you at the time that I would ask a favor of you some day. Did you forget? Did you think *I* would forget?"

"I had kind of hoped," Holt grumbled. He placed a nervous hand on the back of his chair. Talys gestured for him to sit. Holt hedged a moment longer, then sank down into the seat. His shoulders bunched forward, almost like he was collapsing into himself.

"How long have we known each other?" Talys asked.

"Long time."

"A very long time. Most of our lives, right? And who has been there for you all this time? Helping with your grades and your family problems, stepping in when you had trouble with the law? Now you have this career. Practically handed to you! You've built quite a reputation for yourself out of it, too, haven't you? That's something to be proud of, but it is important… *always* important to remember where you came from."

"What… what do you want from me?" Holt asked quietly.

"Have I ever done anything to harm you?" Talys asked. "Have I ever betrayed your trust?"

"No. I, I know that I owe you. I know that. It's just…"

"Just what?"

Holt looked up, anguish in his eyes. "I don't hurt people anymore, Talys. I don't want to hurt anyone."

"Oh, my old friend," Talys said gently. "My dear friend. I don't need you to hurt anyone, I promise." He uncrossed his legs and slid to the edge of his chair. He traced a fingertip along the underside of one of the monitors. "No, Holt, it's information that I need your help with. Specifically, I need help tracking down a ship. The departure date, the tags. I need to find out when it left, and then I need help finding out where it was going."

"We don't log departure destinations," Holt said, frowning. "Not as a matter of course, anyway. To track a ship's tags, I mean… I can think of a couple ways to do it, but they aren't exactly legal."

"I'm not concerned about the legality," Talys said. "And you shouldn't be, either. Remember my position. If there's any blowback—not that there should be any, but if there is—I'll say it was a matter of, mm, species security."

Holt's frown deepened. He rocked back and forth in his seat, massaging his knees. He moved his hands to the desk, drummed his fingers along the top, just beneath his keyboard. He looked up at Talys.

"Whose ship is it?" he asked.

"I'm not quite sure, but I have a short list and a general timeline."

"The spaceport they took off from?"

Talys spread his hands and smiled. "Again, a short list. I'm aware this will take some time, and while you're searching, I will do my best to narrow it down even further. You do have access to the region's spaceport records, correct? There are no problems there?"

Holt shook his head. "No, no problems. Uh. So. You have a short list of parts, a short list of ships, and a narrow time frame. That's still… quite a task, Talys." He saw a hint of darkness cross the Advisor's face and held his hands up. "I ain't got a problem doing it if that's all we're doing. Just trying to set expectations and the like." He straightened his back for the first time since Talys had come in and set about signing into the regional database.

"You gotta tell me, though, what did this ship do to get your attention like this?"

Talys smiled. It made the hair on Holt Simon's arms and neck stand on end.

"Not a ship, just a man. We're trying to find out where Euphrates Destidante got off to."

*****

Days passed.

People celebrated the Rose of the Moon festival on Salix. Every three years the red desert

stretching over half of Martax, the closest of Salix's three moons, would reflect sunlight in such

a way as to resemble a flower in bloom. Elaborate parades took place in cities all around the

planet. Flower petals filled the streets, were woven into lavish costumes, were even baked into

special holiday dishes. In the city of Catalasca, Akers' Storage closed for half a day—a rare

occurrence—ostensibly in brief observation of the event. In reality, ol' Gabber Akers was finally

getting around to beefing up his cyber-security to prevent any further breaches from occurring.

On Peloclade, life continued as normal for the majority of the population. Suki Tuan held their

annual speeder race through the Nhan Canyons. An animal fair was held in Thorery, bringing

together all manner of creatures from biomes across the planet. A slight mishap in the aquarium

zone led to the sudden boiling deaths of three dozen species of fish, including four that were

endangered. A trio of curious workers assigned to dispose of the bodies managed to sneak the

endangered fish away to eat. They were impressed with themselves, if not the meal. In Zeanum,

the Flowing City, the trial of Gorska the Mad Bomber dominated air waves. It was a brief affair,

with Gorska avoiding a drawn-out spectacle by pleading guilty in exchange for a life sentence

aboard the prison ship *APS Tantalus*.

In Odypso, capital city on Elagabalus, in a little office building one block away from the

Headquarters of Universal Discourse, a small, soft-spoken Ryxan named Cryxus discovered a

handful of discrepancies in the reports Euphrates Destidante had presented to the Universal

Council. He transmitted his findings to Ryxol, the Ryxan home world. There, long-necked Tarbanna used her authority as Speaker for the Ryxan to lodge a formal complaint against the Human race for duplicity. Upon receiving a copy of the report, her fellow Speaker Graxus officially requested permission from the Council for acts of aggression against the Humans. Elsewhere on Elagabalus, a vintner taste-tested an experimental new wine with his daughters.

At Fracture, a bar on the moon Outer Springer, Quick Billy Heiser sat in the back of the room in a roped-off VIP section. Bottles of exotic champagne littered the floor around his feet, discarded once they'd been drained, replaced in the bucket by freshly opened thousand-chit bottles of the same. Women dipped, swayed, and twirled around him; he recorded their dancing with a pair of Digi-Save spectacles he had taken from a university student who had picked the wrong place for a weekend vacation. It had taken a little over a year after Colby Tzarkev's murder to seize control of the dome, but Quick Billy had done it and done it smart. He didn't overreach. He kept his nose clean, another cog in the machine. Another strand of the web.

And the days, they passed on by.

*****

"Do you not have much of an appetite tonight?" Nimbus asked. She studied the dessert menu, trailing a finger down through the options.

"Hm?" Euphrates blinked, shook his head clear. He looked down at his plate. The Salixian stag flank was half-gone, but he had been pushing around his vegetables for some minutes. "I'm sorry, my love. I thought this would be a nice night out. Romantic. I do you a disservice by being so… distracted."

"I know!" Nimbus exclaimed in mock admonishment. She set the menu down so she could gesture at the restaurant around them with both arms in large, exaggerated sweeps. "You've only spent an exorbitant amount of money to take me to a place with a six-month waiting list. How careless of you. What a thoughtless gesture."

The corner of Euphrates' mouth turned up in a small smile. She was too kind to him, too forgiving. Even in the extravagant trappings of a restaurant like Chaudhry's, she stood out, a beacon to him.

"You're staring," she said. A shade of pink crept up high in her cheekbones.

"Admiring. And speculating."

"Speculating?"

"I've yet to figure out how an entire universe full of stars and beauty and wonder could fit into a single body. But your eyes betray no secrets, and so I'm left to speculate."

Nimbus rolled her eyes. "You are too much. Cheesiness aside, you've been uncharacteristically taciturn since meeting with the Speaker. Are things that bad?"

Euphrates set his fork down next to his plate, pulled the napkin from his lap, folded that and set it on the table as well. "They aren't ideal. It still isn't any excuse for me to pull away from you. I'm sorry, my love. I'll do better."

Chapter Eight

Home Is Where the Shipwreck Is

Despite the skepticism from his co-captains, Grey really did have a plan to get the *Sol Searcher*

operational again before the *Imagination*'s science tour was over.

The first thing he did was allow himself somewhere between three and four full days to heal.

This consisted of cracking open a bottle of Savaris Crescent gin he had stashed in one of the

Searcher's storage compartments and sleeping for ten or so hours at a time. In between his

hibernation periods, he locked himself away in his workshop and tinkered with small,

manageable projects. Archimedes and Caesar would check on him periodically; he saw these

visits as intrusions and responded with loud variations of "I'm fine!" and "Fuck off!"

Man of many words, was Grey.

Thanks to the medtech on board the IRSC vessel and a nurse he got on well enough with

despite his surly nature, he was able to regain most of the mobility in his arm not long after.

When this happened, he finally began venturing out of the *Searcher* and into the rest of the

docking bay. He studied the ships and surface vehicles, making mental notes on their models and

any custom fittings they had applied to them. The land rigs had the most modifications,

seemingly under continuous work to adjust to Astrakoth's unique terrain challenges. Two more

days passed, all observation, before someone finally approached him to see what he was up to.

"Sergeant Kubo Bremmer," the man said, extending his hand. Grey shook it, taking a measure

of the man. Bremmer was tall, closer to seven feet than six, and had a firm grip. He wore a

mechanic's outfit covered in grease and grime instead of a soldier's uniform, but rank stripes

were sewn onto his upper sleeves. Grey instinctively wanted to fight him, just to see what would

happen. He suspected Bremmer could tell what he was thinking, too.

"Grey Toliver," he said, grinning.

"You're one of the captains of that rig in the corner, right?" Bremmer asked, tilting his head in the direction of the *Searcher*.

"That's right."

"Well, you don't need to worry about any of my people messing with her. We run a pretty tight ship and my guys have plenty enough to occupy them that they shouldn't have any time to bother you or to put their noses where they don't belong."

"Oh, I wasn't worried about that. I've been on the ship. If anyone was looking to dig around what little we've got on board, I'd have dealt with it already."

Bremmer's eyebrows rose. "You've been on the ship? This whole time?"

"Most of it, yeah," Grey said, nodding.

"But not sleeping there."

"Yeah, sleeping there. The *Searcher*'s my home, Sergeant. More than any other place has ever been."

"Sure, but… have you *seen* the room you've been assigned? I'd trade you for it in a heartbeat."

"I'll get you the keycard, if you want. Look," he said changing the subject," you can obviously see my ship has seen better days. My friends and I, we don't really want to be here any longer than we have to be, no offense, and I'm sure a healthy chunk of your crew would prefer us not to be underfoot. But our ship needs to be capable of spaceflight again. That's clearly an issue. I've got a solution in mind."

Bremmer crossed his arms over his chest, curious but cautious. "Go on."

"Your mechanics. They're getting run a little ragged, right? You've got them working full time on repairs, modifications, tests, any number of other things. Then you've got 'em taking turns heading down planetside, right? On-hand work whenever necessary, but the planet is a nightmare, too. From what I've seen and heard, at least one of your guys comes back hurt just about every trip. It ain't always serious, but without time to rest and heal, wounds can get worse, infections can set in. Lingering pain. Exhaustion. It adds up over time, every little bit until they start slipping up. Making mistakes. Getting killed."

Bremmer said nothing.

"So I'm offering fair trade for services," Grey continued. "Let me take over shifts for whoever needs it. I know my way around ships, speeders, cars, you name it. I can fix it or tear it apart and build it better."

"Way I heard it, you got hurt yourself," Bremmer pointed out. He gestured to the lingering bruises on Grey, the careful way he held his arm. "And looking at you, you're not at a hundred percent. What makes you less susceptible than my guys?"

Grey shrugged. "I'm a tougher bastard than your grease monkeys," he said, and grinned. He saw the hesitant expression on Bremmer's face and added, "Work for parts is what I'm asking. You get an extra pair of experienced hands, some of your guys get time to recuperate. I wouldn't even be asking for much." He turned and pointed at the *Sol Searcher*. "The viewport, obviously. You've got plenty of the right glass laying around, and the sealant to bond it to the ship. We need some panels for the hull. Parts to fix my stabilizer, maybe some parts for the thrust drive, but only if our rapid descent—"

"Your crash," Bremmer corrected.

"—our *rapid and forceful descent* burned anything out. That's all little stuff, really, and I can make do with whatever you've got. Fuel, of course. That's about it. All the rest of the stuff—seats, impact foam, all the aesthetic stuff—we can get that taken care of once we're out of your hair." Grey thought for a second. "Paint. *That's* the last thing. I want to clean up her name. I don't like seeing that bit all scuffed up."

The proposal had some meat to it, and Grey could see Bremmer giving it thought. The sergeant looked around at his mechanics, saw the bags under their eyes, apparent even at a distance. A pair of men were passed out under the nose of a light cruiser, their toolkits acting as makeshift pillows.

"Alright, I have an idea," Bremmer said. "Come with me."

Grey gestured for him to lead the way.

A pair of trucks were positioned side by side in the vehicle bay, six large wheels each, racks on the back built to carry equipment, thick steel grills on the front to help protect the engine block. They were silver and black, all metal and no paint. A weary looking mechanic sat in the front passenger seat of one, rubbing at his eyes.

"You alright, Jessup?" Bremmer asked.

The mechanic blinked a couple times, getting the sleep out of his eyes. "Yes, sir. I got all the blood out, Sarge, but I gotta tell you, I don't see much point in reupholstering the seats. They come back filthy every time, and they don't offer much more than creature comforts, you know, and nobody's going down there thinking it's gonna be a vacation. Maybe a metal sheet under their ass'll keep them focused, maybe keep 'em alive. You know? It sure as hell would save me and the others a lot of time and energy we could be using on stuff other than, than these fuckin' *chairs*." He had begun leaning forward as he talked; by the time he finished, his voice had cracked and he slumped back into the seat, his frustration having fully run through him and leaving nothing behind. "Sorry for the language, Sarge," he muttered.

"Don't sweat it, Jessup," Bremmer said.

"We could use upholstery in the *Searcher*," Grey said.

"Yeah, I bet you could."

"We've got a lot of blood and dirt on ours, too. Big ol' hole through one of them."

Bremmer resisted the urge to roll his eyes. To Jessup, he said, "Very good. I'll run the suggestion up the ladder, but you're probably right. Why don't you call it a night for now and sleep in an extra hour?"

"Thanks, Sarge," Jessup said. Not wanting to look a gift horse in the mouth and not waiting for anyone to change their mind, he slipped out of the trunk and headed straight for the docking bay exit.

Bremmer ran his hand along the empty window frame of the truck's driver's side door. "So," he said at length, "here's my problem. *Our* problem, I should say. Astrakoth's terrain, mm, fluctuates. We weren't informed what to expect down there. Big science operation like this, you'd think different, but… anyway, we weren't able to prepare properly."

"Sounds about par for the course when you start mixing the government into your pet projects," Grey said.

"You're not wrong," Bremmer grimaced. "What we're stuck with are these two trucks that have somehow not been fitted to be all-terrain vehicles. We can adjust them for any specific type of environment we want, one at a time. Sometimes we're able to improvise, most times we can't. That means any time we want to switch to a more suitable rig for whatever clusterfuck we come across, we have to find a way to extricate the trucks, bring them back here, swap out parts, fly them back. It's a fuckin' waste of fuel, is what it is, so we've started trying to—"

The sergeant continued speaking, but Grey's mind was already working on solutions. A pair of elevators, maybe, extending from the undercarriage. Rigs on the front and back that could swing down and lock into place. The storage compartments on the back would have to move, probably to the roof.

"Mmhm," he said suddenly, cutting Bremmer off. "Give me twenty-four hours to get a look at your equipment and draw up some designs."

The sergeant laughed. "Oh, yeah? Just like that?"

"Just like that," Grey confirmed. "You can run them by your chief engineers when I'm done, or whoever you've got. If they can't find a way to make it work, I'll figure something else out, but I do think I've got some ideas that will work."

"Engineer," Bremmer said.

"What?"

"We've only got the one, so you'll run it by him. Name's Laske. First name is Warren, but everyone just calls him Laske."

Grey goggled, confused. "You have *one* engineer? On a boat this big?"

"We had a couple more, but they were…" Bremmer frowned. "Well, they were eaten. Laske hasn't gone planetside since."

"Yeah, I fuckin' bet not." The memory of the beast that had unwittingly saved his life came unbidden to his mind. Claws and fur and fangs. The echoes of the screams that followed. Grey shook his head clear. "Twenty-four hours, Sergeant. If I'm right, it shouldn't take more than a couple days to fix those babies up."

Bremmer nodded. "Alright, Captain Toliver. I hope you're right."

"Say, did you ever fight much when you were younger?"

"Did I ever *what*?"

"Never mind," Grey said, grinning. He started backing toward the *Searcher*. "Twenty-four hours!"

Archimedes was not having the time of his life.

That was almost entirely the fault of the *IRSC Imagination* by way of being a spaceship that wasn't going anywhere, perched over a planet that wasn't worth going to. Archimedes liked spaceships! Hell, he lived on one! But even the *Searcher* was constantly on the move, and when it wasn't, he could step out any time to go somewhere: a restaurant, a bar, a club. Even a nice, normal walk under open skies.

The *Imagination* was too large to make him feel claustrophobic, but everything on board looked mind-numbingly the same right down to the people crewing it, and that sameness and monotony bored him near to tears. Normally a people person, his labored healing had left him in no mood to mingle at length with strangers. Spirits were easy enough to find on board, but he wasn't much for drinking alone, either. Not a good look.

He wasn't like Grey, who had immersed himself fully in the docking bay, losing himself in fixing other people's problems so he could fix the *Searcher*. Nor was he like Caesar, content to crunch numbers and run experiments, hunched over a desk in a lab, learning for fun. Both of his friends could happily spend hours locked in a room, and did, and sometimes Archimedes wouldn't see either of them for a full day or two. Ark was restless. He needed fluidity. Fresh experiences. All the *Imagination* offered was corridor after corridor of unimaginative paint schemes and color patterns.

There were small perks. The showers were always hot. With the government picking up the tab, he didn't have to pay for anything and ate as much as he wanted. He got to sleep in more, *actually* sleep, without Caesar bothering him with chores or Grey blaring the disasters he called music. This last, sleeping, was something he found himself doing more and more, letting the days bleed into each other, trying his best to patiently wait for the knock on the door letting him know it was time to leave.

But he could only sleep so much. When he was awake his quarters, spacious as they were compared to his room on the *Searcher*, still felt confining. He made a routine of a half-hour shower, leaving his hair messy (which he never would do normally), and making the bed (something he *also* never did). Anything to keep his mind occupied before he got to wandering the ship.

Weeks went by like a fever dream.

One night in the dinner line, a woman from the docking bay caught his eye from across one of the food stations. Her eyes were a dark green that glittered under the low cafeteria lights. Her cheeks, a light pink smudged with grease, were decorated with freckles. What hair wasn't tucked under her beat-up brown leather cap fell down over her eyes in loose scarlet strands. He averted his gaze, focusing on a bucket full of thick gravy.

"Hey, pretty boy," the woman called out.

Archimedes looked up wildly. The guy in front of him wasn't paying attention. The person behind him wasn't a boy at all. He looked back at the woman in the cap.

"Excuse me?" he spluttered.

"Come around here," she said, jerking her head toward the end of the lines, in the direction of the tables.

Archimedes tried to play nonchalant, piling more food on his plate and keeping his same unhurried pace. Once he had finished making his rounds, he grabbed some silverware and a bottle of beer and walked over to the mechanic.

"What's up?" he asked.

"You're one of them what come up from the planet, right? That we rescued?"

"Uh, yeah," he said, feeling a bit awkward about the word rescue. "I'm one of them."

She raked her eyes over him once, twice. "You seem to be healing pretty good."

Archimedes grinned. "The miracles of modern science. I've still got some stitching waiting to come out, and it feels like my body is just one big bruise, but—"

"What do you say we see if we can't put you back in a hospital bed?" she asked. She had a lop-sided smile that crinkled the left side of her face. It was almost adorable, grease and all, were it not for the shark-like look in those emerald eyes.

"Excuse me?" Archimedes asked again, weaker this time.

"What's your evening look like tonight?"

"…free?"

Underneath that leather cap, her hair had been tied up in a knot. When the knot was done, her hair fell down to her shoulders, as red as strawberries and as soft as lace. He had tried to ask her name, but she clamped her hand over his mouth and kept it there. His stitches did not tear open, nor did he need to revisit the nurse, but it wasn't for lack of trying; when they were finished, it took three stiff drinks in quick succession to dull the ache that had settled across his entire body.

On his way back to his room he had to cross back through the cafeteria. As he limped through the rows of tables, a group of mechanics caught his attention. A handful of them fixed him with a knowing smirk. The rest looked at him with something close to sympathy.

Inconsistent nightly romps with his anonymous assault-lover aside, Archimedes was still a man without pastimes. With his friends consumed by their own interests and his waking hours largely filed with empty space, he eventually settled on an old stable of his childhood, back whenever his parents had grounded him and confined him to his room: making lists. It was an exercise in concentration! he told himself. A reminder of things that he enjoyed! Some people twiddled their thumbs, but Archimedes levied his judgment on the importance of things in a meticulous, itemized fashion.

Starting with a List of Lists, he devised an itinerary of subjects to rank, mentally restricting himself to only filling out two or three a day. Some of them evolved after more than a minute's thought. Top Ten Restaurants, for example, was too difficult to narrow down for a guy whose job took him to different planets and moons all the time. That singular list turned into several region-specific lists. Top Twenty Hobbies Other Than Lists was going to be another tricky one. He decided to save it for last.

He was in the middle of rearranging the Universal Council's Top Ten Most Wanted List according to his personal interest, bouncing a ball (that he couldn't for the life of him remember acquiring) against the wall he was seated across from, when a very prim and proper uniformed soldier, straw-colored hair cut short and coiffed *just so*, stopped and asked what the hell he was doing.

Archimedes caught the ball and looked down at it. "I would have thought the situation sort of explains itself."

"I meant why are you doing it *here*? You could just as easily be doing this in your room."

"My room?" Archimedes asked. "And miss out on this thrilling interaction? I came here to get *out* of my room, man."

"People walk through here," the soldier said, accurately describing the purpose of halls. "There's a science lab just around the corner. Sensitive experiments. Fragile equipment."

"Yeah, I'm waiting for a friend of mine in that lab. You're the first person in ten minutes to walk by, and the only fragile thing you're carrying is your ego, so I think I'm good here. Unless you want to discuss your theory on post-bounce trajectories as relates to force and/or surface material?"

The soldier stared at him for a long moment, clenching his jaw, no doubt clamping down on any number of scathing retorts eager to burst free. He settled on, "We should have left you down on Astrakoth."

"Well, at least there's interesting wildlife down there," Archimedes said. "Big appetites. At least one waterfall I can recommend."

But the soldier was already moving past him, shaking his head and muttering under his breath. Ark watched him go, wondering if maybe he had been unnecessarily dickish.

After a minute, he resumed bouncing the ball.

"Alright. Go ahead and cut out his heart."

"What? Already?"

"I don't see why not. Is that a problem? You're not squeamish, are you?"

"Of course I'm not squeamish. Let me remind you that I was the one that removed his liver. I was just thinking there are other things we can do first. We don't need to jump right to the heart."

"I want to look at it. I want to weigh it."

Caesar glanced up at Koko Noal. "And then what? Eat it?"

Koko's eyes twinkled. "Maybe. Depends on what it looks like. I wouldn't want to eat anything that looked poisonous, for example. What about you? You wouldn't try it? You're not curious?"

Caesar eyed the specimen on the table: a reptilian hound, like the ones that had harassed his friends and him and absconded with their tools. It was fearsome even on its back, even with its limbs all sliced at the joints and pulled back to the edges of the exam table. Its muzzle was ridged, the skin there hard and mottled. Two rows of serrated yellow teeth filled its mouth, chipped and crooked. Black fur, thick and sharp covered the hound's lime-colored flesh save for a narrow patch on its belly, which was bare. Each heavy foot had six scaled toes, the two frontmost ending in wicked hooked claws. It was a nightmare beast.

One that, realistically, had probably never been eaten by Humans.

"Maybe in the pursuit of science," he muttered. "But I wouldn't try it raw."

"Where's your sense of adventure?"

Koko reached over to the scale and poked the purple liver resting inside it. Caesar leaned back over the incisions and pretended to feel around with a pair of forceps. He was watching Koko, though, looking up at her through his shaggy blond hair. Her eyes were electric as she worked, scanning the corpse of the animal, the incisions made, and the flaps of skin peeled back and pinned down. She looked over the organs they had removed and weighed so far—liver, kidney, some kind of bladder—and set about describing them on little cue cards with her neat and tidy handwriting. She was in her element. For once, Caesar felt like he was, too.

The two of them had been working closely over the weeks, cataloguing and experimenting on all manner of specimens pulled from Astrakoth's surface. It gave them plenty of time to get to know each other better.

Koko Noal had grown up in a small city on Salix, the youngest of three daughters. While her sisters had gravitated more toward things like fashion, design, and dressage, Koko loved being out in the woods and the ravine near their home, getting muddy and bringing home small rocks and animals she thought were interesting. Her parents had been concerned early on that her broad interests and unrestrainable urge to adventure would lead to a lack of focus in her studies as she grew older.

In fact, the opposite had happened. Though she did just well enough above average in history and language (they bored her, but she was no slacker), she seized upon the maths and sciences with great delight, eager to explore the wider world of information beyond her backyard. That enthusiasm carried her through all her years of school and into a scholarship at Hervatyne. Two years into majoring in xenobiology, her dissertation on the effects a tidally locked planet had on flora and fauna near the border caught the attention of Professor Sonus Eppleheim. Impressed by the woman's writing as much as her ideas, he had offered to take her under her wing, promising that she could finish her schooling in her spare time aboard an actual IRSC vessel.

And the rest, as they say, was history.

"What about you?" Koko had asked him once. "What's your story?"

"Not much to tell, really," Caesar had responded. He was never comfortable talking about himself—that was Archimedes' bread and butter—and he showed it with a series of awkward fidgets.

"No. Uh-uh. You're a geek like me, Anada, but while I'm up here safe in a lab, you're getting blasted out of space and crash-landing on alien planets. So, spill: what happened to fuck you up?"

"I'm being honest! I grew up in a good home. My mom, my little brother, me. We had a dog. But it was quiet, you know? A normal life, nothing crazy."

"Your dad?"

"Ah. Yeah." Caesar had scratched at the back of his neck, feeling awkward. "He left when I was a kid. Archimedes was staying over at the time—he, Grey, and I all came up together—and I remember my dad was yelling at my mom. Ark and I were watching some show, can't remember which, but we could barely hear the TV over the yelling. Then the door slammed, and... well, he never came back."

"Not so normal," Koko had said gently.

Caesar had shrugged. "What's normal?" And, after a long pause to collect himself, he said, "Anyway, I did fine in school. Better than fine, really, but not Hervatyne fine. Or Ilius, or Pazion, or Su-Ani Ky. None of the big names. I graduated from Cynosure—"

"That's not bad!" Koko cut in.

"No, it isn't, but I couldn't find any work out of it. Not even an internship. Money started to run out, Grey found a ship for sale, and he and Ark got the idea for all of us to pitch in on it. Several more bad decisions later, and here I am."

"In a lab," Koko had pointed out. "On an IRSC ship, just like me. Just like the professor." She grinned. "The universe is a big place, Caesar. There are a lot of ways to get where you need to be."

Getting to know each other was the turning point for their relationship. They no longer felt like passing strangers with a shared interest or two, but genuine friends, colleagues working neck deep in the sciences, the thrills of new discoveries rushing through their veins. Koko treated him with respect because she understood him. She shared the same dreams.

Even if those dreams occasionally included tearing the heart out of an alien pack predator.

Caesar switched the forceps to his left hand and selected a slim scalpel with his right. As Koko watched, eyes alight, he reached into the hound's chest cavity and began carefully removing the heart.

"It's getting to be about that time," one of the other scientists called to Koko.

"Couple hours yet," she called back.

"Yeah, but I want to get cleaned up," the man said. "I'm not going up to a party smelling like chemicals or animal guts, and you know it takes some serious work to scrub the smell out."

"Shit, Chuckie's right," said a smaller man by one of the computer terminals. "I'm going to get going."

Caesar's eyes flicked up to Koko. "You've got a party?"

"Focus," she said.

Caesar's lips twitched, just a hint of a smile. He stepped onto one of the crossbars beneath the examination table to give himself more leverage and a better view. As he worked his way carefully around the heart, severing the arteries holding it in place, the scientists in the room began filing their paperwork into the record cabinets and putting their specimens away in freezers and other containment modules. One by one they left the room. None of them paid Caesar any mind; he had never been officially granted access to the labs but was in there often enough with either Koko or Professor Eppleheim that he'd been more or less accepted as a fixture.

Caesar set the scalpel aside and used the forceps and his hand to slowly extract the heart. It was a rich blue in color, and thick. *Not very appetizing*, he thought. He held it out from his chest and carefully carried it around the table to the scale. Koko lifted the liver out and set it in a small plastic box; Caesar replaced it with the heart, which came in at just under two pounds. The weight went down on another little note card. Caesar began to take measurements, and Koko wrote those down, too. When they were finished the two of them began placing the organ trays in a refrigerated chest, then wheeled the table with the hound's body still attached into a walk-in freezer. Job done, they pulled their gloves free, tossed them in a hazardous waste disposal unit, and washed their hands in tandem.

"There's a party on the bridge tonight," Koko said, toweling off. "At dinner time. The whole science lab is going, pretty much, except anybody planetside or sleeping through it."

"What's the party for?" Caesar asked. "We find something cool?"

Koko snorted. "No. Well, yes, but no. The party is for the professor. He's receiving a lifetime achievement award for his contributions to the sciences. The ceremony is out of Ilius, so his grandniece is accepting the physical award on his behalf, but they're video conferencing the whole thing and Professor Eppleheim is expected to give a speech."

"That sounds fun!" Caesar said, and meant it. "That's tonight?"

"It is." Koko put her hands on her hips and looked him over. "You know, you could probably come if you want."

"Yeah? You think so?" He did his best to contain his excitement.

"Why not? Everybody likes you, Anada. Just come up to the bridge around dinner, say you're there for the party. Ask for me if nobody'll vouch for you, but I don't think it'll be a problem."

There was a sharp beeping sound at the door to the lab as someone used their keycard to enter. The door slid open and a fresh-faced soldier with straw-colored hair stepped inside. He let his keycard go and the cable it was attached to retracted to his back pocket. He looked around the room, found Koko, gave her a smile.

"Hey, babe," he said. "You're still working?"

"Just finished." Koko hooked a thumb at Caesar. "He and I were tearing up wild beasts. Gonna cook 'em up and eat them later."

"Uh…"

"She's joking," Caesar rushed to say. "I think."

He had seen Koko's boyfriend around (hard not to notice him, really, the way he filled a room with his confidence), but he hadn't properly met him. As the idea of making new friends crossed his mind, his old friends suddenly re-emerged in his thoughts. A mad idea came to him.

"Caesar Anada," he said. He stepped forward, hand extended for a shake.

"Connelly Abren," said the soldier. "I've heard a lot about you."

As Caesar got near the man, he misstepped, tripping his left foot up against the back of his right. He fell forward, flailing, and Connelly's own extended hand turned into a wide-armed embrace so that he could catch him. It took a couple moments of jerky shifting, but the soldier was able to put Caesar back steady on his feet.

"You alright, buddy?" Connelly asked, clapping him on the shoulders.

"Yeah, sorry," Caesar said sheepishly. "I don't know what the hell that was. Two left feet, I guess. Not exactly the first impression I was going for."

"It's fine, really."

Koko chuckled. "Anada, I swear to God, you ever pull a move like that while you're carrying a specimen…"

Caesar laughed and the awkwardness of the moments before casually slipped back into something more lighthearted. Connelly tipped his head toward the door of the lab, and Koko nodded.

"We're going to head out," Koko said to Caesar. "We can play with the monster more tomorrow. You going to come up to the party?"

"I mean, yeah, maybe," Caesar said. "I should probably check in on my friends, but I can try to swing by afterward."

"Good. Somebody to keep me company, since my boyfriend is abandoning me."

Caesar looked at Connelly, who shrugged.

"Squad stuff," the soldier said. "Got to meet up with my guys in the mess hall. Science stuff…" He shrugged dismissively. "That kind of thing doesn't really do much for me. You two would have much more fun without me moping around."

Caesar wasn't really sure what to say to that, so he smiled and said nothing. He led the couple out of the lab, then, keeping ahead but not by too much.

He hoped that the lights in the hall weren't bright enough to show that he had begun to sweat.

The cafeteria again. Archimedes was beginning to think of it as a second home and had started getting to know the regulars accordingly.

Florette, for example, ran the salad station during the late-night shifts. She hadn't started yet, wouldn't for a couple more hours, so she was probably vid-chatting with her grandkids like she did every night before work.

Kanto Riley, missing all the digits on his left hand but his index finger, managed the best full-plate omelet breakfasts Ark had ever had. One day after his shift, over a few too many beers, Kanto had told him all about his pre-military life as a dope smuggler living on Dephros.

"Do you still keep in touch with anybody there?" Archimedes had asked.

"A few folk. A couple who helped me get out of the game after my accident. A few who'd probably kill me as soon as help me out of a bind. I still feed those guys some tips, still working at paying off some old debts, so we've got a working relationship of sorts. Bit tense, though, innit?"

"What kind of tips do you give them?"

"Can't tell you that, or I'd have to kill you," Kanto had said. He had smiled friendly-like, but Archimedes believed him.

Nat Color and his siblings, Ducky and Jan, were less intense. They all worked the lunch shift, all at different stations. Together they formed some kind of synth-heavy country band called Tearful Waters. Nat had let him listen to a handful of songs one evening; Archimedes wasn't sure which 'country' the music was supposed to represent, but he was sure he'd pass on a visit. Nice enough people, though.

None of them were working at suppertime, which was good, if Caesar's tone were any indication as to the type of conversation they would be having. In fact, the cafeteria itself was largely empty, with most of the science crew up at a party on the bridge. Of the military contingent, what men and women weren't either working or sleeping were huddled around in circles and at tables, clique-like. Archimedes saw the soldier from the hallway jawing it up with a group of his friends and rolled his eyes, immediately annoyed.

Caesar and Grey joined him a moment later, each with a plate piled with food. They eyed Archimedes' dark cocktail, the only thing he had grabbed from the lines.

"What is that?" Grey asked.

"Beats me. I asked for whatever grog they had saved behind the counter for the cooks, just so I could mix it up a little. Wish I hadn't. Tastes like a wet fart."

"Aren't you going to eat anything?" Caesar asked.

"I've already eaten today. Several times. All I do is eat, Caesar, it's the only thing that excites me on this ship and the lines over there never close. I've got to get out of this fucking place before someone has to roll me down the hall. What are we doing, guys? Why are we still here?"

"Ship was fucked," Grey said, chewing with his mouth open. "S'gonna take a few more days, maybe a week, but she'll be up and running again. I've been doing the repairs almost entirely by myself on top of busting my ass fixing all sorts of things around the *Imagination* while you've been freeloading and whining. You're welcome."

Archimedes sighed.

"Okay, but besides that, I called you both here for a different reason," Caesar said excitedly. "I figured out a way to find out what our package is. Or at least get a good idea, anyway."

"Who cares?" Grey said.

"How long is that going to take?" Archimedes asked.

"Not long at all," Caesar said, and, to Grey, "Who *cares*? You don't? After all that happened on Astrakoth and at Akers' before that? They nearly killed us. They wrecked our ship. Your *baby*."

Grey grunted. His eyes worked back and forth, considering. "Alright, good point. So what is it?"

"I'm not sure yet. But Professor Eppleheim has this machine that can run a full analysis on biological materials and breaks whatever you put in down to its base elements." Caesar saw the blank look on his friends' faces. "So in addition to giving an idea on how something functions, digestive properties, what organs process what, what something breathes and how… if whatever we put in is composed of something rare, we would find out what it was."

Grey laughed. "Are you expecting the lizard to be made of gold?'

"Maybe it has a diamond gizzard," Archimedes said.

"Birds have gizzards," Caesar snapped. "Lizards do not."

"Maybe it's the first lizard to have a gizzard, which would not only be rare and potentially valuable, but phonetically convenient for the science community."

Grey laughed again and Archimedes joined him. Caesar scowled at his plate until they quieted.

"Anyway," he said, "I know how to use the machine. The professor has been showing me, and I'm pretty sure I've got it down. I was thinking, you know, nobody is in any of the labs tonight on account of the professor's celebration—"

"Wait, wait," Archimedes said, holding up a hand. "Tonight? You want to do this tonight?"

Caesar nodded, He forked a bunch of vegetables and chewed them up. "Yeah," he said, swallowing. "I mean, it's the perfect opportunity, right? I don't know another time the place would be guaranteed to be empty."

"How would you get in?" Grey asked. "If we were to do this, the labs need keycard access, right?"

Caesar's face lit up. He pulled something from his pants pocket, something square, and set it down in the center of the table. It took Grey and Archimedes a second to register what it was: a thick, laminated white badge with a photo on it. Thick black letters under the picture identified him as Petty Officer First Class Connelly Abren. Caesar knew him as Koko's boyfriend. Ark knew him as kind of a prick.

"What did you do?" Archimedes hissed. He slapped his hand on the badge, covering it, and slid it across and under the table so it was out of sight. He looked at Grey. Grey was staring at Caesar, jaw dropped. Archimedes said, "Seriously, Caesar, what did you do?"

"I lifted it back at the lab as I was leaving. You only need the card to get into the room, so I was counting on him not noticing it was gone as we left."

"That's great," Grey said, regaining his ability to speak. "What about the next time he needs to get in somewhere else? Like, say, the barracks. Where he sleeps every day."

"That's another reason why we need to do this tonight," Caesar said.

Archimedes scooted up to the table, pressing his chest against the edge, his butt barely on the bench.

He looked over, past Grey, to where Petty Officer Abren was joking with his friends. He looked back at Caesar.

"Listen to me. I didn't teach you sleight of hand for this. I taught you for, like, a fun weekend afternoon of pickpocketing at the mall, or for magic tricks at kids' birthday parties when we inevitably lose our pilot's licenses. This—if we get caught—is prison time at best and getting shoved into an airlock at worst. You get that?"

Caesar swallowed hard. "Yeah. Yes."

"And there is a lot that could go wrong with this plan of yours," Archimedes continued. "Not least of which is you fucking up that machine. Are you sure, *absolutely* sure, that you can use it unassisted?"

"I have been," Caesar said. "The last week or so."

"You don't think we could just ask the professor for permission?"

"I don't think that's a good idea," Grey cut in. He pushed his plate aside, food forgotten, and looked around the room. He spoke softly. "ACG and everyone on board thinks that package was either stolen or destroyed. If we plug in that sphere and we get any surprises back, we'd have to explain why we lied to everyone about keeping a package with a high payout to ourselves and why we smuggled it onboard."

Archimedes nodded. He glanced at Caesar. "You still want to do this?"

Caesar looked back and forth between both of his friends. He looked down at his plate, realized his appetite had got up and left at some point in the conversation.

"I want to know," he said.

Archimedes and Grey glanced at each other, an agreement passing silently between them. Ark handed the badge back to Caesar beneath the table.

"What do you need from us?" Grey asked.

Caesar's eyes widened. He was surprised enough at himself for his audacity. After everything the three of them had been through over the years, he had hoped for his friends' support, but the confirmation still came as a relief.

"First thing is making sure the lab is empty. That's as simple as opening the door and looking inside. If it's all clear, I'll need someone to stand outside the lab and keep watch while I'm using the machine. I'll need to come up with a plausible story, too, about where I found the badge. If I get caught with it, I mean."

"A distraction wouldn't hurt," Grey said. "Some additional misdirection, keep attention focused away from the labs."

"Risky," Archimedes said.

"The whole thing is risky," Grey shot back.

"Mm." Archimedes looked back at Abren. He downed the rest of his cocktail with a gasp and a grimace. "I have an idea to get you your story and a distraction both, but I'm going to need a few more of these if I'm really going to sell it," He raised his brow at Caesar. "Then you're going to need to move fast."

"I still need to grab the cooler from the *Searcher*!" Caesar said.

"Just grab the lizard," Grey said. "The cooler's too conspicuous." To Archimedes, he said, "We'll wait for your signal, but you wait until you see us hovering back in the doorway."

Archimedes nodded and pushed himself up and away from the table. The food lines were thinning out. The cook with the grog saw him coming and nodded when Ark pointed at his empty cup. All he could think about was how his body had just stopped being sore. That, and how this was the most excited he had been in weeks.

Chapter Nine
Men of Action

"…so in the end, I guess you could say they were a real Dyr in the headlights."

Connelly felt the familiar flush of validation as his punchline was met with a chorus of groans and laughter. He drained the rest of his beer and set his cup on the edge of a nearby table. His friends—Taddy, Karl, McGovern—still had spirits in their glasses, so they tapped them together in a mock toast and drank.

This is what joining the service is about, Connelly thought. *Camaraderie, traveling through the stars. Stability. Direction. Good times and good memories.*

He had gone through enlistment training with Taddy and McGovern. They hadn't met Karl until they got stationed on the *Imagination,* but Connelly had quickly bonded with him when he found out they had attended rival schools in the same hometown. The antagonism of their youth transformed into something more in line with friendly competition now that they were serving together.

They had been on the *Imagination* for four years now. Traveling to different planets, partying in their off time. Meeting new people and taking their stories with them. Drinking on the ship when their shifts were over (or boring, why not?). Hell, Connelly had even found himself a woman on board, even if she—

"You really got a cushy job, don't you?"

The words cut into his thought stream. He turned to see who spoke and found the white-haired courier from the hallway. The courier stepped forward, joining the friend circle. *What's his name?* Connelly thought. *Carnegie? Carnahan… something.*

"Are you drunk?" he asked.

"Oh, absolutely," the courier said.

"Don't you have your own friends to drink with?"

"Hyp… theoretically. Couldn't tell you where they are, though. Seems like soon's we got up here, they'nt want anything to do with me."

"Small wonder," Taddy muttered.

"*Anyway*," Carnahan continued on, louder, "since my friends have abandoned me, the cowards, I thought I'd find new cowardly friends."

The mood in the group slid immediately from annoyance to barely constrained anger.

"Care to repeat that?" McGovern asked, voice chilly. "Sounds like you called us cowards."

"I said I'm *lookin'* for cowardly fiends. No, friends. Like my friends." Carnahan looked at each of them in turn, swaying as he did so. "But yeah, I mean, if the shoes fit, then I guess that's what I was calling you."

"You should shut up now, package jockey," Connelly said. "Before you say something else that you can't walk back."

Carnahan gave him a confused look. "Ain't nothing wrong with being cowards. It's how you stay alive, right? Right. Like Astrakoth. I went there, didn't mean to, but I did. Let me tell you, after seeing the things I seen, seeing how many of your buddies are coming back up in bags, I don't blame you lot for hiding up here where it's—"

The courier's sentence ended in a spray of blood as his lips split open. He fell backwards, sprawled out on the mess half floor. It took Connelly a moment to realize he had been the one to strike the man. His mouth dropped open in slow surprise, and he nearly apologized until he saw Carnahan smiling from his back. Then Karl's voice cut in with, "Call *us* cowards, you piece of shit?"

Four on one wasn't the best way to plead the case that they weren't, but it sure felt good anyhow.

They had been expecting the punch—it had been part of the plan, after all—but the sudden viciousness of it still made Caesar and Grey flinch. They had taken up position next to the drop-off area for dirty dishes, edged just enough around the corner to look like they were casually loitering. Nobody paid them much mind coming or going. They were forgotten entirely when Archimedes crashed onto his back.

"Good God," Caesar gasped as Ark disappeared beneath a flurry of fists and boots.

"Come on," Grey said, tugging at Caesar's arm.

"But what if—"

"Come on!" Grey hissed. "We have somewhere to be. That's the whole point!"

They peeled themselves away from the cafeteria entrance and retreated down the hallways, Caesar reluctantly in the lead. They only encountered a few people on the way to the lab; Grey put on his best wild-eyed expression each time and told them there was a fight in the mess hall. Each time it successfully got them running in that direction.

The lab itself had nobody in sight by the time they reached it. Grey positioned himself against the wall opposite the door, not quite directly across. Caesar fumbled Connelly's identification badge from his pocket.

"You sure that thing's going to work?" Grey asked.

"It did earlier."

Caesar held the badge to the little gray box next to the door. A beep of affirmation sounded and the door slid open. Caesar cast a quick look back at his friend and stepped inside.

The science lab was devoid of life. No enterprising scientists working late, no curious soldiers. The room was as meticulously clean and organized as he had left it a couple hours earlier.

Caesar grabbed a rolling chair and wheeled it over to the molecular deconstructor. His temples were pounding with adrenaline, his heart was a jackhammer in his chest, and yet he had to admit… he was excited. His hands moved over the sides of the silver box in fluid motions, tapping panels that would input the shape, size, and weight of the item he wanted analyzed. He gripped the handle on the front and pulled the machine open. A thin black shelf with circular holes cut into it extended from inside. Caesar pulled the translucent green sphere from his pocket. His own body warmth had removed the chill from the cooler, but it seemed unchanged otherwise. The sphere felt kind of like plastic or rubber in his hands. The lizard suspended inside still appeared to be sleeping. Caesar ran his hands over the slots until he found one that would fit the orb and he placed it in gently. Another quick panel tap on the deconstructor's side retracted the shelf and Caesar closed the door. There were no lights or motions to indicate when the machine started working, but a soft *vmmm* sound could be heard.

"God, this thing is so damn cool," he said under his breath.

He sat in the chair and used his feet to drag himself over to the computer terminal. It was password protected, locked to all but approved user names. Caesar had known this when he had come up with the plan to sneak into the lab, but he had kept this detail from his friends. His dashed dreams of being an acclaimed scientists had left him plenty of time to develop new hobbies; that said, hacking into an IRSC vessel's programs was a completely different animal than some understaffed, underappreciated police station's records.

He reached down to his ankle and pulled free a small data drive he had stuffed into his sock. He ran his thumb over both sides for good luck, took a deep breath, held it, then pushed the drive gently into an open port. A moment later, lines of code began running over the log-in screen.

Caesar cracked his knuckles and got to work.

Grey Toliver wanted to fight, which was not a great urge to have for someone whose job was to keep watch and draw as little attention as possible. He knew it was a problem but couldn't help himself. It was his natural gut reaction to seeing one of his closest friends getting his ass kicked.

He knew Archimedes wasn't afraid to get into a fight, knew he could even be a decent scrapper when he wanted to be. He knew that Ark fighting back hadn't been part of the plan, and that he could take a hell of a beating. He even *liked* it, the sick bastard. But none of that made him any more comfortable with the situation.

Grey and Archimedes had been friends since they were five years old, pretty much from the day Ark moved across the street and asked if he could explore the neighborhood with Grey and Caesar. He'd been a natural third to their party, the youngest but also the most daring. Caesar had been a lot more of a troublemaker back then, too, but he still had his limits; Archimedes didn't seem to be fazed by anything, often doing things or going places just to see what would happen.

He had a big mouth, always, for as long as Grey had known him. He could just as easily use it to win over a new friend as he could to start trouble. Problem was, nobody was ever quite sure which option he would choose. It all depended on his mood, really, so yeah, he got into a lot of fights. Half the time they were with Grey, whenever he got in a mood. But when the chips were down and someone came in looking for a scrap, they had each other's backs. Always. As kids, in alleys and bars, even on an inhospitable planet. Always, until now, when Grey had to turn and run the other way.

The door to the lab hissed as it slid upward. Caesar stood back a bit, out of sight, until Grey gave him the all-clear. When he stepped into the hallway, Grey could see his face was flushed red, his hair plastered to his forehead.

"Why are you sweating? Are we good? Did you get what we need?"

"We're good. The security was, uh, just a little bit tougher than I expected. There were a few close calls, but we're good."

"Security?" Grey asked. "I thought the badge—"

"Don't worry about it. Here," Caesar said. He glanced both ways to make sure they were still alone, then handed Grey the orb and the data drive. Both disappeared into Grey's pockets. "Put the package back in the cooler. The drive has all the info on it. I tried to cross-reference it with the IRSC catalogue to see if there were any records that matched whatever it is, but nothing came up. Take this, too." He handed over Connelly's identification badge. "I was thinking, if you place it in the cafeteria near where the fight was, it'll look like he dropped it in the scuffle."

Grey stared at him. "Is there a reason you're unloading all the evidence on me?"

"Yeah, I've got to go. There's some place I've got to be, and I can't go looking like this. Obviously."

"Obviously."

"So I've got to clean up."

Grey nodded. "Caesar, what the fuck are you talking about?"

"There's a… a party thing. For scientists. A science party." He was already backing down the hall. "I've got to go put in an appearance. It's the optics, right? Looks good if we're all split up. Read what you can, see what you can find out!"

Grey watched, dumbfounded, as Caesar ducked around the corner and disappeared from sight. He blinked, remembered himself and his surroundings, and shoved the ID badge into the pocket with the data drive.

"I swear on Terra Prime's broken-ass moon, I'm the only sane one on this ship," he muttered.

There were two brigs aboard the *IRSC Imagination*, though they were hardly ever used as more than an occasional drunk tank. The brig near the bow, in fact, had filled half of their cells with extra supplies for the ship.

Archimedes was half-escorted, half-carried into one of the remaining empty cells near the back. His lips were both split in half, his left eye swollen shut, and that side of his face was settling into a sickly yellow shade smeared with purple. His right ear had a cut along the top fold, a side effect of having his head bounced off the corner of a bench when he tried and failed to get up. It hurt every time he touched it, but he couldn't stop. The rest of his body didn't fare much better: nothing seemed broken, but every little movement hurt like hell, and he was sure he would have the marks to show for it come morning.

A cot with a thin cushion was bolted into one wall. A deflated-looking pillow lay at one end, while a pale green blanket was folded at the other. Archimedes sat on the edge of the cot and placed his head in his hands.

"You think you'll need a doctor?" the guard asked from the other side of the cell door. He was a big man, nearly as broad as the door. His hair was buzzed nearly down to the skull, giving him a bullish look.

"Nah. Some ice, maybe. Think you could swing that?"

"Yeah, man, shouldn't be a problem," the guard said and left.

Archimedes grabbed the blanket and pulled it over himself as he lay down gingerly. The only light in the cell came from the hall outside, so he stared at the dark metal ceiling and let his mind swim. The alcohol haze was fading, and the hangover began to set in, compounding the ache in his head.

"Anything to help out," he said under his breath.

The guard returned a few moments later and tossed a bag of ice through the bars. Ark caught it one-handed from his back and pressed it against his swollen eye.

"Thanks. You're a big dude. Glad it wasn't you pounding on me out there."

"Ah, I'm a big softie. They just put me down here because I look intimidating."

"Are you supposed to tell your prisoners that?"

The guard snorted. "You might be stuck in here for a few days, but you ain't really a prisoner, man. Just need a break from the crew. You're a courier, right, you and your friends? Moving around place to place all the time? I don't blame you for getting twisted up some. These IRSC stints—four to eight months at a time over some place—they're not for everyone. It might help to hear, though, most of the people onboard worth talking to wouldn't give two shits about you punching Connelly in the face."

Archimedes propped himself up on one elbow. "I don't know if you've seen *my* face, but he's the one that threw the first punch."

"Maybe," the guard said, "but I heard you got your licks in."

"Yeah, well, it was four on one," Archimedes said. "I had to start fighting back at some point."

The guard rapped his knuckles against one of the cell bars. "Either way, it's like I said: nobody's real mad about it. Just can't be having fights on board when everyone's going to be stuck here for ages, you know? Look, I'm sure you're feelin' all kinds of ways, none of 'em good. Why don't you try to sleep some of it off? If you need more ice, I'll go grab it for you. If I'm still on shift when you wake up, I'll drag the table over here and we can play some cards. Sound good?"

Archimedes closed his good eye and laid back down. He had been on more than a few cots in more than a few cells, and this one was up there with the most comfortable. "Yeah," he said, already drifting off. "Sounds good."

Caesar found the bridge without too much trouble, but it was gaining entry that took some doing. At first the two guards stationed on either side of the door ignored him completely outside of barring his entry when he tried to walk in. They rolled their eyes as he tried to convince them he had been invited to the party ("Just ask somebody inside!" he had pleaded, to no avail), only to have half a dozen scientists and lab technicians walk past him without so much as a hello, much less a corroboration. Finally, annoyed by his unyielding persistence, one of the men slipped into the bridge to ask around. After a couple of minutes, the door opened and the guard returned to his position. Koko's arm snaked out after him and grabbed Caesar by the shirt, pulling him inside.

Most of the partygoers were gathered on the massive deck where sat the captain and first mate's chairs. Two curved staircases led down to the lower deck on either side. Three long tables had been set up down there with a potluck style variety of appetizers, entrees, and desserts. The technicians, navigators, communications specialists, bridge engineers, and pilots on duty were all working diligently at their stations. Cordons had been set up to give them room to work, but several still chatted with party guests. Still more had at least one plate of food in front of them.

A large video projection played near the front of the room, a live stream of the science convention and award ceremony. The sound was being broadcast through the surround sound speaker system clear as a bell. Professor Eppleheim stood up there, facing the projection, a smile on his face and his hands clasped behind his back. He was wearing a sharp white suit with a blood-red vest and tie. He looked positively regal.

"I'm glad you could make it," Koko said. "You want to head down there, grab some food?"

"Hmm?" Caesar tore his eyes away from the stream. "Oh, no thanks. I don't have much of an appetite tonight. Did the professor give his speech already?"

"Not yet. Coming up soon, I think. The captain made a cardboard replica of the award to hand him on this end." Koko gave him a once-over. "You look nice. Where did you get that outfit?"

"Uh, I own it?" Caesar had made himself comfortable in the quarters assigned to him by moving most of his clothes and a handful of books from the *Sol Searcher*. For the party he had selected a black suit jacket over a white button-up shirt, a pair of black slacks, and the only pair of dress shoes he owned, also black but with some light scuffing around the toes.

"No offense," Koko said. "I just didn't think, you know, with you guys…"

"There are occasions in our lives, believe it or not, when we've got to look presentable. "

The ceremony continued. More and more people in the room turned their attention to the hologram as a panel on fuel drive developments concluded and the host returned to the podium. Professor Eppleheim's award was next on the agenda, and the speaker launched into a smooth breakdown of the professor's personal history beginning with his childhood and gradually working his way through his academic accomplishments.

Caesar was transfixed. He had been transfixed through what he caught of the panel, too, truth be told. He was probably the only person on the bridge—with the possible exception of the professor—who'd had a hand in creating a new fuel drive, and though the experienced had left a bad taste in his mouth they still fascinated him. In fact, he had been working on some plans for the *Searcher* that he planned on eventually running by Grey.

Koko was taken in by the ceremony as well, right up until a uniformed soldier came up and touched her on the elbow. She started at the contact, turned to him with questions on her face. The soldier leaned in and spoke softly in her ear. Caesar, watching in his periphery, saw her eyes widen. He heard the words 'boyfriend' and 'fight' and saw her hook her hair behind her ear, distressed.

"Thank you for telling me," she said in a low tone.

The soldier nodded, turned and left the bridge.

"I've got to go," Koko said to Caesar.

"You do?" Caesar asked. "Professor Eppleheim is about to give his speech!"

"I know. Let me know how it goes."

"Are you alright?"

Koko scowled. "I'm fine. I've just got to go see somebody all of a sudden."

She didn't stick around to elaborate, heading instead for the exit. Caesar knew it wouldn't make any sense to follow her, knew he wasn't supposed to have any idea what was going on. He stayed where he was, heart pounding all over again.

A sudden thundering applause proved to be the distraction he needed.

"My deepest gratitude to the board," Eppleheim said. The captain handed him his fake award. He held it up with as much pride as if it had been the real thing. "And to everyone in attendance who live, breath, and bolster the sciences and their crafts. My gratitude to those who have worked with me directly, helping me perform my experiments, revise my reports, and who have bolstered me as well…"

Grey sat in front of the monitor in his lab atop a rolling stool he had picked up from a junkyard a year and a half previous. The frame and the seat had been separate when he'd found it, and so he had managed to convince the yard dealer to part with it for free. Ten minutes of work and some generous application of grease later and it was like new, save for a few small tears in the seat and a lingering smell of motor oil. Grey loved it.

He made himself comfortable while the computer finished filtering through the information on Caesar's drive. When it was done, he spent another few minutes further separating the data into two different categories before digging into it: the genetic makeup of the sphere and the creature inside it, and the origins and similarities of those components. It was tedious work full of unsurprising information.

The sphere itself was a gelatinous containment module modified to decompose naturally in a humid environment. Simple. Straightforward. Non-toxic. No surprises there.

The lizard seemed to be amphibious, capable of storing and even absorbing oxygen. As each element making up the creature was identified, a list of known planets and moons where they could be found had also been drafted. Long, boring lists.

This thing could have come from just about anywhere, Grey thought.

But as he kept scanning the files, one thing became clear: this creature was not a naturally existing thing, not even a specimen that had been taken in and experimented on. There were just *too many* components to it. Its skin had the ability to camouflage itself. It was resistant to high temperatures. It seemed to be capable of asexually reproducing. Grey wanted to get Caesar's eyes on the data, get a confirmation that he was reading it right from someone who was better with the science jargon. From what he could tell, though, somebody somewhere had cooked this thing up and tossed in every evolutionary advantage they could think of.

"For a goddamn lizard, though?" he wondered out loud.

He was bothered by the idea. Why would somebody do this? Why would they make it so small? Why would they ship something clearly so absurd to Peloclade? He swiped through element after element, planet after moon.

When he came to the last two elements, he froze.

"Pantrillium… that's an explosive," he breathed. "Have we been traveling with a bomb? Did we *crash* with a *bomb* on board?"

He read the information closely. Read it over twice, three times. The traces of pantrillium were scarce. Harmless, even, but they were still there on the lizard. That narrowed down where the thing could have been before being put into the sphere. Mostly government-owned or otherwise restricted locations. Several other places were open to travel and commerce, but Grey knew that any place where pantrillium could be found would be just as forbidden to unauthorized visitors. One planet in particular stood out from the list: Vyroan, some place he knew nothing about. He wrote it down on a note pad.

The last element on the list was even more mysterious: a soil sample found roughly in the center of the sphere, likely in the lizard's stomach or intestinal tract. Only one planet came back as a match.

Vyroan, again.

Grey leaned back on the stool and ran a hand through his hair.

"Okay," he said. "We found you. Now where the hell are you, and why do you sound so familiar?"

Koko Noal stormed down the halls of the *Imagination*, the anger in her face softening into profound irritation before flashing back into anger, over and over, a cycle that kept the people she passed from greeting her. Her steady march was only stopped at the door to the brig, her identification badge not being cleared to give her access to the cells within. She banged on the door with her fist until it slid open.

"Miss Noal?" the guard inside asked, confused. "If you're looking for—"

"It's *Doctor* Noal," she snapped back, interrupting him. "And I know where he is."

"Oh, sorry. I didn't mean, uh, I wasn't trying to imply nothing. Look, I'm not sure it's appropriate for you to be here."

"I want to see him." She stood on her toes to look over the man's shoulder. "He's in here, right?"

"Doctor…"

"Right?" she asked again.

The guard looked past her into the hall, cautious of any of his peers. "He's sleeping," he said uncertainly. "And I'm really not supposed to let anyone in that hasn't been approved by a sergeant. It's the rules, you know?"

"Are you going to physically restrain me from coming in?"

"I would prefer not to…"

"Good," Koko said. "Then get out of my way."

She pushed past the large man and resumed her storming. Her head worked on a swivel, looking into each cell as she passed, not finding what she wanted until she had reached the very end. She lifted one foot and propelled it as hard as she could into the door.

The clanging noise startled Archimedes so violently from his slumber that he fell off the cot to the floor. The ice pack, mostly melted, burst beneath him, soaking his back. All of his varying aches, pains, and injuries screamed in concert; he writhed there, dazed and confused.

"Why?" he groaned. "What did I do? I thought we were going to play cards!"

"Sounds like a pretty sweet arrangement for a guy going around picking fights," Koko said gripping a bar in each hand.

Archimedes stopped squirming at the sound of her voice (squirming wasn't very dignified, after all), and struggled to his feet. His shirt clung to his frame uncomfortably, but the cold water felt surprising nice against the bruises.

"Koko? What are you doing here?"

She flinched at the sight of his face. "You look awful."

"First time for everything." He smiled. It hurt. "Your boyfriend hit me first."

"Did you deserve it?" she asked.

Archimedes laughed sharply. "Maybe. What are you doing with a guy like that? I'm not just asking because he tuned me up, I'm genuinely curious. He seems so, so…"

"Immature?" Koko offered.

Ark snapped his fingers and pointed at her. "Yes!"

"Like you?"

"Exactly!"

Koko sighed. "It's none of your business, Archimedes."

"You're a doctor, Doctor. You can do better than some meathead who beats up handsome couriers in an uncontrollable rage."

"You said you deserved it," she said.

"I said I *might* have deserved it. That seems to leave a lot of room for interpretation." Archimedes spread his arms to either side. "What are you even doing here? Have you visited Connelly yet?"

She shook her head. "How bad did you hurt him?"

"You know how a guy gets beat up and someone like you goes, 'You look awful,' and the guy goes, 'Yeah, but you should see the other guy?'"

"Yes?" Koko asked, suddenly alarmed.

Archimedes grinned. "Well, I'm the other guy. I might have stuck a couple in his ribs, maybe one or two under the chin. I'm sure he's fine."

"Gods above, Ark. You know, I liked you. You were a little much the first time we met, but I did like you. I really thought we'd be friends."

"Me, too!" he exclaimed. "Me, too! And what happened? I hardly ever saw you again, because you're in your lab all the time."

"That's my job!" she shouted at him.

"I know it is!" he shouted back. He worked his jaw, trying to find the right words to follow. His jaw responded by clicking at the hinge. He threw his hands up and limped back over to the cot to sit down.

"The lab is your job, but Caesar gets to be in there all the time because he's interested in that stuff, and he's good at it. The *Searcher* is busted, so Grey gets in at the docking bay and makes himself useful. He's into *that* stuff, and he's good at that. What am I good at? Talking to people? These aren't my people, Koko. The only two people I know are never around, and neither is the one chick who seemed to ride my wavelength. All I'm left with are the goddamn cafeteria weirdos and one lady that has been doing her damnedest to murder me, uh…" He stopped and looked at her sheepishly.

"Carnally?" Koko supplied. "Everyone's heard."

Archimedes rolled his eyes. "Great. I guess that's the nicest way to put it. And although I never thought I'd say it, it gets old after a while. I'm bored, Koko. I'm lonely. Worst of all, I feel pretty damned useless. I couldn't even get my last package where it was supposed to go."

He fell silent. She didn't rush to fill the emptiness where his words had been, but the anger she had felt when she'd first arrived had begun to fade. She stood there, watching him while he looked between his hands at the floor.

"It's possible," she said, "that you're not… entirely useless."

He glanced up at her through the bars.

"You seem to make a pretty good punching bag," she said, smiling.

Archimedes laughed so hard he worried he had finished cracking his ribs.

Koko glanced back at the guard. The large man kept looking anxiously back and forth between her and the door. He rolled his hand in a hurry-up motion.

"Get some rest, Ark," she said, looking back at the courier. "And lay off the sauce some. It's not going to bring you happiness."

"It brought me you," he pointed out.

"Yeah, and if you were allowed to have a mirror, you could see what else it brought you, you gigantic sap."

Koko gave a small wave. Archimedes watched her go, a little sad but a little lifted, too. He shook his head and scooted back until he could lean against the wall.

Like a great many nights before, Archimedes hoped that the things he had done would be worth it in the end. He always felt like it might be, like it probably would be. But he was never sure.

Chapter Ten

The Sol Searcher Flies Again

In the back of the docking bay, tucked away from the government ships and the tired, filthy, and occasionally bloodied busybodies tending them or making trips to or from Astrakoth, the *Sol Searcher* rested, looking immaculate. The soil and foliage had been scrubbed away, the scratches beneath buffed out. Gouges had been filled and dented plates replaced. The viewport had been swapped out for an undamaged one of even higher quality. The seats in the cockpit had been taken out and new seats with fresh upholstery bolted in. The blood that had been splashed all over the consoles and the halls had been fully washed away. The stabilizer had (finally) been fixed, the thrust drive tuned up. The hinges and the gears in the loading ramp had been straightened out and greased up. The fuel tanks were topped off. The Aventure logos and the ship's name had been carefully repainted.

And finally, when all was said and done, Grey Toliver had spent a full day polishing the hull nose to tip, just to give his girl that extra sparkle.

There were a couple things that still needed doing—impact foam needed to be replaced, the dispensers fixed, and posterior cameras would need to be purchased and installed—but none of that was new. All said, the *Searcher* was already in as good a condition as it had ever been. Maybe even better. It had taken nearly a month. A month of hard work and bargaining for parts. A month of dedication and concentration to fix everything so that she would give the best performance possible.

But finally, finally the *Sol Searcher* was ready to return to the stars.

The *Imagination's* bridge looked a lot different with all the tables and most of the crew removed. A lot bigger. Caesar marveled at the size of the room, surprised that he still *could* marvel at the ship after so much time on board. Then he remembered that he was leaving, that he would never get an opportunity to grow used to it, and he felt a twinge of sadness.

"Captain Anada, thank you for coming!"

Caesar turned. Captain Richards had pushed himself out of his chair and walked toward him, a tall, lanky man with silver hair. Caesar shook his hand enthusiastically, only mildly insecure about how soft his hand felt in the captain's callused palm.

"Not bad, right?" Richards asked. "I know you've got your own ship, but stepping on the bridge of an IRSC vessel for the first time has got to still give you chills, right? It still does me, and I get to be here every day. Feels like a dream."

"Oh, uh, I was actually here last night," Caesar said. "For Professor Eppleheim's party."

"Oh," the captain said. He seemed mildly disappointed. "Well, welcome back."

"But you're right!" Caesar added hurriedly. "I was actually just thinking that, how magnificent this place is. The whole ship, really. It has been a real pleasure to be here, and my friends and I truly are grateful for everything you've done for us."

Richards nodded. "It's been a pleasure for us, too, you know. The professor said you really seemed to take to the ship. Sergeant Bremmer said the same thing about Captain Toliver in the docking bay. His advice, and the modifications and repairs he's provided have all been invaluable. As for Captain Carnahan…"

"He's more of a free spirit," Caesar said. "He hasn't felt very free here, unfortunately."

"Well, we're not for everybody. How does that work, by the way, three captains for the same ship?"

"Like a dysfunctional marriage without any benefits except a bit of a tax break."

Richards chuckled. He placed a hand on Caesar's shoulder and gently turned him toward the door.

"Walk with me, would you? It's a beautiful view up here, but I still need a break every now and again."

Caesar was a bit let down that his final bridge visit would be cut short but did his best to hide it. He let the captain lead him out into the halls, passing the first officer on their way out, a handsome dark-skinned woman. She had had coffee with Caesar a few times in the cafeteria and had insisted he call her Jocelyn. He never did learn her last name. They smiled and nodded at each other.

"I hear your ship is finally space-worthy again," Richards said. "You plan on leaving soon?"

"Tomorrow, I believe. We're in the process of moving some stuff back into the *Searcher*. Grey and Archimedes will do some final tests, and if everything clears out we'll be on our way."

"You've got enough food? Enough fuel?"

"Plenty enough of both," Caesar confirmed. "Again, we're grateful for everything. The supplies, the parts. Room and board. Hell, rescuing us at all."

"Trust me, rescuing some poor shipwrecked souls was good P.R. for the *Imagination*," Richards said, chuckling. "As for the parts and supplies, well, you and Captain Toliver worked off that debt." He paused in the hall and touched Caesar's arm to stop him as well. "From everything I've heard, you and Captain Toliver have a lot of talent and potential. You're wasted on a courier ship. It wouldn't be difficult for me to pull a few strings, call in a couple favors. You two could start earning a proper commission here, doing what you guys are good at."

Flashes of what could be ran freely through Caesar's head once again: making new discoveries, publishing papers alongside the greatest minds in the galaxy, becoming universally respected and having access to the most cutting-edge scientific technology. Exploring uncharted worlds.

Maybe not that last one, he thought. *Considering how poorly the first go-around went. Leave it to the professionals.*

Then he thought, *But then I would be a professional!*

"What are you thinking?" Richards asked. "Am I winning you over?"

"It's… tempting," Caesar said. He gave a small smile. "It really is. But Grey wouldn't part with the *Searcher*, and we couldn't just take her and leave Archimedes with nothing; we're all three on the loan, you know, and we wouldn't be able to pay him out for his share. So… for now we're a three-man team, same as we have been for years. Wherever one of us goes, the other two follow."

The captain looked disappointed but nodded and took Caesar's hand to shake it again. "I understand. It's a duty thing. Duty to your crew, duty to your friends. You've got a good head on those scrawny shoulders, Captain Anada. The offer's open if you or Captain Toliver ever want to patch in a call and revisit it."

Caesar thanked him. They chatted a bit longer, mostly about the *Imagination* and what remained of her Astrakoth expedition. Eventually a call came in for Richards to return to the bridge, and Caesar went his own way. He still had plenty of clothes to move back to the *Searcher*.

"Read 'em and weep!"

The guard groaned as Archimedes splayed his cards out in front of him, a full run of Novas. The courier's arm reached through the bars of the cell and swept the pot—a small pile of Salixian blacknuts—over to his side of the folding table. Ark peeled the shell from one of the nuts and popped it into his mouth with a satisfied grin. The guard, seated across from him on an overturned bucket, fixed him with a dead stare.

"You're eating your wealth," he said.

"Don't we all," Archimedes replied.

The guard opened his mouth to respond again but just then his watch began to beep. He glanced down at it, glanced at the courier, stood. The rest of his blacknuts were swept back into the bag they had come in. He gestured at Archimedes' winnings; Ark shook his head and started stuffing them into his pockets. The cards were piled back into a deck, the deck slipped back into its box. The table was folded and set aside, up against the wall.

"You coming in to rough me up?" Archimedes asked. "Can't handle your losses?"

"Quite the opposite," the guard said. "Your cool-down time is officially over. You know, considering the last time you were out in the world you picked up that shiner, maybe you want to stick around an extra day or two."

Archimedes laughed and shook his head. He waited patiently while the guard unlocked the door, then stepped out and clasped the man by the forearm.

"Thanks for the ice," he said, "and for killing the time with me. I didn't catch your name."

"Petty Officer Leo Gratz," the guard said. "And you're Archimedes. If they hadn't told me when you came in, Doctor Noal would have burned it into my memory."

"That was something," Archimedes said, thoughtfully. "Yeah, that was something, alright. Well, I've got to get ready. I think my co-captains have got just about everything ready. No offense to the *Imagination*, but if I miss the boat out of here, I'm going to kill myself." He clapped Gratz on the shoulder and headed for the brig's exit. "Don't let them keep you down here forever, Leo! You're a big boy. Intimidate them!"

The halls were mostly clear as Archimedes navigated back to his guest quarters. When he did pass someone, they averted their eyes; the swelling in his face had gone down but he couldn't imagine it looked much better. His shirt had a not-insignificant amount of blood on it, too, most of which had come from his split lips and nose.

His room was just as he had left it: used towel draped over the back of a chair, bed neatly made, scattered pieces of generic IRSC clothing littering the floor. He took it in for a moment, feeling almost like he was looking at a scene from his life from somewhere outside of himself, then set about cleaning up the room. Quietly, methodically. The towel was returned to the shower rack, the chair tucked back into the desk. The dirty clothes were folded and set at the foot of the bed. It looked nearly unlived in by the time he was done.

He paused by the door when he was finished, taking a moment to reflect. The knowledge that he had acted petulantly during his time on the *Imagination* came to him grudgingly, and he grudgingly embraced it despite that thought making him feel small. He knew he should just be grateful to have survived this long, and for being legitimately saved by strangers. He had always known that their time aboard the IRSC vessel would be temporary, and that he probably should have just enjoyed the little moments as they came, as if he were on the galaxy's most boring vacation.

He knew all this but still couldn't shake the impatient, near-loathing feeling. He would be glad to go.

Archimedes tossed his room card on the bed, turned and left, letting the door slide shut firmly behind him.

Though it lacked the space to move comfortably around in, any of the expensive equipment, or even a modicum of the respectability afforded by the *Imagination*, Caesar had to admit he had missed his personal laboratory aboard the *Sol Searcher*. It was his private zone in a way not even his room on the ship could be, his work space, his think space, the place he could indulge his interests and work on even the wildest hypotheses. It was where he could play at being the scientist he had always dreamed of being.

Caesar had stopped by the *Imagination*'s lab to say goodbye to Professor Eppleheim and Koko, and they had basically repeated Captain Richards' offer of legitimacy. Hearing it from two esteemed scientists gave it additional weight, but he had turned it down again all the same. He had more pressing matters to focus on at the moment.

Grey had printed off a hardcopy of the data and had scrawled notes on several pages. Caesar hunched over his desk, those papers on his right, writing his own notes with his left, and found himself falling fully into the work, this clandestine stuff, picking his way through information he could go to prison just for acquiring.

That fear—and the exhilaration that came with it—only grew more intense as he gained a clearer idea of just what it was they had been transporting. What they had lied about not still having.

A knock sounded at the door. Caesar turned in his chair to see Archimedes leaning against the frame, arms crossed.

"Hey. You're back?"

"Yeah, they let me out this morning," Archimedes said. He dropped his arms and stepped into the lab. He cleared a few books off the room's second chair, setting them on the ground, and took a seat. "I didn't really have anything in the room they gave me, so I'm ready to go when you two are."

"I think Grey's planning on running a final diagnostic on the *Searcher* tonight. He'll probably want your help."

Archimedes didn't say anything. Caesar set his pen down and looked over his friend. The bruises looked brutal, a swirl of purple and yellow, and he wondered if there might have been a less punishing option they could have gone with for a distraction. Then he remembered it had all been Archimedes' idea in the first place.

Archimedes broke the silence first, pointing at the pile of papers on the desk. "Is that the stuff?"

"Yeah. Grey went over some of it already last night. I've been comparing his notes with some details he missed, trying to make a more complete picture out of everything. And, uh… Ark, I think I know what the lizard is."

Archimedes stared at him.

"You're not going to ask?"

"I figured you were just going to tell me. I didn't think we were going to have a guessing game."

"It's a biological weapon."

"See? Not really game material," Archimedes said. "Now what is it really?"

Caesar took a deep breath. "The thing in that cooler most resembles a Necolian thicket lizard. They were an invasive species that was deliberately hunted to extinction. They had natural camouflage to blend in with their surroundings, and toxic skin to avoid being eaten even when they were discovered. They were capable of asexual reproduction and laid massive egg clusters, which would then lead to massive population explosions.

"This," he continued, tapping his notepad, "is some kind of clone of that species, a species that everyone thought was dead. Built from the ground up, Ark, and modified even further. For one, it will thrive in virtually any environment. It has temperature-adaptive cells that allow it to function in extreme heat or to brumate in extreme cold, kind of like it's doing now. You'd have to crush it to kill it, I imagine, some kind of extreme force. But you'd have to avoid making any contact with your skin, because it will poison the absolute shit out of you. If someone were to release one of these in the wild without anyone knowing? You could have thousands to deal with before anyone realized it was a problem."

"You're serious," Archimedes said softly.

Caesar scooted to the edge of his chair and leaned forward. "Oh, I'm deadly serious, man. There's something else that this thing has that the original species didn't. I've read the data on this particular point five times. I've looked up everything I could to verify the effects, because I wanted to be sure. I needed to be sure."

"Spit it the fuck out, Caesar!" Archimedes urged.

"The toxin it releases coats the skin but based on the deconstruction of the sphere I'm also seeing a high concentration in what looks like the mouth or throat. That means that anything it brushes up against is getting some of this shit wiped off on it. Anything it bites into is getting a full dose of it, any plants or trees, maybe a leftover carcass. It's going to leave the stuff behind. The toxin has been given necrotic properties. Transmittable ones."

Caesar's words hung in the air between them. The exhaustion that had been sitting on Archimedes' shoulders seemed to slough off, forgotten.

"You get a thousand of these things running around, spreading a rot that spreads and kills whatever it touches… you're not just talking about an invasive species. This is an ecosystem destroyer!"

Caesar nodded.

"Who… who would do that? Who *could* do that?"

"That's the thing." Caesar reached back to his desk and rifled through the papers until he found the lists he was looking for. "These are the elements that make up the lizard and the sphere it's in. I've been going over it and Grey's notes, and the thing that stood out to both of us are traces of pantrillium."

Archimedes started. "Isn't that—"

"An explosive, yeah. There's not enough to there to *be* explosive, but—"

"But that stuff's hard to come by, isn't it? Government lockdown, government regulated." Caesar nodded again, more slowly this time. Archimedes whistled. "Creating this thing is starting to sound like a war crime."

"Yeah, Ark. A war crime we're in possession of."

"We could space it."

"No, we couldn't. First, I don't think the cold is enough to kill it. Extreme heat, maybe. Magma? Launching it into a sun, that would do it. If we crushed it, it would have to be extremely careful, in an extremely sterile environment, but if this toxin gets on anything organic, it's fucked. And what if we tossed it out of an airlock and someone found it?"

"How the hell would they find it?" Archimedes asked, skeptical.

"I don't know, but what if they did? A hundred years down the line, even, this thing is still a potential world-ender. And here's the other thing: the pantrillium. That shit got in the lizard *before* it went the sphere. If we ignore it or we destroy it without finding out who did it or why, we're basically turning our back on this. What if they—whoever they are—can get more? What if they *have* more?"

"We can't just turn it in somewhere, though, Caesar. If the government is involved, we don't know… like, anything about it! If it's sanctioned. How deep it goes if it isn't."

"And we've been sitting on this, a package we weren't ever supposed to have opened. If someone wanted to turn us into scapegoats or wrap us up into a conspiracy, we'd make the perfect patsies."

Archimedes was quiet for a long moment. He reached out and took the list of papers from Caesar. He flipped through them without really reading them, his mind wandering elsewhere to concepts of morality and obligation and responsibility. They had already been through so much. Where did the obligation end? As couriers, it was well past time. But as Humans? As sentients in a general universal society?

"Goddammit," he whispered.

Grey Toliver found his friends sitting in the lab in quiet contemplation. He had walked by to grab some tools from his workshop, spotted them, turned back. His eyes flicked to the notes on Caesar's desk and then to the papers in Ark's hands. He took in the expressions on both men's faces.

"You catch him up?" he asked Caesar.

"Yeah."

"We're going to expose them, right?" Archimedes said. "Whoever made this?"

The words came out of him slow, like he didn't want to do it, like he was fighting for any reason not to do it. Grey knew him better than that.

"We don't even know where to start," Caesar said.

"Sure we do," Grey said. "The planet I circled. The soil sample is the giveaway. That's the only element that doesn't match any other place. Right?"

"What planet?" Archimedes asked. He began looking through the lists again, scanning the notes.

"It doesn't matter, because I can't find any record of it," Caesar asked. "The soil sample was unique, but maybe it was just tainted by all the other random shit that's been plugged into this thing."

"Vyroan?" Archimedes said suddenly, holding one of the pages up with the circled name facing his friends. He had spoken in surprise, and his voice cracked. "This is the planet you found soil from? You're sure."

Caesar and Grey stared at him.

"Of course you're not going to find anything about it," Archimedes continued. "Every record was supposed to be scrubbed after the Rostal Insurrection and the Elta Pentembra War. Vyroan was the single largest source of pantrillium ever located in the universe. There were concerns about one government gaining control of it, or even one civilian with the right resources, and it led to a lot of…" He trailed off, suddenly conscious of the looks his friends were giving him. "What?"

Caesar and Grey looked at each other, then back to him.

"You're messing with us, right?" Caesar asked.

Archimedes grinned, bemused. "No. Why would I be? I only know about this because one of my professors let it slip once during a lecture. Do you guys not remember what I was going to university for?"

Caesar and Grey looked at each other again. Archimedes' grin faded.

"Seriously?"

Grey cleared his throat. "Look, man, you never really talked about it. You always said you were going to jet off to be rich and popular in the poli circles while I broke my back in a second-hand shop and Caesar got dusty, or crusty, whatever it is you said, in a lab somewhere. You never really talked about school. Frankly, we're surprised you graduated."

"*You're* surprised I graduated?" Archimedes crowed. "*You?*"

Caesar shifted uncomfortably in his chair. "I think we're getting off topic here."

"Astropolitics, astrocartography," Archimedes said, ticking the subjects off on his fingers, "history of universal commerce, history of universal conflict." He stood up, his anger rising with him. "I have two bachelor's and an associate degree, you thick oaf. Do you even know how many goddamn languages I speak?"

"All that, and you're stuck on the same ship as us," Grey said, "with half the usefulness."

Archimedes stepped toward Grey with clenched fists, but Caesar was faster. He shot to his feet and shoved Ark back down into the chair opposite him. The chair rocked back, teetered, settled. Grey smirked until Caesar smacked him hard across the back of his head.

"You're both being ridiculous," Caesar snapped. To Grey, he said, "Ark is the only one here who apparently knows anything about Vyroan." Then, after a moment's consideration, he said to Archimedes, "But you said your professor only let the name slip."

Archimedes was slow to respond. He said, "Do you remember the two weeks I spent in jail during second year?"

"For sleeping with the dean's wife?"

"Is that what I told you?" Archimedes asked, snickering. "Why would I get arrested for that? No, man, I got arrested for sneaking into a government institution. Specifically, a restricted library database. The professor seemed flustered after he realized he'd mentioned Vyroan and got even more so when I asked him about it after class. He wasn't giving me anything, so I went to the public library. Found a whole lot of nothing, like you guys did. I thought that was weird, so…" He shrugged. "I didn't find out much more than what I mentioned: some mining operations were set up there to stock up on pantrillium. Everyone realized it was essentially a planet-sized bomb factory, a couple major conflicts were fought about it, and everyone collectively decided that it was best left alone and forgotten about. That's about all I found out before I got arrested. I doubt you'll find anything else out unless you do what I did, which… you know, good luck. Otherwise the only way you'd be able to find the planet would probably be getting your hands on an old astrocartographer's map."

"Maybe a smuggler's map," Grey mused.

"Not much to smuggle, I'd imagine."

"The pantrillium would be enough. Either way, a map like that would be black market material. No respectable auction house is going to be putting up a map with a government secret on it. That's a good way to get raided."

Caesar fixed Grey with a curious look. A moment later, the same thought crossed Archimedes' mind. A slow, wondrous smile formed on his face.

"What's wrong with you?" Grey asked when he noticed their attention. "Why are you staring at me now?"

"Didn't you say you had a friend on Dephros?" Caesar asked.

Grey closed his eyes and gave a long, long sigh.

"Let me make a call."

Goodbyes aboard the *Imagination* were in short order the following morning. Archimedes and Grey took a brief break from the ship after waking and showering to say goodbye to the kitchen staff and the engineering crew respectively. Professor Eppleheim and Koko Noal stopped by the docking bay to wish Caesar well and to remind him that he would always be welcome back. Koko and Archimedes gave each other a smile and nothing more. The rest of the IRSC vessel went on working as normal, the excitement of having unexpected civilians onboard having long worn off.

Farewells given, Caesar slipped into the *Searcher*'s galley to prepare breakfast while the final diagnostic checks took place. From the cockpit, Archimedes ran through system functionality and pressure checks. Grey cycled the engines, the thrust drive, and the stabilizer from the engine bay, finding the readings optimal. He joined Archimedes in the cockpit afterward and patched through to the *Imagination*'s bridge to get clearance to take off from the docking bay. The bridge conferred with the workers in the bay, then came back with an affirmative.

Archimedes engaged the *Searcher*'s thrusters and carefully navigated the ship from the back of the docking bay while engineers and crew members helped clear the way and direct him. Moments later they passed through the gravity field into the great black canopy of space. The *Imagination* stayed floating behind them, a blue and silver behemoth. Astrakoth stretched below them. Grey looked down at the planet through the new viewport and then checked their data display in the console; their month aboard the IRSC vessel had seen them transported to the opposite of Astrakoth from where they had crashed.

"Good riddance," Grey muttered.

"I'm saying," Archimedes said, meaning something different. "People sign up for ships like that. I still can't believe it. Full tours, willingly, and here just a taste of it nearly killed me with boredom."

"Yeah, well," Grey said, "we're headed to Dephros now, bud. Boredom won't kill you, but I'm sure there's plenty else itching to give it a shot."

Chapter Eleven

Blood In the Water

Thorus, like most major capitals, was the largest city on its planet and so consisted of a great many bustling parts comprising its whole. There were poli centers and offices, including the Parliament of Universal Interest where the majority of legal and extralegal Human business and sociopolitical action took place. Most of the upper-class residences in the city were located nearby, housing Councilmembers, magnates and industrialists, and all but the most secluded or eccentric artists, actors, and sports icons. Thorus had its shopping districts, of course, separated into even more specific categories: technology, jewelry, clothing and so forth. Arenas and playing fields separated the commercial districts from the residential districts, and monetary divides further separated the residential neighborhoods, from the upper middle-class Golden Hills all the way down to a series of slums, the best of which could be described as, 'Not too bad, but I'd stay in after dark.'

Euphrates Destidante wasn't native to Thorus. Not even the planet, really, although he had long reached a point where he had spent more of his life on Salix than off it. His father had taken on a contract with a small commercial shipping business when Euphrates was in his early teens, relocating them from a small town on Agnimon.

He had taken to the city immediately, finding opportunities for an enterprising young man around every corner and connections across every race. As his father's contract grew less and less profitable and his father more and more drunk, it was Euphrates who discovered new ways to make the money needed to keep them afloat. The years passed, and his opportunities and connected had spread into a complex universal network.

Still, he found the bulk of his work—personal, professional, and unsavory—could be handled right here at home in Thorus.

Like, for example, the work that took him down to the Swallows. Officially, the area was ten full blocks starting somewhere around Delta Avenue and ending roughly around Aurine Street, but everyone knew it as the patch of territory that swallowed the people the rest of the city chewed up, spat out, and forgot about. At night the streets would be lit up by trash can fires and filthy yellow street bulbs crowded with moths. By day it was more or less a barter town. People unrolled blankets full of knock-off products or set up folding tables to display stolen goods. Rusty grills and hot panels were rolled out to cook food that was as delicious as it was unsanitary. What legitimate shops did still exist rolled down metal slats over their doors at night and kept bars in their windows. Most homes did the same.

Euphrates stepped lightly through the crowded streets, moving around collapsible stalls and taking care not to bump into anyone. He was dressed plainly, a light brown cardigan and black pants that looked modest but still cost more than some of these people would see in a year. He finally spotted the store he was looking for—tucked between a bicycle shop and a butchery selling any number of mystery meats—and went in. The sign above the door read "Hidden Treasures" in Trader.

The inside of the shop was packed floor to ceiling with junk. Cheap and broken electronics spilled over from their shelves to create uneven piles. Children's toys had their own corner, pieces missing and their paint half-peeled off. A handful of open toolboxes were lined up against one wall, while more tools hung from hooks in the wall above them. A small plastic storage bin sat nearby with nuts, bolts, screws, and nails separated in separate drawers. At the back of the shop was a register. A young, red-haired boy with pockmarked cheeks stood behind the counter working on an old radio. Three other radios of similar make and model sat on the counter to his left.

"Good afternoon," Euphrates said as he edged toward the back. He glanced at the wall just past the cashier. It was a chain link barricade terminating in an electronically locked door. A number of crates were stacked against the wall beyond it, no doubt containing more miscellany. A narrow hallway twisted around out of sight.

"What can I do for you?" the kid asked. He didn't look up, focusing instead on a panel on the back of the radio that was proving difficult to remove.

"I'm here to see Raygor Stahl."

"Don't know no Raygor Stahl, pal. Sorry."

"Mm."

Euphrates stepped up close to the counter, running a finger over one of the radios, then looking at the thin coat of dust he took away from it. The cashier paused to glare at him.

"I find that unlikely," Euphrates said, "seeing as he's the one that pays you. He *does* pay you, doesn't he? You never know in the Swallows."

The cashier set the radio down but kept a hold of the screwdriver. "Look, man, why don't you buy something or get out? I'm sure you've got something more important to do than hassle me about how I get my money."

"I do. Specifically, speaking with Raygor, so if you wouldn't mind…"

Before the kid could say anything else, a small black speaker box in the upper corner of the room crackled to life. "Huxous, please stop arguing with the most important Human in the galaxy, and let him into the back, would you?" it said.

The kid, Huxous, scowled and reached under the counter. A loud buzzing sound came from the door as the electronic lock folded back.

"Much obliged," Euphrates said. He pushed through the door into the cluttered corridor, Huxous sealing it again behind him. He turned a corner, down the hall, and eventually found himself walking into a small office.

Three video monitors were built into one wall, two of them showing different angles of the store interior while the third was focused on the area just outside. Another wall held a set of shelves, each one filled with crystalline figures of all colors. They were each a different kind of animal, a display of life from several different planets across a number of star systems. They were beautiful, out of place in the drab room.

More fitting was Raygor Stahl. The fat Lodite was reclined behind his desk, belly poking out from beneath a white sleeveless shirt. His pale green trunk was curled in frustration over his top lip while he worked at a cobalt sphere covered in long divots. His twelve spindly fingers twisted segments of the sphere left and right, moved them up and down where they expanded or constricted as needed to keep a perfect shape.

"It's a Murasi pentasphere puzzle," Raygor said without looking up. "You have to move the pieces around, matching pathways until the maze is completed. Once that's done the thing pops in half to reveal a smaller, trickier one. The centermost holds a blue diamond as a prize."

"What number sphere is that?" Euphrates asked. He shut the office door and took a seat.

"Only the second. The damnable things are difficult."

"You could always just pry it open with something and retrieve the diamond. Put it back correctly afterward. No one would ever know."

Raygor grunted. "For all your great qualities, Destidante, you lack finesse. Besides, *I* would know, and it would bother me. Enough things bother me already without adding to the fuckin' pile." He twisted the sphere a few more times, gave up, and set the puzzle on his desk. "Anyway. Forgive the kid. He knows who you are, I'm sure, but not *who* you are, although being an Advisor should really be enough. He's got bigger stones than brains."

"It's fine," Euphrates said, dismissing it. "Does he know who *you* are?"

"The guy who pays his bills, didn't you hear? Most folks stop asking questions once their pockets start filling up." Raygor laced his fingers over his stomach. "What brings you to my little hole-in-the-wall, Euphrates? Not that I don't enjoy seeing you, but a man of your status risks a great deal coming on down to the Swallows."

"I'm not particularly concerned about my safety."

The Lodite chuckled. "I expect not. You've probably got some kind of posthumous vengeance contract arranged in the event of your untimely death, and a half-dozen more arranged with other freeguns in case the first one tries to take the money and run. Something complicated like that, right? You fancy yourself a practical man, but for as long as I've known you, you've had a flair for the dramatic the instant anyone really pisses you off."

"You know," Euphrates mused, "I've always thought that for an occupation with 'free' in the name, mercenaries tend to come pretty costly."

"They call themselves that because they're free spirits. Not beholden to anyone."

"I know why they call themselves that. I still think it's idiotic. The minute you agree to a contract, you're beholden to someone." He reached into his jacket pocket and removed two items, setting them on the desk. The first was the data drive Jeth Serrano had retrieved. The second was an immaculately sculpted crystal figurine of a four-eared felid ready to pounce.

Raygor picked up the figurine in his long, thin fingers and turned it over. Even in the dim light of the office the facets glittered.

"It's a Direxian devilcat," Euphrates said.

"I know. I have one in blue that lays on its back. It's adorable." Raygor set the piece down gingerly next to the puzzle sphere. "Thank you very much. And now that you're done flattering me," he said, patting the data drive, "this is why you're really here."

"It is. I need you to decrypt it, and I need an extra copy made."

"There are a thousand shady people you could go to for a fraction of my cost. Why are you here?"

"Because you do have finesse," Euphrates said, smiling. "And discretion. I'm unsure what kind of protections might be on there, but I need the information to be recovered in full. Additionally, the nature of the information is such that I don't trust in the hands of anyone, ah, lesser."

"But you trust me," Raygor laughed.

"I trust you to do what's best for you."

The Lodite considered that. He reached out and touched the drive with his fingers, sliding it around the desk. "You know what's on here?" he asked.

"I have some suspicions. I just want the confirmation and the proof."

"*You* need the proof, you mean. You specifically, which is why you came to me. So if it's something like that, you know the arrangement."

Euphrates relaxed in his seat. "I'm willing to pay what it takes for you to sit on it for three weeks, and whatever it takes if I decided to release it myself."

"One week," Raygor countered.

"Fifteen days from the date you return the information to me. Then, if I don't need to handle it myself, you can sell the information. I'll throw in a favor as well, to be named at a time of your choosing."

"Deal," Raygor said. He slipped the drive off his desk and out of sight. "But only because you brought me the devilcat."

Euphrates steepled his fingers and smiled.

*****

It took less time than Talys expected to track Euphrates' movement from Thorus, but it turned out he hadn't gone very far at all: Galos, on the planet Agnimon, staying in the Agapetos system. It was a decent enough city with plenty of respectable establishments, but Talys didn't think Euphrates would have gone to such lengths to hide his activities if it was respectable he was going for. To find out had taken a few thousand chits, mostly slipped into the hands of the local law enforcement and business owners in exchange for their silence and a good look at their security cameras. Four men had exited the ship Euphrates had allegedly commissioned, all wearing technology that scrambled their digital appearances. Another thousand chits went into retracing their journeys through the city, greasing the palms of potential witnesses: sailors, fishmongers, business owners, and a feisty drunk who kept a well-maintained tent in a wide alley nicknamed Snow Daisy Row for the white walls that framed it.

Snow Daisy Row, which faced the Reishus Sea, just two blocks from the Ruby Swell.

The doors to the Swell opened at sunset, letting a happy and anxious stream of patrons in. The first twenty got their free drink, the rest paid their cover, and Talys waited for a couple hours across the street, enjoying the sight of the smooth waters and what seemed like an all-too-rare moment of tranquility in his life.

When he bored of it, he headed for the strip club. A quick and quiet word saw him bypass the line without fanfare, and a minute later he was seated comfortably at the bar, taking in the scantily clad spectacles gracing the stage. The bartender finished wiping down a glass and came to greet him. There was a moment of hesitation when he saw Talys, trying to place his face, then shock as he recognized him.

"Advisor!" he said, not quite sure what to do with himself. "What, uh… what are you doing here?"

"I've come for a pleasant distraction. Much like I imagine most people here have."

"But… but sir, this place, it ain't the kind of place for you."

"On the contrary, I can think of no more perfect place at the moment. The proprietor, his name's Hewitt?"

The bartender nodded. "Yes, sir. Shelby Hewitt."

"He here?"

"He is, sir."

"Tell him I'm here," Talys said. "And only him. Tell him that I'd like a private audience." He slid a 200-chit marker across the bar. "And I'll take a beer. A Gentle River, if you've got any."

"Yes, sir. Right away."

The bartender stepped away to retrieve a light blue bottle from a small refrigerator, opened it, returned to set it in front of Talys, then stepped away again to find Shelby Hewitt. One of the serving girls took his place behind the bar, setting her money tray out of reach from customers. Talys tipped the beer back against his lips and took a sip. The golden liquid inside splashed against his tongue, sweet and silky, a gentle river. One of the girls on stage did a handstand and split her legs to either side, becoming a T. She lifted her head, caught sight of Talys watching her from the bar, and winked. He took another drink and tilted the bottle in her direction.

A pleasant distraction, indeed.

****

The call came in the late afternoon, after Euphrates had returned home. Nimbus had been in the middle of telling him about a surgery she had coming up that was set to be performed in front of a live gallery. It was a review of sorts, one that would determine her salary for the upcoming year, additional accreditations for her personal record, and that would put her one step closer to a spot on the Medical Board. Euphrates had offered to call in a couple favors to expedite the process. Nimbus responded by angrily pointing out that she had built her career up to that point by herself and that she had no intention of riding anyone's coattails to the finish line.

Euphrates, unaccustomed to so fully putting his foot in his mouth, found the sudden vibrating in his pocket a welcome excuse to crawl out of the hole he had dug.

"It's Speaker Volcott, my love," he said. "I've got to take this."

"That's convenient timing, considering we're talking about pulling strings and granting favors. Who expedited the process so that you could advise for both Speakers instead of just the one you were assigned to?"

It hasn't exactly been a kindness, he thought. "Would you like me to give him your greeting?"

She scowled and said, "I've got studying to do," and left him there in the kitchen. He watched her go, then took the buzzing phone back to the office where he could answer it securely.

"Destidante, where are you?" Volcott asked, when he realized the call had been picked up. "You should be here. You need to be here." The words were slurred and came in a rush. Rors sounded worried, which in turn worried Euphrates.

"You sound out of sorts, sir. Is everything alright?" Euphrates moved around his desk and unlocked one of the bottom drawers, thumbing through the files within.

"No. No, they very well aren't. Are not. And I would think my Advisor should be here with me and be just as concerned with me."

"Talys Wannigan is your Advisor," Euphrates gently reminded him. "I'm still assigned to Speaker Suvis."

He found the folder he was looking for, pulled it free, shut the drawer, and placed the file on the desk. He opened it to the front page and read the header: *A Comprehensive Ryxan-Human Resource Arrangement Report, Requested and Approved by Human Speaker Rors Volcott*. A bit wordy, even by Council document standards, but Euphrates had always found that the duller a document seemed, the less inclined anyone was to sift through the details. The Ryxan had, of course, and tensions between the two races were higher than ever, but full-blown war hadn't broken out.

Yet.

"Look," Rors was saying over and over. "Look, look. Look, Destidante, just look for a second. I'm not calling Wannigan, that dog-snake, that... how that man ever got voted..."

"Yes, sir. It's not an uncommon concern."

"Well, if it isn't uncommon, and you know about it, how about you get your ass over here?" Rors snapped.

Euphrates said nothing for a long time, knowing a proper silence would make him seem chastised. The Speaker was breathing heavily into the receiver, not quite drowning out the sound of his heavy shuffling across the carpet. He was pacing, agitated.

"Nimbus won't be happy," Euphrates said slowly. "She accepts that our jobs have certain responsibilities, but she's only just come home. Still, our stations must come first, I suppose. If we don't stand up, what lesser men would come in our stead, right?"

"Good. Very good."

"Besides, I was going over some old reports earlier today and found some that I had forgotten to have you sign. It's my fault that I didn't get these to you sooner, but between juggling the tasks assigned to me by Speaker Suvis and the additional tasks you've given me—"

"Destidante, if you want to air grievances, just bring the fucking papers over and you can complain here."

"Yes, sir, soon as I can."

Rors disconnected the call and Euphrates slipped the phone back into his pocket. He realized his hand was shaking. What was that? Fear?

No. Anticipation. The papers in front of him were just one part of a slowly closing noose. They matched the official report in the Universal Council records, the ones he had personally delivered, almost exactly but with one crucial difference. One that could still give him plausible deniability. It wasn't perfect, but too clean a case could be suspicious in its own right.

He used his index finger to delicately close the file folder.

For the most part, the perks that came with being a chosen representative for a species weren't public knowledge. Humans, ever and always focused on wealth and rank as indications of social importance, often took the liberty of flaunting their salaries and the concessions afforded them anyway, pleased with how it made them look.

Rors Volcott, soldier down to the marrow of his bones, was one of the exceptions. He took his paycheck without complaint but never took advantage of it. His home, for example, was large but conservative. He had no wife, no children, and so he had picked a building just big enough to fit his needs with a little extra room on top to breathe. Coarse stone, thick and gray, made up the structure. Blocks on blocks, it looked like a government base in miniature. The interior was equally spartan, each room minimally furnished and fastidiously kept clean. There was a study and a strategy room, a gym with an adjoining sauna. A guest room was set near the back, seldom used and even less enjoyed. The house was a clinical space built to the interests of one man, all it needed to be and nothing more.

Euphrates had opted to drive himself that night. It wasn't every day one of the Speakers demanded an audience. Rarer still that they would do so in obvious distress. With everything that had already happened, the fewer people involved in any new developments, the better. He parked his car just outside of Rors' garage, a three-vehicle storage monstrosity that looked like a mausoleum.

The Speaker met him at the door. He was wearing a sleeveless shirt made of white silk and a pair of black slacks secured around the waist by a silver belt. His lids were heavy, his eyes unfocused. Euphrates didn't need to be near him to smell the booze.

"Come in," Rors said, holding the door open with one hand. He flapped his other hand at the interior of the house. "Get in here."

Euphrates moved past him, the file folder clenched in both hands. He had only been inside the man's home a couple of times before, but he remembered where the living room was and headed there. Neutral ground. Two chairs that reclined. A couch to relax on. He saw a half-dozen empty cans of Oaken Cider—not quite illegal yet, but on the regulatory chopping block—crushed and turned over on the coffee table

"Just sit wherever," Rors said. "I'll get you a drink."

The Speaker moved one heavy leg in front of the other toward a bar built into the wall separating the living room from the kitchen. Euphrates did a quick scan of the living room, saw nobody else, gave a quick glance back at the entryway and saw no eyes peeking out anywhere, heard no shuffling footsteps. As Rors took deliberate, intoxicated time to manipulate his liquor bottles into a position where he could pour without spilling anything, Euphrates decided they were well and truly alone.

But maybe still recording? Taping?

He took a seat on the couch and opened the folder, shuffling the papers until the pages needing signatures were on top. "Before we get into anything else, could you please sign these? It really is important that I get these filed as soon as possible."

"What are they?"

"They're the reports from the presentation we gave to the Council. The one regarding the Ryxan's celaron embargo."

"That was over a month ago," Rors said. He stepped back into the living room and set a glass full of plum-colored liquor in front of Euphrates. He kept one of his own tucked close against his chest. "What have you been doing all this time if not getting this shit done?"

"A truly shocking amount of running around, sir. Apologies for losing track of this in the meantime."

Euphrates pushed the papers across the coffee table so that the signature lines faced the Speaker and set a silver pen on top of them. Rors leaned over to look at them, nearly fell forward onto the table, caught himself with his free hand. A small splash of liquor rolled over the lip of his glass and hit the table, not quite touching the paper. Rors' eyes narrowed as he tried to make sense of the documents. He gave up a moment later, picked up the pen and scrawled an approximation of his name across the lines. When he was finished, Euphrates took the pen back and tucked it away. The papers were shuffled back into order, slipped into the folder, the folder itself closed and set aside.

Euphrates leaned back into the couch and left his drink untouched. Rors seemed not to notice, focused instead on pacing back and forth across the living room, relentlessly drinking until his glass was empty. He returned to the bar for a refill, then resumed the cycle all over again. His eyes had grown red, his hair disheveled. His movements were sluggish. All the same, he cut an imposing figure. Euphrates almost admired him.

Breaking into the visible arena of politics from a life of crime hadn't been terribly difficult for Euphrates—polis were people like any other and subject to the same flaws and vices as your average citizen—but he had built a criminal network of titanic proportions because he was careful and because he made sure to know more than anyone else in the room. To that end he focused minimally on platforms to preach from and more on discovering every piece of information he could about even the least influential poli on the spectrum. He figured out which judges could be bought, blackmailed, or beaten into submission. He figured out which Councilmembers were devout believers in the law and which would bend over backwards looking for any obscure loophole they could use to exploit the system.

Inch by inch Euphrates worked his way into the scene. Over the next near-decade his security measures and firewalls protected his extensive history of underworld activity from being directly traced back to him. A handful of trusted contractors, like Jeth Serrano, helped patch any holes before they became leaks. His outward appearance and reputation were that of an independently wealthy investor in tech expansion. His access to digital development companies, cutting edge security experts, computer enhancers and more provided a perfectly legitimate excuse for his money, his connections, and the tech he had access to both at work and in his home. His access to money no one could prove he had and contacts no one else would want helped provide a smooth transition into the upper-class movers and shakers. It wasn't seamless, of course. He sparked a lot of rivalries, even earned a few enemies, but his alliances became countless, built on respect and more than a little fear.

He rose near the top, and that was when he reached his first true frustration: Rors Volcott. He had done some acting when he was a student, then became an infantryman right out of school. Both paths were breeding grounds for controversy: drugs, infidelity, prostitution, abuse, murder, even war crimes. And yet he was clean outside a few minor misdemeanors in his youth. Nothing remotely controversial. Nothing ruinous. Nothing there to exploit the charismatic, commanding presence that rose through the ranks due to his keen mind.

Recognizing that there was only danger in staying close to someone like Rors, Euphrates switched to lobbying for Magga Suvis' Advisor position, opened up after the previous holder had suffered a sudden fatal aneurysm. Magga was almost as untouchable as Rors, but she was a kindred spirit: manipulative, cautious, ruthless and connected. When she threw his support behind him to get him the votes he needed, he suspected she had seen the same in him.

Rors, meanwhile, had become saddled with Talys Wannigan. Another cipher, top to bottom. Euphrates didn't think Talys was traditionally brilliant, but he was shrewd and adaptive. A survivor. There was talk that he had served as well, in some kind of intelligence capacity, but Euphrates had as yet been unable to find any records of that time. Talys seemed a natural fit for Rors due to their shared service history, but their personalities had never meshed, and Rors had become increasingly paranoid of and less reliant on him as time went by.

Of course, Talys' personality doesn't really mesh with anyone, Euphrates thought, *and there was what Magga said about him blackmailing his way into the votes he needed.* Had the other Advisor found out something that Euphrates hadn't? A worrying thought.

Either way, Euphrates had found himself in a unique position: being relied upon by the two most powerful Humans in the universe, both seemingly untouchable, and subtly at odds with each other. A challenge, sometimes infuriating, but not without its opportunities.

"Rors," he said softly. "Why have you called me here?"

The big man stopped, swayed in place for a moment, fixed Euphrates with his bloodshot eyes. For a moment it looked like he was planning on dropping down onto the couch next to him, but he switched tracks and slumped into one of the recliners instead, whatever strength that had been holding him up seeping now into the seat cushions. Some of the liquor jumped from his glass again, this time landing on the arm of the chair. Rors spent a furious minute trying to wipe it off the leather but only succeeded in moving the liquid to the floor.

"These fuckin' Ryxan," he muttered. The words were so hushed that Euphrates almost didn't realize he had spoken. "Now they're trying to pick a bigger fight, spread some blood. I'm trying. It shouldn't have gotten this far, I've been trying, and you're the only one. You're the one knows what needs to be done. What the needs of the Human race are, and how to... how to do it."

Euphrates felt a chill run up his arms.

"They're powerful," Rors continued. "No doubt about that. None. Nobody would say they, that they're not. Big. Strong fuckers, too, of course. Of course. But they're petty. Vin… ah, what's the, vindictive. That's it. Vindictive. With their oil and their trade, their other trades. Imports and exports. They're a danger, Euphrates. Rolling over the Humans with the celaron. What's next? Food? Building stuff, materials? Weapons? When do they start moving in on our territories, our homes? When do they start… when do we get wiped out? Who's next to do what they do?"

The Speaker had been staring at a spot on the wall next to the fireplace, lifting his glass halfway to his lips and then back down again as new thoughts came to him. He turned and looked at Euphrates, mouth slack from intoxication. He lifted an index finger, and the ceiling lights caught a thin white scar there, running vertically from the tip of his finger down to the second knuckle. There was likely a story behind it, but Euphrates wasn't going to interrupt his tangent to ask.

"A lesson," Rors said. "A *lesson*! That's what needs, what we need to be done. What I *planned* on doing. What do they say about best intentions?"

Euphrates watched him, morbidly fascinated, waited for him to finish the thought.

"Destidante!" Rors barked instead. "What do they say?"

"Uh… I think the phrase runs along the lines of the road to Hell being paved with good intentions, Speaker."

"*Best* intentions. That's what it is, what I tried to do. Put a stop to them. Put a stop to them for good, before they could snuff us out. Show the rest of the Council that Humans belong among them, and we get… what *everyone* gets. YOU DON'T CUT US OUT!"

Euphrates hadn't realized exactly how quiet the house was, how empty it felt, until Rors' booming declaration. He wasn't afraid for his own safety, but he had misjudged how deeply the Speaker's hatred and resolve ran. Not for the first time, he considered the potential ramifications the past month's dealings would have for the Human race. Rors seemed to be so fixated on outside threats that he didn't realize he had become a threat himself.

"What did you do?" Euphrates asked.

Rors mumbled something under his breath. He was rapidly losing any sort of coherency, which seemed to have been the goal all along. The hand holding his glass slipped and the drink nearly upended in his lap. He caught it, held it aloft in front of his chest, tipped it back and drank the rest of it.

"Made a deal," he said. "A deal for help. A deal with people, but people, they always know how to not do it. Do things right, I mean, and now I don't know where… now it's gone. It's missing. Should've gone to you. You know what to do, Destante. Destin… Euphrates. You know. You know what's best for Humans. Above all. Everything else doesn't matter. We matter. I was just trying to win and protect us."

Like his legs, the rest of his body had grown heavier. His arm slipped back onto the arm of the chair. His fingers relaxed and the glass tumbled from them to the carpet, rolled to rest against the side of his foot. His head sank until his chin was pressed against his chest. His eyelids closed, fluttered halfway open, closed again and gave up their battle. There was a cemetery stillness for a long moment. Euphrates watched him, wondering if the poli had truly lost all hopes and decided to end it. He was grateful he hadn't touched his own drink.

Then the snoring started, and any thoughts of poison faded away.

Euphrates gathered the folder into his hands and stood. He studied the unconscious Speaker, respected him, pitied him for a few breaths, then silently cursed him for putting the Human race in a precarious situation. He walked over and bent down, setting Rors' glass upright and to the side of the chair, away from any fidgeting the man might do in the middle of the night.

He briefly considered murdering the Speaker.

Euphrates left instead, locking the door behind him. The hum of his car as he started was a welcome break in the silence. He set the file folder on the passenger seat, adjusted his rearview mirror, and drove home.

__Chapter Twelve__

Bandit Moon

Tui-san.

A gas giant known for its stunning pastel pink and green coloration, its turbulent atmosphere, and for the swirling vortex at its north pole originally called the Silver Toilet, later renamed Kam's Funnel after the first poor bastard that tried to fly into it. The storm contained a whirlwind of jagged shards, what would be an enticing target for treasure hunters if the speed and ferocity at which the shards were whipped around didn't send them ripping through ship hulls and retrieval equipment like paper. A few lucky souls had succeeded in coming away with a haul over the years, but the expeditions were so traumatizing—either on an investment level or in the degree of personal danger involved, sometimes both—that the "funnel rich" typically lived out the rest of their lives quietly wealthy instead of boastfully as might be expected.

Still, the allure of the storm brought in people from across the universe, most of whom settled on Dephros, Tui-san's largest habitable moon. It was prospectors at first, the majority of which quickly realized that Kam's Funnel was a death trap. Their interest transitioned from the diamond shards in the vortex to looking for any precious gems or minerals that may have been cast off from the planet to the moons around it. Investors and intellectuals moved in next, funding expeditions and founding small institutions of science and research. Dephros was still mostly green then, save for a short desert that connected the moon's two large lakes (Lucent Shallows to the east, Nearly Young to the west).

But with all the talk of diamonds and the potential for riches, it was only a matter of time before the wrong crowds started paying attention. When they came, they came in droves. By the time they figured out there wasn't much more value to the moon than the money and businesses that had been brought to it from outside, the mentality had shifted from plundering to settling. Not right away mind you—they pickpocketed, burgled, and outright robbed everything and everyone they could, first—but you know, eventually. When that time came, the shops were repurposed, and the houses that had been built gained new tenants. When all of those were full, new houses, shacks, and tent cities were pieced together on whatever spare land was available. They even settled out in the desert, under the shade of tarps hung from half-buried scrap metal. Even on the lakes, atop man-made rafts until junk and other debris started piling up from the lake bottoms, and then people camped out on the islands of dirt and trash that emerged.

The original settlers who survived the incursion (and the families of those who didn't) began hiring freeguns to try and regain their lands. Failing that, they tried to get back the money invested in any businesses or real estate. When *that* failed galactic authorities got involved. Then the Universal Council itself. The smugglers and crooks were driven away for a time but surveilling a moon with no inherent value or resources was an unsustainable expense. The greens of the land had turned muddy and yellow. The blues of the lakes had turned murky and black. Eventually the Council relinquished control of the moon to anyone willing to live there, in full view of a planet with an inaccessible fortune.

Those people returned, the fugitives and outlaws, the thieves and killers, the maniacs and heistmen, sociopaths and psychopaths. A hundred thousand assorted villains were permanent residents on the moon. Twice that were regular visitors. Twice again first-and-second timers, people needing to lay low for a bit, people needing to buy something that couldn't be found in shops of positive repute, or to find something that had been lost (read: most definitely stolen).

Enter the *Sol Searcher*.

"Hey," Archimedes said. He stepped up into the cockpit, peered out through the viewport at the moon, then sat down in the co-pilot's seat. He wriggled around a moment, gave the armrests a couple of firm squeezes. The new seats were taking some getting used to, but they were a damn sight more cozy than the chairs the ship had come with.

Grey gave his friend a small nod, tried to ignore him otherwise. He gave up after a few awkward seconds and leaned back from the controls. His jaw was sore from the nervous clenching and unclenching it had been doing for the past hour. "Hey. Caesar?"

"Trying to dirty up his clothes, I think. Mess up his hair some, more than it usually is. He's worried about sticking out like a sore thumb."

"Tell him to quit it. These guys are going to spot him a mile off anyway, and they'll probably get more pissed at him for trying to be something he isn't than they would if he just looked like the mark he is."

"I did tell him, but he was insistent. You know how he is when he gets all panicky. I'll tell him again before we disembark."

Archimedes studied the readings on the screen. Grey had done a decent enough job piecing back together the dashboard controls and the infomonitor from what materials the *Imagination* had provided. The *Searcher*'s individual access to the universal network combined with the ACG database allowed them to pull up a detailed image of Dephros along with a number of related information files. Most of the files contained things they already knew, facts about the environment, the population, the history, but there was a healthy amount of conjecture, too, mostly in regard to the more infamous residents and the moon's main 'imports and exports'.

"I can tell you, Grey, I'm not feeling super comfortable landing here with just the three guns between us."

"That's one gun for each of us. I mean, Caesar's pretty much useless with a firearm, but you're a good shot."

"You going to fit him with another bomb?"

Grey's brows went up, as did the corners of his mouth. "Should I?"

"I don't think you should have armed him with the first one, if we're being honest."

"It worked out, didn't it? Saved his bacon."

Archimedes snorted and rubbed at his earlobe, scratching an itch. "It almost turned him *into* bacon. Give him another knife or something. Granted, he did nothing with the one you gave him the last time, but maybe there's a… stabbing learning curve or something."

They both smiled at that, both turned away from each other to look back at the moon. They were nearing its atmosphere, and Grey began pushing buttons and flipping switches across the control center to prepare for entry. Archimedes read the data output for the ship and found himself pleased. They had operated so long without a reliable stabilizer that he had forgotten what kind of difference it could make for the ship.

"Are you excited to see her again?" Archimedes asked.

Grey cocked his head to the right, then to the left, thinking. He chewed at the inside of his lower lip. "When you were about to pick a fight with what's-her-name's boyfriend back on the *Imagination* and you knew you had to get your ass kicked in order for the plan to work? It feels a lot like that."

"So, thrilling? Like you've come alive again?"

"There's something seriously wrong with you, Carnahan," Grey said, looking sideways at his friend. "You know most people don't like getting punched in the face, right? And let's be clear:

she and I did not end on good terms. It's not long we're going to be running into each other's arms across a field of roses. Don't forget your gun."

Archimedes toggled down the thrust drive, checked the readings one more time. Satisfied, he pulled himself up and out of the chair so he could check on Caesar before they landed. "You'd really shoot an ex-girlfriend, huh? Pretty cold."

"Well, I'm hoping you'd do it if I end up getting in trouble. That would take the weight off my shoulders. But if it were her or me? If it came down to it?" Grey nodded. "I'd at least wing her. For old time's sake."

Though the landing pad was large, it was crowded to a nearly unnavigable degree. In addition to the regular assortment of stopovers and short-term visitors, several more spacecraft were derelict or near-enough as not to matter. Their hulls were weatherworn and in varying states of disrepair. Viewports were cracked or missing entirely, the open spaces loosely protected from the wind and rain by sheets and curtains, boards, or thick films. Some crafts had broken or missing landing gear and rested flat on the pad or listed queasily to one side. Fifty people or more were milling about between the spaceships, drinking, fighting, moving to and from a half-dozen bedrolls set up underneath the ships. The entire thing looked halfway to a homeless shelter and Grey had needed Archimedes to help him land without clipping some bootlegger or counterfeiter drunkenly staggering about.

Once they had landed and secured their ignition keys, the crew of the *Searcher* took some time to get their gear together and go over their plan, loose as it was. Grey took the shotgun and slung it across his back in a loose rig he had pieced together with some spare leather laying about in his workshop. Archimedes slipped one of the handguns into a thigh holster and had helped Caesar fix a holster at his waist for the other gun. Nearly a dozen blades had been pulled together for Caesar to choose from. He picked the same knife he had carried on Astrakoth, tucking it into a sheath on the other hip. He grabbed a paring knife as well, slipping it into his boot.

"For emergencies," he said, and his friends laughed.

They departed the *Searcher* side by side, into the hot, thick air. It reeked of cigarette smoke, making Caesar's eyes water and, busy rubbing the tears away, he missed the approach of a large, bovine Dyr. The alien's one dark brown eye was fixed on Grey. The other, a bright blue stone, stared at nothing. His meaty four-fingered hands were a network of pale scars, both tugging at the tattered, oil-stained shirt he wore.

"You boys down here on business?" he asked.

"Excuse me?" Archimedes replied in Dyrian. In Trader, he snapped, "Grey, close the ramp." First impressions were important, and Ark could tell Dephros was a place that held to that idea a bit tighter than most. He stepped up to the Dyr and looked him up and down slowly, unimpressed, and spat off to the side. In Dyrian again, he said, "We've got business, sure, but it ain't none of yours."

"Bold of you lot to deliver here, of all places," the alien said, switching to his native language. "I thought the moon was off limits to ACG."

"What do you mean, delivering? Are you high?"

The Dyr pointed a stubby finger at the *Searcher*. "That's a courier tag on the side there, ain't it? You saying you ain't couriers?"

Behind Archimedes, Grey triggered the ramp mechanism with a small device attached to his ignition key, sealing the ship once more. Caesar was crowding him, nervous and fidgeting, his hand on his own belt and inching closer to the knife.

"He's saying something about the tags," Caesar whispered. "You probably should have waited to paint the logos back on."

"I can speak Dyrian," Grey whispered back. "And you might have mentioned that before we took off."

"You had already painted it on by the time I saw it. I didn't think you would want to scrape it off again just to do the job all over down the line."

Grey looked at his friend, annoyance writ in the corner of his eyes. "What are you talking about, Anada? Working on the ship is literally the only thing I enjoy doing."

"Well, and fighting."

"And fighting."

"And drinking."

"Will you shut up and let Ark figure this out?"

The small stand-off had started to attract attention, small groups of people as curious about the newcomers as they were bored with the day. They inched in, eager to see if any violence would break out.

"No, we ain't couriers," Archimedes said. "What kind of dead-end, no-pay, dumb-fuck job…" He jerked a thumb over his shoulder. "We jacked the damn thing. Going to get it chopped over on Peloclade."

"This is just a pit stop," Grey barked in Dyrian from behind him.

"That's right!" Archimedes said. "Got a few meetings, setting up some work for later. Looking for a drink that might goddamn blind me. But again: that ain't none of yer fuckin' business, is it?"

The Dyr stared up at the spacecraft thoughtfully, scratching at his snout. "Looks pretty new."

"I'm not going to sell a piece of garbage, am I?"

"You could sell it to me instead. Save you a trip to Peloclade."

Archimedes rolled his eyes. "Look, I already got an arrangement with a guy I know and halfway kinda trust. No offense to you, cow-face, but you just showed up here and started eye-banging my meal ticket, keeping me and mine from moving on with our day. I ain't selling, and since I ain't selling, you got no further reason for jawing at me. Are you going to get out of our way, or am I going to have to kick your ass up and down this landing pad?"

The Dyr narrowed his good eye. The socket with the stone stayed wide open. "You think you can?"

"You think I won't?" Archimedes held his hands out to either side, flexed them open, closed them tight into fists. Motion on the landing pad stopped, people now fully invested in the exchange. Grey and Caesar held their breaths, the latter now tightly gripping the hilt of his knife.

Then the Dyr laughed, a booming thing that eventually settled into a broad grin full of blocky yellow teeth. "You boys are alright. Welcome to Dephros. You been here before? Need help getting where yer going?"

"We've been," Archimedes said, switching back to Trader. "Never long enough to get comfortable." He glanced back over his shoulder, flashing a quick wink at his friends. "Grey, what's the name of the place we're looking for?"

"A bar called Crater," Grey said, never taking his eyes off the alien.

Archimedes turned back to the Dyr and grinned. "Right, then. Where do we find a shithole called the Crater?"

It was a twenty-minute walk from the landing pad to the rendezvous point. The Dyr (Aester Togg, as he had introduced himself) escorted them most of the way solo, after he offered and the *Searcher* crew accepted. Caesar and Archimedes kept their weapons near at hand, and Grey was tense throughout the journey, but their caution seemed unwarranted. Togg was less interested in leading them into an ambush than he was providing an impromptu history lesson on the buildings and businesses they passed by.

The Crater, for example, was one of the oldest establishments on the moon. It had started out as a farm built inside a collapsible habitat with artificial soil and hydrocollectors, all devised to provide nutrient-rich food for the earnest early settlers. But as the population on Dephros increased so did the prevalence of imported supplies. Time passed. The farm was eventually deemed an outdated concept, a minor success but largely irrelevant. It was abandoned in the face of commerce, the module stripped of its most important parts, leaving little more than a frame.

In a controversial decision the building was eventually rebuilt from the inside out into a humble church, a singular structure meant to provide a quiet place of reflection for faiths of all kinds on a moon that was more and more focused on science, culture, and greed. The concept was ignored at first, scoffed at as it grew closer to completion, then largely ignored again. People did filter in and out, occasionally for prayers or to look for guidance, more often just for a few moments of peace and quiet, but it never sparked any pious movements of note nor did it build a stable congregation. The society of Dephros began eroding into bald-faced illegality. While the business and homes were repurposed, closed, built and torn down, remodeled and reopened, the church alone remained untouched. It only became emptier and emptier until it became a ghost instead of the skeleton it was before.

And then, as only the best churches do, it became a bar.

The Hollowells—triplet brothers rumored to be from slums somewhere on Agnimon—picked up the abandoned property for almost nothing and immediately set about making their dream come to life. Structurally it stayed largely the same, a mixture of wood, fiberglass, and hard plastics, although they reinforced it with metal at the support beams and in all of the corners. Steel slats were fitted against the walls on both the inside and outside. The former pulpit was removed and replaced with a bar that stretched along the entire length of the elevated floor so that the bartenders had to hand the drinks down to their patrons, or on trays to the servers that circled the dirty, battered tables. A handful of pews had been retained, their cushions replaced, the wood refinished, then pushed up against the walls to act as couches. A neon sign was hung over the door: THE CRATER, it said, though the R had lost its light. It wasn't the best bar on the moon, as Togg told it, but it was a popular one and the drinks were worth a damn.

The Dyr left them at the door. Someone had chipped out the word 'Welcome' in the dark wood. Archimedes gave it a thoughtful rap with a pair of knuckles, then pushed it open, heading inside with his friends close behind.

Caesar, not knowing who they were looking for, stared around at the men and women huddled over their tables, drinking, talking, scheming. Most of them were well-dressed. Not fancy, exactly, but in clean clothes without rips or tears and that fit well. With a few notable exceptions they didn't seem at all like the filthy, scarred killers he had anticipated. These seemed like his type of criminals, the ones that committed victimless crimes, aside from the very occasional killing that was less intentional and more because their friend didn't tell them they were lugging around a very innocent-looking grenade.

One of the men near the center of the room was resting his head down on his arms. He reached for his mug, realized it had run empty, and raised his head just enough to shout at the bartender for another round. He and Caesar caught eyes, and Caesar quickly looked away.

Archimedes and Grey spotted their connection immediately, tucked away at the back on one of the pews. Short hair, legs stretched out in front of her, hands clasped behind her head. Two of her own crew were sitting at a round table facing her. Her fiery hair had been longer the last time they had seen her; now it was sticking out in oiled spikes, cut just above her ears. Archimedes nudged Grey playfully in the ribs. Grey resisted the urge to punch him in the face.

"I'm going to go sit down with her," he said instead.

"You going to tell her I said hi?"

"Not if I can help it."

"You're just afraid she's missed me more than you," Archimedes said. He took Caesar's elbow and started pulling him toward the bar, ignoring his protests by pushing an index finger against his lips.

Grey went the opposite direction, toward the back. Toward Estella Vang, the captain of the *Stormy Bellows*. He adjusted the strap holding his shotgun, felt the weight shift off the edge of his shoulder into the more supportive groove of his collarbone. He was sweating under the gun and it trickled down his back. It had to be from the heat of the weapon pressing against his body. Definitely not because of nerves. He wasn't nervous.

Captain Vang saw him coming and pulled one hand from behind her head to wave him over, smiling a smile that shot through his sweat theory like a bullet.

"Estie," he said when he reached her, pulling a chair from the table and plopping into it. He had to reach one hand back to move the shotgun so it wouldn't be trapped between him and the chair. The other two men looked at him dispassionately, but he gave them a polite nod all the same.

"Ressler," he greeted the Human on his left. Ressler Carta was Estella's first mate, a handsome, cold-blooded sharpshooter with a granite jaw. The first time Grey had crossed paths with the *Bellows*, he and Ressler had turned a minor disagreement from adjacent seats in a bar into a full-blown brawl. They had both drawn firearms at the end of it, but Estella had made her man stand down. Something in the way Grey bled seemed to excite her.

There was a purple-skinned Murasai with a droopy eyelid sitting to Grey's right. His canines had been replaced with long, dark silver implanted fangs, mean and vicious. *Overdramatic*, Grey thought. He didn't recognize him, and he'd seen most of Estella's crew during their brief times together. "You, I don't know," he said.

"Ain't really looking to make friends, either," the Murasai said.

"Suits me fine." Grey turned his attention back to the captain. "You look good."

"Thank you," she said with a lop-sided smile. "You look tired. The courier life really wears a man down."

"I suppose it does, you do it long enough. Or wrong enough. Or right enough, I guess, and then everything turns into a shit sandwich, anyway. Where's your contact, Estie? This guy," he said, jerking a thumb at the Murasai, "or is he just some stray you've picked up along the way?"

The Murasai sneered but didn't say anything. Estella laughed. "That's Monserat," she said. "He's my new navigator. Not half bad. Last one caught a bullet during a shipment transfer."

"That sort of things seems to be running around these days," Grey muttered.

"What's going on with you, Toliver?" Estella asked. "Why so eager to jump right to business? It's been long enough that I expected a kiss hello at the very least."

"I'm not kissing you in front of a room full of perverts."

"Perverts? Aren't those your friends over there? That's definitely Archimedes. He's much too pretty for the Crater."

"*Especially* those perverts. Aside from them, in a room full of roughnecks and renegades I expect more than one lowlife deviant to be in here getting deep in their cups."

"Grey," Estella scolded, spreading her hands to indicate the room, "these are my people. I keep telling you Dephros isn't as bad as they say."

"Yeah, and now that I've been here half an hour, I've been wondering which of our standards you've been putting that opinion up against." He fussed at his cuffs until he realized what he was doing. He scowled, irritated that he had shown any sign of discomfort in front of the pirates. "Archimedes wanted me to tell you hello."

"You should have had him come over with you. He makes me laugh."

Grey's scowl grew deeper. "He's better off by the bar. He gets testy after long flights and we've had a number of them. Besides, Caesar's kind of shy. Doesn't usually do so good around new folk."

"That's the blond boy?" Estella asked.

"*Shy?* That's adorable, Toliver," Ressler said at the same time.

"Watch your goddamn mouth, quick-draw, or I'll rearrange it on the other side of your skull," Grey snapped.

Estella pulled her legs in, leaned forward and slapped the table with both hands, her smile gone, her eyes flinty as she looked between Grey and her first mate. The Murasai leaned away from the confrontation, crossing his arms over his chest and looking around the room, staring down anyone that had turned their head at the sound.

"That's enough," the pirate captain said in a low voice. "I've stopped you two idiots from fighting before, and I'm not particularly inclined to do it again, so don't make me just shoot you both and be done with it. I have a feeling Ark Carnahan would be sad, and I so hate to see a pretty man cry. Now, if you can keep the blood in your body somewhere around your abdomen instead of rushing to either head, we'll be in good shape."

The rest of the bar carried on, their interest in the table at the back dissipating. Ressler and Grey kept their eyes locked for a long moment more before they leaned back into their chairs nearly simultaneously and let out their breath. Ressler scratched at the edge of the table with his thumbnail for a second, stood, pulled his coat up from the back of his chair.

"I'm going to go get a drink," he said.

"Good," Estella said.

"You want anything?"

"No. Fuck off. Take Monserat," she said, and, looking at the Murasai, added, "Go with him."

Her navigator stood up without argument. He looked down at Grey, opened his mouth as if he was going to say something, cast a sideways glance at Estella, thought better of it, and followed Ressler to the bar.

Grey pulled the two men's chairs back into the table, then straightened in his seat and looked at the captain across from him. The short hair worked, he decided. Her longer hair had framed her face (and that had been lovely), but this was tougher, a little punk rock, and it made her dark green eyes pop, the freckles on her cheek glitter. She had a pale scar across the bridge of her nose, but he couldn't see it well in this light. He only knew it was there because he had put it there.

But if she was thinking about that, it didn't show in her smile. "You're staring," she said.

"Yeah."

"You're being silly."

"If I am, it's your fault, Estie. I like to think I'm normally a practical man."

"Except around Archimedes."

Grey snorted. "He brings out the worst in me."

"And the best, I think. I'm glad you two are still traveling together." Estella reached out to touch his hand, lingered briefly there, then gave him a quick pat and pulled back. "But you've got to stop teasing Ressler."

"*Teasing* him?" Grey laughed out loud. "What is he, twelve?"

"He has a temper," she warned.

"So do I."

"Yes, I remember," she said. She reached her hand up and Grey thought for a moment that she was going to touch her nose, that he had said the absolute wrong thing. Instead, she made a move to tuck her hair back, forgetting it wasn't there anymore. She smiled a little, embarrassed. "Anyway, to business. I wasn't able to find you anybody that actually works in the store where the maps are. It's pretty tight over there, one of the few holdovers from the old days, taken over by some dangerous folk who sell their stock to high-end private buyers. Collectors and treasure hunters, smugglers and the like." She raised a mischievous eyebrow. "Is *that* what you're doing, Toliver? Going treasure hunting? Because let me tell you about a diamond tornado…"

"I know about the Toilet," Grey said irritably, "and I ain't looking for treasure. What do you mean you couldn't find anyone who works at the shop? How am I supposed to get in?"

"Nobody who works there now is going to sell out their supply to a nobody they've never heard of. Not for any kind of money. They've already got buyers, remember? Filthy rich ones.

So I got to thinking: why not the next best thing?" Her eyes looked past him, to the entrance. Her lips spread into an almost wistful smile. "I got you a weird little dude who *used* to work there."

There was music playing in the Crater, something low and mean and mostly inaudible over the din of the crowd. Caesar couldn't place it—not his thing—but it felt very much at home in the place in a way he certainly did not. He kept waiting for the other shoe to drop, anticipating the moment someone would call him out for his relative innocence.

By contrast, Archimedes seemed to be in his comfort zone. He was splitting his attention between making two one-eyed men laugh and trying to wave down the bartender. The bartender, a Bozav whose coarse black mane was flecked with silver and who barely seemed to fit behind the bar, finally caught sight of the courier's flailing arm and headed over. He leaned down to look Ark in the eye.

"Beggin' ain't a good look," he said. His breath was hot and sour with onions even from where Caesar was standing.

"Agreed, but it's been a long trip. My friend and I are parched. Archimedes leaned away and pointed at the bar display, then at the shelves full of bottles behind it. "I don't see any signage saying so, but do you guys have any kind of drink special going on? Or a house cocktail?"

"We got a drink called Lasting Impact. Fifteen chits apiece, but it'll put you on your ass."

Archimedes made a face. "Sounds awful. I'll take two."

Caesar shook his head in protest, then tried to grab Archimedes' arm when it seemed he didn't notice. Ark shook him off and handed his money unit up to the Bozav, who disappeared further down the line to run the charge and make the drinks.

"I don't want one," Caesar said. "I'm not in the mood."

"Neither am I," Archimedes said in a low voice. "But we're going to get the drinks anyway. We can't be standing around looking sober in a place like this. At least keep it in your hand, alright? Hey, here we go!"

The Bozav handed down Archimedes' money unit, then the drinks, one of which was then passed on to Caesar. Ark took an experimental drink and immediately recoiled, his mouth turning in on itself. "I thought you said it would put me on my ass, not that it tasted like—"

"You don't like the fucking drink, there are other bars, Human," the bartender snapped.

Archimedes held up his hand to make peace and took a second drink to show he was serious. This time he kept his face neutral, though his eyes watered and he paled a bit. The bartender huffed and moved on to his next customer.

"Yeah, I'm not drinking this," Caesar said.

"Don't make me be the only one who tries it."

"It smells god-awful."

"That's part of the charm, really."

Caesar rolled his eyes. He lifted the drink to his lips and turned away, pretending to drink and using the opportunity to scope out the situation with Grey. He found his line of sight blocked by a Murasai and a Human walking right toward him. He flinched backward violently, hitting the bar, spilling some of the pungent liquor on his shirt.

"Hey," Archimedes said, putting his hand on his friend's shoulder. "What's wrong? You okay?" He gave his friend a look of appraisal. "You tried it, didn't you?"

Caesar wasn't paying attention. *It's not him*, he thought. *The freegun had red skin. This one is purple. It isn't him.*

Then why are they still coming right for me?

But when the pair reached them, they took up position at the bar on the other side of

Archimedes. The Human, a clean-shaven sandy-haired fellow with dangerous eyes, turned so he

was facing Archimedes' side. Ark turned to look at him dead-on.

"Package jockey," the man sneered.

"Asshole," Archimedes said cheerily.

"Surprised nobody's shot you, yet."

"I bet it's my natural magnetism."

"That doesn't even make any fucking sense." The man looked past Archimedes, to Caesar.

"And you. What's your deal?"

Caesar blinked and checked either side of himself, but there was nobody there. "Me? I don't

have a deal. I don't even know you!"

"No, but you know him," the man said, nodding at Archimedes. "That's enough to get on my

shit list, so I'll be seeing you." He slapped the Murasai's chest with the back of his hand and

gestured to a spot further down the bar. The two moved off, Caesar gawking after them.

"Insufferable guy, right?" Archimedes asked, taking a long gulp of his drink. "You know, I

can't tell if this actually gets better the further down you drink it, or if it's just melting all of my

taste buds."

It took an effort for Caesar to pull his eyes back to his friend. "You are incredibly difficult to

be friends with sometimes, you know that?"

Archimedes looked stunned, eyes wide, lips pursed around his straw as he finished draining his

drink. He tossed the cup off to the side indignantly, then took Caesar's drink from his hand and

lifted it in a mock toast. "If you're not going to drink this, I'm not going to let it go to waste.

Now talk to me, what do you mean? Because of Ressler? Captain Vang's first mate?" He laughed. "Because that one's not on me. Grey's the one that put that guy's face through a chair. I was just there, you know, watching. Might have made a few colorful remarks."

"Okay, two things," Caesar said. He snatched his drink back. Archimedes let it go without a fight. "You're not drinking this, that's the first thing. Alright? We have business here, and I would prefer that we focus on that, finish that, and then leave as soon as possible. If anyone's going to drink this, it's going to be me."

"Be my guest."

"I might well do."

Archimedes gestured for him to proceed.

Too far in it to back out now, Caesar took a hesitant sip of the drink. He looked up, caught the expectant look in Ark's eyes, and went from sip to hard swallow. The liquid drew across his tongue in a line full of sweetness that belied its smell. It was pleasant, almost delectable.

And then the fire came. Like lighting the end of a gasoline trail, it erupted in his mouth and throat and the taste of old smoke and fermented… something, maybe many things, seemed to consume him. He gagged and added his other hand to the cup to keep from dropping it.

"I'm proud of you," Archimedes said. "Now continue."

"What?" Caesar gasped. His stomach recoiled at the thought of drinking more of the Lasting Impact. He felt impacted quite enough.

"You said there were two things you wanted to say. What's the second thing?"

"Oh. Hold on." Caesar huffed, catching his breath, wiped at the tears that had come to his eyes, and then some flecks of spit at the corners of his mouth. "The woman. And that guy, what's his name? Ressler? What's your and Grey's deal with them?"

Archimedes leaned back against the bar and slipped his hands into his jacket pockets. His eyes turned up to the ceiling, thinking, maybe remembering. "It's not really my story to tell. Just one of those adventures he and I would get up to that you never wanted to know anything about, and I was really more along for the ride on this one. We met them out one night. He was a brute. She was a pirate." He grinned. "Can I make it any more obvious?"

Caesar looked again at the table at the back of the room. Again, he was just in time to catch the occupants walking toward him. This time it was Grey in front, with the redheaded woman just behind him. Trailing last was a Peran looking nervously around with his large black oval eyes. Caesar couldn't remember the last time he saw a Peran, let alone interacted with one. They weren't an uncommon species, nor were they reclusive. His job just didn't seem to take him anywhere they lived in abundance. This one was an adult, judging by the mottled grey tone of his skin, but he was short, standing at about a height with Grey. When the motley crew got to the bar, the woman flashed a toothy grin at Archimedes.

"Long time, Carnahan," she said.

"Estie," Archimedes said, grinning back. "Wait, sorry, it's *Captain* Estie."

"Still an irreverent shit, I see. You know, if Ressler ever caught you talking to me like that…"

"He and I already had words. I think he's mad that I'm a captain and he isn't."

Estella's eyebrows went up, and she looked over at Grey. "You guys are still doing the three captains thing? I still don't understand how that works."

Grey just shook his head.

The pirate captain looked over at Caesar, who looked away, at anything, at a table full of canid Dyr, then at a wall. He ran out of things eventually and turned back to her. He admired her haircut.

"Uh, hi," he said.

"Hello. You must be the third captain. Caesar, right?"

"That's right. I didn't realize Grey had been talking about me. Socializing isn't exactly his best quality."

Estella grinned, devilish. "Oh, I could tell you all about his best qualities." Archimedes laughed, then faked a retching noise. She winked back at Grey, then turned back to Caesar. "I heard you're shy."

"Not really," he said, narrowing his eyes at his friends over her shoulder. "Not normally. I'm just adverse to dangerous situations."

"Strange bedfellows, then."

"Tell me something I don't know."

Estella Vang stepped back and appraised the three captains of the *Sol Searcher*. She nodded at Grey and cocked a thumb at Caesar. "I like this one."

"So do we," Archimedes said.

Grey nodded again.

Satisfied that introductions had been made and measures more or less taken, Estella grabbed the Peran's gangly gray arm and pulled him into the center of their small group. "Okay, listen up. This is Xolop. He's a lock-picker, a codebreaker, a petty thief, an information broker… not great at that one, but he tries. Most importantly, he is the one person I was able to find who previously worked at the shop you three are looking to purchase from. So he'll be going with you, Archimedes, and you, Caesar to get whatever it is you're looking for."

Archimedes, surprised, turned to Grey for an explanation. Caesar did the same.

"She wants me to stay," Grey said, shrugging. "It's been a while, and I figure one less person makes it less conspicuous. Besides, what's a guy like me going to do in a place like that? I don't know shit about maps, that's Archimedes' thing."

Archimedes looked to Caesar to gauge his response. Caesar was still staring at Grey, his heart pounding again, nervous sweat starting to bead at the back of his neck, just behind his ears. And yet, here's where he was now, right? On the tail end of a slow escalation from lightly illegal pranks to hacking the government to whatever was coming next.

Then again, was robbing from robbers illegal? Was that really what was holding him up?

"We're in," Caesar said, and Archimedes agreed. "I trust Xolop knows the way?" He looked at the Peran, who gave a meek nod.

Estella Vang ran her hand against Grey's stubbled cheek and smiled at his lips. "Very good, then. The boys are going to run off and play. And you… you belong to me."

Chapter Thirteen
Love and Shrapnel

Dephros had never got around to developing separate cities so the population was spread out into a number of neighborhoods that sort of bled into each other, instead. The journey through them was an interesting one to Archimedes and Caesar as Xolop led them down avenues named things like Bloody Smile Street and Fortune Road. They walked past people gambling in alleys and bareknuckle boxing on wide porches. They even passed a couple corpses, a Human propped up against the outer wall of a tavern, and a massive Bozav stretched out in the middle of the road, having misplaced its head.

Charming roadside attractions, Archimedes thought. *Exciting adventure opportunities, bring the whole family.*

Their Peran guide seemed to loosen up once they were out of the crowded bar and back underneath the open sky. He spoke to them in a lilting, almost musical voice, saying little about himself but happily filling them in on the history of the black market shop they were headed to, the story of an erstwhile explorer named Harlan Marticelli.

Marticelli had, over the course of a lifetime spent traveling the Causeways, collected a wide assortment of maps and charts from all over the known universe. Places he had been, places he had discovered, some places he had only heard about in wine-soaked stories on the edges of star systems. Having finally reached his fill of cheating death and living like a nomad, he traded in his ship for a smaller personal cruiser with a gate guard and settled down on Dephros. He hoped the draw of Tui-san's diamond cyclone would bring other starry-eyed vagabonds through who might be looking for a map that could guide them to similar wonders. And travelers did arrive, and merchants, and Harlan's map collection expanded into other areas, swelling with rare items of all kinds, not all of which had been come by honestly. He carved an elaborate sign to sit on top of the store, naming it Marticelli's Adventure Emporium. A sign went in the front window to match, with an extra message promising to sell the ticket to a trip unlike anything his prospective buyers had ever experienced.

For a price, of course, and not an insignificant one.

The problem with marketing sought-after, unique, expensive items and the idea of lost locations and potential treasure troves is that it draws in less reputable people like flies to the dung pile. The Emporium was targeted in fits and starts. The windows would be broken out as an intimidation tactic. The big wooden sign up top was torn down in the middle of the night and broken up into its individual letters, the letters then scattered all over the moon. Harlan was furious but not intimidated. He had seen and lived through too much in his life to flinch in the face of some hooligans.

The bullet in the knee, that changed things. Getting dragged through half a dozen neighborhoods after the fact helped drive the message home that the moon wasn't what he thought it would be, that it would never be quite that. Out of respect for his past exploits (but with a gun barrel to his head all the same), Harlan was given the opportunity to take his life, his cruiser, and enough chits and fuel to get him through the Kolesov Gate and on to Peloclade, the only condition being that he leave his stock behind. Harlan, well, he was no coward, but he was no fool either. He took the deal. A doctor saw to his knee, a small group saw to the rest, and they sent him on one more journey.

The group of bruisers and petty thieves that took over the building—the adventure emporium that adventured Harlan directly into a permanent limp—found themselves facing a new problem: they had no idea exactly what it was they had procured. There were no intergalactic journeymen among them, no experts in maps and charts. They were hesitant to sell off the stock to the first interested hobbyist that showed up because they had no basis on which to determine whether or not they were being swindled. So they sat on it all.

In Zeanum a few months later, in a shack of a bar near Timeless Bridge (or perhaps Stokely Bridge, Xolop said, as he had been told both things by different people over the years), Harlan was drowning his sorrows, selling stories of his exploits for pints of beer. A relatively unknown grifter named Sylvain Abalos overheard him one night and, over the course of several frothy drinks, got the full account of Harlan's rise and fall. More importantly, he got a full-fleshed idea of the business that had been left behind.

Abalos took off for Dephros the next day. Within weeks of landing on the moon, he had brought a certain ruthless efficiency to the former emporium. His previous cons had brought him in touch with both the high-class kind of folks that would buy his wares and the shady fences that knew what they were selling and how much they could hike the price up to. Most of the crooks involved with the initial takeover fell in quickly behind Abalos. The rest… well, the grifter had never taken a life before Dephros, but he found he had a real talent for it (or maybe he had been a killer for some time, but Dephros honed his skills, Xolop said, as he had been told both things by different people).

And that was the state of things: a building full of relics from all over the universe and maps of all kinds, collected by one of the universe's most celebrated travelers (as Xolop told it), held hostage by a resourceful killer.

"Yeah, no, sounds like a piece of cake," Archimedes said, casting a sidelong glance at his friend. Caesar didn't notice, focused on looking both ways for anybody that might be taking too much of an interest in them. The sky darkened into a moody orange, what passed for night on the moon.

"No problem, no problem," Xolop said. He pointed out a building just ahead, a squat thing with a roof made of rusted slats that hung over the sides, casting shadows. The two windows set on either side of the door were dark. No signs of life behind them. No signs of life outside, either.

"Hey, man," Caesar said, turning toward the Peran. "How many men are we expecting?"

"What do you mean?"

"Guards, security. Are we going to run into Abalos in there?"

"No problem, no problem! We go around back. There is only three, always three. Maybe up to five. No more than that."

"So… not always three," Archimedes said.

"At least three," Caesar said, "but up to five. And you don't think at least one of them is going to be guarding the back door?"

"Big alarm, big locks, both doors. No need to stand guard. Nobody wants to do that. Mostly they just play cards."

"What about cameras?"

"On Dephros?" Xolop asked. "If he add cameras, I take care of them, too."

They reached the shop and circled around to the back. Caesar scanned the roof and the walls, saw nothing that indicated surveillance equipment. He pulled the knife free from the sheath at his waist and held it anxiously, his hands clammy around the hilt, the pits of his elbows and behind his knees feeling hot. He glanced over at Archimedes and saw that Ark had unstrapped the holster on his thigh and pulled his pistol, holding it low, along his leg.

The back door was a thick red metal thing set a few inches into the wall. Five broad steel bars extended across it through holes in the wall. Xolop felt along the wall until he found the area he was looking for and gave it a light push. A square section not much bigger than his hand popped open, revealing a small compartment with a tiny black box inside. Xolop ran his fingers along the top of it, the sides, was apparently satisfied when he felt the bottom.

"What are you doing?" Archimedes whispered.

"Shh. Talking while sneaking, bad luck."

Xolop pulled out a thin silver apparatus with a small knob at one end. He angled the other end underneath the box, pushed up until something clicked into place. A beeping started as he fiddled with the knob, increasing in frequency. Archimedes' grip tightened on his gun. The beeping stretched out into a single keening sound, something like a flatline, an indicator of death.

Then it stopped.

Xolop pulled the device free and returned it to his pocket. A second passed, two, then the bars across the door began to retract, disappearing into the wall. The door behind it had no knob, no handle. It just sat there, inset, imposing. Xolop pushed on it with both hands and it swung in silently, revealing a deep rectangle of shadow.

The Peran turned and grinned, his teeth glittering sharp and a little yellow under the orange night sky, his eyes black pools. He held up his hands, the gesture reading, *Told you I'd get us in,* and backed into the building. There were no alarm bells, no shouts of surprise.

Archimedes and Caesar looked at each other, nodded once, and followed the alien in.

Grey stood staring at the night sky with his hands in his pockets, shotgun all but forgotten, a comfortable weight across his back. Less comfortable were his feet, sore from traversing the hard dirt road. He shifted his weight from one foot to the other, still looking at the sky, wondering when the last time was that he saw something so beautiful.

"You coming?"

He looked away from the shades of purple and orange to Estella Vang, standing a good ten feet away. Ressler and the navigator, whatever his name was, were standing just behind her.

"Yeah," he said. He started over to join her, pulled a hand from his pocket to push his hair back. It was longer than he'd let it grow in years, but he hadn't trusted the *Imagination*'s barber enough to let him touch his head, and the barber wouldn't let him borrow the equipment to do it himself. Estie said she liked it, but Estie said a lot of things, and a pirate's opinion was unreliable by nature.

"What's wrong with you?" she asked him. "You look almost pensive. It's weird."

"I have thoughts," Grey said, mock offended.

"Oh, yeah? Name one."

"I was thinking I was surprised by the sky here at night. It's gorgeous Not something I'd expect… you know, here. You think outlaws and freeguns, you think of a bunch of people skulking about in the dark, some kind of oily blackness. Not," he said, pointing upward, "you know, that. So then I was thinking, damn, that might be the most beautiful thing I've ever seen. Then you called for me, and I took a good look at you and thought…"

Estella grinned. "You're fucking cheesy, Toliver."

"What? Why? I was thinking, yep. Definitely the sky."

She punched him in the arm and laughed. Ressler rolled his eyes and muttered something to the navigator. *What the hell is his name?* Grey thought. He wrestled with it a moment longer, gave it up as irrelevant, and let Estella continue leading him along, her arm looped in his.

They hadn't stayed at the Crater much longer after Archimedes and Caesar left with their guide. One drink was all, recommended by the pirate captain and tasting like someone had dumped a bunch of fruit into a barrel of gasoline. The "lasting impact", Grey suspected, was the stump where his tongue would be after it finished dissolving. He powered through it anyway after seeing Ressler down his like water, refusing to let the arrogant prick show him up. Estella suggested they leave after that, though she was coy about where they were going.

"But seriously, where are we going?" he asked again. They had been walking for a quarter of an hour, but there had been little conversation. Grey had no interest in engaging the other members of the *Stormy Bellows*, and they felt the same, so he was left making small talk with Estella. It was nice, brought back a whole heap of good memories, but she was too clever for him by far.

"You don't like surprises?" she asked, giving his bicep a light squeeze.

"I actually hate surprises," he said mildly, "but I was thinking more about Ark and Caesar showing back up at the bar and me not being there."

"Are you worried about them?"

Grey laughed. "Not really. Maybe a little worried about Caesar, but he's got Archimedes with him."

Estella didn't say anything at first. They walked in silence, Grey making sure to keep Ressler and the Murasai off to the side, nowhere close to directly behind him.

"Archimedes… he's fun, but he's not really the responsible type. He doesn't seem much like an aggressive type, either. What makes you so confident that Caesar is safe with him?"

"Yeah, Ark likes people to think he doesn't care about anything, or that he doesn't take anything seriously." Grey shrugged. "You hung out with him, what, twice? I've known him a long time. All the years of my life that matter, and I can tell you that most of it's an act. He cares. Not much about himself, but the people close to him? He's an absolute animal about them."

Estella was skeptical. "Carnahan? The guy who once told me he wouldn't invest in a new bed because he spent so much time in other people's?"

Grey smiled a little at that. "You laugh, but… look, one time we were stopping off somewhere. I can't remember the place off the top of my head, some rinky-dink town where everyone knows everybody else. Good place to get a drink and a home-cooked meal and not much else, you know the type?"

"Heard of 'em, sure. Not much business for my line of work in places like that, but I imagine you see plenty."

"Yeah. We deliver just about everywhere, and it turns out we had been to this place before. Can't remember… Drywall? Dry Run? Whatever you call it, Archimedes had met a girl there the first time around and they hit it off. We wound up staying in town that night, the first time, and he didn't come back to the hotel until morning, all grins, absolutely insufferable.

"Anyway, we wind up back in this place a year or two later. Turns out Ark has been keeping in touch with this girl, sending a letter here, making a call there. Staying friends. So we drop off the package, get our payment confirmation out of the way, decided to stop in one of the local pubs for a cold drink and a hot meal before taking off back to an ACG office for the next job. Archimedes hits up this girl and she meets up with us." Grey took a deep breath and looked sideways at Estella.

"Well, it turns out someone blacked this girl's eye. She wouldn't say who, but Ark is persuasive, and he's observant. He's a fucking goof, I know, but he knows how to read people when he wants to, can figure out what it is that makes somebody work. So he keeps asking, she keeps giving him the runaround, but her eyes are darting over to this group in the back of the bar. I didn't see this, mind you, this is what he tells me later. At the time, he just acts like he's upset but he's giving up. He'll let her keep her secret. He switches to talking about sports. This town didn't have much going for it, but they had these quarterly heavyball tournaments that they would get up to, and Ark spent some time trying to convince me and Caesar to stay so that he could try out. He's talking up his talent to this girl, asking her what she thinks about it. Archimedes has never played heavyball a day in his life, but he keeps talking, I keep drinking. Caesar headed back to the *Searcher* early. Eventually Archimedes excuses himself to go to the restroom."

Grey paused as they reached a long, mostly deserted lot with a low building stretched out at the end of it. A few cars, speeders, and personal cruisers were parked here and there. The bulk of the people milling about were clustered around the sides of the building and up on a short porch pushed up under the front door. A handful of lights hung from cables from the underside of the roof, casting a pale white shroud over the smokers loitering around outside. Most of them were drinking as well, tossing the empty bottles and plastic cups on the ground when they were finished with them.

"Oh, this place looks great," he drawled.

Estella unhooked her arm from his and waved her crew on. "Ressler, you and Monserat go ahead and save us a spot. We'll be in in a minute."

Monserat, Grey thought, before trying to forget it again.

The two men headed for the building. Grey pushed his hands into his pockets again and looked at the pirate captain with questions in his eyes.

"I want you to finish your story first. I think it's the most I've ever heard you talk at once, and it isn't even about me." She winked at him. "Carnahan should be flattered."

He snorted and rolled his eyes. "Yeah, alright. Anyway, there's not much more to tell. The girl and I, we thought he got up to take a piss. And maybe he did, I don't know. All I know is a couple minutes go by and then this huge commotion breaks out. I'm talking flipped tables, smashed bottles. It looks like a pack of squids going at it on account'a how many limbs are flailing about. There's beer and liquor everywhere, then I see a bunch of red flying with it once people start bleeding. And right there, right in the thick of it, I see a head full of white hair that is *also* quickly turning red. Ark went and picked a fight with five guys."

"Bullshit," Estella said, brows knitting together, skeptical.

Grey placed his right hand over his heart and lifted the other to the heavens. "Hand to God, Estie. I wish he'd told me ahead of time. I would have had his back. Always have. Now he's never told me why he didn't, but I'm thinking it's just because he didn't want to freak the girl out."

"Wouldn't starting a full-blown fucking brawl freak her out anyway?"

Grey grinned. "Well, yeah. Archimedes is a smart kid, but he's got a problem with impulse control."

Estella chewed at her lower lip, trying to visualize the scene. Across the lot, on the porch, one of the smokers suddenly laid out another with a haymaker. There were hoots and hollers and laughs from the rest of the group that echoed across the empty space. The puncher finished his cigarette, flicked it on the guy he'd hit, and went back inside. The punchee lay there for a minute, slow in coming to, then climbed to his feet and staggered off into the night.

"Well?" Estella asked.

"Well, what?" Grey asked back. He watched the man limp off until he disappeared down an alley.

"You can't expect me to believe Archimedes fought five men by himself."

He barked a laugh. "Oh, no. God, no. By the time I got over there and started pulling people off, he'd gotten his ass kicked pretty bad. Cut over one eye, broken nose, busted ribs. He broke two fingers on his right hand. But he got the guy that gave the girl her shiner. Hit him with a bottle, broke his jaw, dislocated his knee. Every one of the others was bleeding, too, from one place or another. Then *I* showed up. Ark, man… you don't hurt his friends, and you don't hurt any women."

"Mm, fascinating. And Caesar is the soft one."

"Diplomatic, let's say. He ain't much of a fighter, but he's no coward."

Estella bit her lip and looked up at him with her green eyes, those damn emerald eyes, and Grey remembered grabbing a handful of her body and pulling her in so that he could lift her lips to his. Flashes of their last encounter broke in and he frowned.

"And you?" she asked softly, seeing his expression darken.

"I'm the mean one," Grey said. "And the angry one. And the better fighter."

She laughed. It was a light laugh, music to his ears. He stared down at her, remembering how dangerous she could be, still having a hard time giving a damn. If she hadn't brought up what had happened, he wasn't going to. She was a pirate, after all. Some things came with the territory.

"Ressler and Monserat are probably getting impatient," she said. She turned on her heel and began walking toward the building. She lifted one hand and crooked her fingers, beckoning him.

"What is this place?"

"I told you, it's a surprise!"

Exasperated, he said, "And I told you: I fucking hate surprises."

There was a sound coming from above them as they moved through the building, up in the ceiling or high in the walls. A buzzing noise, soft and constant, that helped mask the *pat-pat-pat* of their footfalls. Not a lot, but every little bit helped.

It's not an alarm, Caesar thought. *A temperature regulator, maybe, or an air filtration system. Maybe both? And look at Archimedes. Like a kid in a candy store.*

They moved through a seemingly endless number of aisles, maps lining the ends of the shelving. What physical copies had been obtained were now carefully preserved in glass frames, their conditions ranging from pristine to tattered and barely legible. One map looked to have been drawn in miniature on the back of a cocktail napkin, but Caesar could tell even in passing that the detail on it bordered on unbelievable. Digital maps were arranged in displays of their own, glowing softly in the low-lit interior of the warehouse. Glass cases crowding in on either side of them contained even more merchandise, artifacts from all over the universe positioned carefully on velvet cushions inside. Ceremonial masks, ritual weapons, frayed and faded garments, each with their own title card listing additional details and price points. Caesar saw Archimedes' mouth moving as they walked, describing the items to himself with wide-eyed wonder.

There was still no sign of any security, no sounds other than the soft ones they were creating. Ark didn't seem to care, absorbed as he was in his surroundings, but it made Caesar uneasy. Millions of dollars in rare items just laying about in a dark building that could be so easily hacked by a fidgety Peran? Was it reputation alone, then, that kept people from skulking about? And the captains of the *Sol Searcher* were simply being audacious in their ignorance?

He opened his mouth to say something, but Xolop, some steps ahead of them, stopped at the far wall and waved them around the corner.

"This way," he said, pointing with one long, thin finger. He fixed his big black eyes toward them, but Caesar couldn't tell if he was looking at them or past them. He tossed a nervous glance over his shoulder just to be sure, saw nothing.

"To the pre-war maps?" Archimedes asked in a hushed tone. "You're sure?"

"I only worked here," Xolop replied sarcastically. "I was only in charge of inventory, only cataloguing everything in and out."

"Alright, alright," Archimedes said. "Lead the way."

The Peran fidgeted for a moment, almost hopping on each foot, then turned and led them once more. He began muttering in Perasi, hushed, just above a whisper. His head turned to the left and to the right, though there was nothing to see but the wall on one side and tall shelves stuffed with chart books on the other.

Caesar felt the hairs on the back of his neck go up. This was too easy. The whole thing had been. And he didn't like Xolop, hadn't liked him since they met. Too twitchy to be trustworthy.

"What's he saying?" he whispered to Archimedes.

"What?"

"Xolop. He's muttering to himself. You speak Perasi, so what's he saying?"

Archimedes frowned. "He's *muttering*, Caesar. I can't make out a word. What's wrong with you?"

"Something's not right. I don't like the way he's acting. He—"

But Archimedes' attention was already pulled away. The shelving had transitioned into a series of chest-high silver cabinets with long, locked drawers. Each drawer was labeled by years, by Causeways, and by coordinates. Xolop had crouched down to examine one, second from the bottom. He pulled another instrument out, a slim pick with a narrow hook at the end. He gave the grip of the tool a small twist and it began to hum softly.

Caesar and Archimedes checked both ends of the aisle once more, both convinced that they would be discovered at any moment.

Nobody came.

A click sounded from the drawer a moment later and it popped ajar. Xolop twisted his tool the other way and the buzzing stopped. He put it away, stood, stepped back away from the cabinet. He pointed at Archimedes, then pointed at the drawer. Ark took his meaning and replaced him in the spot. He slipped his gun back into his thigh holster and gripped the edge of the drawer carefully with both hands, pulling it slowly out from the cabinet until he could fully look inside.

Caesar took a few steps forward so he could look over his friend's shoulder but kept enough distance that he could run without getting tripped up if need be. The drawer was filled with a number of rectangular black storage boxes, each with a dozen slots for data drives. Each drive had a silver label stuck to the end of it with the same parameters as had been on the drawer. Archimedes cast an excited look back and then began looking through them, dragging an index finger across each drive. Caesar felt a thrill run laps around his heart. The thrill of danger, the thrill of discovery.

Neither captain noticed Xolop pull a pistol out until he had centered it fully on the back of Archimedes' head and cleared his throat.

"Archimedes," Caesar said in a low voice.

"Just a minute, I think I've almost figured out—"

"*Ark*." Caesar didn't raise his voice, but he added some flint to it. His friend froze, one hand in the box resting on a handful of data drives. He turned his head slowly, caught a glimpse of the edge of the gun barrel pointed at him.

"Ah. So, what is this? Did Estie set us up?"

Xolop shook his head. The gun shook with it. The Peran was nervous, and small beads of pale blue sweat started to break out across his wide gray forehead.

"She doesn't know anything about it." Xolop had switched to his native language. Archimedes understood him, having studied a number of alien languages in university, but Caesar was left clueless and increasingly agitated. "I'm tired of people looking past me, looking down on me. Nobody pays poor Xolop any attention until they need something from me, and then more often than note I get stiffed on my fee. Get me into this place, Xolop. Disarm that door, Xolop. Well, I want a payday, too. I never get to be part of the con. I never get the cut I deserve." He spat off to the side. "When Abalos switched up the security protocols, I knew it was just a matter of time before someone like you came along looking to take advantage of it. The guards? They're long gone, let go not long after I was. The security system just got an upgrade, that's all. Easy enough for me to figure it out. Now tell your friend to hand over his gun."

"He wants you to give him your gun," Archimedes said to Caesar.

"Should I?" Caesar asked, eyes saucers.

"He's pointing *his* gun at my head, so please do."

Caesar shakily unstrapped the pistol at his waist and held it by the butt as he handed it over to Xolop. The Peran took it in his free hand and stuffed it in the back of his pants.

Archimedes slowly pulled his hand out of the box and lifted his arms above his head. He stood, turned, half-waved his fingers at Caesar in an effort to calm him down.

"He says there aren't any guards here, anymore. Just the disabled alarm." To Xolop, Archimedes asked, "Look, man, what's your plan here? You want maps, or relics, or whatever… they're all over the place. Take your pick. Any one of these things are worth a ton of chits to the right collector."

"Oh, I'll take my share," the Peran said. "Now that we're in here, I can clean up just fine. But you're looking for something specific, yeah? You've got a bead on something. And if you're walking past all these things and trying to zero in on a specific map, I'm betting it's worth a lot. So I'll take that, thank you."

"He wants the map," Archimedes muttered to Caesar. To Xolop, he said, "Or what?"

The skin around his wide black eyes puckered in bemusement. "Excuse me?"

"Well, I mean… I haven't pinpointed the drive I'm looking for yet. I've got a general idea, not that I'm inclined to share it with you, but there are a ton of drives in there. What are you going to do if I don't give it to you? Shoot me and take all the drives? You don't know what you're looking for. Caesar won't crack. I saw the guy respond to two freeguns pointing weapons in his face by dropping a grenade at his own feet, the guy's a fucking lunatic. Now, if I gave you the right drive, what's to keep you from shooting us after? If I gave you the wrong one, tried to pull a quick one on you, same thing. And how would you tell the difference? You pulled your gun too early, Xolop, and now we're at an impasse."

The Peran's mouth worked angrily as he considered what Archimedes was saying. The shaking in his arm began to increase, either from anger or from the growing weight of the gun.

But whatever he was thinking, whatever he was planning to say or do, it all fell by the wayside as a sudden loud scraping sounded from where they had come in. Slowly, the three of them turned to look back at the head of the aisle. Xolop's gun moved just a bit, pointing now at Archimedes' shoulder, a less fatal but no more fun place to get shot. Then the gun dropped to his side completely, in shock, as the sight of a massive golden form shuffled into sight.

The suit of armor (if that's what it was) or the golem (which is what it looked like) loomed even at a distance. It must have been eight feet tall hunched over, with two polished arms resembling massive pistons supporting it. At the base of the arms were two giant hands that curled in on themselves, so that it was resting on its knuckles, ugly things, and sharp, all scraped edges. Three thin pipes extended from each of its bunched shoulders, thin wisps of dark gray smoke drifting from each. The face, if you could call it that, was a flat slab of white metal connected to the body by a series of thick cables. It was featureless save for three blue 'eyes' ringed in black and arranged in a triangle formation in the center.

"Is that a goddamned robot gorilla?" Caesar breathed.

Whatever it was, it charged.

There had been no signs on the outside of the building, but a neon light hanging above the bar inside named the establishment *The Hangnail*. It was an appropriately disgusting name for a place whose floor was covered in sawdust and grime by inches and where sweat and the smell of narcotics hung like curtains in the air. Smoke from any number of recreational flammables made everything hazy, and the sounds of raucous debauchery blended together into a kind of thundering monotone.

Estella pushed Grey through the crowd, one hand on the square of his back while his broad

shoulders did the rest. At the bar he ordered a Rithian stout, but the acoustics washed him out.

What came back was not a beer but some kind of light yellow concoction with a heavy dose of

gin in it. It tasted pretty good, but a feeling tugged at his short hairs that this was the kind of

place where even the bartenders might slip something extra into your drink just to see what

would happen. After a couple of sips he decided to keep the drink as decoration only.

Ressler and Monserat were nowhere to be seen, not that Grey much cared. He focused instead

on the interior of the *Hangnail*, the scarred walls filled with tattered advertisements for bands

and films, and with wanted posters sporting faded mugshots. He noticed the conspicuous lack of

windows and the thick splinters of wood sticking out in every direction from the gray

crossbeams that supported the ceiling. A pair of doors were situated at the back, one each to the

left and right of the bar. The door to the right, red, looked heavy and reinforced. He suspected it

led to a back office, some place to tally up the night's profits. The other door, as gray as the

crossbeams, had an EXIT sign lit up above it in blue.

He felt Estie's hand on his back again, steering. They passed a pair of nasty looking bathrooms

and headed for an alcove. A steep set of metal stairs was tucked in there, and the pair of them

descended to the lower level, pushing past a number of rough-looking folk heading up. Grey

noticed a theme among the patrons of the bar, one of dusty skin and greasy hair, torn clothes and

bloodshot eyes. The bandit moon might have some well-off outlaws on the run from the law, but

you wouldn't find them frequenting the *Hangnail*.

The stairs terminated in a modified basement. Crushed cans and shattered plastic cups littered

the dirt floor next to half-smoked cigarettes, needles, and even a handful of discarded blades,

more than one of which looked to be crusty with dried blood. Crowds of people huddled around the six thick support posts, all looking to the center of the room, all screaming, some waving slips of pink paper in the air.

"Come on," Estella said, taking his hand. She led him through a knot of rumpled clothes and excited limbs until they came to the spectacle pulling everyone's attention.

A square pit had been dug into the center of the room and a waist-high chain link fence put up around the lip of it. Onlookers pressed their thighs against the fence as they cheered, careful not to stretch so far over that they lost their balance and fell in. Grey found himself at the front of the crowd, feet pushed up uncomfortably against the bottom links. He was disappointed to see what had everyone so excited.

Pacing back and forth around four feet below the crowd were two leonid creatures, each half the size of a full-grown Human man, one colored red, one black with streaks of white across its flanks. Both had two pairs of ears. The larger pairs, covered in fur, were currently cocked back as a warning, a sign that both animals were ready to let blood. The smaller, hairless pairs of ears stayed pressed against the creature's skulls, their sole purpose being to register noises while they were sleeping and to trigger a subconscious alert for any approaching threats.

"Direxian devilcats," Grey said, more to himself than anyone else. He had only ever seen them in zoos and, once, for sale by a man who specialized in exotic pets. That particular beast had looked miserable, the cage it was stuffed into much too small to suit it.

"Twice a week," Estella said, stepping up next to him. "Not always devilcats but always something with a little flavor to it. They're not all bred and trained on Dephros, but people fly in often enough with new challengers or champions from some other backwater city on some other moon." She pointed out the pink slips being waved around. "Lot of money can pass through even a dive like this. If you want to make a bet, I'll go upstairs and place it for you."

Grey made a face, disgusted. "I'm good, thanks."

"Didn't know you were an animal lover."

"Even if I didn't like animals, which I do, it would still be an extra level of sick to make them fight for sport. Bunch of unwashed lowlifes screaming down at the poor things. They're hunters, you know, in the wild? People box them up in crates, put them in small, loud places. Beat 'em, starve 'em. It's fucking wrong."

Estella studied him. She looked down at the circling animals, watched them take a few cautious swipes at each other, bared her own teeth when the black one suddenly snarled.

"You know, Captain Toliver, I think you're right. Maybe we should put a stop to this."

Grey turned away from the scene to look at her, something in her tone putting him on edge. Someone's elbow dug into the middle of his back as they yelled at the cats to start biting each other. Someone kicked his heel as they tried to get a closer look.

"I'm not saying I don't agree, but there's a whole lot more armed folk here cheering for it than ain't, don't you think? What's your plan?"

"Easy," she said, smiling. She met his eyes, looked down to his mouth, sucked on her bottom lip, teasing. "I'm going to give them something they want more."

Her hand shot to his holster, grabbed the strap of the shotgun and pulled it over his head in one quick move. She coiled her leg behind his own and pushed hard against his chest with both hands and the gun, sending him staggering back against the chain-link fence, back and over and past it. Grey was about to ask what she was doing, had the question on the edge of his lips, and then he was falling. He landed hard in the center of the pit, high on his back, between his shoulders. The breath shot out of him. The devilcats sprang back at the same time, retreating to opposite sides of the pit, equally frightened at the sudden addition to their melee.

Senseless, Grey's first instinct was to try and curl up on himself. He knew he was lucky not to have broken his neck falling in, but agony was already starting to spread across his back, the muscles around his spine tightening in violent protest.

But no, he needed to move.

He somersaulted backward, pain and all, coming up on his feet and putting his back to the dirt wall. A heavy red paw slapped down, claws out, where his head had been seconds before. He lashed a retaliatory kick out to his left, but the animal sprung away, too quick for him. Grey cast his eyes up to the top of the pit, searching for Estella and finding a mob of angry faces leering down at him, stunned, waiting to see what would happen next.

There, a shock of spiky red hair.

"What the actual fuck, Estella?" he snarled.

"Sorry, baby, but I just kept thinking about our last night together. You think you could just punch me in the face and there weren't going to be any repercussions?"

"I only hit you *after* you tried to rob me, and after you *shot me in the fucking leg*. That still seems like you came out ahead."

A devilish grin broke out across her face. "I'm a pirate, Grey. I enjoy you, but I take what I want. I wanted what you had, you got in the way. I didn't kill you, didn't even shoot you anywhere too serious. You should have just let me get away."

"Yeah, I enjoy you too, that's why—" The black devilcat had started creeping closer. He broke off to kick dirt at it. "That's why I didn't shoot you the fuck back."

Estella winked and turned to address the crowd, arms spread wide. "Ladies and gentlemen, it looks like we've got a new contender in tonight's fight! Adjust your bets if you'd like, but above all enjoy the show! I've got a courier ship I've got to go plunder."

She tossed one last happy look over her shoulder, then disappeared into the crowd. The cheering and screaming and ticket-waving resumed around the pit, cacophonous. The blood pounding in Grey's temples did its level best to drown it out and only partially succeeded. The devilcats had circled outward, positioned diagonally from him. They were still wary of each other but had found a mutual interest in the smell of new meat.

Grey quickly checked himself over for injuries, mostly found dirt. A small patch on his left elbow had ripped open when he landed in the pit and oozed a thin line of bright red blood, more enticement for the animals. The pulled muscles in his neck, shoulders, and back were really coming alive now, too, distracting him with hot slices of hurt.

He bared his teeth and clenched his fists.

"Alright, then," he said.

Pop! Pop! Pop-pop-pop!

The gunshots were loud in such close quarters but were still nearly drowned out by the towering golden robot barreling down the aisle toward them. Xolop's bullets bounced off the metal plates and chipped away at the shelves and walls on either side. Archimedes turned away, frantic, and started pulling data drives from the drawer by the handful, shoving them into his pockets.

"Ark!" Caesar urged, voice rising.

"I know! Run!" Archimedes grabbed, pulled, stuffed away. His pants were getting heavy, but he had cleared out three rows of data drives, and he was almost positive at least one of them had the map they were looking for. Almost. He looked over at Caesar, eyes wide, almost high off the adrenaline pumping through him. "Run, I said! Why aren't you running?"

"Why aren't *you*? What are you doing? Do you not see the—"

"I see the fucking thing, Caesar, I'm getting what we came here for! I think." He paused, muttered. "I hope."

Pop-pop!

Xolop's last shot cut in under the robot's face plate and collided with the cables underneath just as it reached him. A small gout of blue flame puffed out from where its neck met its shoulder, but if it did any real damage none of them could tell. One of the massive arms shot out and grabbed the Peran around the waist, pulled him up into the air like a tuft of grass, and slammed him hard into the wall halfway to the ceiling. There was a wet crack, like someone taking a sledgehammer to a coconut, and the back of Xolop's head split open. Black blood sprayed across the wall, up toward the ceiling, and Archimedes was reminded of the time he had knocked over a professor's inkwell while trying to lift the answer sheet to a linguistics exam. The memory passed, ripped away as the robot hurled the Peran's body at him. He ducked and Xolop hit the cabinet Archimedes had been digging through, dropping down into the open drawer.

"Time to go!" Archimedes yelled. He grabbed Caesar's sleeve and turned, pulling him along and running in the opposite direction of the robot. Heavy thumps and mechanical whirrs followed, though there were no calls for the couriers to stop, no warnings given as to what would happen if they didn't return what they had taken. The message was clear: break in and die.

Caesar was gasping for breath, face flushed, eyes bugging out of his head. Xolop's sudden transition from betrayer to corpse was emblazoned in his mind, and he didn't seem keen to go through the same process, which was good, because fear was a powerful motivator. But he was also hyperventilating, which was bad, because panic wasn't terribly conducive to split-second, life-saving decisions.

There came the briefest pause from behind them, a stagger-step. Archimedes set his foot hard on the floor, put as much of his arm strength into shoving Caesar's shoulder in one direction, then pushed off with his foot to dive the opposite way. A massive golden fist clubbed through empty air, then swung around, grasping. The metal fingers missed getting a grip on Archimedes (*Flughlehgahh!* his mind vomited in response), but they did make contact. Ark, being mostly airborne, was sent fully so and he pinwheeled over a low counter to crash into a glass case full of ceremonial headdresses. Glass dug into his back, into his palms as he pushed himself back up into a sitting position. Three sharp feathers were poking into the meat at the back of his left arm, ripped from the fringe of one of the relics. He ripped them out, thought about picking the glass out of the palms of his hands, saw the robot slowly turn and focus its full attention on him. He decided he should probably survive first so that he could save his hands later.

The blow had deposited Archimedes in the next aisle over, so he looked both ways for a clear path out, praying to any god that might listen that there weren't any more robot sentries. He caught sight of Caesar on his right, peeking around the corner at the end of the aisle, momentarily out of sight of the gorilla. Archimedes lurched to his feet, wobbled for a minute, steadied himself. Keeping an eye on the robot, which was approaching more cautiously now that merchandise had been damaged, he unstrapped his thigh holster and held it and his gun in one hand. With the other, he unbuckled his belt, dropped his pants to the floor, and shuffled them over his shoes. He hooked the inside with one foot and slid them down the aisle toward his friend.

Caesar goggled at the sight of Ark standing there in his boxers, dripping blood from his hands, arms, and back.

"What the… whatthefuckareyoudoing?" he hissed.

"Grab the drives and get the hell out of here," Archimedes responded, keeping his voice low and trying not to move his lips. "I'll lead it the other way."

"How are *you* going to get out?"

Archimedes glanced over at his friend and grinned.

The robot placed both of its hands on the ground and stood still. A hydraulic groan came from its arms, and a second later its limbs began to expand, growing taller, lifting the gorilla from the ground. The massive construct's body was pushed forward at the shoulders until it began to pass over the low counter and into Archimedes' aisle.

Ark's grin faded. He ran for it, ignoring the sharp pains in his hands and the ache in his back, trying his best not to focus on the fact he had no plan.

Caesar watched, stunned, as his friend ran off cackling and half-naked, pursued by a golden giant. So stunned was he that it took him a moment to remember what he was supposed to do. The robot moved out of sight. Caesar peeked back around the other corner and found the coast was clear there as well, save for Xolop's crumpled form, the top half of the body thankfully slumped out of sight.

He broke from cover and moved as quickly as he could, grabbing Ark's pants and tucking them under his arm, careful to keep the pockets pointing up so none of the data drives could slip out. He took two steps toward the way they had come in and stopped. A thought had come to him, maybe a stupid one.

He turned and ran back to the aisle with Xolop's body. His gun. It had dropped to the ground when the Peran had been snatched up. Xolop's weapon hadn't proved to be any use against the robot, but that wasn't the only threat on Dephros, and Archimedes had taken his own gun with him. Caesar needed more than just knives.

He spotted the pistol, dulled chrome and ridged grip, tucked almost neatly against the wall. It was just below where Xolop had had his skull crushed, knocked free from the back of the Peran's pants. A thin trickle of dark black blood had slithered down the wall toward it. Caesar snatched the gun up and checked to make sure it wasn't damaged, not quite sure what it would look like if it were. It seemed okay, so he slipped it back into his holster. A quick-draw position, Grey had called it, not that he had ever needed to draw a gun quickly in his life. Not that he had ever hit what he was aiming at when he'd had the luxury of time.

"It's the thought that counts," he breathed. "It's the, the symbolism of it that holds power."

He repeated that to himself a few times—symbolism, power, symbolism, power—and then made his way back to the rear entrance, toward the door that poor, duplicitous Xolop had hacked them through. It was a straight shot, or it should have been, but the tense stillness and quiet of the warehouse had been replaced with chaotic electricity. The robot's thick arms and posterior… appendages? pistons? paws? seemed to be slamming down all over the place. The warehouse was built with weird acoustics; thumps and groans and the screeching of the construct's parts as it wheeled through aisle after aisle seemed to come from everywhere. Archimedes both helped and didn't, his taunts and maniacal laughter ringing clear and providing a more precise idea of where the action was, but it also abandoned any pretext of this being a stealthy thieving operation. And sure, the booming sounds of the robot as it pounded down the floor after Ark were thundering enough, but it still felt like tossing shuttle fuel on a gas fire.

Caesar stepped lightly as he did his best to stay away from where the noise was coming from, sticking to shadows and corners where he could, any place that might afford him a warning glance. One aisle at a time he worked his way back through the building, pants full of priceless maps under one arm, pistol an uncomfortable weight on his hip. He caught glimpses of white hair darting past an aisle and brief, terrifying sights of the massive gorilla-bot following him— *thum thum thum thum*—and somehow staying remarkably agile. Though it cut off some of its speed, it could still work its way around sharp corners, careful not to even disturb, let alone damage, any of the merchandise.

Caesar got one good look at the thing, at its posture and its mostly featureless face. The sight of those three lenses sitting alone in an otherwise blank slate almost gave Caesar a sense of pity for it. For its seeming regret at having destroyed a display and its fear of repeating the mistake.

Poor thing realizes not everything can be a solid brick wall to bash a skull against, Caesar thought, then immediately followed that thought with, *I can't believe I'm feeling bad for a murderous robot that's trying to kill my friend. I've got to get out of here.*

Archimedes' hands *hurt*. On four occasions since crashing through the display he had clenched his hands reflexively, agitating the glass puncturing his palms. He had tried to remove the larger pieces while he ran but staying out of arm's reach—a reach that could evidently extend itself— remained his priority. His saving grace, the thing that gave him hope, was the robot's size. The way it was built, hunched forward and propelled by its massive arms, meant it had some trouble navigating corners swiftly. It could have just barreled through them, had the weight and power to do so, but it had some kind of programming installed that made it conscientious of the valuables.

That was fine with Archimedes, who used the crucial extra seconds he gained dashing around corners into new aisles to catch his breath.

Not a great design, he thought. *Not for a building like this, not when every third stop is something worth more than a house. I guess it lacks the capacity for greed, the desire to steal, but it'd still have made more since to craft several smaller bots. Maybe Abalos was relying on the intimidation factor?*

There was a flash of gold through a break in the cabinets to his right as the robot's massive hand shot in to grab at him. Archimedes yelped and leapt over it, pushing down on the hand with his own to get the leverage needed to make the vault. The move pushed glass deeper into his palms and the world went white, his brain playing nothing but static. He hit the floor on the opposite side of the arm awkwardly and fell onto his stomach. His chin bounced off the floor, grinding his teeth into his tongue, and he tasted blood. The robot was too large to fully fit through the gap, so it adjusted its position until it could better reach its arm in after him. Archimedes felt a metal finger scratch against the bottom of his shoe and scrambled onto his back, blood dripping down his chin, glass pushing into the space between his shoulder blades, red bubbles frothing at the edges of his mouth. The hand slapped against the floor in vain for a moment longer, blue lenses flaring as the gorilla stared at him, and then the arm withdrew. The robot thumped away, the acoustics of the building making it difficult to discern which direction.

"This thing sucks," he groaned, then picked himself up and ran.

The robot met him at the end of the aisle, lumbering into place until it blocked the exit entirely. The thing had no face, but its three blue eyes somehow conveyed a sense of eager hungriness.

Archimedes nearly drew his gun, but a million things were running through his mind. The ineffectiveness of Xolop's firearm. The speed of the construct in front of him. The glass in and the blood all over the palms of his hands. His options were limited, and those that were there didn't look good. Could he run, or would the thing catch him before he reached the far corner? He suspected the latter.

"Shit," he said, looking around. "Shit." A painting on his left looked back. A portrait, rather, of some prince or royal consort or whatever, Ark didn't have time to read the accompanying card, he just ripped the thing off the wall.

The robot went still. Its lenses grew bright. Cautious, calculating.

"Don't ascribe people thoughts to parts and pieces," Archimedes muttered to himself under his breath. "That's a very Caesar thing to do."

He took one trembling step forward, then another. The glass in his hands was sending bolts of agony through his forearms. The frame felt slippery, but he gripped the edges of it tightly with his fingertips, knowing it was a death sentence to let it drop, knowing death might be in store for him anyway. He held it out from his body, used it to cover as much of his body as he could. He wasn't sure what the robot deemed to be an acceptable risk or what was acceptable damage, and he would hate to find out by suddenly having an ankle or the crown of his head suddenly pinched between two giant metal fingers.

But his plan, off the cuff and reckless as it was, seemed to be working. The robot certainly recognized that there was a target behind the painting—enough of him *was* still visible and it didn't suddenly forget the pursuit that had led to this point—but it couldn't reconcile the potential damage to the merchandise. As Archimedes strode closer, the golden gorilla shrank back and back again until its bulk was pressed firmly against a wall. Enough room was left for Ark to squeeze by, painting and all, and he took advantage of it, the frame held forward like a weapon, one eye peeking around the side of it.

"Easy, big guy," he whispered. He glanced back, saw the open door, saw Caesar fidgeting just outside, his pistol in his hand. He backed up slowly, step by step, mentally classifying the pain he was feeling as a throbbing, willing it to not to feel worse. The robot followed him, one heavy footfall after another. *Thum. Thum.* The lenses flashed.

He backed up toward the door, step, step, the weight of the portrait bearing him down, making his arms ache, making them loose. He could hear Caesar urging him to hurry from outside. "Come on, come on," repeated the record. "Come on, come on."

When he was about fifteen paces from the door Archimedes hurled the painting as best he could at the gorilla's feet. The robot *flinched*, its massive arms coming up to try and catch the artwork. Archimedes didn't wait around to see if it would. He ran for the back door, air whipping around his naked legs, pistol bouncing against his thigh, his hands feeling like two blocks of raw meat at the end of his arms. He ran, breathless, yelling the same thing until the cold night air of the moon hit him: "Shut the door! Shut the door! Shut the door!"

Caesar did exactly that, reaching in past Archimedes to grab the edge of the door and yanking on it to bring it closed. A whirring from the door frame started as the bars began to come back out, crossing back across the door. Archimedes stared at the back of the building, wide-eyed, as several hard slams against the other side of the wall shook the whole structure. Dirt and debris filtered down from the roof.

Archimedes, chest heaving as he gasped for breath, asked, "What were you going to do with the gun?"

"I don't know. Xolop's didn't seem to do shit. I thought maybe, you know, if someone else showed up…"

Archimedes nodded, hunched over, the outer edges of his palms pressed against his knees as he tried to stabilize himself. "You get the maps?"

"Everything you shoved into your pockets, yeah."

"Alright, good. We've got to get back to the *Searcher* to stash them. Give me my pants back." Archimedes stood up and threw his head back, letting a hoarse laugh burst free. "Shit, we almost died. I love you, man."

"I love you too," Caesar said, mildly embarrassed. He held Archimedes' jeans out until his friend took them. "You think Grey will meet us at the ship?"

"I don't know. We'll figure something out," Archimedes said, shoving a foot through one of the legs. "Keep that gun ready, though, and try not to shoot me by accident."

When Grey went for the edge of the pit, the devilcats went for his legs. One of them, the red one, was successful, wrapping its front paws around his ankle and sinking a dozen sharp teeth into the back of his calf. The black one with the white stripes just barely missed, catching the side of his boot with its claws as Grey frantically pulled it up and out of the way. He placed the palms of his hands on the lip of the pit and used his arm strength to push himself up, forehead grinding against the mesh of the chain link fence. He kicked back with his free leg, the one with the scored boot, and caught the red devilcat in its haunch, its side, its groin, finally dislodging it and sending it back down into the dirt. His leg was hot and wet with blood. He could feel it trickling down beneath his jeans, knew it was going to pool in his sock. He got angrier.

Above him the crowd had started getting wild. Slips were being exchanged, as were yells and curses, and men and women alike jostled each other for a better look as Grey tried to get a firm grip on the fence. A man with a scar cutting through a milk-white eye put a hand on Grey's head and tried to push him back into the pit. The cats had taken residence on either side of Grey,

standing up against the wall so they could paw at his hips. He felt hooked claws tear into his

pantlegs, behind the pockets, felt the holes rip wider, then felt the claws tear bloody cuts into his

flesh. Grey grabbed the one-eyed man's wrist in his right hand, leaned back, and *yanked*.

The man, not expecting the resistance nor the surge of strength, was pulled perilously far over

the fence so that he was dangling nearly upside down, feet kicking, his crotch on the railing the

only thing keeping him from falling. Grey got his feet under him on the lip of the pit and stood.

He centered his weight, then leaned down and whispered in the man's ear.

"Hope you like cats."

He quickly got a tight grip on the top of the fence with his left hand, moved his right hand from

the man's wrist to the man's leg, gripped the flap of cloth there, and pulled back. The man slid

the rest of the way over the fence and fell, sprawling on his back in the center of the pit not far

from where Grey had landed. The devilcats sprung away to avoid being landed on, then darted

back in so they could attack the man. The red one went for the throat; the black one started

tearing at the shirt covering his ribs.

The space where the one-eyed man had been was quickly filled with two more, slender but

rough-looking types, one with a mouth full of cracked and browned teeth, the other with a hook

attached to his right arm in lieu of his hand. The hook was grimy and red and glinted sharply in

the basement's low lights. Grey moved first, leaning over the fence and into the crowd, and

throwing a quick right jab at Brownteeth. The man leaned back out of the way, flashing his

rotting grin. The hook hand flashed in overhead, aiming at the crown of Grey's skull. Grey

flinched back, shot his hand out again, grabbed the hook by the curve. The tip of it dug into the

back of his wrist, and as they wrestled for control the small puncture turned into a deeper horizontal groove and more blood. Grey let go of the fence to grab Hookhand by the forearm and, with both hands, was able to twist the hook and drive it down until it sank deep into Brownteeth's collarbone. Both men shrieked, although the one with the hook in him was markedly louder.

Grey swung one leg over the fence and used it to kick Hookhand in the hip, sending him off balance. The crowd moved away from them, and Hookhand fell, dragging Brownteeth with him with an accompanying spray of blood. Just under the wailing, Grey could make out the rending of flesh from the pit. He tossed his other leg over the fence and landed back on the filthy floor of the basement, amongst the crowd, and had a second to catch his breath before a fist appeared out of nowhere and crashed into his cheek, sending him staggering back into one of the support pillars.

He looked around but couldn't see who had hit him. Everyone was looking at him with hungry eyes and nasty smiles. He saw a few blades come out and, pressed tight against the pillar so he could protect his back against any opportunists, crouched down until he could grab a discarded bottle by the neck. His calf burned in protest as he squatted, and he felt a fresh stream of blood spring forth. A woman, black eyes shining dangerously, reached down to her thigh, pulled free a nicely polished hand cannon, and pointed it right at him.

That's a Frazee Thunderclap, Grey thought inanely. *I always wanted one of them.*

"No fuckin' firing guns in the bar!" someone yelled, and a large man barreled into the gunwoman, knocking her arm to the side. The pistol fired anyway, startling the crowd who had expected a more hands-on experience. One of the devilcats screamed from out of Grey's line of sight, and someone from the other side of the pit yelled, "You shot my fuckin' cat!"

All hell broke loose.

Taking advantage of the distraction caused by the pair wrestling over the gun, Grey rushed forward and hit the person closest to him—a purple-skinned Skir—right between the nose slits. It wasn't enough to break the bottle, but it sent the alien reeling backwards, its spindly arms pinwheeling into the mouth and neck of the two Humans behind it. The Humans' pained surprise quickly turned to anger; they seized the hapless Skir and started in with their fists.

Grey didn't stop, swinging the bottle again, backhanded this time, and this time it shattered when it connected with the base of someone's skull. That man dropped like a rock, maybe dead. Grey didn't check. He was too busy jamming the jagged remains of the bottle into a Murasai's chest, pushing him back into three more people looking to rush him. He could see the bottom of the stairs, not too far, maybe thirty feet.

Then someone grabbed him from the right. He cocked his left fist back, ready to swing, and then someone else entirely hit him in the kidney, again, three times. Grey's legs buckled and he went down to his knees. Someone else's knee decided to join him, and he brought his forearms up just in time block most of it. The collision was still enough to drive his own arms back into his nose hard enough to pop something. His mouth filled with the taste of hot copper. A pair of gunshots sounded from the opposite side of the pit and the chorus of excited screaming swelled once more.

"What the hell did you do that for?" someone yelled.

"She shot my cat!"

"Fuck your cat! It can't compete, so you forfeit the match!"

"She shot it, what about her? What about the guy that got tossed in with 'em?"

"Which one?"

"The first one, dammit, the first one!"

"Yeah! Where did he go?"

Grey would have laughed if the hail of fists and feet blocking him from sight didn't hurt so much. He covered up as best he could from his knees, arms protecting his face, although someone's heel managed to break through and score a gash through his left eyebrow. A thin waterfall of blood started flowing. He wiped at it with his sleeves, trying to keep it out of his eyes. He was able to get a foot back underneath him and twisted it into the ground to secure his footing. He was worried more about his back now, it being unprotected, and he swiveled at the hips, throwing elbows whenever he felt an opening, trying to keep anyone attacking from behind from landing a focused blow.

The basement of the bar had gradually turned into a full-blown riot once everyone who had placed a bet realized there wouldn't be any kind of payout for the devilcat fight. One man was already dead, and as demands that bets be returned to the bettors grew louder, more and more people were turning their frustration into physical violence. Before long Grey was no longer the center of attention. People were still hitting and kicking him, but his assailants were getting pulled one by one into scraps of their own as they got jostled, or spit on, or punched and kicked themselves by mistake. Grey's low position was suddenly an advantage as those crowding him were turning, aiming to hit each other in the face.

Grey kept an eye on the legs in front of him, letting himself be shoved about here and there, until he found just enough space to move. When it came, he pushed off the floor with the foot he had set firm and wrapped his arms around the knees of whoever was just ahead, unsure what species he had scooped up, keeping his head down and barreling forward, kidney screaming. He used whoever he was holding as a battering ram, pushing back the crowd and clearing a path for himself. Those he ran into were taken off guard and too hemmed in to get a solid strike through or to correct their balance and push back.

The staircase appeared through a sliver of space to his left. He dropped the man he was holding and kicked him in the stomach, nothing with much force but enough to keep him on the ground. The people trying to reach Grey found themselves stepping on and tripping over the body at their feet, giving the courier a few more precious seconds to escape. A pair of Serobi women stood in front of them, their pearlescent skin shimmering, their teeth bared, and their knives out.

They'd be pretty if they weren't trying to kill me, Grey thought.

He grabbed the woman on the left and threw her into the woman on the right, knocking them both down and clearing his way. He took the stairs up two at a time, pushing past a handful of others that were smart enough to know it was time to leave. His entire body was wet with sweat and blood, sore with bruises. Nothing felt broken, though the blow to his nose still had percussion playing behind his eyes.

At the top of the stairs a small group of curious people had gathered to look down into the basement. He pushed through them at the waist, firmly but not violently, uneager for a repeat performance of what he had just gone through. He looked around the bar, realized he must have looked a horror with his face covered in blood, pointed at the stairwell and yelled, "They're shooting guns down there! People are dying!"

Two Bozav, what must have passed for security in the *Hangnail*, were already headed for the stairwell. A porcine Dyr sidled up next to Grey, a yellow drink in each hand.

"You should grab yourself a bar towel to wipe your face off, and get yourself one of these," he said. "Artinian Toe-Rag. Tastes better than it sounds, but I guess that wouldn't be too hard." He laughed at his own joke, and added, "It'll mellow you right out. People are always dying on Dephros. Almost like a hobby. I wouldn't sweat it."

Grey stared at him for a long moment, his mind still trying to catch up with his body. "Yeah?" he asked, shaking his head. "Well, leave me out of it."

The Dyr was right about one thing, though. The Artinian Toe-Rags sure did mellow out the person drinking them. So much so that the Dyr didn't even notice when Grey slipped the alien's gun right out of his holster and took it with him out the front door.

The journey back to the *Searcher* didn't take long. Now that he had seen the uglier parts of Dephros, the streets made a certain kind of sense to Grey. Add to that the knack he had always had for reading body language. Face sticky with its mask of drying blood, gun held openly in his hand, nobody bothered him while he studied the men and women looking for their next drink or fix, the armed groups on their way to some kind of revenge or business deal. He watched for patterns, found some, narrowed them down to those that seemed likely to end in a landing pad.

The *Sol Searcher* sat just where he had landed it. Still beautiful. Still lean, save for a layer of dirt that had started to coat the bottom of the hull. That, and the three treacherous, backstabbing goddamned pirates standing next to it. Estella was actually touching the ship, rubbing her hand over the side, a thoughtful look on her face as if she somehow knew it had recently undergone severe repairs. Ressler and Monserat (*Yeah, that's his fucking name*, Grey thought) were behind her, Ressler with his arms crossed, the Murasai with his hands in his pockets.

Grey lifted the pistol, closed one eye to aim, and shot Monserat. The bullet hit clean, square in the center of his chest, and knocked him flat on his back. His hands convulsed, clawing at the wound. Monserat lifted his head from the ground to stare incredulously at the blood gushing from his torso, but his eyes were already losing focus. A moment later he stopped moving entirely.

"Guess you're going to need yet another navigator," Grey said. "Now, if you don't mind, please get your hand off my fucking ship."

Ressler went for his gun and another gunshot sounded. A plume of dust kicked up at the pirate's feet, red with blood, and the leather of his boot split apart. Ressler howled and fell onto his side, nearly landing on the dead Murasai. His hands grabbed at his ankle, unwilling to touch the bloody hole in his foot but needing to squeeze something all the same. Estella backed away from the *Searcher*, hands up.

Archimedes and Caesar stepped up next to Grey. Both were carrying guns, but it was clear which one had shot Ressler. Grey looked at Ark's bloody hands and arms and raised his eyebrows.

"Nice shot. What happened?"

Archimedes shrugged. "Betrayal. Faceless robot gorilla. You?"

"Betrayal," Grey said, gesturing toward Estella with the gun. "Devilcats and an angry mob."

"Nice." Archimedes fired again, hitting the ground between the two downed pirates. "Ressler, you even think about going for your gun again, you're going to have more than that piss-poor thought passing through that turd you call a brain."

Grey walked toward the pirates, kept his eye and the pistol on Estella. To her credit, even with her hands up she didn't seem concerned in the slightest. Archimedes followed a half-step behind, watching Ressler writhe on the ground. Caesar moved past all of them and keyed in the code that would unseal the *Searcher*'s ramp and lower it. Grey cast a quick glance over at him, saw that he looked ruffled but otherwise unharmed.

"Unbelievable," he muttered.

"Can I put my hands down?" Estella asked. "You have quite the advantage. Surprised me, really. I always figured you boys as tough, but nothing like this. You'd fit in nicely on Dephros, I'd say."

"Shut up, Estie," Grey said. He pinched the bridge of his nose to try and help his headache, wound up making it worse when he grabbed where the cartilage cracked. "But you can put your hands down. Don't try anything, please. I'd hate to knock you out again, but that doesn't mean I won't do it."

"Not shoot me?"

"After the shit you pulled in that bar, nobody would blame me for shooting you, but no. I'd rather we just call it quits. Got my shotgun?"

"It's on my ship. Want to go get it?"

"Nah. It wasn't really mine to begin with."

Estella nodded and looked down at her dead navigator. "Ressler won't forget this, you know. Neither will I. I can't."

Archimedes snorted. "Not making a great case for keeping you two alive."

The *Searcher* suddenly came to life, engines humming, exterior lights snapping on and cutting through the dusty air. Ark glanced back at Grey, who tilted his head toward the ramp. Archimedes nodded and backed up the ramp.

"Always a pleasure, Estella," he said before disappearing into the ship.

Grey followed him up but stopped when the pirate captain called his name. He turned back to her and sighed. "I don't want to hear it. I don't want to hear that it wasn't personal, or that it's just the pirate's nature. Whatever other half-dozen excuses you have. Things have been so extraordinarily bad for us on its own without having someone I—"

"Trusted?" she asked.

"God, no," he laughed. "But cared about. Someone I thought I shared something with despite the fact you shot me last time we saw each other. Thanks for the favor, I guess, although from the look of Ark, I guess even that was loaded."

Estella held her hands up. "I don't know anything about that. I had nothing to do with it."

"Maybe. You still did enough on your own. Let's call this goodbye and leave it at that." He flicked his gun in Ressler's direction. "Keep him away from us, too. A third confrontation between us, I'm gonna stop holding back."

"For what it's worth, I'm glad you survived, lover."

Grey rolled his eyes and backed up the ramp, watching her disappear a fraction at a time. That fiery hair. The soft lips. Her dangerous body. Once he was fully inside the *Searcher*, he hit the control that closed and sealed the ramp. Then, as the ship began to rise, he dropped down to the floor, leaned back against the wall, and buried his face in his hands.

Caesar sat in the *Searcher*'s cockpit, comfortable as he took the ship up. He angled the ship away from the pirates, turned the nose up toward the sky, and headed for space. He had had quite enough of the bandit moon, though he knew the experience, brief as it was, would never leave him. Like Astrakoth. No doubt like wherever they were headed next.

Picking up a lot of those life experiences, he thought.

He felt unreal, like he was living someone else's life. Scientists didn't get into gunfights. They (probably) didn't fight robots. They researched and built things, they developed breakthroughs in science and technology. You didn't get killed for that kind of work, not unless you were notoriously bad or kidnappingly good in the field. He would have been content just toiling away in his lab somewhere with a lovely sky, normal sun cycles, temperate weather, minding his own business. Now he could barely remember the last time he had a solid night's sleep.

It must have been aboard the Imagination, he thought. *Which, true to its name, I'm beginning to think I conjured entirely in my mind as some sort of sweet release from this nightmare.*

A shirtless Archimedes moved gingerly into the cockpit and leaned against the doorway with his forearm. A giant purple-black bruise at his hip had begun to spread up from his waistline to just below his ribcage. That and the bloodied bandages wrapped around his hands were a glaring distraction from the dozens of healed, puckered scars that criss-crossed his arms and abdomen.

"How are you doing?" Caesar asked.

"Got the glass out of my hands, at least. All the big pieces, anyway, although I'm sure there are little chunks trapped in there somewhere that'll just have to work themselves out. I can't reach the rest, so I'll need you or Grey to help me with that, but I've tracked down some painkillers and chased them with whiskey in the meantime. Should right my ship here in about twenty minutes."

"You shouldn't do that, you know. Drinking with painkillers. It's dangerous."

Archimedes' eyes widened in mock surprise. "Oh, is it? Good God, I wouldn't want to put myself in *danger.*"

"Alright, point taken," Caesar said, shaking his head. "How's Grey?"

"Upset. Physically, I think he was probably worse off after Astrakoth, but I didn't ask. He looked like he needed some space."

Archimedes moved around to the co-pilot's chair and sat down on the edge, careful not to touch his back to the seat cushion. He looked out through the viewport at the stars, thoughtful. Caesar glanced over. Archimedes' back had some bruises as well, though not as bad, a gross yellow that darkened to green in a few small patches. There were a couple dozen small cuts, seemingly shallow enough, easily treated with some salves and bandages. There were also at least three larger shards of blood-stained glass poking out of his skin, each about half the length of his little finger. Those would need to be removed, the wounds cleaned thoroughly and stitched.

Caesar said, "Hey, so I'd like to get at least a Causeway away from Dephros before we start… I don't know, relaxing? Or whatever, debriefing? I can take a look at your wounds, fix them up a little bit better. If you don't want to wait, we can see if Grey is in good enough shape to take over."

"Whiskey and painkillers, brother," Archimedes said. "I can wait."

Caesar looked his friend over one more time, saw him hunched forward, elbows on his knees, a content expression on his face. Looking at the stars. Caesar was sure he was in pain, even with the medication, but his friend didn't look uncomfortable. He just looked tired. Caesar nodded to himself and turned back to the controls. He had never been an ace pilot like Grey or Ark, but he was a good one. He enjoyed flying. He enjoyed the quiet of space, the relative stillness once you for away from the moons and the planets.

That stillness embraced the *Sol Searcher* and her crew now like a cool blanket on a hot night.

Chapter Fourteen

Final Preparations

Morning. Thorus, on the planet Salix. The estate of Euphrates Destidante.

The sun had been up for only an hour. Euphrates had not slept long the night before, but what few hours he did get were deep, fulfilling, and left him feeling well-rested. He stood now in front of his bathroom mirror, naked to the waist, studying his reflection. The years had aged him but only seriously around the eyes. There were crow's feet there in the corners, and the faintest hint of bags beneath them, though he used creams—expensive and imported—to help with those. As he had grown older, his eyes had recessed some. Not enough to make him look gaunt, but enough to make his gaze more severe. He liked to think it lent him a hint of dangerous wisdom.

A silver hair caught the bathroom light, poking out just above his right ear. He gripped it between his index finger and thumb and gave it a sharp tug. It came free with little resistance and no pain at all. A minor inconvenience snuffed out because Euphrates willed it, the same as he had other inconveniences around the universe. He let the hair drop in the bathroom sink and turned the faucet on to wash it down the drain.

There are other problems, though, aren't there? Euphrates thought. *Severe ones, stubborn little bastards that refuse to go away. You've come a long way from that filthy little shack on Outer Springer, a long way from the dozens of other grimy holes-in-the-wall over the years, but sometimes you've just got to handle things personally if you want them handled right.*

He slipped a dark green button-up shirt off of the hook on the bathroom door and put it on. As he did up the buttons, he turned his head back and forth, checking for any other rogue hairs hiding in the slick blackness he meticulously prepared each day. Satisfied that he had eradicated the sole offender, he buttoned his cuffs, straightened his collar, and stepped from the bathroom back into his bedroom.

Nimbus Madasta was sprawled out on her stomach in their bed, her hair splayed out like a purple halo around her head. At the sound of the bathroom door opening, she made a small noise of contentment, the sound of someone who had become one with their mattress, and turned her head to look at him. Her eyes squinted at the light spilling from the doorway behind him. Euphrates reached back and flicked the switch, taking the bathroom back into darkness.

"You're up early," Nimbus murmured. "S'usually me."

"It is," he agreed. "Unfortunately, I've appointments to keep. The universe never sleeps."

"Get better assistants and come back to bed."

Euphrates' smiled faintly. "If only I could. Would you like me to put the coffee on, or will you be a while yet?"

Nimbus turned her head back the opposite way and lifted a hand to wave him away. *Go do your duty*, the wave said. *You're keeping me up.* He left her to it, venturing into his office to retrieve his jacket, his pistol, and a few papers that needed filing to keep the bureaucratic machine rumbling along.

The ride from his home was uneventful. Rollo had attempted playing classical music, an enjoyment normally shared between them, but Euphrates had asked him to turn it off, preferring silence for the morning's drive. He watched the buildings swim by one by one, the reds and oranges of dawn splashing them where their own lights had yet to turn on. They drove down Araman Way and through the Golden Rails district. The crossed the bridge over Opinti River and went around the Bends instead of continuing straight toward the Political Discourse and

Development district, driving on until they finally reached their location: Bradamar Square, a large shopping center located halfway between a residential area and the freight yards.

The area contained two concentric circles of strip malls filled with retail stores and restaurants, neither with any consistent theme. The centerpiece was the Sabraudio, a towering mall filled with more stores and more restaurants and that made up for its modest base area by boasting twenty stories that also contained two theaters, a bowling alley, an in-door ice rink, an arcade, half a dozen bars, two emergency treatment centers, and more. By the time Rollo pulled into one of the mall's parking spots early morning had settled in to just about opening time, and several more cars were parking around them.

Rollo turned around in the driver's seat. "You want me to come inside with you, boss?"

"Absolutely fu…" Euphrates cut himself off and rubbed his temples. "I've come to realize, Rollo, that sometimes my immediate responses can come off rude, and I would like to work on that. So, to that end, let's just say that I would prefer that you didn't, and that you should assume that to always be the case unless I state otherwise. I hardly think I'll be in any danger in a mall, and you would contribute nothing of value to the conversation I'm about to have." He opened the car door and stepped one foot out, paused, leaned back in. "Not that you aren't valued. It's just that… you… hell, never mind."

It was still early enough in the day that the crowds in the mall were few and spread thin. As Euphrates worked his way through the halls and around slow walkers, storefronts were pushing up their security gates and finishing their till and inventory counts. Euphrates took the escalators (elevators were too confining for him in a place like they mall; they made him nervous, despite what he had told Rollo) to the third floor. From there, it was hard to miss the little restaurant he had been asked to attend.

Boncho's Pizza Palace wasn't large by any standard, let alone that of the tower it was located in. There were only five little booth tables and a kitchen that shared most of its space with the front counter, but when Euphrates had researched it, he found that it still managed to open early each day, received high marks on all of its health inspections, and had a reputation for creative and delicious dishes.

He still couldn't help but hate it on sight.

Raygor Stahl was seated at the second-to-last booth, facing the entrance. The portly Lodite was stuffing a slice of pizza under his trunk when he caught sight of Euphrates and paused just long enough to give him an upward nod of acknowledgment. Euphrates strode through the restaurant, lifted his hand as a greeting when the cashier welcomed him, and sank down into the booth.

"Humans crack me up," Stahl said, finishing his slice. He licked all six of his thin little fingers. "A universe full of fruits and vegetables, oils and broths, peppers, spices, herbs, all manner of beasts to broil, cook, bake, and eat raw, and places like this still exist. They thrive! The longevity of your people's simplistic inventiveness is truly admirable."

"Places like this are beneath me. I suppose it's too much to hope they serve salads."

"They do, but you're not eating a fucking salad in a place like this. Get over yourself and have a slice, Destidante. You're embarrassing me."

Euphrates scoffed. "Yes, that's likely." He hedged for a minute, then slid a small plate over to sit in front of him. He picked up a piece of pizza, almost delicately, hating the grease, and took a bite before setting the slice on the plate. It was his first food of the day, and it was oily and arguably too cheesy, but the vegetable toppings and whatever they used in the sauce were both tangy and savory.

Euphrates made a face.

"You like it," Stahl laughed, trunk quivering.

"I won't give you the satisfaction of saying so."

Stahl laughed again and pulled another slice free. He grabbed a glass shaker full of pepper flakes and unleashed a healthy coating. "I've got to say, Destidante, as stiff as you can be, I truly enjoy your company. Off the record, and I'll deny it and kill you if you tell anyone."

"Naturally." Euphrates' stomach rumbled, loud enough for both of them to hear. Stahl grinned. Euphrates glared, then picked up the slice for another bite. "I will admit that my feelings are… similar. It's rare for me to find someone I can regard as a peer. A confidante, even."

"We're honest in our dishonesty," Stahl said.

"Just so."

"You ever worry about what people might think?"

Euphrates' brows pinched together in confusion. "Not particularly, but what specifically do you mean? Seeing me in a place like this? You picked the place, so I'm not sure what you're getting at."

"I did pick the place. You can't be seen skulking around the Swallows all the time. Again, I'm glad to see you, but on the rare occasions we meet up, a Lodite getting together with one of the top five most influential Humans in the universe… I'm not exactly one of your constituents, you get what I'm saying? It's no skin off my back, but you ever think people might start getting some notions in their head as to why you're meeting with someone like me when you have better things to?"

Cloaking technologies for the cameras, Euphrates thought. *The rest is rumors and hearsay from nobodies, easily snuffed out should the rumors ever start getting too big for their britches.*

He cleared his throat. "Even a man like me is allowed to have… friends." He rolled his finger. "Rewind a moment, because I'm curious: you said top five. I assume you meant Rors, Magga, Talys—loathe as I am to admit it—and myself. Who is the fifth? Do you know something I don't?"

"Undoubtedly. In this case, however, I have nothing but conjecture. I assume it's one of your generals. Maybe one of your celebrities. Your people's obsessions with disproportionate military responses and the mundane idiocy of rich people is basically bred into you." Stahl laughed through his trunk. "That's why I like the Dyr so much. You two and the Ryxan come from three near-identical planets, so why is it the Dyr are the only one who know how to mind their fucking business?"

"The Dyr, *as a species*, exist only to look like animals Humans eat, or have tamed, or have driven to extinction."

Stahl looked amused. "And yet which of you is getting mollywhopped by the Ryxan over trade agreements?"

Euphrates said nothing. Only fools railed against irrefutable fact.

"To that end," Stahl continued unperturbed, "I have this for you." He pulled up a box, gift-wrapped in dark blue wrapping paper, crossed over and bound with silver ribbons and topped with a silver bow. He slid it over to Euphrates' side of the table.

"Raygor, what the hell," Euphrates protested.

"A whole lot less conspicuous than kicking a briefcase over to you or trying to slip a data disk over in a secret handshake. A gift box, though? It could be your birthday, or congratulations for a notable political achievement. You had any of those lately? Besides nearly starting a war with the Ryxan?"

Euphrates' eyes narrowed. "Careful, Raygor."

The Lodite tapped the edge of the box. "What you wanted is in here. I have the copy, as requested. Whatever you thought was on this, it's worse. Enough to transform the universal landscape on an unprecedented scale. And if the... item were to get out, it would be something else entirely. Even if it were never used."

Euphrates took the box in his hands, gently, lost in thought. "The information, you're thinking it has value to you personally, now."

Stahl barked a laugh. He pushed the tray with the remaining pizza off to the side so he could look at Euphrates directly, no obstacles between them.

"This information would be valuable to *anybody*. If you were anyone else, I would have sold it already. I don't need to rehash our history, how you and I got to where we war, what we've done for each other. But the universe is bigger than you and me, bigger than Humans and Lodites. What's on that drive..."

"I'll pay you an additional 50,000 chits to honor our original arrangement. Fifteen days. I've been on this since the item's initial delivery and have been attempting to track its journey since. Give me the fifteen days to find the item and to make arrangements as I need them. If I've not contacted you about using the information, you have freedom to sell it however you want."

Stahl studied him, folding his twelve fingers over his abdomen, thinking. "You're going to need to add a zero. If you have as strong an idea as to what's on here as you led me to believe when we met in my shop, you'll know it's worth the money. Anyone but you, you'd never have seen me again the minute I unlocked the little fucker, but out of respect I gave it all back to you. Could have told you it got lost or deleted, could have doctored up some shit, and I didn't. Out of respect. My original fee bought you the information. Half a million chits will get you the two weeks."

Euphrates clenched his jaw so tightly that his molars clicked together and he though, just for a second, that he might have cracked his teeth. "Fifteen days was the deal."

Stahl smiled. "Sure."

"Then it's a deal. I trust the usual account is still active?"

"It is."

"I'll have the money wired within the hour." Euphrates reached into his pants pocket and removed a slip of yellow paper. He slid it across the table. "The copy… I may need it delivered somewhere."

"You've got my number," Stahl said. He scooped up the paper, tucked it away, then slapped the table and started scooting out from the booth. "Help yourself to the rest of the pie. My doctor says I've got to lose weight. I've paid ahead for appointments through the end of the year, so I've got at least look like I'm putting in an effort. A pleasure as always, Destidante. I'll see you on the other side of this."

Euphrates nodded. He didn't bother watching the Lodite leave. He just ran his hand over the lid of the gift box, feeling validated but tired, electrified but frustrated, and feeling just a little bit, though he would never admit it, afraid.

*****

The hospital, as always, was a flurry of activity. Patients checking in, patients being wheeled out, patients being rolled around on gurneys. Doctors and nurses walking briskly to and fro, noses deep in clinical files and treatment notes or carrying an assortment of medical equipment, using their peripheral awareness to keep from bumping into anyone or anything. In one corner of the lobby, a family was crying while a doctor did his best to remain emotionally detached. A child was wailing in another corner, her arm bent at an odd angle. As Nimbus Madasta walked through she passed a thin woman with a headwrap who was smiling and telling a younger woman, her daughter, perhaps, that the treatments she had been going through were a success.

Nimbus, awake now and ready for the day, loved it at the hospital. There was an efficiency to things among the emotional chaos and the urgency of pain and illness. Procedures were followed and backup procedures in place, waiting in the wings if the first steps went awry. Even something as simple as drawing blood could be broken down to a matter of steps once the equipment was sterilized and prepped: find the vein, apply the tourniquet, swab the area, puncture the flesh. She liked to think of herself as an agent of order.

One of the nurses at the front counter noticed her as she walked by. She begged a quick pardon from the red-eyed, pink-nosed woman checking in and waved Nimbus over.

"Good morning, Cheryl," Nimbus said, leaning into the little office. "What's up?"

"Good morning! A package came for you this morning, so I had security run it back to your office. Is that alright?"

"That's fine, yeah." Truthfully, Nimbus was surprised the woman didn't take it upon herself to open the package and see what was inside. She had always had an interest in other people's business that could most positively be described as overly enthusiastic. "I wasn't expecting anything. Who dropped it off?"

"No idea. Somebody from one of those courier groups. Aventure or Tigen Delivery, whatever." The woman waiting to check in was getting impatient. She fidgeted uncomfortably in front of the little window and placed her hands on her hips. Cheryl held up a finger, telling her to wait just a second more. "I pulled up your credentials to prove you worked here, and they let me sign for you on behalf of the hospital. They took off without giving me any details. No name on it that I could see, just that it was from some city on Agnimon."

Another surprise. Nimbus didn't know anyone on Agnimon. Not that she could recall, anyway, nor could she recall anyone saying they were even heading over to the planet for a visit. If she told Cheryl that, though, it might kick off a whole set of unsubstantiated rumors. "Thanks again for taking care of it. You're all good up here?" she asked, tilting her head in the sick woman's direction.

"Oh, sure! Business as usual. You'll have to let me know later what you got."

Nimbus smiled and stepped out of the room, letting the other woman get back to her responsibilities. Big Dave Andler was working security. He smiled at her through the glass of the surveillance room and buzzed her through the doors. She gave him a little wave as she passed, Big being her favorite of the hospital's armed guards.

Her office was located in the surgery center despite her appointments seldom including any kind of surgery work. She had been gifted the room once she had gained her residency, a place to call her own and a solitary dark red wooden desk inside for furniture. She had added an ergonomic office chair for herself, a pair of tidy little chairs for her patients and visitors, two filing cabinets set in the back right and back left corners, and a little rug she had picked up on a beach vacation on Inner Springer. A fan in the corner helped keep the windowless room cool. Her walls were dressed with several fine art pieces she had picked up at auction or that had been gifted to her by Euphrates. A picture of her parents, a calendar, and a cup full of pens helped occupy the surface of her desk so that her computer wouldn't look so lonely. Slowly but surely, she had transformed the office into her home away from home.

And there, sure enough, was a small square package in the center of her desk. A gift? Euphrates could be spontaneous when he wanted to be.

Nimbus took off her jacket and draped it over the visitor's desk. *Need to get some coat hooks,* she reminded himself. *Set them up near the door.*

Cheryl was right about one thing: the box had no name on it, no return address, no indications as to who might have sent it beyond Agnimon's custom stamps. It had been addressed to her, at the hospital, in neat handwriting in black ink. The box was about the size of a child's lunchbox and wrapped in thick brown paper. The flaps at the ends seemed untampered with. She slid her nail beneath the edge of the flap on one end and began tearing the tape away. It came up easily enough and she tossed the wrapping in the waste bin. The box itself was plain black wood with silver hinges on the back. It bore no locks, had no clasps. It wasn't ticking or hissing or scuttling. She placed her thumbs on either corner of the lid and pushed it up and open.

Inside were mostly papers—stories, they looked like, or statements—but there was a recording device as well. A small data drive was taped to a flyer for a club called the Ruby Swell. A note written on a small square of plain white paper read, "Do you know where your lover is?"

Nimbus' heart began to quicken.

*****

With the Parliament of Universal Interest being as well-oiled a machine as it was, Euphrates' work didn't take him long to finish: a couple hours of tedium, a small pile of paperwork, a pair of meetings, a few e-mails sent, and a reminder of his invitation to a socialite's ball with an auction that night. It was all just detail work, nothing mentally taxing, and Euphrates attacked it until he was finished and alone again in his office. Only then did he slip a data drive into his work computer. He waited while the files contained within decrypted themselves for his viewing, secured themselves against any outside interests, and then pulled up on the screen one by one: financial records and account balances from scores of cities across two dozen planets and moons. At the bottom of each list, beneath the most recent balance report, was a bulleted list of recurring expenses—payoffs, maintenance costs, the prices of supplies—followed by a second list of potential emergency expenses. In nearly two decades of dealing with various underground elements and the political arena (which could often be just as undermining and ruthless), he had rarely suffered a dramatic loss of income.

But then again, he had never before been confronted with a situation such as the one he was in now. He studied the lists and jotted down notes on a small pad as needed, figuring out where to pull funds from, which accounts to reinforce. Raygor had demanded a heavy price, but his word was good with Euphrates, and he would be a dangerous man to cross besides.

The door to his office opened suddenly without announcement or ceremony. Talys Wannigan stepped inside and leaned back against the doorframe, keeping the door open. Euphrates slid his notepad to the side, out of sight, and set his pen down on it. Talys couldn't see the computer screen either, not from where he was standing, but Euphrates tapped two keys on his keyboard anyway, and the display turned black.

"Did you forget where your office was, or just common courtesy?"

"Apologies for not knocking. I just figured you would want to hear the news."

"What would you have done had my door been locked?" Euphrates asked, remembering storming into Talys' office a couple months before.

"I suppose I would have stood there a bit embarrassed." Talys stuffed his hands into his oversized pants pockets and grinned. Whatever he was happy about, Euphrates was sure he wouldn't feel the same way. "I've been speaking with Rors."

There it was.

"Have you," Euphrates said.

"With Magga's health improving some, there has been more than a little buzz about her returning for the next Council meeting. With her need of you as her Advisor, I'll be returning to my role as Advisor for Rors full-time. I do appreciate your diligence working with him while attentions and duties called me elsewhere."

"Yes, and what was it that you've been doing in the months I've been speaking in your place?"

Talys shrugged, grinned again. "Rors has plenty of other responsibilities away from the Council. He asked me to make sure those were taken care of so that he wouldn't be distracted during this trying time with the Ryxan."

Bullshit, Euphrates thought.

But a sudden sliver of doubt crept into his chest. He hadn't heard the rumors about Magga's return, nor any updates about her health. Was it true? Had he been too distracted to notice, or was he being kept out of the loop? Or was Talys lying to his face? And while Rors had more or less dismissed Talys entirely while confessing his guilt, the possibility that the other Advisor may also be complicit suddenly reared its head.

His resolve to eradicate the problem that was Talys Wannigan deepened.

"Is that all?" Euphrates asked, turning back to his notepad. "You just wanted to tell me my workload has lightened? Appreciated. You can see yourself out."

"Do you have any news for me?"

Euphrates flicked his eyes up. "Other than that we're still on the brink of war over an oil that eight out of ten people could not tell you a single application for? No, no news."

"In that case I'll leave you back to your thrilling afternoon of inaction. Best regards to the doctor."

Anger flashed in Euphrates, but before he could stand or even say anything in return, Talys was out the door, closing it behind him.

Temper, temper. Everything in its own time. And if all else fails, maybe you can just shoot him in the street.

Euphrates turned back to his computer. A few more taps on the keyboard brought the files back up. He briefly considered locking the door to prevent any more unwanted intrusions, but he was nearly done. He just needed to figure out where he could divert one more large sum of money. Just in case he needed it—and he suspected he would—for one last major play before the house of cards came down.

*****

"And now we've come to our spotlight item of the evening: an original Domingo Santano Flores painting, *The Plight of Valerie's Stars*. Painted two hundred and two years ago in Flores' hometown of Daraska, on the planet Salix, this particular piece has been well-maintained and kept in near-mint condition despite the passage of time and despite being transported through several Causeways over the last two centuries. This magnificent work of art would be at home in any collection or would serve as the perfect painting to start a new one. Bidding will start at 250,000 chits."

"Two-fifty!" a voice called out.

"Three hundred!" cried another.

"Three-fifty!"

The painting was indeed beautiful, one of several acclaimed productions from one more tortured creative soul in the universe. It hadn't been depression that so plagued Domingo Flores, however, nor any kind of substance addiction. He had been a compulsive gambler in his spare time, a vice he quickly discovered he was no good at but couldn't tear himself away from regardless. In his later years, after a brief period away from the canvas, he turned to his art with a renewed passion, desperate to finish and sell as many pieces as he could that he might use the profits to stay ahead of the debts he had accrued. It worked for a while. Right up until the day it didn't.

Valerie's Stars was one of the pieces completed near the start of Flores' decline, when his concentration and affection for the craft still bled into the paint. The painting depicted a woman rising toward the stars in a personal spacecraft, wonder in her eyes, while two lovers stared forlornly after her from the ground. As the auctioneer said, it would be a vast improvement to anyone's home.

"Five hundred thousand," a man growled from the back of the room. Euphrates glanced back over his shoulder, spotted him almost immediately. Dalton Hess, early fifties. Salt-and-pepper hair. He had a bushy mustache that he once confided made him feel more distinguished. Euphrates had found it was an efficient tool for storing the soup served at the poli potlucks.

"Eight hundred thousand," Euphrates said, looking back to the front. His jet-black hair had become tousled at some point; he smoothed it back into place with one hand.

The massive jump in the bid brought the crowd to a stunned silence. Hess shifted in his seat to gape at him.

"Eight hundred thousand," the auctioneer said. "Eight hundred, do I have eight-fifty? Let me hear it, eight-fifty, do I—"

"Here," Hess croaked.

"Nine hundred," Euphrates responded immediately.

"One million chits!"

"One million and two."

Silence again, save for the uncomfortable fidgeting in seats, the disbelieving whispers. A few of the attendants had turned to look at Hess openly, curious to see what he would do next.

"One million, two hundred thousand. One million, two! Do I have one million and three? One million, three? We've got one million, two. Anyone? Anybody. Going once. Going twice."

"Damn you, Destidante," Hess snarled. He stood from his seat and stormed through the parlor doors and back into the ballroom. The rest of the crowd gradually followed suit, the auction officially over. The whispers grew louder and, like, the people, followed Hess out.

Euphrates smiled to himself.

The dinner in the ballroom was an immaculate affair, with close to two hundred tables set up in a space larger than some homes. Servers hustled as quickly as they could without causing an accident, carrying trays of hors d'oeuvres that could fetch four hundred chits apiece in a restaurant somewhere. Glasses were filled with exotic brandies and champagnes, never fully empty for long. The smells of gourmet dishes mingled with each other in the air as plates were hand-delivered to seated dinners engaged in conversation.

Euphrates was enjoying himself, having left the transportation of the painting to the movers provided by the auction. He eschewed liquor for the evening, opting for sparkling water while Gladys Kane, the heiress to a chain of high-end jewelry stores, regaled him with tales of her third husband, a well-known hunter and outdoorsman who had died some years before when his canoe overturned on Direx. Euphrates detested the heiress but nodded and listened politely all the same; you never did know what might slip out once someone really gets going.

Dalton Hess found him less than ten minutes later. Euphrates feigned surprise when the older man grabbed him by the elbow and asked for a private audience. Euphrates apologized to Mrs. Kane for the interruption, but she waved him off and told him she was grateful for as much time as he had allowed her to take up.

The two men walked away, equal in stride.

"You're wrinkling my suit," Euphrates said as soon as they were out of earshot. Any sign of geniality he had put on for the jewelry baroness had vanished.

"Sorry, sorry," Hess said, releasing his elbow. He brushed at his own lapels, jittery. "Look, I wanted to talk to you about the painting."

"The painting? You mean the Flores piece?"

"You know damn well I mean the Flores piece. It was the only item I came here for, and just about everyone knew it. I want to buy it from you, Euphrates, everything that you paid for it plus another thirty percent for the trouble. It'll take me a little bit of time to get the funds together, but if we can come to an agreement on that and you keep the painting safe in the meantime…" He trailed off when he heard Euphrates chuckling. "I'm not joking, dammit! I had plans for that piece, for my collection. Is thirty percent too low for your rich blood? Because I can go up to thirty-five if you're looking to prove a point of some kind, but you're pushing me with that."

"I'm not laughing at your offer, Dalton," Euphrates said. He finished his sparkling water and placed the glass on a table as they walked by. "And thirty percent would be more than enough, but you're right about me looking to prove a point. In fact, I've already sold the painting for thirty percent of what I bought it for."

Hess stumbled. "What?" he spluttered. "When the hell did you even find the time to sell it?"

"It was a pre-arranged deal in exchange for a favor. I've never been much of one for paintings, personally. I prefer sculptures. There's a much smaller margin of error. As far as *Valerie's Stars* goes, it's as you said: just about everyone knew you wanted it. I figured I could kill two birds with one stone."

"You threw away eight hundred thousand chits? To *spite* me?" The older poli's face was growing bright red. His hands were working themselves into and out of fists.

Euphrates gave him a toothless smile. Something deadly danced behind his eyes. "To spite you," he acknowledged.

The rich and bitter moved around them, oblivious or apathetic to the unsettling quiet that had settled over the two men. A waiter hovered for just a moment, intending to provide them with new drinks. He thought better of it and moved on at a brisk pace.

"Why?" Hess rasped.

Euphrates nodded, pleased that he had fully captured the other man's attention. "Walk with me, Dalton."

He slipped his hands into his pockets and began working his way through the crowd, trusting that Hess would follow him. The poli didn't disappoint; he stayed two steps behind, working his head on a swivel to see if anyone was looking his way, appearing very much like a man who had stepped in a puddle much deeper than he had expected. Neither man spoke a word until they had left the ballroom and stepped into an elaborately furnished smoking room. Euphrates closed the door and locked it.

"Is it because I've spoken against your proposals?" Hess asked softly. "You and Magga, Talys and Rors, you're our representatives, but the polis have a voice, too. It's supposed to be a collective effort. If I see or hear something I don't agree with, I believe it's my civic duty to say something about it. To take a stand. But it hasn't ever been personal."

"Dalton, I would never accuse you of being a stupid man," Euphrates said, turning away from the door to look at him. "Misguided, perhaps, and occasionally lacking foresight, but I think you value your career enough not to risk it because of how you feel about somebody. I also think it would be foolish on my part to expect you to agree with me on every little thing. So no, I don't think it was personal, and I don't hold it against you. I do, however, need you to agree with my most important plans when they come up. I need that to be an absolute surety."

"I can't guarantee that," Hess said. He paced around the room, shaking his head. He faced Euphrates and brought a finger up as if to scold him. "You know I can't guarantee that, and I won't. You piss away a *painting* and you think that's enough of a power play to make me bend over for whatever half-assed schemes you bring to the arena? Petty nonsense. All you did was piss me off and you've guaranteed that I would be turned against you. You best believe I'll be tearing apart any proposal you do bring up now, looking for any one thing, any singular detail that I can use to derail it when it comes time to vote."

Euphrates waited until he was sure the man was finished ranting. He watched Hess' chest heave, watched the blood that had so quickly rushed to his face start to settle. "The painting was a warning. I needed to get your attention. I needed you to understand that I am willing to do anything, spend any resource to get what I want and to get where I need to be. See, I don't need you all the time, Dalton. I only need you to back my play when I truly need it backed. When it would matter the most in the larger scheme of things. And I need you, specifically, Dalton, because I have a feeling you will soon be gifted with an opportunity unlike anything you have ever expected, one that I intend to do anything in my power to make sure is granted you."

"What are you on about?" Hess asked, narrowing his eyes.

Instead of answering, Euphrates took a seat in one of the leather-bound chairs in the room. He gestured across the way at a companion seat. Hess hesitated but curiosity got the better of him. He sat.

"We can get into the details later. The point is that I believe we would work better together than as opponents. The painting… I admit that what I did was kind of cruel. Like I said, it was a warning. A showcase of what I can accomplish when I set my mind to it. The right resources in the right places at the right time, they can benefit me, they could hurt you. I might get a piece of art, for example. I might get information, instead. Information like where your money has been going besides auction houses and gifts for your better half."

Hess froze everywhere but his eyes, which gave a bit of a nervous shake. He said nothing.

"The off-planet vacations," Euphrates continued. "Vacations you write off as business trips and have been embezzling government funds for. Expensive dinners, lavish travel accommodations. The escorts. A *shocking* number of escorts, really, considering your history of cardiovascular issues. It's impressive in its own way. That I should be half as virile as you when I reach your age."

"Euphrates—"

"I wasn't able to confirm the use of REM powder, but the rumors have been circulating for some time. I had nothing to do with those, but I could certainly speed them along. A urine test would sort things out one way or another. Either way, the locations you've checked into, the audio and visual records of your… unique kinks, well, it's enough right there to paint a damning picture." He gave a thin smile. "And you, so fond of paintings."

"Please. My wife—"

"Dalton, I don't give any more of a damn about your marriage than you seem to. That ship launched long ago, and I'm sure she knows it. The poor woman is just too kind to leave you, although I'm sure she's working something on the side as well. But *your* crimes and extracurricular activities are downright salacious. Those are just the things I found out, the things that *actually* exist. Now imagine if I were to turn my undivided attention to creating a work of art of my own."

"My career," Hess muttered. He seemed to fold into himself, sinking back into the chair. His eyes had dropped to the floor between Euphrates' feet, and it was there that they stayed.

"Your career, yes. It would be ruined, your supporters tarnished. Your wife would finally go, along with the shreds of your reputation. Prison is almost a given, for the embezzlement at the very least. Any attempt your allies might make against me would be rebuffed, soundly, by plans I had prepared before I even stepped into the building tonight. That's what you've never understood about me, Dalton, as a person: everything I do is just a piece of a larger puzzle. You have always focused too hard on the subject at hand, not what it can lead to or transform into."

"Why would you want to do this to me?"

Euphrates' eyes grew wide, sympathetic. "Dalton, you haven't been paying attention. Those resources… right place, right time, they can swing things back just as easily the other way. They don't have to *ruin* your career. I don't want that. They can elevate it. Just as long as I know I've

got your support when I need it. For your sake. For the sake of the Human race."

Hess closed his eyes tight, struggling to stifle whatever tornado of emotions was tearing

through his chest. He lifted his hands—big, meaty things with scarred and knobby knuckles—

and covered his face with them.

Muffled, he said, "I'm listening."

*****

The painting was delivered in late evening, after the sun had gone down. The knock at the door

surprised Nimbus, pulling her out of a daze that had seen her sitting on the couch in the living

room, staring at the fireplace, her third glass of wine held between her knees. She set the glass

down on the coffee table and went to the door, pausing to grab a taser from her purse.

The two men at the front porch held the painting between them. It was wrapped in a protective

cloth, only the sharp edges of the frame sticking out. The men had been resting the weight of the

item on the tops of their shoes but lifted it again when the door opened. They both saw the taser

at the same time, looked at each other, then smiled back at Nimbus sheepishly.

"Pardon the bother, ma'am," said the man on the left. "We know it's late, but we were asked to

deliver this to the estate of Advisor Destidante immediately. We were under the impression—"

"You're at the right place," Nimbus cut in. She held the door open wider. "Come on in."

"You want this somewhere in particular?" the man on the right asked as he shuffled past her.

"No, anywhere is fine," she said, then pointed at the living room. "Maybe in there. Just prop it

up against the wall, behind the recliner."

"We could hang it for you, ma'am. Wouldn't take more than a second, and it's in the job description." Lefty said it with a smile, so she would know he really wouldn't mind. She shook her head all the same.

"That's good enough for now, thank you," she said. "Euphrates and I can hang it up tomorrow. When it's light and we're both awake enough to enjoy it."

Besides, I've opened enough unexpected packages today.

The men took their time in setting the painting down and making sure it was secure enough not to fall in the middle of the night. The cloth remained wrapped around the frame, but neither man presumed to lecture her on how to properly care for the painting; they had seen the end of the auction and suspected anyone willing to shell out that much money for a work of art probably knew not to mess around with it.

Nimbus transferred a tip to their money units and walked them out. She never let go of the taser, and the men both kept a respectful distance. When they were gone, she locked the door and went to retrieve her wine. The painting peeked up at her over the back of the recliner, reminding her again of the package she had received earlier despite not bearing the slightest resemblance to it. She had left that box and its contents locked away in one of her file cabinets at work. Better there than in the house, a place Euphrates might stumble across it before she was ready. Before she had decided what to say, what to ask.

Until then, she thought, smiling wryly over the lip of her glass, *I guess we can just talk about art.*

Chapter Fifteen

Passing Through

The small moon they had landed on had no name, but the trading post and fuel depot located on it were collectively called Hooper's Hope after the retired soldier who had moved out there to the edge of the Hesperos system to set up shop. Hooper Caldwell was getting on in years, but he was still quick with his temper and quicker still with his gun. His sons, three of them, were more of the same. Hooper's Hope wasn't a place for gossip. It was a place people showed up to, bought what they needed, minded their business, and moved the hell on.

It was perfect, and the captains of the *Sol Searcher* invested just about all of their remaining funds there filling up the ship's fuel tanks and the kitchen's cabinets.

Archimedes spent most of their time on the moon and the day after they left in his room, on the bed, poring through the data drives from Dephros. He had been at it for hours at a time, drive after drive, taking breaks only to eat or to use the bathroom. And at long last, after an increasingly desperate search for clues, he believed he had found what they were looking for. He set his datapad off to the side and leaned his head back against the bedroom wall, a mixture of emotions washing around inside him.

"How's it going in here?"

Grey had appeared in the doorway quietly and leaned now against the frame, arms crossed over his chest.

"I'm exhausted to be honest," Archimedes said. "Sitting in one place, staring at a screen all day. I don't know how I used to do this as a teenager. I feel like my legs aren't more than a suggestion at this point." He reached over and removed the drive from his datapad, tossed it over to the doorway. Grey snatched it out of the hair with his left hand.

"This it?" Grey asked, turning it over between his index finger and thumb.

"Think so, yeah. If I haven't started hallucinating." He gestured to the rest of the drives, scattered on the bed around him. "I've been thinking, we could probably get some good money for the rest of these, f we could find a discrete buyer."

Grey grunted and slipped the drive into his pocket. "Yeah. I know a guy who could probably take these off of us. Not for a fair price, but probably the best we'd get without a target getting put on us."

"Why do you know so many criminals, dude?"

Grey snorted. "Why don't you know more? Keeps things interesting." He looked around the bedroom. "You've cleaned up in here. Looks almost adult."

"Did I?" Archimedes asked, acting as if he was seeing everything for the first time. "Does it? Shit, I *must* be delusional." He perked up. "Hey, since you're here, do you have any painkillers stashed away? I ran out."

"Top drawer of the cabinet next to my bed," Grey said, hooking a thumb over his shoulder. "Caesar gave 'em to me. You want me to grab some?"

"I can get them, if that's fine with you. I should stretch my legs, anyway, make sure they still work."

"Go for it. I'm headed to the cockpit to touch bases with Caesar." He turned halfway into the hall, hesitated, and asked, "You doing alright? Your hands are still bothering you, huh?"

"Only when I use them," Archimedes said, trying to smile. It looked more like a grimace. He held his bandaged hands up. "Turns out I use them a lot."

"Well... I don't know, man. They'd probably heal a lot faster if you quit jerking off."

Grey stepped back into the hallway and headed for the front of the ship, Archimedes' laughter following him out.

And when the cataclysm's done

When the world is ash and bone

When yesterday's shadows cover tomorrow's sun

It'll be my brothers who take my home

The lyrics to Fire and Willow's "The Last Tonight" were repeating in Grey's head as he walked through the *Searcher*'s halls. His workshop was calling him from below, a handful of his projects needing tuning up, his weapons needing reloading. He had taken some of his private savings into Hooper's Hope and picked up some ammunition and some spare parts that he had needed, things he hoped would better prepare the three of them for whatever was coming next. But the data drive was burning a hole in his pocket, and he figured they would have time enough on the way to their destination to make final preparations.

He ducked into the cockpit, found Caesar sitting in the pilot's seat, a leather-bound journal in his hands. He didn't look up from his writing when he asked, "Did he find it?"

"He thinks so," Grey said. He fished the data drive free from his pocket and held it out to Caesar. And kept holding it for nearly a minute while Caesar finished the paragraph he was working on. Finally, he set his pen down, took the drive, and plugged it into the navigation system.

"How's he doing?" Caesar asked.

"He's hurting. And quiet." Caesar looked up, concerned. Grey added, "Well, quiet for him. I think he's just… I think we're *all* just feeling bounced around. Am I wrong?"

"No," Caesar said, shaking his head. "We're a long way from ringing doorbells and running."

"As I recall, you were always the one hiding in the bushes while Ark and I rang and ran." Grey settled down into the co-pilot's chair. "None of the risk, all of the reward. It's amazing we let you hang out with us."

"Yes, how magnanimous of you," Caesar said dryly. He began typing commands into the navigation system so the map would pull up. He studied it closely, opened his journal again. Jotted a few notes onto the back page.

"What is it?" Grey asked.

"Uh, I would ask Archimedes if you're looking for a technical description of our travel plans, but it looks to me like it's a mostly straight, very long flight."

"Well…" Grey laced his hands behind his head. "Take us away, Captain."

The coordinates Archimedes found led them out to a Causeway far removed from the known travel routes or from any semblance of sustainable life. The wormhole had cropped up behind a small, uninhabitable moon that had long since detached from the gas giant it once orbited and had been discovered quite by accident. The gate that was built around it after its discovery was done so quickly and was just as quickly consumed by bloody conflicts. According to the map the system beyond the Causeway was a desolate one called Urden, named after the first ship that dared to venture there. There were only three planets in the system, a half a dozen large stone bodies, and a single small star around which they orbited. Only one of the planets, Vyroan, had ever attracted any interest, and only for the explosive elements that occurred there naturally.

When the Universal Council decided collectively that the battles being waged were too costly and had too much potential to throw the whole universe into war, they forbid any further journeys to Urden. The mining operations were stopped, people were paid for their silence, and the Council did everything it could to erase any evidence of it ever existing. Even the gate had been torn down.

That is, until a group of co-conspirators decided to rebuild the passage through, scaring up old ghosts.

The *Searcher* pulled up to the reconstructed gate, wary of any satellites or ships that might be waiting for trespassers. There was nothing. Space was a void as it was, but the area around the abandoned gate seemed almost haunted in its emptiness. No lights flashed on the gate signaling right to passage. It just hung there like an echo, like an answerless question. The three captains huddled together in the cockpit gave a collective shudder.

"What do you think is through there?" Caesar asked.

"Nothing good," Archimedes murmured.

Grey just grunted and pushed the controls forward, leading the *Searcher* through the gate. He had broken more than a few laws in his life, but never one that the Universal Council had decided was worth erasing history for. He tried not to think about it.

The journey through the Causeway was the same as any other, to the mild relief of the couriers. Archimedes took over in the captain's seat and monitored the *Searcher*'s outputs. Caesar, in the seat behind him, looked out of the viewport at the blue-white streaks passing them by. Just about everyone called it the Ice, because of the color and because of the flow, and Caesar had always found it beautiful.

Fifteen minutes went by, and then fifteen more. This went on for a while. By the time they came through the other side nearly seven hours later, Caesar had fallen into an uneasy sleep, and Archimedes and Grey had exhausted their trove of childhood stories to reminisce to. The *Searcher* drifted smoothly out of the gate on the other side.

"Ark…" Grey said, leaning forward far enough that his chest pressed against the control console. "Where are the stars?"

Archimedes stared, slack-jawed. There *were* stars out there. You could see them, truly, if you tried, but they were so few and spaced so seemingly far from each other that they could just as well have been specks of lint on a black blanket. The navigation system still charted the path to Vyroan, still showed the other bodies. The galaxy's sun was most visible, centered to the right of their ship, but it still felt like they were traveling through a graveyard, or trespassing in a dark and empty room, one with living shadows reaching.

"Ark," Grey said again, louder this time, an edge of tension in his voice.

"We said," Archimedes rasped. He cleared his throat and tried again. "We said we'd do this. We owe it to ourselves at least, right, to check out the planet." He turned away from the viewport to look at Grey. "Right?"

Grey said nothing. He checked the navigation system. After a moment, he set a course for one of the stone bodies.

Caesar stirred awake in his seat. He blinked at the viewport, rubbed at his eyes. "What's up?" he asked. "We're out of the Ice?"

"Yeah, buddy," Archimedes said. "So far, so good, although it's, uh… well, it's a little strange out there."

"Hmm? Are we at the planet?" Caesar, eyes rubbed clear, looked out into space once more. He was shocked back to full wakefulness and put his hands on the glass. "What… what the hell?"

"Yeah, told you."

"We're heading some place out of the way," Grey said. "Out of sight of the gate, not near Vyroan. Not yet. Figure we can take a night to get our bearings. Rest up." Grey tapped the navigation screen. "We made it through. Didn't get blasted to pieces at either end of the gate, so we're in good shape relatively speaking. You got any readings, Ark? Radio transmissions, ship signals?"

Archimedes checked his displays, flipped a few switches, checked them again. "Nothing. Not yet, anyway."

Grey seemed satisfied. "We'll hide the ship, then. Get some sleep. Tomorrow we'll put this to bed."

According to the ship's internal clock, it was nearing midnight by the time the *Searcher* got settled in behind a giant ice rock Archimedes dubbed Cover. The ship's exterior lights were shut off and all the power was routed to life support and temperature regulation. The interior lights stayed operational, tied to a backup generator. They decided six hours of sleep would do, with Caesar having already caught some shut-eye and Grey and Archimedes being used to truncated sleep schedules. With the other two captains headed to their room, Ark dragged a pillow and blanket up to the cockpit to get his rest in the captain's chair.

And there, in a dark and empty galaxy, the three captains of the *Sol Searcher* slept.

Archimedes, curled up in the chair, dreamed of a beach he had never seen before, one with white sand and light pink waters. The sun was setting along the horizon, splashing the sky with citrus colors. He dug his hands into the beach, letting each grain of sand trickle over his skin, between his fingers. He felt the wind tousle his hair and took a deep breath every time the waves crashed into the shore, exhaling slowly as the water then folded back on itself, returning to the ocean. Things were calm. No deadlines, no obligations, nobody demanding his attention, nobody pressuring him to act, to move, to challenge himself. Things were calm. Crash, inhale. Swoosh, exhale. The beach, warm and empty and bright.

Caesar Anada slipped into slumber, which then slipped him into a younger version of himself. Back in Gamemon, at the Cynosure Academy. He was a student still but stood up at the front of the class, teaching a lesson on rare minerals, and the chemical reactions you could form with them. The class was enrapt, hanging on his every word, and his chest filled with pride and confidence. This was where he was meant to be, where he was always destined to be. Teaching the youth, when he wasn't making groundbreaking discoveries and winning prizes for his writing. The back door of the lab opened. Professor Sonus Eppleheim stepped through, brows furrowed, disappointment in every step. He began to accuse Caesar of being a fraud, a plagiarist, of stealing another's work. *This isn't right*, Caesar dreamed himself saying. *I'm a scientist!*

And Grey slept, but not deeply. He tossed and turned in bed, shaking off every attempt any dreams made to latch onto his subconscious. His blanket was too hot, but when he moved it off of his legs, or even only off his feet, a chill started to sink into him. He turned his pillow over once, then again an hour later. He slept, but in fits and starts. At one point in the night, he woke long enough to reach under his bed, search for a moment, seize onto a bottle of whiskey and bring it up. He took three long slugs, letting the liquor sit in his mouth for a moment, sizzling, soothing, before letting it burn its way down his throat, into his chest. He set the bottle on the nightstand and rolled over. Grey slept.

Intermission

Koko Noal Makes a Discovery

After months orbiting the planet Astrakoth, the *IRSC Imagination* was finally ready to head home. Like any successful exploratory mission, the expeditions to the planet's surface had seen a great many tragic losses of life, but they had been rewarded as well with countless new scientific discoveries. New flora! New fauna! New rocks and minerals! In addition to finding a bounty of previously unknown fruits, vegetables, beans, and nuts (many of which would find their way into government-funded genetic replication laboratories for eventual commercial distribution), the number of new animal species they had discovered was staggering. Already scientists and officers on the ship were arguing over who got to name what, anticipating telling their children about the things most of them had only seen once it had been dragged up and tossed into a lab onboard.

And then, of course, Astrakoth really had been a beautiful planet to visit when it wasn't trying to kill you.

As the remaining members of the expedition were packing up their equipment on the ground and taking shuttles back up to the main ship, activity on the *Imagination* itself was pretty subdued. Some scientists had taken to the smaller labs to continue their studies and experiments, but the larger lab was being methodically scrubbed of Astrakoth-related findings to make room for wherever their next expedition would take them. Specimens were being dissected and placed in storage containers that were then carefully labeled and separated by type. Data was being backed up from the ship computers onto external drives, then sorted by similar methods.

Koko Noal had taken lead on cleaning out the molecular deconstructor. It was scrubbed thoroughly after each use per protocol, any biological materials lingering in the machine after the specimens were removed wiped thoroughly, then burned away via an internal furnace system, then sterilized once the machine cooled down. Koko's final cleaning was more formality than anything, but the Professor had asked, and so she had complied.

While the furnaces was going Koko took to the main lab computer and began pulling up and purging the deconstructor's data log, everything having been copied and moved to the drives in the days preceding. She lingered on some of the items, reading their molecular makeup, recalling discoveries she and Professor Eppleheim had made, usually followed by an excited high-five and then several hours of paperwork. Mostly, she just ran through the slides, deleting them, only taking a break to sterilize the machine.

And then she moved on to the back-up files. These were passcode protected and stored in a separate databank, designed as a failsafe in case the original programming was damaged or tampered with. Still, now that everything was stored away, these files needed to be purged as well so that they wouldn't conflict or be confused with any future analyses.

It was during this process that she found herself befuddled, having stumbled across a file with no name, number or classification. A scan had definitely been done or no record would have been made, but the lack of a title meant it would be impossible at first glance to determine where the file should be stored. Koko opened the report and found herself staring at a translucent orb with some kind of animal suspended inside it. Living, according to the read-out, but in some kind of stasis or hibernation mode. It wasn't something she recalled ever seeing in the lab, on this trip or on either of the two that had come before. So where did it come from?

"What have you got there?" asked a voice. Koko jumped in her seat, turned her head to look over her shoulder. Professor Eppleheim had come into the lab and was rifling through a file cabinet at the far side of the room.

"Just one of the Skeviraptor eggs we found," she said, and immediately wondered where the lie had come from. "I'm just going through the backups and reliving some fond discoveries before deleting everything." She minimized the window so that the image was directly in front of her instead of plastered across the entire screen. "Anything I can help you with, Professor?"

"That's alright," he said. He found the file he was looking for and pulled it from the cabinet, waving it at her. "See you for dinner! We can go over some theories about that waterfall the young captain found."

"Yep! Sounds good!" Koko called, without looking at him. Her eyes had been drawn back to the data in front of her. Surely these elements couldn't be right. She hadn't even *heard* of pantrillium being used in anything that wasn't a bomb in years, there's no way it could be part of this thing, because if it were… and all of these other elements seemed to imply….

"Oh my God," she whispered.

Chapter Fifteen, the Sequel

Straight Up Terror Science

On Salix, often in forested areas but occasionally where you would least want or expect them to be, there existed a type of two-stingered wasp. It had an official science-y name, but most people called them Winged Screamers. Not for the noise *they* made, but for the one you would once one of them stung you. They were hard to outrun but easy to see coming, each of them the size of a Human thumb and patterned bright red and black.

That's what Vyroan reminded Caesar of as they cruised through the atmosphere, red and black and mean as it was. Most of the planet was covered in jagged black rock. The rest was magma, which crossed through in angry veins, inflamed and throbbing, with visible explosions popping up here and there as it came in contact with traces of pantrillium. There didn't seem to be any way for life to sustain itself—and indeed, they saw no signs of vegetation or wildlife—and yet the atmosphere was somehow oxygen-rich and breathable.

The *Searcher* had spent most of the day crossing over the planet looking for any hint of activity. They had passed over dozens of long-abandoned constructs—mining shafts, quarries, and drilling rigs, mostly—but they saw no figures moving around, saw no ships on the landing pads, registered no signs of machinery running. They had nearly decided to break off back into space for a lunch break when they saw it.

"Is that a…" Caesar trailed off, stunned.

"It sure as hell is," Archimedes said.

One of the drilling rigs had been extensively modified, with nearly every inch of exposed surface covered with white paneling so that it shone brightly, a beacon on a desolate planet. It looked almost perverse in its nonconformity. The platform itself had been expanded from its original design, additional spaces crafted to grow it outward and upward. Towers had been built on all four corners of the rig, complete with battlements. The landing pad had been left untouched, but the door, large enough to fit a truck through, had been altered to include a portcullis, which was raised.

They were staring at a castle.

"What do you think?" Grey asked. "Should we take the ship down?"

"I mean, that's got to be the place, right?" Archimedes asked. "It has to be. The only person crazy enough to build a castle on Lava Rock Planet is going to be the guy who put a lizard in a bouncy ball, right?" He looked at Caesar, who shrugged.

"I'm going to take her down," Grey said.

There was a single ship already on the landing pad, a model none of the captains had seen before. It was an ugly, box-framed thing, obviously capable enough of galaxy-hopping but unlikely to do much more than that. It had no name emblazoned on its hull, nor did it seem to have any registered tags. Grey set the *Searcher* down next to it.

They sat there in the cockpit, looking at the other ship, looking up at the castle, not moving, not speaking. There was a feeling in the air like the silence right after a break-up, a kind of restless dread.

Grey was the first to move, pushing out of his seat with a grunt and heading out of the cockpit.

"Just like that?" Caesar asked. "We're not going to talk about it first?"

"Nothing left to talk about," Grey called over his shoulder. "Let's get armed up with everything we've got and go say hello. Bring the sphere, too. This place is as good as any to unload it."

"What if we've set off an alarm? What if there's an army or something in there?"

Grey said nothing, already out of sight, heading below to his workshop.

"I don't think an army got hauled here on that piece of shit," Archimedes said, tilting his head toward the other spaceship. "The point is moot, though, because I don't think Grey really cares one way or the other. And neitherr do I." He clapped Caesar on the shoulder. "Let's get you strapped up again. We're storming the castle!"

Caesar groaned.

As it turned out, the doors—big, heavy, wrought iron things—were unlocked, though it took the combined effort of Grey and Caesar to pull one open. The three captains proceeded inside, guns out, ready to fire at the first hint of movement.

What they weren't expecting was the well-lit foyer they walked into. Whatever had been in the space before had been cleared out, leaving an open square covered in thick rugs of red fur. The walls were painted black with ornate silver whorls. A chandelier had been fixed in the center of the ceiling with cascading crystal lights.

"Really makes a decent first impression," Archimedes noted.

There were no places for anyone to hide. No furniture, no windows. Just a black and silver room with shiny lights, soft rugs, and a pair of swinging double doors that led further into the rig. The captains pushed through them into the next room, and down a small hall. To their right was the remains of an office, the door hanging from the top hinge, the interior empty except for a sagging desk and a splintered wooden chair. To their right were a pair of doors labeled as locker rooms. Another pair of double doors sat at the end of the hall. A white sign above it said, 'CAFETERIA' in red letters. Caesar's stomach growled. They went on through again, leading with their handguns.

And stopped short.

Whatever tables had been in the cafeteria were gone, replaced by three hospital beds and a chair with manacles on the arms and footrests, and a band that looked to snap into place around someone's forehead. The beds were covered in a reddish-brown crust. The chair, on the other hand, glistened dark red under the bare bulbs in the ceiling. Scattered around the room were small piles of sheets, towels, and clothes, all stained with blood and other unidentifiable substances. The pile next to the chair looked nice and wet. A rolling tray was next to the chair, as well. Grey edged toward it, saw an assortment of scalpels, forceps, and scissors, all freshly used. The drill, too, was red, pieces of ragged flesh still stuck in the flutes.

Caesar turned away from the sight and tried walking away to an emptier part of the room. His shoe hit something and sent it skittering away into the side of a discarded black sock. It was a toe, he saw, one that had had the nail removed.

He vomited.

Archimedes glanced over, hoping to ease the situation. No quips came to mind. Instead, a deep, abiding horror began to creep along his spine. He could see bones around the room now the more he looked. Peeking up and out from beneath the clothing piles. Small bones, mostly, but there was a femur propped up against one wall. A skull had fallen on its side underneath one of the hospital beds. He joined Grey.

"Do we still want to do this?" he asked in a low voice. He looked down at the tools and flinched.

Grey looked at him, eyes the size of dinner plates. He opened his mouth to respond. A loud crackling, almost a screech, came to life overhead, interrupting him. All three captains looked up, startled, and moved together toward the center of the room.

"A true surprise, and a welcome one!" The voice was speaking Trader, like them, but it took them a moment to understand it all the same. The words came out rough, like rocks going through a tumbler. It was unpleasant to hear, and it continued on, saying, "To have come so far. Here, to me. What pleasures are in store for you."

"We're doing this," Grey said to Archimedes under his breath. "We're definitely killing this guy."

"We're just killers now?" Caesar asked.

Archimedes pointed hard at the skull under the bed.

"I will give you a tour. My pleasure to do so, as I have accomplished so much here, created so many things, but I so rarely have company to appreciate my work. Come, travelers. Visitors. Find me in the next room and let me lead you."

The speakers clicked off. The captains waited a moment to see if there was anything more. Any voices, anyone walking through the doors on either side of them.

Nothing.

"There's no fucking way he's in the next room," Archimedes said.

"Probably not," Caesar muttered.

"There's only the one set of doors," Grey pointed out. "If we want to go deeper, we've got to go that way."

"Yeah," Caesar said.

It didn't take them long to decide; turning back had ceased being an option once they had walked into an abattoir. Staying in the room wasn't an option either. It smelled of viscera and fear, hopelessness and dead memories. They didn't need to say anything to each other. They moved as one through the doors, a bunched triangle with Grey at point.

They realized, one by one, that the place was affecting their sense of perception. There was no telling how long it had been since the structure had been used for its original purpose, but it wasn't fully the castle it appeared to be from outside, either. It was something else, something other. The rooms were emptied out, molded, built to hide some parts and expose others. The structure itself was a mutation.

The third room they walked into was perfect evidence of this. Grey, Caesar, and Archimedes walked out of a drab, low-lit chamber of filth into a bright, pristine, octangular room. Whatever the original design had been was impossible to decipher. All they knew was that the space was roughly half the size of the room before and that the walls, ceiling, and floor were covered in nearly spotless panels of white iroplas. Iroplas was a light, affordable, nearly indestructible material that served little practical purpose for interior design.

There were seven other doors besides the one they had walked through, one in each of the other walls. Each was a metal slat, white like the walls they were set into. The room was bright to an almost disorienting degree, reflecting the light from seven clusters of three bulbs each set into the ceiling. Caesar, the last to pass through into the room, held his pistol over his eyes.

"What the hell kind of—" he started, but was cut off by a *VMMM* sound. A metal partition slid down from the ceiling to seal their entry point. Caesar turned back and ran his hands over the surface of the panel, trying to push it up, trying to push it in. His efforts yielded no results; they were trapped in the room.

"*Fuck*," Grey snapped. He lifted his pistol and pointed it at the door, thought twice about what a ricochet might do, and swore again.

Somewhere above them, unseen speakers crackled to life once more. The voice said, "My deepest apologies. I know I said I would be present to greet you. It's rude to lie, but a true scientist must constantly introduce new variables to their experiments. Surprise, for example, or

disappointment. Confinement. Confrontation. Please forgive me, and be proud of yourselves.

You are, after all, helping advance science through your contributions."

The captains looked at each other, bemused. The speakers buzzed, then clicked off.

Caesar shook his head, trying to understand. "Confrontation, he said. With who? Each other?"

"Maybe he'll keep us in here until we have to draw straws on who to eat first," Archimedes

said.

His suggestion was met with another *VMMM* sound. The door directly ahead of where they had

come in retracted into the ceiling, leaving a hole full of shadows, darker by comparison to the

bright room in which they stood.

They watched the doorway cautiously.

A figure materialized, stepping from the black, filling the door frame and ducking so that it

could join the captains in the room.

The thing towered over them by at least two feet, a humanoid creature with gray skin stretched

tight over corded muscle, stapled to stay in place. It was naked but had no genitalia to speak of. It

opened its mouth to hiss at them, and they saw its teeth had been replaced with sharp metal

implants. The thing had no eyes, just smooth flesh over the sockets where they should have been.

Its hands both had one finger too many, the extra fingers' nails replaced with metal claws that

had been fused to the skin.

Archimedes and Grey opened fire simultaneously.

Four, five, six red holes appeared in the thing's torso, each generating a slow drooling of dark

brown liquid. The creature became furiously animated but otherwise unfazed, charging forward,

twisting its head left and right. Caesar dove out of the way, pressing himself against one of the walls. Archimedes wasn't as fast; one of the creature's heavy fists swung forward and caught

him flush in the nose. There was a sound like dry twigs snapping underfoot and he went

sprawling in a spray of blood.

Grey had sidestepped just enough to avoid the flailing limbs, close enough still to press the

barrel of his gun against the creature's ribs and fire twice more. The thing tilted his head back

and screamed at the ceiling, a raspy, bubbling cry. It turned at the waist, lightning fast, and

grabbed Grey by his right wrist, lifting him into the air with seemingly no effort. There was a

sudden crisp crunch and Grey threw his head back and screamed. He punched at the creature's

face with his left hand, flattened its nose, smashed it into a pulp. It did nothing. He tried to dig

his thumb into the skin over the creature's eye socket but found it heavily callused and

unyielding. The creature turned its head upward, fastened its metal teeth on Grey's left hand and

bit. Grey screamed again. He slammed his forehead into the creature's crushed nose but only

succeeded in reopening the cut in his own eyebrow.

The spotless white room was now splattered with red and brown, Grey and the monster both

flailing their limbs, sending strings of blood across the ceiling, walls, and floor. Archimedes,

groaning, was contributing, too; he had turned over on his side and let the blood from his nose

pool beneath him. Caesar edged around the room until he reached Archimedes, too shocked to do

anything else. Ark pulled on Caesar's clothes, then his arm, until he regained his balance. He

looked through teary eyes for his gun, finally saw it on the other side of the monster where he

had dropped it.

"Give me your pistol," he said to Caesar.

The words felt like mashed potatoes in his mouth. He worked his jaw, probed the inside of his

mouth with his tongue, tasted blood. He was startled when he felt cold steel in his hand and looked down to see that Caesar had done what he had asked. He aimed the gun carefully, fired off a shot. It whizzed past the back of the creature's head and hit the far wall, ricocheting twice off the iroplas before spinning to a stop across the floor. He took a step closer and fired again. A large chunk of the monster's skull blew apart at the back, near the crown, a flap of skin and bone flopping forward over its face. Gore splattered in every direction, including across Grey's cheeks and forehead.

The monster flung Grey to the side. The captain hit the wall hard and left a streak of red. He landed on his shoulder and stayed there, too stunned to move and unable to put any weight on his injured hand and wrist besides. Archimedes stepped up to the creature again, close enough not to miss, and fired into the thing's head twice more, until the only evidence a head had existed there was the chunks of flesh and bone and metal teeth that were suddenly strewn about the room. The monster dropped to its knees, then fell onto its stomach and was still.

Caesar had made it over to Grey and helped him back to his feet. Grey's face and left hand were covered cloaked in red. His right wrist was bent at an ugly angle, the hand at the end of it already turning an ugly purple. Archimedes picked up his own gun, holstered it, and returned Caesar's pistol to him,

"I think that thing broke my nose," Archimedes said. He put one finger gently against one nostril and blew out a wad of snot and blood. The pain nearly took him to a knee.

"You got off lucky," Grey said, grimacing. "It even made you look better."

"This is enough," Caesar said. He took a handkerchief from his pocket and used it to clear some blood from Grey's eyes. "We obviously have no idea what's going on in this place, but this is… we're out of our league here, guys. Let's just get out of here. Take what we know to, I don't know, the press or something. They'll send people out here to investigate. People will get involved. We've done enough, haven't we? We've hurt enough?" He pulled his hand back and looked at Grey. Grey scowled but said nothing. Caesar looked at Archimedes, who shrugged sheepishly.

The *VMMM* sounded again. A second door slid open, to the left of the one the monster had come through. Then a third door, to the right. More doors opened, one after another, until each one of them had a black entrance yawning in their direction. Every door was open except the one that they had come through. Every door but their exit.

Then they heard the buzzing. And it was getting louder.

<u>Intermission</u>

A Bit of a Mess

Sylvain Abalos cut a dashing figure. A Serobi, his skin shimmered a translucent blue-green, a color he had been told several times over the years reminded others of a tropical ocean getaway. He often wore dark colors to make his skin stand out more, and this day was no exception. He stood in his warehouse in a double-breasted suit that was black at every layer, save for his tie, which was a delicious purple. His shoes were recently polished and reflected the lights above like obsidian under the sun. He was careful where he stepped with those shoes, proud of how much he had spent on them, proud of his appearance in general.

And so he was exceptionally pissed that he had scuffed them wading through the carnage of his private collection.

Abalos stared down at the crumpled body of Xolop the Peran. He had barely recognized his former employee with the back of his head was gone, plastered all over one of the warehouse walls. There was blood everywhere, black and red, staining the walls, the ceiling, the display cases, and dried in puddles all over the floor. Judging by the mostly empty drawer Xolop's body was folded into, someone had also made off with a neat little chunk of his prized galactic maps.

"What the fuck happened here?" he asked one of his two bodyguards, a towering blue-haired Bozav named Garron.

"Looks like somebody broke in, boss," Garron said, mouth twisting awkwardly around the words. He had broken two-thirds off one of his bottom tusks in a brawl three months back and had yet to get used to the feeling.

"Oh, does it?" Abalos snarled.

"If I may, boss," said his other bodyguard. Dagrilla the Skir was a newer hire, but one that had come highly recommended after five years working as a freegun. What he lacked in the brute power and intimidation factor Garron had, he made up for with ruthlessness. He wasn't half bad as a conversationalist, either, whenever Abalos had the inclination to indulge him.

This wasn't one of those times.

"You may not," Abalos snapped. "It's clear to anyone with eyes what happened. Xolop snuck somebody in, that somebody stole my things, and the sentry *you* convinced me to buy," he said, jabbing a finger at the Skir, "trashed my place but didn't stop the theft."

"He stopped Xolop," Garron pointed out.

Abalos whirled on his feet, ready to shout. He saw the dim look in the Bozav's eyes, realized chastising him further would be pointless, and rubbed at his temples instead. "I've got to get a hold of someone who can figure out which of these fucking relics are salvageable. Garron, get a cleanup crew in here to get rid of this mess. Don't help them, just supervise them. Make sure nothing else of mine goes missing, or *you* will go missing. Dagrilla, I want you to find people who can reliably construct some replacement storage cabinets and display cases for the ones that have been damaged or…" He made a face. "Tarnished. After that, you can get rid of that *fucking gorilla* and start working on finding whoever stole my *goddamn maps*."

Chapter Fifteen, Trifecta

How to Make Monsters and Terrify People

It was a swarm that separated them, a thick cloud the height and width of the doorway it poured through, a mix of biology and cybernetics. Each individual bug had been about the size of Caesar's fingernail, but there had been so many that they overwhelmed the senses. The captains couldn't see anything but *the swarm*, couldn't feel anything but the tiny stings, over and over, by the dozens. Later, once Caesar had successfully fled from the octagonal room, he found one of the bugs trapped in the cuff of his pants. The insect was nearly unidentifiable, the majority of its body encased in a small metal carapace with a blinking red light that Caesar took to be some kind of control chip. There were holes in the shell that allowed the wings, delicate silver things, their mobility. Likewise, the head was exposed, revealing a hairy brown face with three multi-faceted eyes and two thick black fangs.

When Caesar saw the fangs, he had flung the bug away and set about checking his hands and arms, anywhere on his body where he had been bitten or stung that he could see. The bites were there, flushed pink and slightly swollen, but there was no itching, no severity to the pain. No dark red or black tendrils spreading from the bites. No pus.

Doesn't seem like the bites were venomous, he thought. *Just really, really goddamn annoying.*

The swarm hadn't followed him through the door he had chosen, which he found curious. It had stayed in the white room, buzzing threateningly, zipping from entrance to entrance without passing through.

Programmed to herd us? No, separate us. Sow confusion, leave us vulnerable. A castle full of horrors on a dead planet, I must be out of my fucking mind.

He stood in a dark hall, the only source of light coming from long, thin halogen lights set up near the ceiling that glowed a dirty white. The walls were a patchwork mess, only half-covered with the ivory-colored panels that had adorned so much of the exterior of the rig. The other half was the exposed skeleton of the original building, brown metal, hard and jagged.

The hall was long but straight, the only two offshoots both leading to maintenance closets. Caesar had checked both out, found nothing of use, and continued on. The bulbs flickered as he crept along. His hand dropped down to the pistol at his hip. He flicked the safety strap off but didn't draw the gun, instead playing nervously with the strap, eyes focused dead ahead. He could see that the hall curved to the right down at the end. When he finally reached the turn, after what felt like a mile's worth of walking, he paused and took a breath before rounding the corner.

The room he walked into was awash in a blue glow. It made sense to him in a way the other rooms had not, filled with a practicality and a purpose. This kind of room was a necessity on a planet like Vyroan where there were no animals to hunt, no soil to grow food in.

The light came from either side of him, from recesses in the walls where thick vegetation grew in concrete beds filled with dirt. There were hundreds of plants, the room barely large enough to accommodate them. Each recess was glassed off, but Caesar could see control panels to open them built next to each one and sprinklers set into the ceilings. Fruits and vegetables such as he had never seen grew in abundance.

There's the food supply. And cleaner oxygen than whatever is outside, probably.

Caesar moved further into the room. Six long tables were arranged in pairs with ample walking space cutting through them. There were no chairs, no stools. Each table was cluttered with test tubes, beakers, scales, scalpels, scissors, flasks, funnels, tubing, and trays. Most of the trays contained dried flowers of all kinds and colors. One had bad been thoroughly plucked, the purple petals laid out in a concentric pattern around the silver pistil. Another tray held nothing but an inch or so of congealed green fluid.

"What the hell…" he said as he came to the end table. A cutting board had been laid out, away from the rest of the equipment. A pair of pale green thumbless hands and a pair of what appeared to be toeless feet ridden through with knotted roots sat on either side of a splintered black jawbone.

Nope, Caesar thought, backing away. *I want none of that.*

The back of his foot clacked against the base of some kind of metal cylinder. He turned to look at it, jumped as the top half of the cylinder detached and raised toward the ceiling, hoisted by dark cabling. Another blue bulb was plugged into the center inside, rising up like a thin column. A vine coiled around it, covered in beautiful maroon flowers. Caesar leaned in to get a closer look at the flowers, at the faint checkered pattern that seemed to cover their petals. The petals quivered, like a butterfly shaking its wings. A puff of golden pollen shot out and landed directly in Caesar's eyes. More invaded his nose. He swallowed reflexively and tasted something like honey gone bad.

Caesar reeled away, panicked, rubbing at his eyes. They didn't hurt, didn't even sting, but they *throbbed.* He sneezed but hardly felt it, nose numb. He spat but his mouth still felt thick. He blinked tears from his eyes and found the room swimming, the blue lights from the walls pulsing, the hallway entrance he had come from puckering in and out like the mouth of a fish. He was standing back next to the cutting board, and he looked down in horror. The hands were tapping a beat with their fingers (*no thumbs, where did the thumbs go??*) and the slabs of meat that had once been feet were dancing a jig, the roots that twisted through them groaning with the effort. The jawbone leered up at him.

"Thought you were a scientist," it seemed to say to him. "What kind of scientist is so disgusted by science? Am I joke to you? Do I gross you out? You ain't looking so hot yourself, buddy."

The ceiling flashed red. The sounds of a thunderstorm raged somewhere in the distance. The windows in front of the fruits and vegetables shattered, pieced themselves together, shattered again.

Caesar screamed.

Archimedes bolted down the first open door he could find, naked from the waist up, having stripped his shirt off to use as an improvised weapon against the swarm. Thick, dark red blood streamed down his chest from his broken nose and he saw everything through a haze, the swelling in his face threatening to pull him into unconsciousness. He bounced off one wall with his shoulder, pushed off the opposite one with his hand, kept running. The swarm eventually faded away, though the scores of bites and stings across his arms and torso ached.

Finding himself alone and unable to hear any cries or calls from his friends, Archimedes pulled his pistol free with his right hand and carried his knife in his left, trying to ignore the pain in his wounded palms. He continued on through a series of twisting corridors, ignoring the closed doors and finding nothing of interest in those that were open. His mind flashed back to the surgical room they had walked into, and the blood there, and the pieces of tissue scattered about on the floor. He hoped neither Caesar nor Grey had stumbled across anything similar. Or worse. He didn't know what he would do if he came upon either of them being vivisected.

"Don't think like that," he muttered, shaking his head clear. "That doesn't help you or them. Just got to find a center point, a place to regroup. This was a drilling rig, right? There's got to be, like, a barracks or something. A mess hall? No, that was the damn nightmare show…"

He came to an open room at the end of the hall that was both wide and long, with doors set in

the center of the other three walls. There were four large metal containers, one in each quadrant,

with electronic hatches on the ends. Digital displays were set into the side of each container,

though the screens on the two at the far end were dark. The ones closest to Archimedes as he

walked in were lit up green and ran lines of text and numbers. He leaned in to study one; he

didn't recognize the language, but figured the numbers to be some kind of biological readout.

"Some bodies take to enhancement less readily than others."

It was the gravelly voice again, booming from more unseen speakers. It seemed to come from

all around Archimedes, like he was being surrounded. He wiped some blood from his nose,

winced at the sharp pain even that minor touch elicited.

"Others take to it like a babe to the teat, ready to evolve, ready to become superior. The change

is… not without its difficulties. Some become ravenous. Others become more aggressive, more

territorial. Like a personality, each case is different. It's beautiful, though, like a shedding of

skin, or the emergence from a chrysalis. I wonder, visitor, will you see what I see? Before your

skin is flayed, before your eyes are torn from your skull?"

"Sweet stars, what is wrong with you?" Archimedes breathed, turning in circles in the center of

the room, trying to spot the speakers, the cameras.

"Will you appreciate their unique characteristics? I wonder." There came a click, the

microphone shutting off.

"Thank God for that," Archimedes muttered. "I don't know how much more of that

pretentiously macabre…"

He trailed off, a whirring sound from behind him breaking his train of thought. He turned

slowly, brought a knuckle to one of his temples and rubbed at it, trying to break the incessant pain spreading from the center of his face so that he could focus. The hatches at the end of the two containers he had passed popped open a couple of inches. A red light from inside bled through the open space, casting two glowing lines on the floor. Shadows passed over both, accompanied by shuffling sounds.

And low growls.

The doors began rising even more, inch by inch. Some kind of appendage swept out from the container on Archimedes' left, something pink and fleshy on top, half-fused with tarnished silver metal. Three sharp claws, also metal, scraped against the floor with a shrill noise that set Ark's hair on end.

Not wanting to wait and see what monstrosities came out of the containers, having had more than enough of the castle's secret terrors, he turned and ran through the door at the back of the room. His head began pounding once more from the exertion, and his lungs began burning with each tortured breath. Somewhere behind him came a flurry of scraping and scratching, and a yowl that sounded like a car accident. Archimedes ran down hall after hall, taking turns at random, trying door handles as he came to them and finding them all locked.

Are you watching, you psycho? he thought, trying to picture the face behind the voice. *Are you locking these ahead of me, hemming me in?*

There were crashing noises now, as whatever beasts followed him slammed each other into the narrow corridor walls. The heavy, clanking footfalls were getting louder, sounding closer. Some thing or things were screeching under the yowling, metal on metal. Something wet hit Archimedes' hand: blood, he saw, dripping from his nose again.

I bet they can smell this, too, considering I'm basically wearing it like a shirt. Enhanced, superior pieces of shit.

Caesar had no idea where he was, but he knew he was in trouble. He had wandered away from the plant room, back through the black hole he had come from. He had stumbled down the dim hallway (*an alley*, he had thought, *I'm in an alley somewhere on Salix*, before reminding himself that he couldn't be nearly so lucky) and back into the octagonal room. The swarm was gone, to his relief, but the white room seemed to have transformed into a strobe light. It flashed all manner of colors at him, disorienting him. He didn't know where he went after that, which corners he had turned or which doors he passed through.

He walked through a fever dream. The shadows in every corner were laughing at him. He caught glimpses of his father, always disappearing from sight a split second later. Caesar had tried calling to him, had tried asking him why he had left so many years before. He gave up after the third try.

"The delius perum-zergalium," boomed a voice from all around him.

Are you there, God? It's me, Delirium, Caesar thought.

"In lay terms, the flower is called the Parting Veil. It hasn't been seen in bloom in nearly a hundred and thirty years. The seeds, of which there are still many, have been believed by many so-called great minds to be inert. Stillborn. But theirs are brutish, archaic methods of cultivation. Some things, as cliché as it may sound, only require a little love. I don't believe the effects of the pollen are fatal, but I've not yet had the chance to test it on anyone. Be blessed, little interloper. You are experiencing something I don't believe any other living soul in the universe has."

Caesar was crying. He didn't know why, or when he had started, but the tears were flowing freely. He used the balls of his hands to wipe his eyes dry and continued on.

Another door, another horror.

Archimedes couldn't believe his eyes.

He had come to a long, pale green corridor that ended in a catwalk surrounding a massive open space. A drill of astonishing size was suspended in the center of the hole, built to descend to the planet to conduct its work. It was large, and gray, and daunting, but Ark's eyes were drawn past it to the catwalk on the opposite side. There, a pale-faced Caesar Anada stood, pressing his shoulder against the wall for support.

"Hey!" Archimedes called as he ran. "Head's up!"

Caesar whirled around, caught sight of him. Even with the distance between them, Archimedes could see his eyes were wide, almost crazed.

"Are you real?" Caesar called out.

"What?" Archimedes asked, confused.

"Oh my God!" Caesar shrank back against the wall, gawping.

Archimedes risked a glance over his shoulder and immediately regretted it. The monsters had finally caught up to him, and they huddled together at the end of the corridor. They looked almost like giant cats, what parts of their facial features were visible, and with the arch of their backs and the way they swished their tails. What flesh was exposed was equal parts raw pink and a faded gray, stitched together in a horrible patchwork. The rest of their bodies, including parts of their jaws, their skulls, exposed vertebrae, and parts of their ribcages were replaced with or covered by metal, gears, and electronics. Murky tubes pumped some kind of thick liquid from one organ to another. Red glass shields were bolted into their faces, covering the eyes. Of the swishing tails, one had a wicked-looking serrated blade sutured to the tip, while the other was fused to a metal cap containing two syringes full of a bright green fluid.

They pawed at the ground, and then charged.

"What the fuck is it with people and robot animals?" Archimedes gasped, pumping his arms and legs as fast as he could. The catwalk grew larger in his vision, more immediate. He tried to mentally calculate the distance across the gap, decided it would either work or it wouldn't, but he was definitely doing it. He leapt, got his foot squarely on the top rail, and pushed off into the open air. Caesar watched on in horror, one hand covering his mouth. Archimedes looked down, saw his foot clear one of the ridges of the drill, saw the opposite rail coming up, so close, and then he was falling. He reached out, managed to get both hands on the middle rail at the cost of his pistol, which spiraled off into the dark. He gripped the rail tightly, his left hand wrapped desperately around the hilt of his knife as well. The wounds in his palms all stretched open at once in a surge of agony, the feeling like nails being driven through his hands. Blood poured down his arms. His torso slammed into the bottom of the catwalk, and he thought a rib might have broken. Archimedes screamed, and then suddenly a pair of hands were grabbing at his arms, pulling at him, pulling him up, underneath the middle rail so that he could roll onto the catwalk.

"You're real," Caesar said. "You're real, thank God, which means you are a goddamn lunatic."

"The cats," Archimedes wheezed.

"What?" Caesar was checking Ark's hands, gagged at the sight of the blood, and started looking for something to bind the wounds.

"*The cats!*"

They both looked over in time to catch the cyborg beasts taking a cue from Archimedes and leaping from the rails toward the catwalk the couriers were on. The weight of the first animal tilted the railing, putting the second one off balance. While the first one—the one with the syringes on its tail—easily cleared the hole and the drill and slammed into the wall next to the two couriers, the second landed at the edge of the catwalk, roughly where Archimedes had. Its metal claws ripped the middle bar of the railing free; as it scrambled for purchase, its claws started tearing more of the catwalk apart, ripping huge gouges in the grated metal. Caesar kicked at its face, got his boot momentarily caught on two of the beast's teeth, and then Archimedes was kicking at it too, pushing it away, screaming at it until Ark drove his knife through the glass over one of the thing's eyes. It jerked back and fell from the catwalk into the dark hole the drill had torn in the ground far below. The knife went with it.

The supports of the catwalk squealed in protest as the other monster turned around to square off with its prey. It screeched at them, that dreadful skin-crawling yowl, and a wave of rancid breath washed over them, stinging their eyes and making them gag. The monster's tail lashed out, down, at Archimedes' face. Caesar flailed his arm and managed to score a glancing hit against the tail, just enough that the strike meant for flesh hit the grate next to him instead, breaking one of the needles off. The tail whipped back, and the metal cap caught Caesar flush in the mouth, splitting his lips and chipping one of his front teeth. The catwalk lurched again, tilting downward toward the hole as the supports weakened and began to pull away from the wall. The couriers dug in as much as possible, pushing themselves up, away from the edge.

"Shoot it, shoot it!" Archimedes urged.

"With what?" Caesar cried.

"With your fucking gun! Did you forget you've got a fucking gun?"

Archimedes could see from Caesar's expression that he had indeed forgotten. Both of them scrambled to free it from Caesar's holster. Ark fought through the pain to put his bloody hands over Caesar's; they fired together, over and over until the magazine ran dry, aiming for the animal's head. Most of the bullets missed, Caesar apparently aiming for something Archimedes couldn't see, but the ones that landed did terrific damage, tearing bloody runnels down the beast's open gullet, punching through the thing's skull and obliterating large chunks of brain tissue.

The monster snapped its great jaws, the metal teeth clanking, but it seemed to lose any idea of where they were or what it was doing. Blood and some kind of black fluid mixed together and ran from its mouth in a thick stream. It listed to one side, then took a heavy step forward that would have crushed Caesar's calf had he not pulled it out of the way in time. It opened its mouth to roar at them once more, unleashed a torrent of yellow-green bile instead. It tottered, then collapsed, its head landing between Archimedes' widespread legs.

The pair of couriers took a moment to catch their breath. When it was apparent that the creature would not be stirring again, Caesar took the pistol back and holstered it. He stood up, hooked his arms under Archimedes' own and dragged his friend back onto a more stable section of the catwalk.

"Grey and I have really got to teach you how to handle a gun," Archimedes said. He clambered up to his feet and looked at his friend, resisted the urge to smile at seeing Caesar's bloody mouth. He still said, "It's about time you picked up a battle wound. Are you okay, though? Did that thing stick you with the needles?"

"No," Caesar groaned. "Chipped a tooth, though. And I'm seeing three of you right now, all with different faces, each one uglier than the last."

Archimedes hesitated. "I can't tell if you're joking."

"I'm not. Where's Grey? Have you seen him?"

"No. I've been too busy running away from these things," Archimedes said, gesturing at the monster. "You still have the sphere?"

Caesar patted his pants pocket and nodded. "Any more of these things after you?"

"I don't think so."

"Alright. Let's go find Grey. I'll try to tell you what I remember on the way."

Vyroan was beautiful in a way, with the reds and oranges of the magma glowing and pulsing through the black rock. Grey had somehow made it to one of the rig's outer passageways, and in a rare moment of silence took time to admire the planet through large windows of the oil rig. His bloody left hand was pressed against the glass, leaving a print.

As far as he could tell, the swarm had not gone after him in the octagonal room the way it had his friends. It overwhelmed his vision, stung him repeatedly any time he tried to press through it, but it seemed content to push him back, leading him through one of the open doorways instead of actively attacking him. He hadn't tried that hard to resist, hurt as he was. His right wrist was broken for sure, and a couple ribs cracked at the very least. The cut across his eyebrow was still seeping blood, as were all the various bite wounds he had acquired both here and on Deprhos; if he survived this, he planned on going to the doctor to make sure he hadn't contracted anything. At some point, he had twisted his right ankle, too. Hadn't noticed at the time, but it was screaming now; he started walking again, and the crimson trail his hand left across the glass was uneven from the limp.

Grey breathed in deep, let it out slow. He let the aches of his body wash over him and swallowed the pain.

"Come, little lamb," coaxed a harsh voice, interrupting his reverie. It was the voice that had greeted them when they had entered the castle. The one that had sicced that mountain of flesh on them. "You are so close. See what you have come for. Enjoy the sights, just a little more, a little further."

Grey ground his teeth together and pushed off from the window. He dragged his foot behind him as he continued down the hallway, forced himself to stay focused and look ahead instead of distracting himself with the beautiful, violent scenery outside. As he progressed, the metal wall on his left gradually transitioned into a series of glass panels. And, as he passed, they lit up one by one, the lights triggered by his movement like the frozen food displays at a supermarket. But unlike the supermarket, the things behind the glass were not quick and easy meals. Grey glanced at them as he passed, pulled a muscle in his neck doing a whip-fast second look, and recoiled.

Each glass display was a tank set into the wall, filled with some kind of dark liquid. Suspended in each tank was a body… or most of one. Grey saw a Murasai without its limbs, a Peran without its head. Three Humans in a row had been heavily experimented on, body parts replaced or covered with cybernetic attachments. One man's arms had been swapped out for grotesque, oversized chitinous claws. Blissfully, none of the bodies seemed to still be alive. Grey had no idea what he would have done if any of them had blinked at him or gestured for help.

He moved quicker, down toward the end of the hall. He saw where it ended in a wall ahead of him, saw the dark recess of a doorway on the left. He limped toward the doorway, fumbling his gun out of his holster and into his left hand. The bite wounds made his grip sting, and the blood made it slippery, but it was better than trying to manage the recoil with a broken wrist.

"You've made it," said a voice as he entered the room. The lack of speaker distortion did nothing to make it wear less on the nerves; it still sounded like it was coming from a throat full of gravel and glass shards. "I am glad you've come. I do not get so many visitors out here. Not many to share the delights of my science with."

Grey looked around, saw that he was in another laboratory. This one appeared significantly cleaner than the surgical horror show that had greeted him; it was a large and circular room with at least two other entrances that he could see, and one exit, an open space in the opposite wall that led to an outside platform. There didn't seem to be much use to the platform except as a viewing area, though you could just as easily look out through the windows set on either side of the exit. Two long rows of computers with a path between them broke up the center of the room, at one time used to monitor the drilling rig. Coils of red and black wires spooling out from their bases implied tampering, however, most likely to help facilitate the structure's terrifying new purpose. The computers' screens were suspended from the ceiling: wide, thin, visible panes of glass that glowed a pale blue. The light from outside, the screens, and the blinking lights on the computer consoles were the only sources of illumination in the room. All the rest were shadows.

But Grey was never much scared of shadows.

He walked further into the room, biting the inside of his cheek whenever his ankle protested. He could make out a large figure at the back, and a crumpled form at its feet. Grey's breath caught, already picturing one of his friends as the body. The figure standing over it stepped forward into the pink light coming from outside.

"An Ilo Eronite," Grey spat. "No wonder your Trader sounds like shit."

"And your Iloni is proficient?" the alien replied.

Grey didn't speak a single word of Iloni but didn't bother saying so. It had been a long time since he had seen an Ilo Eronite, and even longer since he was this close. They weren't a race known for their social graces, preferring to travel by themselves and only participating in things that interested them, though to Grey's knowledge that didn't typically include experimenting on sentient creatures. They were intimidating, though, often reaching eight or nine feet in height by adulthood and even bigger on occasion. They had long, leathery ears that folded down their back, broad chests, and four thick arms, two at the shoulders and two more mid-torso. There was no wasted space on an Ilo Eronite, no fat, pure muscle, a fact that was putting a serious damper on Grey's hopes of thrashing the guy about.

"You appear pained," the alien said.

"I've had worse." Grey sized him up. The Ilo Eronite was shirtless underneath a blood-spattered apron, his mottled blue flesh rippling. He had two feet on Grey, but if he could twist that apron around, maybe strangle him with it…

"All the same, I'm sure my flesh golem surprised you. It surprised me as well. Creating him was not my favorite project, but I quite enjoyed the results. The muscle stimulants I developed did more for the brain activity than I had anticipated, coupling nice with the increased aggression. Still, to be taken down by three couriers. I expected him to endure more than that."

"A bullet to the brain's kind of a catch-all for a bad time," Grey said. "I take it you ran the ship's tags."

"Yes. The *Sol Searcher*, registered to the Aventure Courier Group. I wouldn't have guessed that by looking at you. You look mighty haunted for a courier."

"You try carrying people's shit all over the universe with no gratitude, see how you look." Grey tilted his chin up in the direction of the crumpled form on the floor. "Is that one of mine?"

"No," the alien said, shaking his head. 'No, just something to pass the time. Here come your friends now."

The alien gestured to one of the entrances just as Caesar and Archimedes stumbled through. They took a moment to look around, their eyes adjusting to the darkness. Archimedes spotted Grey at the same time Caesar saw the Ilo Eronite.

And then chaos was unleashed.

Caesar moved first, surprising them all. He stepped away from Archimedes to get some room and pulled a metal disc from his pocket. Grey had given it to him before they left the *Searcher*, had explained how to activate it, but none of them thought they would need to use it. Caesar took a split second to size up the distance, one eye closed, then pushed in a tab on the top of the disc and hurled it at the scientist.

Grey held his breath as his invention spun across the lab, not daring to hope, astonished when it defied all odds not to miss or hit the apron. Instead, the bottom of the disc smacked against the Ilo Eronite's arm and attached itself. The scientist looked down at it, more curious than afraid, and then his body was wracked with electricity. Blue bolts of lightning coursed out of the device and wrapped around the large alien, a crackling ribbon of energy. The Ilo Eronite jerked his head back, a scream clawing itself out of his throat, primal, full of rage and pain.

The three couriers watched as the alien's muscles spasmed, the coarse hair on his arms and chest smoking, and then after a tense ten seconds the electricity ceased all at once. The Ilo Eronite's shoulders sagged, his knees nearly buckled. But he stayed upright.

Archimedes looked sideways, across the lab. "Grey, you said—"

"I know." Grey lifted his gun, found it hard to get a good grip on it.

"You said it would *drop* an Ilo Eronite!"

"*I know what I said!*" His finger found the trigger and tightened. The gun bucked in his hand, his blood-slick palms and the pain shooting across the pulled muscles in his shoulders rendering him unable to control the recoil. The bullet missed, ricocheting off one of the computers and firing through one of the windows facing the pad outside.

The Ilo Eronite tore the metal disc from his arm and threw it into the shadows at the back of the room. The skin beneath it had burned raw and red, and the air was filled with the smell of burnt hair and cooked flesh. His top two arms grabbed the lab apron and tore it apart down the middle, dropped the shreds to either side. The curiosity and intellect that had been in the alien's eyes were replaced with sheer animal rage. He stomped forward, charging toward Archimedes and Caesar, and his foot came down on the skull of the body at his feet. There was a wet crunch, but it didn't slow him even a second.

Grey charged from the side, trying to reach the crazed scientist first. He took his gun in both hands, fired once, twice, ignoring the pain in his hands, his wrist, his ankle. Both shots hit, the first taking the Ilo Eronite in the top of his left shoulder. The second blew through the back of his bottom left hand. The Ilo Eronite pivoted, far faster than Grey could have imagined, and the courier was suddenly yanked hard and fast into the air by four rough hands. In the same motion he was swung around and hurled through the air with as much effort as one might use to throw a pillow. The lights of the control panels whizzed by, streaks of pale color, and he was suddenly reminded of the holidays.

What a strange thing to come to mind right now, he thought, and then he slammed into the window. The glass shattered around him and he felt a deep cut open at the base of his back. The gun flew out of his hand, spinning away, far past the edge of the pad. When he landed, he did so on his right shoulder, cracking something and proceeding to tumble over onto it another half-dozen times before finally settling onto his back. A sob escaped him. He opened his eyes and was surprised to see the sky through his tears. It was orange. He had never seen a sky like that before, except maybe nighttime on Dephros. The air was hot on his face, hot to breathe, and he felt a body-wide sweat break out, the salt stinging everywhere there was an open wound.

Gotta get up, he thought. *You've got to get up, Grey.*

The mind was willing, but the body was not.

Archimedes pushed Caesar out of the way, sending him sprawling across the floor, and faced the charging Ilo Eronite on his own. He leaned back out of the way of a hard right hook, caught a hook in the ribs from the alien's lower right arm instead. He crumpled around it and felt himself carried with the force of it, his feet lifting off the ground. Ark went tumbling awkwardly, ass over teakettle, and stopped at the base of a computer console. He looked up in time to see a foot rushing toward his face, rolled out of the way, heard a crash as the metal folded in around the kick. Sparks flew into the air, a firework display in miniature.

Scrambling to his feet, Archimedes put some space between himself and the Ilo Eronite. He caught Caesar hovering, watching from behind a lab table, and waved at him to get going.

"What do you want me to do?" Caesar yelled.

"Pal, you've got to *figure it out*," Archimedes gasped. His ribs were screaming at him. One was broken for sure.

The alien's lower hands were taking turns cracking their knuckles, the left one streaming dark blood. His upper arms were stretched outward, flexing, getting loose, apparently unfazed by the bullet wound. Archimedes looked around for something to use as a weapon, anything, came up short.

"You know, for a fucking crazy person, I would have expected you to have more… hacksaws and shit laying around."

"Those tools have their uses," the Ilo Eronite said. "But alas, I've left them elsewhere. I'll have to take you apart with my hands."

Archimedes caught sight of the corpse on the floor. The head was little more than mush and splinted bone. Archimedes' stomach turned.

That's not going to be me. I didn't come all this way to go out like that.

He moved, rushing toward the alien, ducking a heavy left from an upper arm. The lower arm came but Archimedes was expecting it and slapped it away. He tried to aim for the bullet hole, didn't quite get it, and the hand clipped him across the hip. Archimedes staggered, used the momentum to turn in a tight circle. When he faced the alien again, he snapped a kick out into the Ilo Eronite's knee. He threw a right, then a left, and a right again, really getting his weight behind each punch, landing them flush in the alien's face. Each blow was murder on his own palms, and flashes of white crossed his vision.

The alien's nose sprayed out thick green blood… but that was it. The Ilo Eronite seemed unaffected by the kick, unrattled by the punches. His lower arms grabbed Archimedes by the waist and hoisted him in the air. The fists at the end of his upper arms repaid Ark's punches one-for-one: a right, a left, a right. Archimedes felt blood fill his mouth and saw nothing but red for a second. His vision came back just in time for the Ilo Eronite to slam him down like a flyswatter on top of one of the consoles. Knobs and dials dug into his back and he felt another rib go, white lightning. A circuit breaker blew beneath him and fire, or maybe electricity, something was burning through his shirt and searing his skin. The hands released him, and Archimedes used his feet to push himself away, off of the console, hitting the floor.

"Hnng," he grunted. He spat a mouthful of blood on the floor and crawled right over it. He could hear the heavy footsteps behind him getting closer but couldn't will himself to move any faster. He turned onto his back, looked up into the mad eyes of the alien. "That… all you got?"

"Most Humans quail and beg, weep and rail in the face of inevitability," The Ilo Eronite said. "But you have spirit. I can't wait to dig it out of you."

Caesar watched as the alien picked Archimedes up off the ground, shook him about like a ragdoll, then tossed him into one of the suspended computer monitors. The glass was apparently made of tougher stuff than the windows, but the weight of Ark's body tore the screen from the ceiling, and the two of them hit the ground in a tangle of cords and a cloud of dust. Archimedes managed to crawl over to the base of the wall, but there his strength left him, and he collapsed.

Frantic for something to do, some way to help, Caesar turned and bumped hard into the corner of a metal desk. The desk pushed something in his pocket firmly enough into his leg that it hurt. He put his hand in there and came out with the sphere. Caesar had completely forgotten about it. The whole reason they were here. The lizard was still motionless in the center, still suspended in whatever rubbery plastic material the sphere was made of, but Caesar's body warmth had begun to soften the outer shell. It was a reminder that they still had to destroy it, too, carefully lest they die a particularly gruesome, poisoned and rotting death.

Wait. Wait, wait, Vyroan has… and if I could find…

Caesar ran around the side of the desk, planning to go to Archimedes' aid. The Ilo Eronite stepped between them, standing in profile between the two couriers, looking back and forth between them. Caesar held his hands up to show that he was unarmed, knowing it wouldn't matter. The Ilo Eronite caught sight of the sphere and grinned dangerously.

"Ah," he said. "So that's what brings you here. My pride. My joy. I wonder how *you* came to possess it. That wasn't the plan." He stepped toward Caesar. The courier took a step back, holding the sphere in front of himself like a shield.

"You're sick," Caesar said. "Sick in the head. Do you have any idea how many people would die if this thing had got out?"

"Of course, little lamb. That was the whole point. I designed it that way."

Caesar kept retreating until his backside hit some kind of counter or console, maybe the desk he had just bumped into a moment before. He didn't check, couldn't tear his eyes off the alien advancing on him. The Ilo Eronite's four arms all stretched out, ready to swing, the hands at the ends of them all clenched into tight fists.

"What kind… of lonely, cowardly piece of shit builds himself a castle in the middle of nowhere? You ever invite anyone out here? Have a coffee date or something?"

Archimedes had pushed himself up the wall and stood leaning against it with one shoulder, his arms hanging by his sides. He was covered in blood from wounds both old and new. The blood vessels in his right eye had burst, leaving it dark red, and his left eye was drooping because of a swollen lump just above it.

He was grinning.

"You got any ideas, Anada?"

Caesar's eyes circled the lab, took in the counters and cabinets against the back of the wall. "I don't know. I think so."

The Ilo Eronite watched him curiously, then seemed to decide Caesar could wait. He waved him off with the hand that had taken a bullet.

"Run along, Human. You are too gentle for a place like this. I'll retrieve my masterpiece from you when I am done with your friend. We'll have plenty of time to catch up.

Caesar looked past the alien to Archimedes, who nodded at him. *Do what you're going to do,* his eyes said. *I've got this,* and Caesar knew that he didn't, but he ran for the back of the lab anyway.

The effects of the pollen had faded away almost entirely, but he was still left with a pink and purple haze at the edges of his vision, and stationary things still seemed to swim a little. He tried not to let it bother him while he went on the hunt.

The back wall of the lab had a trilogy of refrigerators flanked by sets of wooden cabinets. He tore open the cabinet drawers and doors first, frantically searching for both the specific materials he wanted as well as anything that might help them in general. He found an exam table nearby and started placing materials—a rag, a lighter, a small plastic bottle containing some kind of solvent—atop it. Next, he went to the first of the refrigerators and ripped the door open. The head of a Peran was staring back at him, and Caesar immediately dry-heaved at the sight of it. The rest of the shelves were packed full of containers and vials, though, and he forced himself to ignore the head so he could scan through the labels, pushing containers carefully aside with his fingers if they weren't something he needed. Most of the words were written in Iloni, which he couldn't read, but the actual contents were listed by their universal terminology.

He grabbed an armful of jars and bottles that looked promising and carried them the short distance to the exam table, arranging them in a line. Caesar returned to the cabinets, still searching, and found a silver cylinder tucked away by itself in the back of the bottom shelf. He had missed it the first time, but he saw it clearly now, and could read the white label affixed to the front of it.

It was exactly what he had hoped for.

Two birds, one stone, Caesar. Two birds, one stone. You're a scientist; use your science-brain.

That wasn't the technical term for it, but that didn't matter. What mattered now was finding some gloves.

Grey, covered head to toe in blood and grime, had finally rejoined the fight. He had ripped off the rest of his shirt and tore two long strips from it, wrapping them around his hands so that he could have something approaching a dry grip again. As an extra bonus, the layers of cloth served to protect his left hand from the shard of glass he had picked up to use as a weapon. The Ilo Eronite was stomping at Archimedes, landing solid blows against the courier's leg and hip, but missing just as often, Ark covering up the best he could and rolling left and right to avoid him. Grey jumped on the Ilo Eronite's back, wrapping his right elbow around the alien's neck and jabbing the glass into his shoulder, his neck, the side of his face with his left hand. Sprays of blood jetted out each time the glass was pulled free.

The Ilo Eronite roared and twisted his body, reaching back with his topmost arms and grabbing Grey by the back of his head. He pulled him up and over, flinging him down toward Archimedes. Ark moved just fast enough to avoid having his friend land on him, winced at the sound made when Grey collided with the floor instead. The Ilo Eronite hobbled away, probing his various wounds and rubbing the dark, sticky blood between his fingers.

Grey pushed himself up onto his hands and knees and looked over to Archimedes. Ark, laying on his side, eye nearly swollen shut, gave him a bloody grin.

"Fancy meeting you here."

"Can we just kill this prick already?" Grey groaned.

"Already? And here I was having the time of my life."

The Ilo Eronite had wandered to the opposite side of the lab in a daze, back to the body he had been standing over when the couriers had come in. He reached down and grabbed the corpse by what remained of its head and held it up with his two right arms. He looked at it for a long moment, then turned into the light from outside so the couriers could see the mangled remains of what had probably been a Serobi.

"Blood and pain," the mad scientist said. "It has been so long since I have seen my own blood, felt pain in my own nerve endings. Useful knowledge to draw on when I take you on as my next projects. I will take your fingers, your toes, one by one, a knuckle at a time. I will leave you your tongues until the end so that we might talk. That was my mistake with this one. I took his tongue too soon, and he was unable to tell me what he was experiencing. He couldn't sing to me. He only screamed, and even screams can grow tiresome after a time."

"For fuck's sake, this guy," Archimedes said. He forced himself up into a sitting position. Grey turned over from his hands and knees so that he was sitting next to him. They were both ready to move the minute the Ilo Eronite did, though neither of them were confident in how quickly that might be.

Something whizzed past them through the air, then, something bright orange and red. It cut across the room, trailing thin wisps of pale smoke and a stubby tail. A tail, Archimedes and Grey realized, that was made of fire. The Ilo Eronite snatched the object out of the air with his upper left hand out of reflex, winced at being burned, and dropped it into his lower left hand. He held it up between his thumb and index finger.

The three of them turned to see where the projectile had come from and found Caesar standing in the doorway of the lab with his hands covered in thick brown gloves.

"Fire won't destroy my sphere," the Ilo Eronite said, peering at it. The flames were searing the skin at the tops of his fingers, and the smell of it drifted across to the couriers. "Nor will it deter me. A man who is still afraid of the flame has not flown close enough to the su—"

An ear-shattering roar ripped through the room as the sphere exploded in his hand, hurling the alien against the far wall. Metal sheets tore off the control panels near him, blown away in the blast. Cables snapped free and sprayed sparks as they twisted and writhed. Whatever glass hadn't already been broken during their altercation shattered from the concussive sound.

Archimedes and Grey instinctively covered their faces with their arms and curled up defensively; the blast was powerful, loud, and bright but far enough away as to not affect them. When no further explosions were forthcoming, they slowly peeked over their arms. Caesar had come up to them from the entrance and was looking over their wounds for anything imminently fatal. They were both seriously injured, but they would live.

"Whaaat the hell was that?" Grey asked. His voice was tinny in his own ears and he slapped at them with the palm of his hand, trying to clear out the ringing.

Caesar looked back at the Ilo Eronite. There was a bloody dent in the wall where the alien had struck it. The sphere had been obliterated, as had the arm that had been holding it; in fact, the alien's entire left side was a ruin, charred black with wet chunks of red breaking through. The Ilo Eronite's intestines had unspooled between his remaining leg and the crisped stump of the other, a dark blue snake coiled over itself. He was staring sightlessly through one black eye, the left side of his face nothing but burnt skull and lingering strings of muscle and tendon. The corpse he had been holding had been reduced to chunks plastered against the wall.

"Uh," Caesar said, "I found some pantrillium. Coated the sphere with it. Put a thin layer of some kind unima cream over that. Unima is flammable but mostly harmless. It gave me enough time to handle the orb and get rid of it. When the fire burned off the cream and came in contact with the pantrillium…" He gestured to the carnage.

Archimedes was awed. "First off, awesome, but secondly, is blowing people up going to become a thing with you? Is that something we need to be worried about?"

Grey chuffed a laugh and tried to climb to his feet. His leg gave out on him about halfway to a standing position. Caesar caught him and helped him up far enough that he could rest against a desk. Archimedes found a chair that had survived the fight and climbed up into it. His ribs didn't allow him to lean forward much, so he put his hands over his face while sitting upright, shoulders shaking. Neither Grey nor Caesar knew if he was laughing or crying. Neither asked anything to find out. Grey was too busy trying not to pass out from exhaustion. Caesar had set out to find a computer terminal in the room that hadn't been destroyed, something he could patch into for more information about this hidden madhouse.

While they took their time to catch their breath, slow their pulses, and to relax, some realizations came to them. The sphere, and the lizard inside it, was gone. No longer a threat to the universe. The mad scientist who had cooked it up had been thoroughly destroyed, no longer free to conduct his sick experiments.

And the three captains of the *Sol Searcher* were alive. For them, that was enough.

It was finally, mercifully, time to go home.

Chapter Sixteen

Collateral Damage

From NORCAS NEWS, the planet Salix:

When "Rocket" Riley Badcraft came out of retirement to fight one last time, a lot of people thought at first that it was either some kind of publicity stunt, or, perhaps, an exhibition match for charity. We soon found out that it was in response to a challenge, and that there was bad blood involved. Badcraft's opponent, current Boneshaker champion Rostin, had been publicly trashing Badcraft seemingly every chance he could get, landing shots in his promotional interviews and during his victory speeches, each new win notched into his belt giving his words more weight. With that news in mind, "Rocket" Riley's unretirement suddenly became that much more electrifying.

Without Rostin's belt on the line, but with both men's reputation at stake, preparation for their highly anticipated match is now fully underway. Rampant speculation is underway, too. Badcraft, even at the height of his career, was known more for his timing and precision than he was for sheer stopping power. Rostin, a Bozav, not only has significant advantages in height, weight, and reach, but he has also shown that he can withstand a tremendous amount of punishment within the columns. Though "Rocket" Riley has pulled some impressive victories over opponents that seemed out of his league, he's never fought someone like Rostin before. So now that "Will Badcraft fight?" has been answered, the next question is, "Will Badcraft win?" Up next we'll take a look at some of… hold on. Excuse me, viewers, I'm getting reports of some breaking news. We'll have to cut to that right now, and I'm being told to advise you that what you will hear may be quite alarming.

*****

A self-eradicating sphere containing within it a genetically modified reptile of some kind, or an amphibian, the chemical composition of which is supposed to trigger a kind of biological reaction in the flora and fauna it interacts with or maybe is simply near to. I'm to release it in an area with plenty of vegetation but where natural predators seem the least likely, both to decrease its likelihood of detection and increase its odds of survival and reproduction. Out in the wild, Ryxol is mostly fish and insects, so as long as I stay away from populated areas or bodies of water where carnivorous fish are known to swim, the application of the weapon should be simple enough.

I have no doubt, no hesitation in what I've been asked to do. The Ryxan are little more than animals, their reptilian minds never truly adapting to the complications of universal politics. On Terra Prime, dinosaurs were recorded to be nothing more than relics of a bygone age. Their seeming evolution has done nothing to show me that isn't the way they should have stayed: buried in the dirt, forgotten except for brief moments of marvel at a museum exhibit.

But while my thoughts and my beliefs are sound, I've begun to wonder who shares them. Who has the resources to put such a thing in motion? The intelligence to develop such a sophisticated biological weapon? The Nova may have cut ties with me, but that was politics, not because of any fucking lack of investigatory skill on my part. I could run research circles around any of them, except maybe Lynette. A diamond in a dung pile she was, for whatever that's worth.

Anyway, I'm getting off track. Let's start with the communications sent and received. I'll branch out from there.

Euphrates read through several of the correspondences, then leaned back, keeping his hands on the desk. For all of his personal problems, Turner Materas had turned out to be a far better investigator than it seemed anyone had given him credit for. He had managed to start drawing some concrete threads to Rors Volcott, though they never quite got all the way there. He hadn't had the time or the resources.

But Euphrates had the resources. *And* the inclination.

There was a knock at his home office door. A first. Euphrates barely had time to register surprise before Nimbus opened the door and stepped inside.

Another first.

"Nimbus…"

"We need to talk."

"Okay. Of course. Is it a conversation we can have a little later? You've caught me right in the middle of—"

"No, I'd like to talk now. The living room, please."

She turned on her heel and strode out. Euphrates could tell something was deeply wrong, knew he would be an idiot if he couldn't read the glaring signs, and stood. Uncertainty wracked him hard; he hated it. It was not a feeling he encountered often as an adult, especially not with the position he held, and never in his home.

Euphrates left his office, closing the door behind him, and walked down to the living room. Nimbus stood there with her arms crossed. The television was on and turned to the news, the sound muted. A small box sat on the coffee table, open. He could make out some papers, some data drives, but nothing stood out to him.

"What's going on, my love?"

"The Ruby Swell."

Whatever he had been expecting her to say, that was the furthest thing from it. "What?" he said, unable to think of anything else.

"The Ruby Swell," she said again. "A gentleman's club, they call it. A strip joint on another planet is what it is."

Euphrates' mouth was working, but his voice was not. Nimbus continued on without him.

"You were there," she said, gesturing to the box. "Travel records, witness accounts. You did a decent job covering your tracks, and I can figure why. A man of your status going into a place like that."

"It was a business trip," he said lamely.

"At a place like that? On Agnimon?"

"Yes! My job requires me to interact with people from all walks of life and in all manner of businesses. I'm an Advisor to a Speaker for the Human *race*, not just the Humans on Salix. If you've got the records there, Nimbus, you'll see what time I went in there. What exactly do you think I'm going to get out of a trip to a nightclub… in the goddamn *morning*? It was a business trip!"

"With freeguns?" She spoke softly, but the words still thundered across the room to punch him in the chest.

"What?" he said weakly.

"This conversation would go a lot more smoothly if you quit acting like you forgot how fucking words work," Nimbus snapped. "Bounty hunters, Euphrates."

"I know what freeguns are. I just… think it's… a ridiculous name."

"That's the part you want to focus on?"

"No. Sorry." Euphrates shook his head, trying to clear it, trying to think. "Where did you hear I was speaking with... there are elements of my job that are classified or that would be considered clandestine. Not only should you not be privy to those plans and actions, you really wouldn't *want* to know. And, and what was I supposed to do," he stuttered. "Tell you I had a top-secret meeting to attend in the back of a, a strip club as you've put it, and you're not going to have more questions? Questions I might not have the answers to?" He was babbling, and he knew it, but he couldn't stop. "And if I'm vague with my responses about what I'm doing at a nightclub—in the *morning*—then I run the risk of you thinking something more is going on, something that isn't."

"Is there?" Nimbus asked. "Are you having an affair?"

"*No!*" Euphrates cried, aghast. "Nimbus, I would never! Who gave you this goddamn... goddamn..."

He trailed off as he caught sight of the television. The news anchor was sitting stiff as a board, expression neutral but unable to eliminate the traces of panic in his eyes. But it was the chyron crawling across the bottom of the screen that commanded Euphrates' attention. His mind struggled to comprehend what his eyes were seeing.

No, he thought. *Impossible.*

The communicator in his pocket began to vibrate. The communicator for his *other* work.

"Nimbus, I have to go to my office," he whispered.

"Like hell. We're in the middle of a conversation."

"Nimbus!"

Her name burst from his lips in a quivering shout, startling both of them. She took a step back reflexively and Euphrates saw a sliver of fear in her eyes as well. Fear of him. It killed him. He held up a hand, palm outward, trying to calm her.

"I will tell you everything. Whatever you want to know, if I know the answer, I will tell you. No half-truths, no lies. I promise. I *swear it*. But I need to go right now. Please. And please try to remember… anything I do, everything I have done, it has been for you and for the Human race."

Nimbus just stood there, shaking, and said nothing.

Euphrates turned on his heel and retreated back to his office, the communicator still vibrating angrily. He felt sluggish, like he was wading through mud, but he kept moving and kept ignoring the communicator, focusing instead on his computer. His computer with its state-of-the-art encryptions and a staggering amount of illicit material, not least of which was the evidence of Rors Volcott's plot. His fingers flew over the digital keyboard, backing up his files, everything, and sending it to a drive only he knew about, one stashed in a shipping container buried under another shipping container, located on a private lot he had purchased under a pseudonym on a moon half the galaxy away. It was the first time he had ever had to use it and he struggled for a moment while he tried to recall the commands needed to make the transfer possible. Once it was done, he purged the contents of his home computer entirely.

But a blank slate could be just as incriminating in its own way.

He slipped a key from his pocket, unlocked one of his desk drawers, removed a data drive, and plugged it into his computer. A backup of his official Council documents and e-mails was loaded onto the computer. He had added some personal files and half-finished lists and notes for extra effect, all things that fit with his Advisory role and that could be expected on a personal computer.

The drive went into the wastebasket when the process was finished. The communicator would need to go in, too, both items to be destroyed. But there was still work to be done.

The communicator started buzzing again. Euphrates finally answered the call, anticipating the first words he would hear. Raygor Stahl did not disappoint.

"Euphrates, you son of a bitch!"

"It wasn't me," Euphrates said.

"Fifteen days! That's what we agreed upon, was it not? Have you seen the fucking news? Have you turned on any channel that *isn't* the news? Because it's fucking everywhere! Details I didn't know, files I sure as shit didn't *have*, so not only did you fuck me, I find out you've been holding out on me!"

"Raygor, I didn't do it," Euphrates insisted. "I just found out, seconds before you called me. I haven't even had a chance to listen to any of the reports, but I assure you, you have everything that I do. What do I have to gain from welching on our deal? As I'm sure you'll see in the days to come, I'm very likely about to be thrust into an unenviable situation and, quite possibly, a prison cell. Now listen to me: I need you to drop off that duplicate data drive at the address I gave you. I'll pay you whatever you want, for that and for not being able to sell the information as we had agreed."

There was a thoughtful pause on the other end. "How do you expect to pay me from a prison cell?"

"Today's unsettling incident aside, have I ever let you down?"

Another pause. "I'll come up with a price, but I'll want another favor. That's two, you understand?"

Euphrates sighed and sank into his chair. "I understand. It's a deal, provided I don't get executed for some fool reason. I'll have someone get in touch tomorrow or the next day. I've got to lose the communicator."

"Fuckin' Humans, you're like a galactic STD, I swear to the Ten-Armed God," Raygor spat and hung up.

Euphrates squeezed his eyes shut, trying to think of all the angles over the pounding in his temples. Rors was done for. Raygor was appeased, for now. There was no direct evidence linking Euphrates to any of it, save for Jeth Serrano. Serrano would be in the wind, his partner dead, the only other witnesses to their meeting…

The Ruby Swell. Someone had given Nimbus that box, someone with interests in Euphrates' whereabouts. He opened his eyes.

Talys. He almost laughed, but let it die in his belly instead. There was yet more work to be done, and quickly.

*****

They had done it. Like toothpaste and the tube, there was no way to silence the word once it had been whispered into the air. Or, in this case, once it had been loaded onto a time-released self-replicating data file. It had only taken Caesar a day to figure out how to pull it off, having had some recent inspiration. Two more days were spent figuring out a plan for releasing it without anything leading back to the *Sol Searcher* or her crew.

What they did was this:

Step one: After a considerable amount of discussion, they settled on Thorus for releasing the information they had recovered from the mad scientist's castle laboratory. As the capital city of Salix there was a considerable amount more surveillance to be cautious of, but there was also a lot more foot traffic and more crowds to get lost in.

Step two: The *Searcher* landed, their arrival logged into the official docking records. They announced their intention to seek work at one of the Aventure courier offices, but this was a lie. Caesar and Archimedes departed the ship together. Archimedes spent some time in an ACG office for the camera's sake and then returned to the ship without a job, long wait times being the excuse they would use should anyone ask. He and Grey took off for the other side of the planet, to spend a couple nights in Catalasca. After that they would return to pick up Caesar, using the same excuse, looking for work, as their reason for the port authority for returning. This would put the *Searcher* out of the city on the day the information went out.

Step three: Before leaving the *Searcher,* Archimedes helped Caesar come up with a disguise. Walking around Thorus with any kind of digital camouflage—something that Grey and Caesar had been working on in their spare time—would set off alarms. It would be better to stay visible but unrecognizable. Grey had picked up some black hair dye that washed out. Archimedes had some liquid latex on hand, products from his theater days in university, and used it to widen Caesar's nose and to give his right eye a noticeable droop. Caesar's beard had grown out; that was dyed as well. For his clothing, he pulled out an old reversible jacket of his own and wore a pair of Archimedes' athletic shorts under a pair of Grey's pants, which were too big for him.

Step four: Once in the city, Caesar found a digital café, a necessity for people working away from their homes or ships. Once he was able to secure an available computer, he created a fake email address, loaded up the files with his data drive and set up a number of time-released emails to every news station and poli he could think of, set to send an hour and a half after he left the café. The emails would arrive as a story tip for the news stations and as an offer of campaign funds to the polis; not everyone would open it, but whoever did would have the files automatically downloaded to their computer and then sent again to all of their saved contacts.

An old-school virus, really, but one that could start or maybe avert a war.

Now Caesar was in the middle of the fifth and final step. Grey had told him about a bar in Thorus that didn't keep any cameras inside, preferring to handle any in-house issues immediately, personally, and by any means necessary. A hallway inside led directly to the brothel next door, one with a generous matron who would allow you to rent a room for the night as long as you met her price. Caesar entered the bar a bearded brunet in jeans and a black jacket. He would leave the brothel blond and clean-shaven in a red jacket and shorts a couple days later.

Laying in bed, nervous and sick, Caesar hoped it would all be enough.

Either way, he felt confident that they had done the right thing.

*****

It had been some time since Jeth Serrano had visited Sul Torun, the home world of the Murasai, and he was glad to be back. He had taken the *Mathra D'abai* into port at Ordway, a small town a hundred miles from where he had been born. There was a diner he liked there called St'orid Tappan, which translated roughly into Trader as 'High Light'. It was a place he tried to visit every time he returned to the planet, particular to the sandwiches they made with swamp hopper meat, black cheese, whatever vegetables the cooks felt like adding in at the time, and a house sauce that was both savory and spicy.

He had taken one of those sandwiches and a goblet of mulled wine and tucked himself into the back corner of the shop. It wasn't a big place, High Light, but it was warm, cozy, the kind of place old friends would come for a light lunch and a chat about better times. There were no televisions in the building, and no communicators beside what you brought in with you. Soft instrumental music was piped through a pair of small speakers.

Serrano had just taken a bite of his sandwich, closing his eyes and letting the flavors spread across his mouth, when his communicator chirped in his pocket. He set the sandwich back in the basket it had come in, took a quick swallow of wine to wash everything down, and answered the call.

"Serrano," he said.

"Have you seen the news?" responded a voice he recognized immediately.

"I have not." Serrano actively avoided the news, actually, as his interests did not stretch much further than whatever job was immediately at hand.

"I would recommend you get caught up as soon as possible," Euphrates said. He sounded urgent. "I have a job for you that needs to be handled immediately."

"Come on," Serrano groaned. He pushed his sandwich around the basket, grabbed the wine, took a swallow. "You always pay me handsomely, so don't think I'm not grateful for the opportunities, but after this last one, I'm on a break. I'm home. I'd like to enjoy that."

"I imagine you would, but we don't have that luxury at the moment."

The way Euphrates included himself caught the Murasai's attention. "What's the job?"

"The place we had our meeting, where I met your partner for the first time."

"Yeah?" Serrano asked, this time tentatively.

"That place needs to be taken care of."

"Management?"

There was a pause. Serrano heard Euphrates take a deep breath. "The whole place."

Serrano's nose slits flared. "I don't… that's not the kind of work I do, all due respect. I'm not a butcher."

"One at a time or a dozen at once, it all shakes out the same," Euphrates replied, audibly impatient. "Turn on a fucking television and watch it, Jeth, and then keep two things in mind. The first: whatever your asking price is for this, whatever settles your stomach, it's paid. You don't want to work for me again, that's fine. You don't want to have to *work* again, it's a done deal. The second thing is that once you get a grasp of what is going on in the universe right now, remind yourself that the place we met has as many ties to you as it does to me, and that I'm in the crosshairs. Those ties serve everyone best if they were severed."

"Everyone that isn't in that building, maybe," Serrano muttered.

"Will you do this? I need to know now, because I need to get rid of this communicator."

Serrano considered the proposition. He already lived comfortably enough, but comfortably *forever* had a certain charm to it. And he hadn't heard Destidante so shaken… maybe ever. A few more lives for the eternal favor of the most powerful Human in the universe?

"The usual account number," he said.

"Done," Euphrates said, and ended the call.

Serrano slipped the communicator back into his pants pocket. He stared at his sandwich for a moment, then grabbed the goblet and guzzled the rest of the wine. It was hot and sweet, the way he liked it. A taste of home. He waved the man at the front counter over and pointed at his sandwich.

"Can I get this to go?"

*****

From GOLDEN STAR NEWS, the planet Elagabalus:

Police were dispatched this afternoon to the estate of Rors Volcott, Speaker for the Human race, to take him in for questioning in regard to the leaked infodump that has spread across universal news streams like wildfire. The files in question seemed to implicate Speaker Volcott in a plot to attack the Ryxan home world with a biological weapon designed to potentially devastate the planet's ecosystem on an irreversible and uncontrollable level.

Upon arriving at the Speaker's home, officers found that the doors had been locked and barricaded and the windows boarded. Reports state that there was communication between the Speaker and the officers, although the content of those dialogues has not yet been released. With access to the domicile blocked, officers had hoped to reach a peaceful resolution with Volcott that would lead to him leaving the premises voluntarily. Tragically, a gunshot was heard from inside the home, leaving the officers no choice but to make a forced entry. They discovered Volcott in his living room, deceased from what appears to have been a self-inflicted gunshot wound.

In addition to the Speaker, at least two other people have been mentioned as co-conspirators in the plot against the Ryxan. Rab Mool, an Ilo Eronite scientist, allegedly designed the weapon at Volcott's request and with his funding. The Speakers for the Ilo Eronites have officially denied any connection or knowledge of Mool's actions or of the plot itself. According to Ilo Eronite officials, Mool had been reported missing seven years ago after a number of experiments described as "extreme" led to him being barred from the Hervatyne Institute of Science. Rab

Mool had been presumed dead until reports of his involvement in this plot surfaced. He currently

remains at large.

The other implicant was Turner Materas, a forty-year old Human journalist who had lost his job

with the Purple Nova news group on the planet Peloclade. The leaked files indicate that he was

to be the recipient of the weapon, with the intention being that he transport it to and release it on

Ryxol. Materas was found murdered in his apartment some weeks ago, his apartment ransacked.

While investigators initially believed the murder to be the result of a botched home invasion,

they are now looking into possible connections to the terrorist plot.

Finally, but perhaps most importantly, the leaked documents came with an anonymous note

presumably from the source. It states that the weapon in question has been destroyed but

provides no further information and no proof to verify that claim. With the seriousness of the

allegations leveled against the late Speaker, Mister Materas, and the missing Rab Mool, we urge

everyone to remain vigilant and to report any information at all that you think might prove

relevant. And to those who leaked these files, we urge you to reach out to law enforcement so

that a fuller, more informed picture can be drawn.

*****

Talys Wannigan was arrested at home with no trouble but considerable righteous indignation.

Like everyone else, Talys had been surprised by the files plastered all over every major station

in the universe. He had seen the viral e-mails in his inbox promising campaign funds and had

deleted them; even if they hadn't seemed like an obvious scam, his position as Advisor was to

last until death, resignation, or a vote of no confidence, no re-elections held, no campaigns needed. But then he started receiving panicked calls from his peers and turned on his television.

As he listened to the reports and discovered how the files had been spread, he pulled up a deleted

e-mail and read the files for himself. Why not? They had already been spread everywhere else.

His first thought was that the information was part of an elaborate smear campaign designed to

discredit Rors Volcott. The more he dug into the details, however, the more they seemed to be

legitimate. Volcott's suicide, whether a note was discovered or not, seemed to confirm the

allegations. Volcott had always had fight in him, and Talys believed that if it had all been a ruse

he would have railed against it tooth and nail.

Talys' mind wandered next to who might profit from releasing such information, knowing that

it would send the universe into chaos. Euphrates Destidante seemed the obvious choice, being as

underhanded and power-hungry as he was. Throwing Rors to the wolves (or in this case, the

saurian Ryxan) would lead to a vacated Speaker position, the only position that could afford the

man more power than he already had.

But no matter how hard he looked, no matter which angle he approached it from, he couldn't

see any ties to Destidante. That didn't mean anything, of course. The universe was full of people

willing to do anything for a few chits, it wouldn't have been hard to find someone to do the dirty

work for him. But how did he get access to so much data in the first place? Where did he find it?

Talys knew he was missing something. And, just as he reassured himself that he had time to

figure it out while everyone else was caught up in the uproar and in dissecting Volcott's terror

plot, a plot he still had a hard time wrapping his head around and one he was glad he had no part

in, a heavy rapping sounded at his front door.

The police ignored his requests for them to leave and his refusal to invite them in. They

weren't rough with Talys, but they did push him back into the house, leading with a warrant to search the house for any and all evidence pertaining to Volcott's plot against the Ryxan. They received a tip, they said, that implicated Talys as an accessory by way of foreknowledge. Talys claimed innocence, but his protests fell on deaf ears. He was handcuffed, again not roughly, but he was turned firmly around by the shoulders, his arms tugged behind him. Stern actions, like parents restraining their child. Talys was asked if any pets needed to be relocated or if there was anyone that needed to be contacted to take care of them or to meet him at the station. Talys had no animal companions and named nobody to contact, disbelieving the situation, furious and scared, mind racing. He was escorted to a cruiser and lowered carefully into the back seat.

As the car pulled away, Talys watched a small squad of uniformed men filter into his home to begin their search. The men would work dutifully and thoroughly, tackling each room in pairs and twice-over. It took them three hours and a second investigation of the bathroom, but they would find a small data drive taped up underneath the sink. Upon further investigation, they would find that while the drive was password-protected, it was easy to crack, and the contents on it included the first-hand account of Turner Materas detailing his role in the terror plot and a detailed description of the weapon that would have been used to carry it out. This file was formatted differently and contained additional details from the files already leaked to the public, missing pieces from a terrifying puzzle.

Talys was officially charged as an accomplice to the attempted genocide of the Ryxan people. His attempts at being released on his own recognizance were denied, as was bail, the case being directed to the Elagabalus High Court, and the High Court deeming him a flight risk due to the severity of the charges levied against him. He was placed in protective custody, but the Advisor took little solace in that.

A cage with a pretty name was still a cage.

*****

From FEATHERED ARROW NEWS, the planet Agnimon:

Firefighters rushed across town today to combat a five-alarm blaze at popular gentleman's club,

the Ruby Swell. In a shocking sequence of events that responders are calling a freak accident,

faulty electronics not only triggered the fire but also engaged the locks at the front, back, and

emergency exits. Two patrons were able to escape the flames via the upstairs windows but later

succumbed to smoke inhalation-related complications. The owner of the Ruby Swell, Shelby

Hewitt, was not at the location at the time of the fire, but in a bizarre twist, when law

enforcement authorities sought him out at home to question him about the accident, they

discovered him dead of an apparent overdose.

All told, twenty-four people, including staff and patrons, were killed in the fire.

No foul play is suspected at this time.

*****

The trial did not burn long, but it did burn bright and hot. It was the first time in thirty-four

years, since General Torrga of the Skir, that someone was being put on trial for war crimes. It

was the first time in over two centuries that the defendant was someone ranked so highly in the

Universal Council.

Over the two weeks of proceedings, security at the High Court stood guard at an unprecedented

level. None of the guards were Human or Ryxan, the fears of zealous support for Talys or violent recourse against him running high. The Advisor was driven to court each day in a different

armored vehicle, each one part of three motorcades, each motorcade proceeding to the trial on a

different route. His hands and ankles were in proximity cuffs, allowing minimal movement but

magnetically drawing his hands and feet back together should they move too far apart. They had

taken some getting used to, but Talys was a quick study. He was thinner than normal, his skin

sallow, his hair thinning and growing lighter. The courtroom artist, an avid follower of the poli

arena, noted to himself with some amusement that the prison uniform seemed to be the first

outfit to actually fit the man.

With one Speaker dead and one Advisor arrested, the police decided approaching Euphrates

Destidante as well would be prudent, considering him a person of interest but not an outright

suspect. Yet. Having spoken on Rors' Volcott's behalf on occasion, specifically in regard to the

Ryxan, there was some lingering concern about what level his involvement might be. They had

not received any tips about him, however, nor heard any rumors, and nothing at his home seemed

to link him to the incident, so he had not been arrested. Instead, he had been given the option to

stay in a safehouse location in the days leading up to and during the trial. This allowed the

authorities to keep an eye on him while also providing protection from anyone, especially among

the Ryxan, who might assume his complicity before he had a chance to be fully cleared of

involvement.

The High Court, overseeing the trial, was reserved for the most serious of crimes, criminal acts

that affected multiple planets or the universe as a whole. Each race elected a Judge to serve on

the High Court, and each case was overseen by three Judges who would confer during and after

the case, reaching a verdict together. The Judges selected were always of races other than those

standing trial. In this case, Treyisil Pool of the Lodites, Sarina Elianes of the Serobi, and Bas

Orrin of the Murasai were selected, with Judge Ilgen Duffy of the Humans and Judge Loguna of the Ryxan exempt from the proceedings.

The trial moved swiftly and in stages. The prosecution focused first on the ones deemed the leaders of the genocidal plot: Rors Volcott, who commissioned the weapon and funded the undertaking, setting the whole thing in motion; Rab Mool, who developed the weapon itself; and Turner Materas, who conspired to release the weapon on Ryxol. There was no doubt an untold number of others helping along the way, but with no other names given and no clues yet as to which direction to search, it was these three men in the spotlight. The evidence against them was overwhelmingly damning, the leaked correspondences between them and their personal journal logs as good as signed confession letters. The schematics recovered from Mool's computer, wherever it was, detailed the creation of the weapon. A handful of trusted scientists, Professor Sonus Eppleheim among them, reviewed the science privately and came to the conclusion that it was sound and that there was no mistaking its purpose.

Rors Volcott and Turner Materas were unanimously found by the Judges of the High Court to be posthumously guilty of several charges including conspiracy to commit genocide, attempted genocide, attempted use of a biological weapon in a time of peace, and violating the Moon Glow Convention. Rab Mool was on trial for the same charges, as well as the development of an unsanctioned biological weapon, and was convicted on all counts, guilty in absentia. All three were sentenced to death. Mool, the only one not already confirmed deceased and whose whereabouts remained unknown, was declared the Most Wanted Man in the universe with an as yet unspecified reward offered to anyone that could provide information leading to his capture.

The second stage of the trial shifted the focus to Talys Wannigan. To the Advisor's dismay, his habit of concealing his every action on a day to day basis in an attempt to be unpredictable and untouchable to his political rivals worked against him, appearing now to be a deliberate obfuscation disguising what he was doing to further Volcott's plan. Talys' lawyer argued that discretion was critical due to the nature of his job as an Advisor, an argument that held some weight until the prosecutor brought forth the first piece of evidence: recovered from the Parliament of Universal Interest was the hard copy of Volcott's report on the Ryxan's production levels of celaron oil, the one he had Euphrates present to the Council. With it was a typed confession admitting knowledge of the falsified details, subscribing the idea for and the formulation of the report to Talys Wannigan. The letter further admitted to picking Euphrates as scapegoat by having him present the reports instead of Talys, his assigned Advisor. At the bottom was Volcott's handwritten signature, confirmed by three separate handwriting experts to be sloppy but legitimate. Talys finally lost his composure and protested loudly, ignoring his lawyer's efforts to calm him, and declaring that he had nothing to do with the report, that Euphrates Destidante was trying to frame him.

The prosecution then brought out the data drive discovered beneath Talys' sink. The Advisor protested again that he had never before seen the drive in his life. Officers brought in to testify confirmed that none of them were left alone in any of the rooms during their search of the house, and that there had been no signs of tampering or evidence that anyone other than Talys had been in the home before or during the search. The information on that drive, everything that Turner Materas had put together confirming his complicity, was another nail in Talys' coffin.

There was a brief period of excitement when it seemed the Advisor had truly lost his mind. He stood in the middle of the High Court and began to rave, pleading his innocence once more, and again blaming Destidante for the evidence against him. He claimed that he had evidence of his own, proof that Destidante was engaged in illicit activities with freeguns and crime lords. He pointed at where Destidante sat waiting to give his own testimony and began cursing at him, threatening to sink his career. He threatened to *kill* him, which caused an uproar among those watching the proceedings. The High Court Judges demanded that Talys be restrained and threatened to remove him if he would not cease his tirade.

Nevertheless, curiosity had been awakened among the three Judges. Interested in seeing what the Advisor was talking about and how, if at all, it tied Euphrates to the case, a box of evidence was allowed into play. Audio logs were played of Talys interviewing eyewitnesses who placed Euphrates at the Ruby Swell. The manager of the establishment, Shelby Hewitt, confided to Talys that Euphrates had engaged in business at that location more than once and had recently met with a pair of freeguns. While Hewitt couldn't remember their names, he gave detailed descriptions of a red-skinned Murasai and a Human with a cybernetic eye. Travel logs were dictated to the court regarding Euphrates' travel to and from Agnimon, and although no actual video footage of Euphrates was recovered due to some kind of cloaking technology on his person, the ship's pilot and crew confirmed to Talys that they had shuttled him there.

Talys' trial was temporarily suspended while Euphrates Destidante and his defense team were given a chance to address the accusations and evidence. His story was simple: he *had* gone to Agnimon, and he *had* gone to the Ruby Swell. The cloaking technology was military tech, legal to procure and use for government employees, especially someone of his station, but he hadn't procured it through the proper channels. He *had* met someone at the Swell, but freeguns? No. He had met a dancer named Sapphire, a dancer that he had been having an affair with. When asked why Talys would go to such efforts to imply extralegal and clandestine activities, and why Shelby Hewitt would imply the same, Euphrates' defense lawyer suggested it was simply an attempt to both discredit Euphrates and distract the High Court from the crimes Talys was himself committing.

Talys went into another fit of hysterics. The Judges gave him their final warning concerning his behavior.

Doctor Nimbus Madasta was brought up briefly, her credentials verified. She was asked to speak to Euphrates Destidante's character, and she did so, describing him as extremely dedicated to his position as Advisor, and to the well-being of the Human race as a whole. She confirmed her knowledge of the affair and testified that Euphrates had sworn to end it.

Nobody at the Ruby Swell could be reached to confirm either the meeting with the freeguns or the affair; the dancer known as Sapphire and most of the rest of the staff had perished in a horrific fire. Shelby Hewitt was also deceased,

The trial moved on.

The Judges called up Speaker Magga Suvis to the stand as their final witness. No evidence whatsoever tied her to any of the events at hand as she had been away from the Parliament for some time while struggling with her health. As the Advisors and the other Speaker were on trial and under scrutiny, however, she was asked to testify. With help from her medical staff, she took her seat in front of the Judges, adjusted her microphone, and spoke.

She had a lot to say:

Magga spoke of Rors Volcott's intensity and occasional volatility but denied any knowledge of the plot or of ever even hearing him speak of any biases toward the Ryxan. She admitted she did not care for Talys' methods of political administration but denied any intimate knowledge of the man or his intentions, stating he had always seemed to move in his own circles and appeared to be loyal only to himself. She spoke in support of Euphrates and made it perfectly clear that she did not believe anyone, regardless of their station, should be on trial for infidelity. The crowd tittered at that. Euphrates said nothing, nor did Talys, who seemed to deflate more and more as the days went by. The Judges thanked Magga for her testimony and dismissed her from the stand.

The prosecuting lawyers were allowed to make their final arguments. The defense attorneys did the same. The Judges thanked them all and announced their intention to withdraw for final deliberations. The verdict would be announced the following day.

The crowd was dismissed. The lawyers went home. Talys Wannigan was taken back into custody, and Euphrates was shuttled back to the safe house.

Though the halls, lobby, and streets outside of the building were packed with reporters and spectators, the High Court courtroom was closed for the final verdict. Speakers and Advisors of the Universal Council were allowed to be present. The lawyers that had taken part in the trial, and the defendants, and anyone else that had been on the stand were there, too. There was security, a lot of security, armed and ready for anything. The Judges came in and took their seats, Treyisil Pool and Bas Orrin on the ends, Sarina Elianes in the middle.

The room was still. What breath wasn't held was let out shallowly.

Judge Elianes touched one of the data pads set into her podium and a holographic display was broadcast in the center of the courtroom. She began reading the list of charges one by one. These were the final determinations of the High Court:

Talys Wannigan: guilty of deliberately misleading the Universal Council, guilty of tampering with evidence, guilty of accessory to attempted genocide. Sentenced to life in prison. The request of the Ryxian leadership to have Talys extradited to Ryxol. Sentence to be carried out on the astro prison ship, the *APS Tantalus*.

Euphrates Destidante: acquitted of any involvement in the plot against the Ryxan due to lack of evidence. Acquitted of involvement in clandestine activities due to lack of evidence. Guilty of unauthorized use of government and military technology for personal indiscretions. A fine to be paid in the amount of fifty thousand chits.

Magga Suvis: No charges to be brought against the Speaker due to lack of evidence.

Final Remarks: No further charges to be brought against anyone else due to lack of evidence, but should the ongoing investigation uncover any further conspirators, the High Court reserved the right to try them at a later date.

There was a mixed reaction from the Ryxan present. The guilty parties had been named and found culpable, their legacies destroyed, two men dead and one man convicted, but being unable to dispense any kind of retribution themselves left them visibly agitated. The rest of those assembled seemed unsure what to do with themselves. The very nature of the plot had left everyone shaken, and the speed at which things had been decided left them little time to process it all. As they filtered out of the courtroom and into the halls, an explosion of voices could be heard from the people left outside trying to find out what had happened.

Talys was escorted away by security, back to the prison until such time as his transfer to the *Tantalus* could be completed. The guards may as well have been handling a wicker effigy, so unstable was he on his feet, so lightly did they carry him away.

Watching him go was an ecstatic Euphrates, though he took great pains not to show his glee. Justice had been served, and he had come away lightly touched but unharmed.

Nothing that can't be fixed, he thought. *Even financially, now that the danger has passed.* But as he would find out, there was more in store for him yet…

*****

From BROKEN LETTER NEWS, the planet Elagablus:

In the weeks following the universal trial of the century, the Human poli spectrum continues to be in upheaval. With the positions of the disgraced Rors Volcott and Talys Wannigan now vacant, lobbying amongst those searching to take the spots has become particularly nasty. Several polis have used their campaign funds to finance blistering takedown videos of their rivals. Others have taken to insulting each other face to face in hopes of intimidating them out of the race. Instead, the opposite effect seems to have happened; at least seven sanctioned duels have taken place since the verdicts were announced, resulting in four injuries and three deaths. A number of popular frontrunners are becoming clear contenders, but nothing should be considered certain and more turmoil should be expected until a final vote takes place.

In the meantime, another vote has gone through. Euphrates Destidante, Advisor to Speaker Magga Suvis, was acquitted last month of any involvement in both the plot against the Ryxan and of any political interference against former Advisor Wannigan, although the trial did uncover evidence of his using government equipment for personal use, and of that personal use specifically being an ongoing affair. Since then, Advisor Destidante has issued a public apology, and his long-time girlfriend Doctor Nimbus Madasta has also spoken publicly about her decision to forgive him and to give him a second chance while they navigate the fallout from the trial.

Public sentiment, however, doesn't appear to agree with the doctor. Since skating away from any serious legal consequences, Destidante has faced a rapid decline in his approval ratings. It is so low, in fact, that the Human polis managed to set their differences aside just long enough to cast a vote of No Confidence. Advisor Destidante is expected to resign from his position sometime soon. If he does, that will be one more coveted position up for grabs.

*****

Archimedes sat on a large rock in the middle of Ocala Springs Park, finishing the burger he got from Fries, Slides, and Other Sides, washing it down with a crisp, cool soda, and watching the subtitles flash and the chyrons crawl across the large screens plastered along the sides of the buildings around him. They had been on a 24/7 news cycle since before the trial and that didn't seem like it would change anytime soon.

Fall was beginning to come to Thorus and the park was cool with the autumn air. It was Archimedes' favorite season. The changing of colors in the trees and bushes, the brown and orange aesthetics. Weather was never too hot or too cold. A sun that set in the early evening, the streetlights coming on to guide you home after a nice dinner out. It was the season he spent the most time away from the *Searcher* whenever they were between jobs.

"Ark?" asked a woman from behind him. "Archimedes Carnahan?"

He turned to look, spotted a young woman walking across the grass toward him. She was pretty, with honey-colored eyes that turned downward just a little bit at the corner. Her hair was a deep red with a snow-colored lock hanging free at the front. She had a pleasant smile, one that distracted him enough that it took a second for him to recognize the rest of her face. He slid off the rock and walked to meet her.

"Melanie Strannigan," he said in admiration. "It's been, what, three years?"

"Three or four, yeah," she said. "Gamemon. Graduation night, remember?"

Archimedes laughed. "I mean, I don't remember a lot of it, but what I do remains a highlight of my life, sure." He waved at her with the soda cup. "You look fantastic."

"Thank you," she beamed. She held her hands toward him, questioning. "What are you doing out here? Just snacking, hanging out?"

"Yeah, pretty much," he said, laughing again. "People are always rushing around hither and thither, but that's never really been my style. I think it's important to take your down time when you can and really immerse yourself in it when you do. Stop and smell the burgers, eat some roses." He pointed up at one of the screens. Euphrates Destidante was standing behind a podium somewhere in the Parliament of Universal Interest. The subtitles at the bottom of the screen were transcribing his resignation speech. "I still can't believe all this craziness."

Melanie's eyes followed. She watched the speech for several beats, then shook her head. "Weren't you going to be a poli? That's all you used to talk about. Theater, politics, women…"

"Oh, come on." Archimedes rolled his eyes. "I didn't talk about women that much."

"You did."

"I didn't…"

"You did!"

"With you?" Archimedes' face flushed, and he looked around at the other people in the park, pointedly avoiding her gaze. "Jeez, Melanie. I don't know what to say about that except that I'm sorry. Not a great move on my part."

"That's alright," she said, patting his arm. She pointed back at the screen. "I take it you didn't follow your dream."

"No, not really. Not that one. And I've got to say, seeing what happened to Destidante, I'm not entirely sorry I didn't dip my toe into that shark pool." He saw a look cross over her face, quickly added, "Look, I'm not saying what he did was right. The infidelity, the… whatever technology it was he highjacked, the personal flights on taxpayers' money, whatever. In a vacuum, sure, that would be enough to get pretty pissed off. But the guy pulled himself up from nothing to get to the position he was in, an *Advisor*, and while everyone else around him is… trying to commit atrocities or are finding ways to skim millions of chits off their constituents, I mean…" He flapped his hand aimlessly, leaving the rest unsaid.

Melanie looked at him curiously. "You almost sound like he's a hero of yours."

Archimedes shrugged. "I used to think I could be somebody like that. Driven, ambitious, adaptive. Successful. Three years after graduation there are people from our class winning awards, they're millionaire investment brokers. They're doctors." He paused, pointed at her with his straw. "What are you doing now?"

"I'm a veterinarian," she said, smiling. He could see in her eyes that she truly loved it, too.

"The kind of doctor that matters!" he said, throwing his hands up. The lid of his soda cup popped off and splashed his arm with ice cubes and what little soda remained inside. Melanie laughed while he tried to shake his arm dry.

"You're being too hard on yourself, Ark," Melanie said. She reached into her purse and pulled a handful of napkins out, handed them to him. He thanked her and tried to rub the stickiness off his skin. "How many languages do you speak now?"

"What?" he asked, off guard.

"You spoke three when I met you. Trader, Murasi, and..." She reached for it, couldn't quite find it.

"I spoke a little Lodite," Archimedes finished for her. "I've gotten better. Picked up Peran, some Skir. I'm pretty good at Serobi. Dyrian. It comes in handy, working as an intergalactic courier in a ship I don't even own by myself."

Melanie shook her head and gestured at the people walking the streets all around them. "You think any of them knows what they're doing? Deep down? Do you think *I* know what *I'm* doing? It's only been three years, dude. There's no rush." She tilted her head up at one of the news screens. "You think Cheaty McCheater up there gave up after three years? I'd be surprised if this resignation even keeps him down. Wouldn't you be? You work as a courier, so what? That's an awesome job! You travel around the universe all the time, and some people don't even leave their home world. You speak seven languages when other people rely on translators exclusively. So you don't own your ship by yourself, at least you... wait a second." She eyed him closely. "Are you... did Archimedes Carnahan settle down with somebody?"

The laughter burst out of him loud enough to startle her. He bent over at the waist, cackling, hands on his knees.

"Alright," Melanie said, eyebrows raised. "So, still a ladies' man, then. That could be good, too. Keeps you on your toes."

"No, no," Archimedes said, waving at her, still buckled over. "No, it's just... the ship... I own it with my two oldest friends. The idea of 'settling down' with them..." He straightened slowly, still grinning, and wiped tears rom his eyes. "I haven't had time for anything serious with anybody. We've been zipping around moon to planet to moon. Picking up packages, and..."

His words faded, and he looked past her at nothing, remembering. Reliving. He could still feel the vines wrapped around his body, could still hear the robot gorilla stalking him and see the obliterated body of the mad scientist. He gave his head a little shake and smiled at her.

"What about you?" he asked. "Have you found a special somebody?"

"No, actually," Melanie said, shifting her purse to her other arm. "In fact, when I saw you I kind of went back in time for a minute. I was wondering if you had actually been living in Thorus this whole time, but it sounds like you might just be passing through."

Archimedes nodded. "We've been here for a bit, and we'll probably stay here a week or two more before moving along. We've just been taking sort of a break. A breather. Our last job had some unexpected complications."

Melanie's eyes turned up and she smiled coyly. "Sounds intriguing. Well, look," she said, pulling her communicator out. She scrolled through it for a moment, checked something, and continued, "I'm not doing anything tonight. I know you already ate, but what do you say to, you know… spending some time together? Like old times."

He considered it for a long, long moment. He did. They'd had a lot of fun together once, back when he still felt like half a kid, and she was as beautiful now as she was then. Perhaps even more so; she had developed some worry lines around her eyes, no doubt from taking care of sick and injured animals. They seemed to lend her a grace he never appreciated before. She had always been able to make him laugh.

But then he remembered Vyroan. He remembered Dephros, and Astrakoth. He recalled sitting in the cell onboard the *Imagination*, and the things Koko Noal had said to him, the way she had looked at him almost with pity.

"I'm… sorry, actually. I think I'm going to have to give a rain check on that. I've been thinking about a lot of things lately, and I—"

Melanie placed her index and middle fingers on his lips to shush him. He blinked, surprised.

"You don't need to explain anything to me, Ark. You change your mind, just look me up. I'm at the Paws 'n Pals Health Clinic. Think you can remember that?"

Archimedes nodded, once. "Fucking terrible name like that, yeah, I think I can manage." He smiled and held his arms open, embraced her. Her hair smelled like peppermint, and he savored it with his eyes closed, just for a moment. "It's good to see you, and I'm glad you're well. Thanks for understanding."

"Of course," Melanie said, stepping away. "Keep your head up. Or down. Whatever keeps it out of your ass so that you can start enjoying life."

"Why did we ever break up?" he asked.

"You moved away, Carnahan." She lifted her hand and wiggled her fingers, a little wave goodbye, then turned and started walking out of the park.

I'm an idiot, Archimedes thought.

"I'm an idiot!" he shouted after her.

"Who isn't?" she called back over her shoulder, and laughed.

Epilogue

The Sun Always Rises

Euphrates stood on the terrace at the back of the estate, hands on the marble railing, looking out at the gardens. He was wearing a high-collard black duster over a black vest and mauve button-up shirt, black dress pants, and black shoes. The outfit had run him close to two thousand chits, with extra thrown in to have hidden pockets sewn in. They were good for holding switchblades, stoppered poisons, small guns, money units, sensitive documents, or whatever else he could think to put in them. With the sun beating down on him, though, and making him sweat, all he could think about was how much he hated the whole assembly.

"You're looking mighty fancy for a man who nearly spent the rest of his life rotting aboard a prison ship."

Euphrates turned, offered a thin smile. Magga Suvis shuffled out, clacking a walker ahead of her. She had gained some weight and some color, and the IVs were nowhere in sight. She set the walker aside once she reached Euphrates, using the railing to hold herself up instead.

"You look considerably better than the last time I saw you, Speaker."

"Pah," Magga said, waving a hand. "I look like shit. I feel only marginally better than that, but I've still got a few years left in me."

"The miracles of modern science."

"The miracles of stubbornness and spite for the suckerfish that fancy themselves my peers. Who do you think will take my seat once I've gone? Oleg Daniker? Hayden Woodrue?" Magga spat over the railing. "The so-called favorites that have been lining up like vultures are all more concerned with the status the position would give them among Humans than they are about where Humans should be standing among the rest of the universe." She pointed a boney finger at him. "You would have made a great replacement, had you not cocked it all up."

Euphrates would have laughed if he weren't so tired. "I wouldn't have wanted it, I don't think. Where I was, that was about as high as suited me."

"Where you could still work from the shadows, you mean?"

Euphrates glanced at Magga, found her staring at him intently. He shrugged and nodded.

"Yes. And, as it turns out, that may have been too high still."

It was Magga's turn to nod. "Perhaps. Although being Speaker has never stopped me, I expect your operations ran a bit further… underground. It was a very near thing, what happened to you."

"Yes," Euphrates said again, sighing.

"But you weren't the one to leak the information."

"If I were, if I even had access to those who did, I would have never gone to trial."

For want of a nail, he thought.

Magga narrowed her eyes and allowed a moment of silence to pass through the air between them. She turned to look at the gardens, and Euphrates did the same. A pair of gulls flew playfully overhead, cutting low across the backyard.

"How much *did* you know?" she asked finally.

"About Rors? I knew the report was faked. After that it was mostly suspicions." He took a handkerchief from his back pocket and used it to wipe away the sweat that had been collecting on his neck. Magga watched him, unbothered. He said, "I don't know how you can stand this heat."

"I think of it as foreplay to Hell. You knew about the report, but you never mentioned it to me. That's what an Advisor would do, Destidante, is it not? Advise one of a surprising, potentially scandalous situation?"

"What do you want me to say, Magga? It was Rors and Talys' signatures on that paper." The lie came smoothly, even for him, bolstered by his resignation. He made a mental reminder not to let himself fall into believing it. "I was dealing with them alone while you've been recuperating here. Mind sharp as ever, sure, with a body I wasn't sure could last through a stormy night. Knowing they were lying gave me a place to start. More importantly, it gave us more time with the Ryxan, whether or not it was for the wrong reasons."

"Alright, alright," Magga said. "Good God, Destidante, you sound like a teenage girl."

"A bit sexist of you," Euphrates said with a smile.

"I can still unman you quick enough, frail as I am, so bite your tongue on that. How about Wannigan? How much did you know about his involvement?"

Here Euphrates paused. If Magga suspected he had framed Talys, she may suspect he had more knowledge of the whole plot. Maybe she already knew and was just letting him go through the motions. He could feel the weight of her eyes on him, heavy and full of thorns. He met them with his own.

"The less said about Talys, the better," he said.

It was a gamble, one with the shrewdest high roller in the game. Magga dissected his expression, infiltrated his eyes. She nodded, barely, turned back to the gardens. She drummed her fingernails across the marble, *tap-tap-tap-tap, tap-tap-tap-tap*.

"Yes, he was a bit of a bastard, wasn't he? It's a small wonder he didn't follow Rors' example, especially after the verdict came in."

Euphrates had nothing to say to that.

"It's a shame you were given a vote of no-confidence despite being acquitted. I've always had the utmost confidence in you." She gave a wry smile. "They've not voted in anyone to replace you, did you know that?"

"I had heard." What he had heard specifically was that things had grown exceptionally bitter among the poli circles, with at least three old blood-feuds gaining new life. It was something he could use, something he should probably look into, but it would require a delicate hand.

The sun was beginning to set, the wind beginning to cool. Euphrates could have shouted his relief. His shirt, clammy at the small of his back, had been threatening to drive him to distraction.

"They think they're clever," Magga sneered. "The polis in their arena, playing at ferocity and originality. They don't think I'll live out the year, but as I've said, I'll show them even old dogs can still bite and this bitch has sharper teeth than most." She glanced at him. "Dalton Hess. Your doing?"

Euphrates shrugged. "My word doesn't hold much water after the no-confidence vote, but I found ways to support his ascension to Speaker, yes."

"I suspected as much. That should make him more agreeable than Rors was." Her eyes were moving, calculating. "They're still voting for his Advisor, too, but I suspect it will wind up going to Breia Yant."

"I'm not familiar with her."

"Why would you be? She isn't a lowlife."

Euphrates scowled. "I resent that."

"You would like her, Breia. She's quite brilliant. A bit too attached to the rules, but she's young yet and the brilliant ones shed naiveté like a snake does skin."

Magga stepped away from the railing and took hold of her walker. She began shuffling back to her estate, leaving Euphrates to follow after on his own. When the air conditioning in the house washed over him, he had to stifle a gasp. He almost wondered if she had made him stand outside for so long just to make him uncomfortable.

Spiteful bitch, indeed, he thought, smiling.

They walked together until they reached the main foyer. Carlito, ever the loyal manservant, checked to make sure Magga was alright, then cleared the rest of the staff from the room. Euphrates glanced over at the front door.

"So this is it? You invited me over to offer your condolences?"

"A man as smart as you should put more effort into not being so fucking droll. I have no Advisor and you still have your uses. I want to know who released the information about Rors, and I'm quite sure you've been losing some sleep over it. You like to work behind the scenes, and it turns out that's where I need you."

Euphrates swallowed hard, a shiver of anticipation coating his bones.

"I still believe that you have the Human race's best interests in mind," Magga continued. You will have access to the resources you enjoyed as an Advisor, though going forward you'll need to be less direct in accessing them. You will answer to no one but me, but you will also stay out of the public eye. I won't ask you to report everything to me—frankly I doubt I'll want to know half of it—but you will not let another clusterfuck like this go unmentioned. Lastly, Rors Volcott and Talys Wannigan behind us, you will henceforth be *completely* honest with me. I'm not your priest. I'm not your lover. I don't give a shit about your sins, I care about results. Understood?"

Euphrates thought of Nimbus, of the long conversation they would need to have about this in addition to the seemingly endless conversations they had been having. But she hadn't left him yet. Not during the trial, not after hearing about some of his actual crimes. Despite the grisliness, despite the public scrutiny.

"Understood," he said.

"Good," Magga said, flinging her arm toward the door. "We'll figure out the details in the coming days."

Euphrates gave half a bow at the waist and headed for the exit, wheels already turning in his head. He started making a list of improvements that needed to be made, things that needed to be done posthaste. The first thing would have to be a letter to Dalton Hess congratulating him on his Speaker position and reminding him of their arrangement.

A smile on his face and his hand on the doorknob, he turned back when Magga called his name. She was still standing in the center of the foyer, thin hands clutching the arms of the walker.

"Just out of curiosity," she said, "have you ever considered having me killed?"

He thought about the question for a long moment, then shook his head. "Not really. Our interests have always seemed to be aligned."

"What does that mean, not really?"

"You know the way a bank employee might dream up the most efficient way to rob their own bank without ever actually doing it?"

Magga laughed, long and hard. In that moment she seemed twenty years younger.

*****

It took three hours for Huxous to sort through the box of maps. There were just shy of three dozen in total and he'd had to load each of the data drives, consult a number of astrocartographical records to find out what set the maps apart, look up what the comparative sale amounts or auction postings were, if there were any, and send the information to the man in the back for review and approval. A few of the data drives had additional information included, things like travel logs or scientific reports, listings of lost ruins, or the rumors of undiscovered treasures. These maps required deeper scrutiny, more thorough research, and their value to the shop varied wildly on a case to case basis. Other customers filtered in while Huxous worked on them, trying to make a purchase or sell their own things. He told most of them to come back later but made a handful of allowances, dragging the whole thing out even longer.

Grey had pulled up an empty fruit crate and sat on it in a corner of the store. Huxous had given him an approximate time to return so that he didn't have to wait around; Grey had declined, unwilling to let the data drives out of his sight even for a second.

Finally the last drive was reviewed, its value calculated, its buying price confirmed. Huxous slipped it back into its protective case and placed it in a lockbox with the rest. He jotted some notes down, tallied up the totals with a calculator, and wrote down a number. He waved Grey over and turned the paper around so the courier could read it.

"We don't *normally* deal with things of this nature," Huxous said.

"Yeah, you've mentioned that six times since I walked in here, and I'm tired of hearing it because both of us know that ain't fucking true. What am I looking at here?"

"It's an itemized list of what you brought in. They're listed by galactic region and then further broken down by star systems, planets, moons, any and all distinguishing features and information. I've taken the liberty of including my personal notes as to what went into determining the final price we're offering. The sum is at the bottom of the page."

Grey's eyes skipped to the bottom, took a look at the number, and nearly lost focus. He exhaled hard through his nose, then tapped the paper.

"I want three money units loaded with five thousand chits each. Let me see your pen." Huxous handed him the pen and Grey wrote a number underneath the sum. "Deposit the rest into this account. I'll be confirming the transfer before I leave."

"Most people try to negotiate for more."

"Would you give me more?"

"We never do."

"Then please just do what the fuck I said." Grey flashed a fake smile. "Thank you."

Huxous harrumphed and took the paper with him, back to the computer. Grey waited, leaning on the counter with one elbow, struggling to contain his excitement. It was about time things started turning the *Searcher*'s way.

A door creaked open somewhere behind the gates that separated the inventory crates and the offices from the store proper. Grey turned his head, watched as a heavy-set Lodite made his way out to the front. The Lodite paused, took Grey in from top to bottom, then gave him a disgusted look. "Captain Toliver. Uglier every time I see you."

"Might be, Raygor, might be. I'll tell you what, though." He touched a finger to the thin white line that cut through his eyebrow. "Every scar I pick up between us meeting, you pick up another ten pounds."

Raygor laughed and the two embraced. The Lodite leaned in and said in a hushed tone, "You've got some brass ones for a Human, flying a shit-kicker around the cosmos on someone else's dime."

"I have no idea what you mean," Grey said, looking over at Huxous.

"He's fine," Raygor assured him. "Would I hire someone who wasn't?" He leaned in, conspiratorial. "I had caught wind of Sylvain Abalos getting hit, but the last thing I was expecting was to find out my little Human courier friend was the one to do it. I've got to know: I heard he swapped out security for some kind of golem or robot or something. Is that true?"

"I have no idea."

"How did you get past it? Certain people might pay to know."

Grey placed a hand over his heart. "Raygor, I didn't go in there. I swear."

The Lodite took a minute to search for any sign of lie or humor. A lightbulb clicked on in his head. He pointed two of his fingers at Grey's chest. "You're still doing the three captain thing."

"Listen," Grey cut in, "leave them out of it. Okay? Is this sale going to be a problem?"

"Of course not," Raygor said, raising his hands in defeat. He winked. "Leave *who* out of it? You're the only one I deal with."

"Okay, sure."

"Look, Grey, I buy and sell information, but product is still a big part of my operation. You and I have had a good working relationship on the occasions that have seen you down to the Swallows. Telling Abalos about you would rob me of you as a patron. He'd probably demand his maps back, too, and that would turn into a whole thing. You did me a boon here, kid."

Grey swallowed that, digested it. He gave a curt nod. "Alright, I'll take you at your word. Honor amongst—"

"Opportunists," Raygor broke in, grinning.

"Opportunists, then. You still lowballed me on these maps, though, didn't you?"

Raygor's grin grew wider. "Oh, absolutely."

*****

After the events at Vyroan the three captains of the *Sol Searcher* had taken her in for another round of hull repairs and polish. The journey had left each of them feeling renewed in their love of the ship, each in their own way, and as they healed physically and mentally from their ordeals, they wanted the same for the *Searcher*. Cleaning her up, making sure she ran well, it kept them occupied in an otherwise vacuum of activity. A return to normalcy, though all of them felt irrevocably far from normal.

They came together that night at the dinner table. Grey set out the silverware and the glasses, filling the latter with nutri-water, leaving a pitcher in the center of the table. Archimedes brought out three snifters and poured a healthy serving of Durelli's Captain's Choice in each. Caesar joined them last, bringing out plates of roasted fennel with cinnamon and melted cheese, garlic mashed potatoes, and some kind of Ryxan waterfowl braised with red wine.

As Caesar set the plates down, Grey placed two money units on the table. "Five thousand chits for both of you, and I've got one of my own. The rest is in the joint account. We *did* get ripped off, just a bit," he admitted, shrugging, "but I don't know where else we would have sold them. We still walked away with enough to pay off the *Searcher*. Maybe even enough to treat ourselves to a vacation after."

Caesar gaped at him. Archimedes, having lifted his fork and knife to start eating, let his utensils drop to the plate.

"Well, alright!" Archimedes exclaimed. "I was going to suggest we toast to being alive, but since I'm pretty sure debtors will follow you to actual Hell, this is probably better." He grabbed his glass of whiskey and raised it. "To the *Sol Searcher*!"

"To the *Sol Searcher*!" Grey and Caesar echoed in unison.

They clinked glasses and drank and began to eat. The room seemed warmer. Perhaps it was the ship's temperature regulator making adjustments, or perhaps it was just them, just the good news and camaraderie that also made their spirits light. They cracked jokes and laughed. They discussed heading to the Aventure office and picking up a job, then decided their break could probably run a little longer.

Caesar's communicator chirped. He glanced at it but didn't recognize the number, held a finger up to quiet his friends before answering.

"Hello?" he said, tentative.

"Caesar Anada?"

"Yes…?"

"This is Koko Noal from the *IRSC Imagination*."

"Koko?" Caesar almost jumped out of his seat. "Hey! How are you? How've you been? I was just thinking about you the other day, wondering what you were up to. You know, I've been thinking about that offer Captain Richards extended."

"You brought a *biological weapon* on board my ship?"

Caesar blinked, unsure if he heard her right. Except he had done exactly what she said, so she must have said what he heard. He looked at Archimedes, then Grey. They looked back at him, hands out, waiting for an update.

"How is she?" Archimedes asked. "Tell her I said hi. Ask her if she's been thinking about me."

"Uh…" Caesar said into the communicator. "Can I call you back?"

--October 1st, 2015-September 1st, 2019

The Sol Searcher

will fly again in

BRIGAND RELAY

51834682R00283

Made in the USA
San Bernardino, CA
03 September 2019